storyland

storyland

CATHERINE McKINNON

FOURTH ESTATE
An Imprint of HarperCollins*Publishers*

Fourth Estate

An imprint of HarperCollins*Publishers*
First published in Australia in 2017
by HarperCollins*Publishers* Australia Pty Limited
ABN 36 009 913 517
harpercollins.com.au

HarperCollins*Publishers*

Level 13, 201 Elizabeth Street, Sydney NSW 2000, Australia
Unit D1, 63 Apollo Drive, Rosedale, Auckland 0632, New Zealand
A 53, Sector 57, Noida, UP, India
1 London Bridge Street, London, SE1 9GF, United Kingdom
2 Bloor Street East, 20th floor, Toronto, Ontario M4W 1A8, Canada
195 Broadway, New York NY 10007, USA

National Library of Australia Cataloguing-in-Publication data:

McKinnon, Catherine, author.
 Storyland / Catherine McKinnon.
 978 1 4607 5232 6 (paperback)
 978 1 4607 0716 6 (ebook)
 Historical fiction.
 Australia – Fiction.
A823.4

Cover design by Darren Holt, HarperCollins Design Studio
Cover images: Illustrations by Darren Holt; images by shutterstock.com
Maps by Map Illustrations
Typeset in Hoefler Text Roman by Kirby Jones
Printed and bound in Australia by Griffin Press
The papers used by HarperCollins in the manufacture of this book are a
natural, recyclable product made from wood grown in sustainable plantation
forests. The fibre source and manufacturing processes meet recognised
international environmental standards, and carry certification.

For Gary Christian

If I wanted a one-sentence definition of human beings, this would do: humans are the animals that believe the stories they tell about themselves. Humans are credulous animals.

Mark Rowlands, *The Philosopher and the Wolf*

Contents

Will Martin 1796 | 1

Hawker 1822 | 46

Lola 1900 | 68

Bel 1998 | 118

Nada 2033 & 2717 | 174

Bel 1998 | 239

Lola 1900 | 267

Hawker 1822 | 302

Will Martin 1796 | 315

Maps | 370

Author's Note | 373

Acknowledgements | 379

Will Martin
1796

My oar stabs the side of the *Reliance*. We push *Tom Thumb* away from the ship. Venus is out but the sky is still light. Lieutenant Flinders takes the helm. Mr Bass and I row until we are clear of the ships docked at Sydney Cove and then we boat the oars and hoist sail. *Tom Thumb*'s sail snaps at the breeze and air-filled we bounce across the water.

'To dare is to do!' Mr Bass shouts our motto.

'To dare is to do!' The lieutenant and I reply as if we are one.

It is Thursday, the twenty-fourth of March, the year 1796. This day we have embarked on our second *Tom Thumb* sail. Mr Bass and Lieutenant Flinders are charged with locating the mouth of the river that Henry Hacking (a ship pilot who likes to hunt) has discovered inland. Hacking has guessed the mouth to be south of Botany Bay, near Cape Banks. Mr Bass says that if we find that river, and it is deep enough to take large vessels, then our names will be shiny buttons on English coats.

Seawater sprays across the gunwale. It is the enchanted hour, where blue water glows and the rocky shores and sandy beaches have a yellowish gleam. On the eastern side of the cove I spy the governor's stone house. Near it, the farmed gardens. On the western side is the hospital, where my friend Na will be sweeping floors. Around the cove, dirt paths snake by houses made of brick, mud, wattle and post, and limed inside and out. Beyond the settlement, it is all forest. The trees have rare and fanciful roots that rise high above the ground. At each step there are fallen trunks, slumped sideways like drunken sailors, or prostrate on the ground; others that are lightning splintered or perished. The foliage is silver-tinged and evergreen. In this land, nature is upended. Birds sing through the night, animals hunt and forage in moonlight.

Dribbling through the trees and over mud flats, and dividing east of the cove from west, is the Tank Stream. Once it was a pure stream, but now it is fouled by pig dung, food scraps and more, so that our small colony is desperate for clean water. The governor hopes that the river we seek may provide new areas to settle. According to Mr Bass, therein lies the importance of our task.

We sail on past stony Pinchgut Island. A man stands on the shore. I see a hand rise to wave. Or is it a trick of the eye? Only the wicked are left there. No one on Garden Island. Behind us, the ships moored in the harbour soon disappear. Larboard and starboard is only darkened forest. Indian fires glimmer between the jungle of skeleton trees.

Our first *Tom Thumb*, owned by Mr Bass and friends, was taken to Timor on the *Nautilus* and did not return. The colony's boat builder, good Mr Paine, clinker built a new *Thumb,* with steamed frames of spotted gum, red cedar planks, and polished copper fittings. We are kitted with a mast of flooded gum, a linen lugsail, a sweep sail and well-crafted oars. Less than twelve foot, so a small boat to sail in. There is no anchor spare in the colony so our anchor is a lump of rock that the sea has speared a hole through and, under Mr Bass's instruction, I have threaded it with thick rope. We have only two muskets to contest pirates or cannibals, supplies for ten days, no more, and the danger is great.

The governor himself tried to dissuade us from the journey.

'We are more than willing,' Lieutenant Flinders said.

'Good fate does not side with every explorer,' the governor warned.

'We are confident,' Mr Bass assured him.

Still the governor resisted. 'No,' he said, his gaze on me. 'The risk of young lives lost, with so much yet to give, outweighs the cause.'

'Sir!' Mr Bass stepped forward, his great shape commanding the room as he spoke our motto in Latin, *'Audere est facere!'*

The governor laughed abruptly and we saw he had relented.

The water melts into the night sky. Mr Bass tips his head to stargaze. He is almost as long as *Thumb.* Lieutenant Flinders sits, hand on knee, reading the wind. I button my jacket against the cold, see the beacon flaming on South Head. On this sail I aim to prove my worth. For it is as Mr Bass says: 'In the new world, a man is what he dares to be, no more, no less.'

The water goes *slap, slap* against the side of *Thumb*. *Slap, slap*, to dare is to do.

Near Shark Bay the wind drops. Mr Bass and I get upon the oars and pull to shore. The surf foams and spits as we haul our boat up onto the sand. Mr Bass and the lieutenant stand on the beach and shake hands.

'Mr Bass, congratulations.'

'Lieutenant Flinders, congratulations.'

They are pleased to have nine days exploring, away from duties on the *Reliance,* and with no pipe whistling orders.

The bay is edged by rocky cliffs. Mr Bass and the lieutenant take off to climb the nearest, and soon become inky shapes. The dark sea is furrowed by starlight. Behind me, tall eucalypts stand like bark-coated marines guarding the beach, their leaves tinted by the moon.

'Will, bring my red waistcoat,' Mr Bass calls.

Yesterday he gave Hoary Bogarty a bottle for the coat. Hoary Bogarty himself had won it in cards from a convict, who had won it at dice from a marine. I fetch the waistcoat and scale the rock to where they stand. For a tick-tock they slip into their Lincolnshire thees and thous, like Quakers at prayer — Think thee, Mr Bass; Would not thou, Lieutenant Flinders — as though our arrival needs marking. Then, games over, Mr Bass breaks off a tree branch to swat mosquitoes and opens the bottle of spirits he has saved for the occasion.

Lieutenant Flinders has lost his customary droop. The change is not the trip alone but also Mr Bass's doing. Many times, on the *Reliance*, I have been below deck and have spied the lieutenant, on hearing Mr Bass's boot above, down pen and hurry to greet his friend. On deck, as they pace, the lieutenant's cheeks begin to shine, as though Mr Bass himself has brought the sun into the day.

The two now sit on the top of a rock, drinking and talking of the governor's latest Tank Stream orders, while I go about wooding. In the first order the governor forbade the pulling down of palings or the keeping of pigs near the stream, it being the only fresh water Sydney Cove has and now badly tainted. But all disobeyed that command. The worst offenders? The *marines* who have huts along the stream. So the governor put out a second order saying that when he gives an order he expects it to be obeyed.

'If I were the governor I would have the marines whipped,' I say.

'Have I taught you nothing?' Mr Bass asks.

'The marines are boorish, I will give the boy that,' the lieutenant says to Mr Bass. 'But they wield a new sort of power. Whipping would only cause them to rise in revolt.'

If the lieutenant speaks to me directly, it is usually to give an order. He thinks me dull-witted; a servant to be suffered for the sake of his friend. In time I will show him different. For now, I play my part.

The lieutenant turns the conversation elsewhere. I set a fire on a flat rock that has a view of the bay. We supped before embarking and, as we intend to sail before sunrise, I stretch out to nap, but with the sea splash, frog croak and insect buzz, napping is all pretence. Mr Bass and Lieutenant Flinders sit fireside and argue politics.

'You take too many risks mingling with seditionists,' the lieutenant says.

Mr Bass pokes at the coals. 'A risk only for the lily-livered who hang on public opinion.'

The lieutenant pays the jibe no heed. 'You made a show by attending Gerrald's funeral.'

'Never a show to grieve a death,' snaps Mr Bass.

I am with the lieutenant on this one, for I did not weep at Mr Gerrald's funeral. Far from it. In the months before his passing he had often detained Mr Bass and me at his house for hour after insufferable hour, giving speeches about universal manhood suffrage. Mr Bass was there to treat him, and this a kindly act, because Balmain, the colony's surgeon, refused to medicate what he called 'that horrid seditionist!' Mr Bass, whose duties were bound only to those on the *Reliance*, took Balmain's place because he has sympathy for those who uphold ideals, claiming it is the mark of a worthy man. Yet, to my mind, the upshot of Mr Gerrald's universal manhood suffrage was that more men should be like him. Mr Gerrald may have upheld ideals, but he was also a pompous drunkard, and, as we had enough inebriates in Sydney Cove as it was, I wagered my sympathy was not worth giving.

Mr Bass and the lieutenant get as noisy in their arguing as convicts at rut-time but when their beverage has spiked their drowsiness, they lie down and snore. I drink what is left, no more than a sip, and stretch out, flat on my back on hard rock. I eye the winking sky and listen to the night. *Swish, swash, swish, swash.*

The sea never stops its caress of the earth. On land, old-bone branches crack and crash. This place is an upturn of the natural world, each step, new and old together.

The next morn, with the world still dark, Mr Bass wakes me. An owl hoots. I sand the fire and scramble down to help haul *Thumb* to the shallows. Mr Bass and the lieutenant are black figures splashing in water. We shove off and jump in, wet feet slapping wood. My eyes do not want to stay open but they must.

Mr Bass and I pull out of the bay, the moon our guide, then hoist sail. The air is cool. *Thumb* skips over velvet water towards the twin heads and the wide-open ocean. The South Head burner is flickering. A lone redcoat should be tending it though I spy no one. Once we are through the heads, the breeze drops, paddles us along until dawn, then departs. The sun peeks over watery dunes. Mr Bass and I set to the oars – *splish, splash, splish, splash.* I know now why sailors say the splash of wood in water is a mariner's dirge. The never-ending of it. We pull at an even pace. Lieutenant Flinders sits at the helm, watching the coastline. Behind him, the English flag is limp. The lieutenant's eyes narrow as he flashes his timepiece and compass, scribbling calculations in a book that he keeps wrapped in seal hide. Mr Bass and I are hour hands of a clock, slow and steady; the lieutenant, the seconds darting by.

The sun fires hot. My arms shake like a fish on a hook. At Mr Bass's nod we boat the oars.

'Water,' he commands.

I roll out the water cask from beneath the thwart. Mr Bass sits side on, fills his cup from the spout, and leans back to drink. In a tick-tock water spurts from his mouth.

'Blasted spoiled!' he shouts.

The lieutenant reaches forward, snatches the cup and sips. He too spits it out, then turns on me, red-faced, and with a neck like coiled rope.

'Will, this water has been put in a wine barica!'

A rush of heat. Silently, I curse Bogarty and his ruddy head, for water held in a wine barica is quickly poisoned. The lieutenant sighs, thinking, no doubt, that his brother would not make such a blunder. Samuel is not a clot but he whines like one. I was chosen for the sail over him, thanks to Mr Bass's stubbornness.

'Will is as strong as a man, Samuel less so,' Mr Bass had argued.

'I saw no evidence of strength at Georges River,' the lieutenant said, referring to our first *Tom Thumb* sail.

'Were you looking?' asked Mr Bass, offended on my behalf. He stayed firm and the lieutenant gave way.

But to be without water is grim. Mr Bass scratches his neck. He is my advocate; I hate to disappoint him.

Bogarty, yesterday morn, was as slow as a wet whistle because his hip was playing up and because of his rotten head, which he said was not due to drink, as I suggested, but caused by *my* mouth going pell-mell. I took the barica from his store without my usual look-to. The error is mine.

'Check and recheck all your tasks,' is what Mr Bass instructed at Portsmouth. One substance should never taint another. Medicines must be stored with care. It is a sin to lose a life through recklessness. These are his commandments, recited again and again.

I burn with shame and hear the creak of *Thumb* above the slap of the sea. Then I remember Mr Palmer's gift. 'Keep safe, young friend,' he had said, handing over melons newly plucked from his garden. (Mr Palmer, like Mr Gerrald, was transported from Scotland for his belief in manhood suffrage, only from Palmer's mouth the term is not only reasoned but followed through with action. Man, boy, even on occasion woman, he treats as his equal.) I scramble to the bow to fetch a melon. Mr Bass eyes me with relief.

'We will search out a stream when we land,' he says, turning to the lieutenant. 'It is that fool Bogarty we should punish. The old goat sniffs rum from ten rods away; surely he has the nose for a wine barica.'

I lay the melon on the thwart. Mr Bass slips his blade along the thick skin, careful as he splits it not to lose any juice. He quarters the melon and we sit in the heat, sucking the moist flesh. We are three, in a small boat on a flat ocean, drifting beneath a forever blue sky.

'Chew the seeds,' Mr Bass commands. He fills his cup with the poisoned water, splashes the contents over his head and shouts, 'To dare is to do!'

This is how he lifts the mood. He fills the cup again, hands it to the lieutenant, who, jolly now, repeats the action. I too take off my hat and pour the spoiled water over my head. For a tick-tock I feel less sore about my mistake but when I glance at the lieutenant, it is clear he has not forgot.

The lieutenant stores a secret ledger in his memory. Each person has two columns, for and against, and the lieutenant always knows where a person is placed. It is not surprising to hear him tell, in bitter words and months after the event, of some small injustice he has suffered at the hands of another.

'Mind, give that barica a good scrub before we fill it,' Mr Bass whispers as we take up our oars.

Mr Bass does not keep ledgers but he does take measure of his fellow man.

How he does it? I sense that he begins to draw a portrait of a particular fellow in his mind and, at every meeting, he shades the portrait one way, then another. It might take several meetings for a full colouring but, once a portrait is complete, Mr Bass sticks to his opinion. From then on he is loyal to that original conception. The lieutenant is more precise and, for good or bad, his ledger is always open. I imagine my own name in that ledger; my against column is nearly full.

We pull southward with the sun overhead. The sail flaps. We set taut the line to catch the breeze at south-southeast and steer for shore, skimming across the waves.

'We are sailing at three knots,' calls the lieutenant, pleased with *Thumb*'s pace.

Mr Bass is at the helm, looking west. 'Is that Cape Banks?' he shouts.

Cape Banks is our marker to set course for land and search out our river.

The lieutenant peers towards shore. 'Looks more like Hat Hill,' he calls, hesitation in his voice.

'Surely we have not sailed that far,' Mr Bass replies. 'Hat Hill is fifteen leagues from Port Jackson.'

Cape Banks is a far shorter distance from Sydney Cove than Hat Hill. I first spied Hat Hill on our *Reliance* voyage to Port Jackson over a year ago.

'There is the hill Captain Cook likened to a hat,' our master said as we sailed by.

I stood on deck eyeing Hat Hill for as long as it remained in sight, stirred by the thought that I was sailing the same sea as Cook.

From that day, all on board called it Hat Hill. We had seen it again only last month, on our return from Norfolk Island.

I scramble to the bow. Yes, there, to the west, is the hill Master Moore had pointed out.

'Hat Hill it is,' I call. 'See the flat top with its slope. No mistaking that.'

Mr Bass laughs. 'Matthew, we have overshot the mark!'

The lieutenant looks at the water. 'Who would suppose it? The current must be strong.'

A fierce north wind forces our sail south. Our aim is to find a place to land and search out fresh water before night falls. Clouds race along the coast, shifting from white to grey to black. The sea-swells become frothing giants hungry for our boat. We toss about and must tack for shore even though the cliffs are still forbidding. To the west the sun dips behind the mountain. Darkness arrives in a rush. The wind drops, but the sea is choppy. The early moon tickles the water with light. We are still four miles from land.

The lieutenant and I pull for a bend in the coast. Soon we can set a fire, roast meat or boil some soup. The promise of supper keeps me alert but, when we near the beach, our disappointment is great for there is white surf gnashing at the sand.

'Landing is out,' the lieutenant shouts.

Nothing for it but to boat the oars. The lieutenant and I heave up the stone anchor and tumble it into the sea. The moon catches Mr Bass's face as he clears the line, but his thoughts are disguised. Stoic is his second name. The lieutenant and I secure the ropes. My belly rattles. There will be no chance to soak the salt from the pork so it is ready for roasting, nor boil soup. No flame to keep us warm, and already I am cold to the bone. The lieutenant and Mr Bass repack our stores for neither is content with the current arrangement. I pull out another melon, place it on the thwart and cut it open. There is naught to add but bread and raw potato. I serve our meagre meal. As we chomp, I eye the stars.

'Mr Bass, what shall we name this place?' the lieutenant asks, as he sucks on a second piece of melon.

On our Georges River trip all had been named before we arrived.

'Moody Bay?' Mr Bass offers.

'The theatrical interpretation?' Lieutenant Flinders is not convinced.

'Too emotive?' Mr Bass asks.

'According to Bligh,' the lieutenant says, 'when naming unknown territory, the name must allow others to imagine its function. How it might serve future settlements.'

'Anchor Bay,' I say.

'That might give the impression of large vessel anchorage,' the lieutenant says. 'And this is not a bay – it opens too much to the east.'

I hear his dismissal and vow not to speak again, except to agree. This is best with the lieutenant. The only way to stay on the right side of his ledger.

'And yet,' Mr Bass says, surveying the surrounds, 'there is something in what Will says. This bay offers shelter. And that shadowy cliff could be an Arcadian barn.'

Mr Bass throws his melon skin into the sea and wipes his mouth on his shirt.

He grins at me. I bite into my melon to hide my pleasure. Sheltering is not so far from anchoring, is it? How I wish to be like Mr Bass. All is ease.

'Barn Cove,' says the lieutenant. 'It has a lyrical touch and perhaps, as you say George, enough description.'

'Barn Cove it is,' says Mr Bass.

We jostle to find a sleeping nook. Not a simple task as Mr Bass's legs, which do seem longer than a horse's, jerk about. The lieutenant, thinking himself in privacy perhaps, begins souring the air with foul odours. I tuck one arm under my head and bury my nose in the other. I do not know if sharks can smell but if they can, I will put coin to it that the lieutenant's inner winds, once released, will keep them distant.

As I wait for sleep I vision fish swarming beneath our small vessel. Do fish sleep? *Slap, slap,* to dare is to do. *Slap, slap,* to dare is to do. Mama, you did never imagine me an explorer. Your stage set could not compare to this. For here, there is no *Reliance* with its shuffle of crew, it is three of us rocking in a tiny boat on the great ocean. This is my second night away from the *Reliance.* I think now that no other tale ever had this shiver or this shine.

Saturday, March twenty-six, the third day of our journey. I wake. My throat is blistered. There is water about but the wrong kind. I am hot even though it is cold. I say this out loud then regret it.

'Remittent fever,' Mr Bass teases.

Mr Bass likes to scare me with horrid diagnoses. He once told me that Mama had a terrible remittent fever. 'She could die,' he said, with a face so grim I nearly sobbed in his presence. The fever caused him to stay with Mama night after night until she was cured. At least that is what he proclaimed. It took me longer than it should have to see through his ruse.

'More like putrid fever,' the lieutenant says with a sniff at my being.

'No,' I say. 'It is every bone in my body rattled by strange foot-kicking in the night.'

Mr Bass laughs, rubs my head. I pull away. Fifteen is too old for such things, yet Mr Bass refuses to acknowledge it. Why, he is only ten years my senior, and the lieutenant only seven. But to Mr Bass I am still that runt he hired.

Mama had just finished singing on stage when he told her of his offer. 'No,' she said, her face puffed and red. She took off her wig and thumped it on the stand.

'Do not do this, Isabella,' Mr Bass replied, calmly crossing his legs as he sat beside her. 'Do not cosset the boy.'

'He has a gift for the stage,' she said, holding out her glass for more liquor.

'He wants the walls cast away, not the walls closed in,' Mr Bass argued, in his deep-sea voice. 'He wants the rise and fall of waves, not the stage.'

Mama laughed. 'Lucky you are *not* a writer, George, your rhyme is too limp!'

But Mr Bass could convince a fishmonger to buy fish and he proceeded to convince Mama to allow me a life at sea, claiming that if not for his *own* mother's restraints he might by now be captain of his *own* ship. I had begged him to argue for me, having had my fill of rigging stage ropes and mending props, of holding cushions for kings while dressed in hot fabric. Mr Bass's efforts to convince Mama included the buying of expensive liquor.

'You are the victor,' Mama finally said to me two bottles later. She put her hand to my cheek and laughed. I jumped around her dressing room.

That was more than a year ago. Since then, I have travelled further than most have ever dreamt. Despite what Mr Bass thinks, I am *not* that same boy.

The lieutenant leans over the gunwale, eyeing the shore.

'Landing is still out,' he shouts. 'Those waves would pulp us.'

North, the cliffs are high for some long way, yet we need water, *desperately* so, and we must land somewhere.

'South! There, see!' Mr Bass calls. 'Low land is visible.'

'South is away from our river,' is the lieutenant's curt reply. 'No, George, we must bide here until the weather turns.'

'If we sail south and go ashore, a stream might be found,' Mr Bass argues. 'Besides, the wind is for the south, there is little choice.'

'To continue south stretches our agreement with the governor,' the lieutenant says.

Lieutenant Flinders does not easily defy an order.

'How can it be a stretch when the weather itself is telling us what we must do?' Mr Bass reasons.

The lieutenant is unsure.

'Remember, this far south no man has stepped ashore,' says Mr Bass. 'Save roaming cannibals and one or two pirates who do not warrant merit as they have made no map.'

Mr Bass strikes the right chord, as mapmaking for the lieutenant is like honeymaking for the bee.

'Cook's map of this area is scant on detail,' Mr Bass adds.

It is all the convincing the lieutenant needs. 'South it is,' he says, as though the idea was his.

We hoist sail and steer south.

At first, the coast is like the walls of a crumbling castle, only walls where shrubs have rooted. It is forbidding and eye-gobbing. This is not a land of elves and fairies, but one full of misshapen monsters and skeleton ghosts. Then, the castle walls fall away, the land shrinks and is covered with scrubby trees. It becomes sandy beach and stony headland, followed by sandy beach and stony headland, as if God himself had been journeying along the coast practising Port Jackson miniatures before creating the main event. We spy a likely spot for a stream and sail through a gap in the reef but cannot land as the surf is in a beheading mood.

'Anchor,' the lieutenant calls.

Mr Bass and I drop anchor well before the surf. My throat is now a hollowed-out log. One of us must swim to shore to search for water.

'Will, are you up for it?' the lieutenant asks.

'Yes,' I say, pleased not only for the challenge but that he addresses me.

I begin to strip off my clothes. The white sandy beach is curved like a butcher's knife. Scrubby trees beyond become a green blanket covering the hills. A man might get lost in such a place. For that matter, anyone or anything could hide there, if they knew how to get about. Before we left Port Jackson, stories of cannibals living down south had been all the talk. I stare at the trees.

'Will, who is the best swimmer, you or me?' Mr Bass asks.

'Your stroke has mightily improved,' I say, unable to take my eyes from the shore.

Mr Bass laughs too loud.

'Together we can fight all the cannibals that come our way,' I add, for I cannot abide being thought a coward.

'Both cannot go,' the lieutenant says, cheerily. 'Two men lost to cannibal supper is unseemly.'

'Then, as I will no doubt make the best stew,' Mr Bass says to me, 'should not I be the one to swim to shore?'

This moment is a mark, is it not? We are in a place where no European foot has stepped. Therefore, my swim to shore is unbefitting. It is Mr Bass who should have the honour.

'In the sea I am a dolphin,' Mr Bass shouts, as he dives into the water.

I empty the barica and throw it to him. 'Do not forget to

scrub it out,' I tease, because the mood has turned easy, and the lieutenant will surely not mind my jest.

Mr Bass floats on his back, takes hold of the barrel in one arm, and begins to stroke with the other. We cheer him on, but the current is strong and, despite our care when dropping anchor, we have drifted to where the waves break.

'Here, Will, take the helm,' the lieutenant orders, spying the danger.

Taking hold of the anchor rope, he hauls us back to our dropping point. When we are safe again, I turn to watch Mr Bass. He is midway to shore, his arm like a great oar rowing his course.

But again the lieutenant shouts. 'Will, the anchor is lifting!'

I whip to attention and spy a growling dog of a wave bolting in. It picks up *Thumb*. A dazzle of blue sky and salt spray. We ride the wave with terrific pace. I steady the helm but the wave shatters and *Thumb* crashes in the surf. I fall and roll about, grip the gunwale. A second wave, even larger than the first, splashes over the boat, scoops me up. I am tossed into the water and tumble in white froth until my shoulder thumps onto wet sand. I thud to a stop, water rushing around me. There I lie, coughing and spluttering, a wet rag in need of squeezing, grit in my nose and ears. My cheek sinks in the sand. I spy shells like white pearls, then see the lieutenant, sand-covered, as if newly born from the earth, staggering to his feet.

'Will,' he calls. 'Quickly now! We must use the next wave to haul *Thumb* to safety.' He starts limping towards our boat.

I stand and splash after him. Mr Bass, having swum to shore, comes wading through the surf and hurls the barica onto the sand. We grip the gunwale of our small boat that is tossing in a turbulent sea, an enormous swell romping towards it. The wave lip splits around *Thumb* and we heave with all our might, running with the smash and crash of water and pushing the boat up onto dry sand. Safe at last. Mr Bass and I whoop with pleasure. We eye each other and, for no good reason, race around *Thumb*, hooting and howling. In our mad calls there is that nameless thing we share, a wild wanting, all fluid and light.

The wind is gusting, kicking up waves that lick the dry sand. It checks our high spirits. The lieutenant begins to pull soggy supplies from *Thumb*. He lays them on high ground to dry.

'Will, bail the boat,' Mr Bass says, taking his cue from the lieutenant but, in truth, having to feign sensibleness as our high spirits will not easily abate.

I climb into *Thumb*, pull out the bucket and begin to bail, remembering the ride to shore, the rush of wind. I want to hoot but dare not. It would displease the lieutenant. I bail until my arms ache and only stop to rest when the water in *Thumb* is ankle-deep. It is now that I spy a thin trail of smoke snaking up from the scrubby trees. The howls of dark nature in my head; my imaginings, bloodied and boned. I see how we are as if from above. We three, caught between the snapping ocean and the scrubby foreshore, with a boat no larger than a young one's toy. I try to speak. No sound comes. Mr Bass and the lieutenant do not see me pointing. I slip from the boat onto the sand, shake Mr Bass's arm. Mr Bass, still naked, turns to gaze at the forest. The lieutenant does the same.

Yes, I have heard tales of cannibals living south of Botany Bay, but hearing tales is different from standing on a beach knowing one could soon hunt me. Here, death and life are wrangling twins and I am standing in between. In a land that breeds animals with enough spring to jump over huts, and where a bird can be taller than a man, run faster, yet cannot fly, who can tell what rarity we might meet this far south.

We three are hushed, for being here is a step too far beyond our knowing. When I first learnt my letters I stumbled over those that would not jiggle together. I whittled away at them until one day I shaped a word. I felt so shiny with myself for having a whole word in my grasp. But a day later, when Uncle Hilton (a stage player like Mama) gave me one of his scripts to read, I became gloomy, and was truly a most miserable wretch. Before I started my lessons I did not notice words at all, but that day I did, only I had not reckoned on there being so many *more* to know. Here in the new world it is like we are all just learning our letters.

The lieutenant cannot take his eyes from the smoke. 'If natives were to run from those trees, there would be no time to get *Thumb* through the surf,' he says.

Mr Bass picks up one of the muskets. It is wet and filled with sand. The second musket is the same.

'Damnation,' he whispers. 'We are unarmed.'

In fright, I look again to the smoke rising above the canopy. If the rising smoke signals a campfire, and if that campfire warms cannibals, and if those cannibals have a mind to sup, we have no way to defend ourselves. I peer into the forest. There! Something moves. Animal or man I know not. The tall trees twist in the wind and bend towards us belching forth a flock of wild birds with yellow crests and enormous white wings. The birds fly above then arc south, winging inland from the coast, screeching like monkeys. *Aark! Aark! Aark!*

Mr Bass is the first to make a move. 'Get *Thumb* out past the surf now,' he orders. 'I will swim the provisions to you.'

'No. You and Will take the boat.' The lieutenant's face is pinched with worry. 'I will wade out with the stores and meet you at the wave break while you swim back and forth to *Thumb*.'

'And when the cannibals arrive, what then? Have us all made savage supper with your poor paddle?' Mr Bass flushes red.

So too Lieutenant Flinders. The air is fine ropes stretched tight. I cannot breathe.

'Bass, my man,' the lieutenant whispers, 'I will not leave you alone on this shore.'

'No more on it, Matthew, you *cannot* swim!'

When he wants, Mr Bass is commander of all.

The lieutenant's face is like furrowed land but he must agree. He knows he has no talent in the water. If cannibals came, he could not save himself, let alone Mr Bass, and without doubt I would not figure in his thinking.

'As you wish,' the lieutenant says, 'but first, I'll pack what might spoil.'

He sets about sorting the stores.

Mr Bass turns to me. 'From your vantage point at sea you can spy the entire coast. If there is movement, holler with all your might.'

My friend, Na, has shown me how to call across distances with cupped hands to push the sound. I tell Mr Bass this is what I will do if I spy a cannibal.

'Matthew, go. I'll bring the rest,' Mr Bass orders. 'If it comes to it, our lives are more important than victuals.'

I grip the gunwale, ready to launch. One of the oars is split. I pray it holds together.

The lieutenant stashes the flour and rice, and signals me with a nod. With Mr Bass's help, we slide *Tom Thumb* along the wet sand into the shallows, pushing through the waves. Mr Bass takes hold of the lead line and wades back to shore. Lieutenant Flinders and I climb into *Thumb* and, sitting together on the thwart, row out past the wave break. We pull to a safe distance and drop anchor.

'Where are the muskets?' the lieutenant asks.

My heart, a thousand tiny drums. In our rush we left the muskets on the sand. The lieutenant goes to holler but I stop him. I put my cupped hands together and call. Mr Bass looks up but thinking I am signalling danger, searches the forest first, then the beach, before he turns to us.

The lieutenant stands and mimes shooting Indians. At another time the mark of it would set me laughing. He does not intend comic, but comic it is.

Mr Bass, finally comprehending, picks up the muskets and waves them at us. Holding the lead line in his left hand, he runs into the surf. When the water is to his chest, we yank on the lead line, pulling him towards us. He raises the muskets high above his head. We heave. *Thumb* creaks. We heave again. Seawater splashes. Heave. Heave. The weight of the man! Heave. Then – snap! The line breaks and the lieutenant and I fall backwards. I only have time to spy Mr Bass sinking beneath a wave. The muskets go under with him. When I scramble up, Mr Bass has already resurfaced and is kicking through the water on his side, holding the muskets above his head once more. The lieutenant hauls in the rest of the lead line.

'Damaged as we were dumped,' he says, picking at the frayed end.

Mr Bass reaches the boat, clings to the gunwale. I take the muskets from him.

'We need a raft,' the lieutenant says.

'We could lash the oars together with the mast,' Mr Bass suggests.

'That will do it.' Lieutenant Flinders is up and at the mast.

I stow the muskets.

'Will, help me here,' the lieutenant says.

We unstep the mast while Mr Bass clambers into the boat. He uncoils the rope and we three tether mast and oars as one.

'Now we have a tolerable raft,' the lieutenant says, grinning. 'But pray *never* tell the marines about our near musket loss. They will taunt us for not preserving our artillery.'

I look to the shore. Our stores are spread on the sand. What if cannibals were to come running from the forest? Can they swim? I wish I had asked more questions of Na, who says he has met a hundred such devils.

We lower the raft. Mr Bass climbs down and I toss him a coil of rope that he slings over his shoulder. He settles himself on his knees and uses his arms to paddle in to shore. When he nears land, he rides the surf to the shallows, and jumping from the raft he hauls it up on dry sand. He checks our supplies and discards what is spoiled. The rest he carries to the raft, fastening it with rope.

I eyeball the beach. Only sand glare and tree shadow. Smoke still rises from the forest. No longer a wispy stream, it appears now in short puffs. A signal? Or have the cannibals left the fire unattended?

Outward, I am calm but inside me there is a great bellowing. For now I sense the true weight of my earlier error. If I had checked the barica when Hoary Bogarty had given it over, we three would not be here. I see how one error tumbles into another.

I think of the story that had been the rush of Port Jackson before we sailed. The events in question happened a way back with the tale written up in a Calcutta newspaper and transported by a vessel from that region to Sydney Cove. The report told of how a small boat, with a captain and eight men, set out from the main ship to explore an island. Rough seas caused them to lose sight of their vessel. As they pulled towards shore, the Indians signalled they were friendly and with waving arms directed the sailors to a safe landing place.

Once on shore, three sailors requested permission to tramp through the trees to the top of the hill so they might eye their ship's position. The captain agreed, said he and the remaining five crew would stay with the boat. Three Indians offered to guide the sailors through the forest.

The six men hiked for some time but, as they were nearing the top of the hill, one of the three sailors, the only one with a musket, became suspicious of the guides. He whispered his fears to his two companions but they, trusting souls, assured him the Indians were friendly.

The men continued on their way. When they reached the hilltop they eagerly searched the sea for their ship but saw only waves and gulls. Their disappointment was monstrous. Would they be trapped on the island for all time?

Heavy of heart they began their trek back to their companions. Halfway down, the man with the musket spied one of the Indians moving towards him, too fast for friendship. He shot off his gun. The Indians bellowed and whooped and attacked all three men, spearing the second sailor and cutting the throat of the third. The man with the musket fired again and the Indians ran into the forest. The musket man was unharmed and helped the two wounded men stagger down the hill.

Arriving at the beach they spied blood splattered on the sand. Warily, they followed the blood trail to the water. There was an arm lying in the shallows. A few steps on, a leg. These, they realised, were the limbs of their captain, now hacked from his body, a body that was nowhere to be seen.

Further from the shore two of the crew were floating, facedown, in bloodied seawater. The sailors waded out and turned the men over – their throats had been cut from ear to ear. The horror of it. The three sailors, one still clasping his own throat, the other pressing on his wounded side, now splashed towards the boat. In it lay two limbless sailors. They clambered in beside the dead men and only now did they see a headless sailor, tossed about by the breaking waves beyond the boat.

Shaken by the ghoulish sight and sick with fear for their own lives, the three pulled away from shore just as the Indians, which they now guess to be cannibals, rushed across the sand hooting and howling. They quickened their row and were soon out at sea, far enough not to be pursued. The Indians set up an unholy racket and began dragging the dead bodies towards a large fire set back from the beach. In despair at leaving their companions to be feasted on by cannibals, the three survivors sailed away.

They had a terrible journey, with only salt water to heal their wounds and no rations. After paddling through too many windless days, they made it to Sarret, near Timor Land, where some kindly Indians gave them food and water. The three survived to tell their tale, although one of them died soon after from fever.

This story I tell to Lieutenant Flinders as we watch the shore for any sign of wild men. The lieutenant says he knows the tale and it smacks of embellishment.

'Do not think on it, Will.' The lieutenant is packing away the goods that Mr Bass has rafted out. He is being his sensible self. 'For a start,' he says, 'why would the cannibals leave the boat and the bodies unattended? Where did they go?'

'To light the fire,' I say. 'Or to chew on the captain's body.'

'Why did they not leave a guard?' he asks.

'Because they are cannibals. They do not have guards and soldiers and armies as we do.'

'And why did the three survivors not see the fire burning before they set sail?'

'They were in a state of great fear and shock,' I say.

But the lieutenant will not be convinced. I curse him silently. If Na was with us we would be safe. Na had begged to come on the journey. Mr Bass had been for it but the lieutenant was against, saying he would first need to secure the governor's permission to allow Na to join us, and that would delay our departure.

'And besides, Na eats for ten,' the lieutenant had added.

'Na is needed to sweep in the hospital,' Mr Bass had said finally.

But Na knows how to ward off cannibals with his death-rattle stare, which he has shown me, revealing the whites of his eyes. I realise now that it falls to me to keep alert for cannibal terror, as the lieutenant is too comfortable in his perceived knowledge.

It is late in the day when a red-raw Mr Bass finally climbs on board and flops down, exhausted.

'The bread is spoiled,' he says. 'The tea and coffee too. I left them on the beach.'

I untie the raft while the lieutenant reports on the rest of our supplies.

'Sugar, half wet. Flour not at all, nor the cakes of portable soup. Six pounds of rice, one piece and a half of salt beef and three of pork, all dry.'

I roll the barica under the thwart. We have failed in our attempt to find fresh water, and feel it sorely in our throats.

'One horn dry, two wet,' the lieutenant adds, checking the gunpowder. 'And I cannot pull the damn rod from this musket.'

Mr Bass lies, gasping like a caught fish. There is no way to quench his thirst. Nothing for it but to leave him be.

'We must be on our way,' I remind the lieutenant, who is taking his time about our departure from danger.

Surprisingly, he heeds my words. We step the mast and hoist sail. A breeze catches and we are off. The lieutenant sits at the helm and navigates towards the islands in the distance. I claim the bow. Mr Bass attempts to dress in damp clothes, but his skin is too sun sore and he can only suffer a shirt.

We near the first island, but it is too rocky for landing.

'Not here,' I call.

Air currents roll around us as if twisting a knot. The lieutenant steers further south; Mr Bass, asleep at his feet. We again pass beaches and headlands that look like practice Port Jacksons. I clamber back to the lieutenant.

'Can we land?' I ask.

The lieutenant looks to the sails to read the wind, then to the trees on land. He reads the invisible by close attention to the visible.

'Not yet. The wind will be against us for some time,' he says. 'See that double saddle?' He points to the south.

'Yes,' I say.

'We will pull to the other side and wait it out.' The lieutenant eyes the water. 'It is the sea currents you need to gauge as much as the wind,' he adds, in a kindly voice, kinder than he has ever used before. 'Come on, we will douse the sail.'

The lieutenant clambers over Mr Bass. We lower the sail and get upon the oars. Squalling winds now come at us from all directions, tossing *Thumb* about. *Slap, slap,* to dare is to do. *Slap, slap,* to dare is to do.

We row to the other side of the saddle and are out of the gale but the sea drums the rocks beneath the cliffs.

'Anchor!' the lieutenant shouts over the noise.

Mr Bass wakes, his skin tight and red. He lies on his side and rocks with the boat. Although he is hot to touch, he shivers.

The lieutenant and I sit by and try to cheer him.

'Will, how do you think those cannibals would have broiled us?' the lieutenant asks, as if it is a serious question.

'The slow broil, I think.'

'Yet our cook might give a different counsel on the best way to broil *human* flesh,' the lieutenant says.

'He might indeed,' I agree.

Our cook on the *Reliance* has seven different broiling methods, one for each day of the week, which he feels a need to test on us. All on ship are in the habit of remarking, Oh, it is the tough broil today, or, Yes, yes, cook has outdone himself with a feat that defies nature, he has given us the dry broil.

'What say you, Mr Bass? What advice would our cook give the cannibals?' I ask.

Mr Bass can only manage a whisper. 'He would suggest roast for my carcass. Too fatty for much else.'

'What if they were not cannibals at all,' the lieutenant says, 'but the kindest of Indians?'

It is hardly possible to think them kindly but I join the game. 'What if the smoke was caused by young ones left by the campfire for the day?' I say.

'What if it were smoke smouldering from a fire caused by lightning?' Mr Bass suggests.

We laugh and our spirits are eased. Yet talking is hard with the drumming sea. Lieutenant Flinders says we must again spend the night on *Thumb*. I prepare melon and bread for our supper. We eat in silence, weary from the day. After, I lie down near the bow and watch the blue sky fade and a fire-orange moon rise.

When I first learnt I was in Mr Bass's employ, for days after, everyone wanted to jaw my journey. I was a bright star.

On the sail out, it was Mr Paine who convinced Mr Bass I would need to improve my letters if I was to contribute to the rise of man.

'Without your letters *properly* learnt,' Mr Paine said to me, 'you are an animal, no better or worse than a pig!'

Yet, though I did not voice it at the time, and nor have I since, if I followed on with Mr Paine's idea of who was animal and who was man, and if it all came down to knowing your letters properly or not, then *most* people I know (back home and on board the *Reliance*) are in the sty with the pigs.

Mr Bass paid particular attention to my spelling, which was poor, for he said it was a sin to stick in and take out parts of the English language without law or licence. And it was he who, with his painterly way of shaping a foreign word, roused my interest in the Indian language.

It came about when Mr Bass was attending our friend, Baneelong, who was mightily ill. This, on the voyage to New South Wales. Baneelong was the first native of this land we ever met. He was journeying back from living the high life in London with Governor Phillip.

For the first part of the journey Baneelong lay on his bunk staring at the boards above. He made no motion other than that made for him by the rock of the sea. I spied him once for a full hour. Stillness itself.

Mr Bass said, after the hijinks in London it would be a cruel trick if Baneelong were not to reach home. But, curiously,

Baneelong rallied once we'd skipped across the equator, as if he could sniff his homeland on the breeze.

It was then he taught us his language. The word for the Milky Way, only seen in the southern hemisphere, he called *Warrewull*. The Pleiades are *Moloomolong*, and the moon, *yennadah*.

Now I gaze up at the stars and moon every night and, moreover, speak them in two languages, where once I did not give thought to them at all.

Now I know how big the world is.

Before, not knowing the world's bigness meant that tomorrow looked like yesterday.

Yet knowing makes it harder to spy ahead, as now I see tomorrow as unmade and know it will always be so.

I wake, cold to the bone. Eye *Warrewull* above. I sit up. It is not only the sky that is rippling with light, the sea too is covered with flecks of shining. All between is black except to the east where the light curves up, as if a stairway to the heavens above.

If the world were being born again, this is what it would look like. The only sound is the *splish, splash* of water.

I uncoil a rope – *splish, splash* – and twirl the end in the sea – *swoosh, swoosh* – like a whirligig – *swoosh, swoosh*. It goes round and round, stirring the water so it throws off thousands of sparklings, as though sea and sky are sending signals to each other by shards of light. I think I will never see anything so beautiful again.

I grow drowsy and fall asleep with my head and arms resting on the thwart. When I next open my eyes I spy a white-bellied sea eagle gliding above. I sit up and shiver.

Mr Bass sighs. He still wears only a shirt. He holds his head prisoner in his hands. I see blistering on his neck but say nothing as he cannot abide fussing.

The lieutenant nods me good morning, then tips his cheek to catch the breeze. We sit, silent monks in prayer with nature. I watch the sun spread light across the water. The air is not warm, but promises to be.

A voice. Heard above the swish of the sea. Mr Bass and Lieutenant Flinders hear it too. We turn our heads together, and look to the shore and see two Indians in the surf, jumping and waving their fish gigs about so as to catch our eyes. In a click I am like a man stiff with death.

'Only fish gigs,' Mr Bass says to soothe us all.

'But fish gigs have four sharp prongs,' I say.

'They can't be thrown,' the lieutenant says. 'But must be thrust at the fish.'

'So you are safe, Will, unless you turn into a fish.' Mr Bass laughs, but I don't see what tickles him so.

The Indians call again. I can pick out words. Only then do I ease. Cannibals would not speak like Na. One of the Indians holds up a fish. My belly yelps.

'They are offering food,' the lieutenant says.

We all have eyes for the fish.

'Is it safe?' the lieutenant asks.

But our hunger answers for us.

The lieutenant and I get upon the oars and row towards the Indians. Mr Bass sits gingerly at the helm. On the beach seabirds squawk and flap their wings. It is calm enough to land, but we stop pulling some distance from the two men and well away from the thrust of their fish gigs.

One is a giant. His body is burnt black and glistening with water. Hair and beard like a bush, knotted and wild. Dark eyes. Like a man born of the earth itself. When he turns to me my chest goes tight. Yet his mouth is merry.

Mr Bass speaks first using what language we know from Baneelong. He asks the giant his name.

'Dilba,' the giant says.

The second Indian does not say his name. He is twig-thin but strong. And a match for Mr Bass in height. Both Indians have bones through their noses. Do they suffer it for a show of strength?

The second Indian wades through the water towards us, a palm leaf bowl held in his long fingers. The bone through his nose is pointed at one end, like some I have seen before.

He offers the bowl to Mr Bass, who takes it and sips, and hands it to the lieutenant who does the same, before passing it to me. I sip and the liquid cools my throat. Yet after drinking I only want for more.

The giant, Dilba, offers fish, but we have no trade. Then Mr Bass remembers his handkerchief. I spot two potatoes wedged under the thwart and pull them out. We offer these to Dilba who takes them, trading two silver fish of medium size. I throw them in the pail.

Despite thirst, Mr Bass has perked up. He likes to practise the language Baneelong taught him. Dilba's friend dimples, his teeth whiter than any on board the *Reliance*.

'Is our new friend from Broken Bay, or did he say Botany Bay?' the lieutenant asks me.

'One from each,' I say, although I have not been listening properly and am not at all sure.

I want to ask the Indians if they sailed down here in a canoe or if they walked. Na swears that he could beat me to any place, he walking and me in a canoe, even if we both set out at the same time. I cannot always discover what is fibbery with Na, as everything in this land is strange, and what appears strange may not be. Na has told me that his uncles walk south for a gathering where they dance their strange dances. He calls it *carribberre*. I want to ask the Indians if that is why they are here. Are you here for *carribberre*? I decide to ask when Mr Bass has finished his gab and sit forward keen to speak, but spy on shore several Indians striding down the dunes. More Indians soon follow, and more again, all calling and whooping and raising an almighty racket. The two Indians with us turn and bellow to those on shore, who start to enter the water with shouts.

'George?' the lieutenant whispers. 'What do they say on shore?'

Mr Bass has his ear cocked. 'A different language,' he replies. 'I cannot make out a word.'

The lieutenant turns to me. 'Will?'

The shouting frightens me, it sounds like one big roar. I mimic Mr Bass. 'Not a word,' I say.

'Pull out,' the lieutenant orders. 'Too many are gathered.'

In haste, we take up our oars and row away. The two Indians, now waving those on shore to join us, turn back, surprised at our retreat.

'To Port Jackson,' the lieutenant calls to them.

I start to pull north, even though the wind is the wrong way about and slaps me in the face.

The lieutenant hisses. 'Will! Where are you going?'

'Port Jackson,' I say.

'We go south to the tip of the saddle!' he snaps.

I change direction. *Tom Thumb* slides about in the water.

'For pity's sake,' the lieutenant complains.

'Matthew, ease up.' Mr Bass laughs. 'We are safe.' Mr Bass does not look scared but with him it is hard to tell.

The lieutenant turns to me. 'When you know not your opponent's next move, make sure your own is difficult to comprehend. I told the natives north precisely because we are going south.'

'Ah,' I say, as though the strategy is clear, although it is not – for surely they will see us going south?

We row out of the bay and around the point. I am weak with thirst when finally we haul *Thumb* up onto the sand.

Mr Bass stands, eyeing the land. 'No blasted water here.'

'We will eat first, then search for water,' the lieutenant says grimly.

Scrubby land lies at the back of the dunes. I gather sticks for a fire but dizziness forces me to sit. Mr Bass takes the pail to the shallows and guts the fish. When I have recovered I pile sticks on top of each other and set them alight with a flint, blowing until I spark a flame.

When the fire is crackling I lay our clothes near it to dry. My stomach has its own voice. The lieutenant laughs at the noises it makes.

'Hunger must be the most fearful death. I would rather a spear through my chest,' I say.

'You may get both!' The lieutenant cat-grins, as though he relishes the idea.

'The land is a book waiting to be read,' Mr Bass says, slapping the gutted fish on the fire. 'Learn to read it and you will never go hungry. But I agree, Will, hunger is a terrible thing.'

'Disagree,' says the lieutenant, lively and spoiling for an argument. 'Hunger can be good, as long as you are not the hungry party. Thinking, France. Thinking, Howe.'

Mr Bass scoffs. 'What? Are you saying Howe won because he captured the grain ships?'

'Yes!'

Mr Bass finds a long, thick stick to stir the fire with. 'It was an unnecessary move on Howe's part,' he says. 'I would almost venture dishonourable.'

'Howe used every tactic he knew in order to win,' the lieutenant replies. 'Hunger was one of his weapons and knowing how to employ it, his wisdom.'

There is a conflict that now and then rises between the lieutenant and Mr Bass. Both have had to battle death but their stratagems are different. Mr Bass, being in the healing trade, thinks more on healing or prevention, while Lieutenant Flinders, being in the business of defending, most often has weaponry on his mind. Thus they confront death differently. But it has to be said that when both are hankering for exploring, their stratagems are the same.

The lieutenant squats before the fire, keen for debate.

'I know the *Bellerophon* story,' I say to him. 'They talk of it on the *Reliance*.'

The lieutenant looks surprised. 'Do they?'

'They do,' I say, though this is not what I mean. What I mean is that when I was first on the *Reliance*, some nights I would settle quietly outside the wardroom and listen to the officers talk, and several times I heard the lieutenant tell his story of the Glorious First of June Battle, led by Admiral Howe. He did not tell his version with the verve of my Uncle Hilton, who is fond of telling that same battle at London inns, his way of getting free grog. Yet, when I overheard the lieutenant, he was not without style.

'What do they say?' the lieutenant asks.

There is no *they*, but I cannot say I was listening in. 'You wish me to tell how *they* say the story?'

'Yes, Will, yes,' the lieutenant says.

I cannot look at him if I am to speak. I stretch out my arms, as I have seen my uncle do before an oration.

'See, the French are hungry after the Revolution,' I begin, improvising on my uncle's version.

'They start that way?' the lieutenant asks.

'Yes,' I say, remembering I must agree with him always if I am to stay on the right side of his ledger. 'The French people have the heads of nobles but they do not have a plan for what to do with the heads. Not only that, but the people are helter-skelter with the business of revolution. With a bit of bad weather, the crops fail and in a tick-tock the whole country is desperate for a feed. War is trumpeted between England and France because cantankerous George does not want dirty revolutionaries crossing the seas and messing up what he has nice and orderly. When someone high up hears, by use of a spy or two, that a hundred and twenty Yankee ships are sailing for France, loaded with grain, this makes English legs quake. The French fed are strong. The French hungry are a weaker foe.'

'Ah,' says the lieutenant, turning to Mr Bass. 'The French hungry are a weaker foe, the men tell it this way too.'

Mr Bass flips the fish and pushes it into the fire. He raises his eyebrows at me but keeps his thoughts to himself, so I continue.

'What happens is George decides he wants to keep the French hungry and so he sends Wrinkly Lord Howe, who is like a wolf when it comes to stratagems and spoils, to capture the grain ships. Lieutenant, you were only two years on my fifteen when you were on the *Bellerophon*, is that not so?'

'It is so,' he says.

'The fleet sails out of Spithead with twenty-nine warships and fifteen frigates. Hundreds of white sails battling the winds. A glorious sight! Lord Howe has a plan. He knows the French will sail out to meet the Yankee grain ships and guard them into port. Howe wants to get to the Yankees first, take hostage the grain ships and guide them back to England, then turn his cannons on the French. Out on the Atlantic, Howe's fleet patrols day after day. Despite their constant watch no Yankee ship appears on the watery horizon. Howe gets a craving for battle so he leaves nine warships on guard and, with the remaining fleet, sails to the French coast.'

'The French are under Admiral Louis-Thomas Villaret de Joyeuse,' the lieutenant says.

'Howe's new plan is to trap the French as they leave Brest. But all goes hubble-bubble when he discovers the French have already left. Howe sails in pursuit. On the twenty-eighth day he sights the enemy. They have twenty-six warships and smaller vessels too. This is a tough match for Howe's fleet. They are now less nine ships and fewer ships means fewer guns.'

'Well observed.' The lieutenant is pleased with my tale.

'The blustering winds cause sea-swells that tower above the English sails. Raindrops turn to ice and pelt the decks. But still the English chase the enemy. Gun ports are flung open and cannons rumble out.'

As I tell the battle beginning, I make noises in the style of my uncle. There must be theatre in the telling, he has often instructed. His style is what assured him free grog. Sometimes, when we were setting up our theatre in town squares, I would join Uncle Hilton as he rallied the crowd with spine-chilling tales. I learnt from him all the old tricks, yet my telling to Lieutenant Flinders and Mr Bass has something firstborn about it.

'The sailors are feverish for battle,' I say. 'The *Bellerophon* sees a frigate and fires. *Bang*, go the cannons and the frigate sails off. The sailors cheer. But now, alongside the *Bellerophon* comes the great shadow of the *Révolutionnaire*. Big and black like a killer whale, this ship has a thousand men on board and a hundred and ten guns. Cannons blast back and forth! The roar is deafening. The smoke becomes so black it is hard to make out the figure of a man an arm's length in front. The maincap of the *Bellerophon* is hit and the ship lurches to one side, like a wounded walrus. The sailors drag the topsail and soon there is a mess of rigging on deck.'

'The *Bellerophon* had to retreat to repair the damage, there was no other option,' the lieutenant says to me. 'So too the *Révolutionnaire*.'

Mr Bass now has his eye on me, as if my telling surprises him.

I continue. 'The *Bellerophon* and the *Révolutionnaire* appear and disappear like giants of the watery deep, but soon lose sight of each other. Night comes. Lanterns flash. The sailors on the *Bellerophon* work on through until morning. All that can be heard above the sea rush is a hellish hammering.'

The lieutenant picks up a twig and traces the *Bellerophon* in the sand.

'At first light,' I say, 'Howe orders the fleet to form a battle line. He has a new cunning plan. He wants the English ships to sail *straight* for the enemy and cut off the rear of the French line to confuse them. This plan is bold and never done before. The English set sail but some cowardly captains do not carry out Howe's order to the letter.'

'They think the plan too dangerous,' the lieutenant explains to Mr Bass.

'Yet the tactic catches the French on the hop,' I say. 'The English have full stomachs but the French do not. There are loud shots – *crack, crack!* – and thick grey smoke. The *Bellerophon* aims for ...' And here I hesitate, for in my rush of Uncle Hilton-style theatrics I forget what the *Bellerophon* did next.

'The *Bellerophon* sails straight for the space between the second and third ships,' the lieutenant prompts.

'The English sailors fire cannons,' I say. '*Boom, boom!*'

'So too the French,' the lieutenant joins in.

'*Boom, boom!* Then comes the loud crack of timber as masts fall. Wails of men. All is desperate. The *Bellerophon*'s forward rigging is slashed to pieces.'

'It truly was,' says the lieutenant, remembering.

'The French, also, are badly mangled. The *Bellerophon* limps off to repair. That night, time slows. A fog covers the sea like a dirty old coat. Bloodied men appear and disappear, carrying hammers and bits of timber. The next morning the fog is still there. All day the only sound is the sea and this infernal hammering, on and on. This is a cold misty hell; not a burning hell, but it is a hell.'

'You tell this tale with style, Will,' praises the lieutenant.

I feel myself swell.

Mr Bass has two sticks wedged beneath the cooking fish. As the skin blackens over the flame, the smell rises, and my mouth waters, yet the urgency of my tale narrows my attention.

'The morning after, fog again,' I say. 'Later, it clears. The English eat but do the French? No. They cannot eat. They have little food. The English wait to attack. They hold out another day, in order to make the French tremble, in order to make the French weak. Then they sail. They set a diagonal course and smash through the centre of the enemy, attacking the ships from leeward. The *Bellerophon*, second in line, opens fire on the French *Éole*. The two ships are so close that any one of the men could reach out and touch an enemy sailor. Fighting breaks out.'

'Black smoke. Gunfire,' says the lieutenant.

'Screams and clashing iron. Turmoil!' I say. 'The *Bellerophon* receives a heavy pounding from the French *Trajan*. You were standing where, Lieutenant?'

'On the quarterdeck.'

'And you were there when a shot smashed through the barricading and hit your patron, Rear-Admiral Pasley?'

'I was there. Pasley's leg was no more than blood and bone.'

'His blood splattered on the faces of sailors nearby,' I add.

'The men say all this?' the lieutenant asks.

'They say this and more,' I reply.

Lieutenant Flinders smiles, pleased his bloody battle is so spoken about.

'Old Pasley has copped it bad,' I say. 'Bleeding, he is carried below. And you, sir, were at the cannons, so fiery was your mood.'

'It was indeed.'

'Yet, Howe's plan has worked,' I say. 'The hunger of the French means seven French ships surrender, too weak to continue fighting.'

Lieutenant Flinders claps his hands together triumphantly. 'And that goes to show that in war there are many ways to defeat a foe and hunger can be used for the good of a nation.'

'And yet the grain ships got through, did they not?' Mr Bass says.

I look to the lieutenant. 'Surely not?'

'Much delayed,' the lieutenant says.

'And strangely, the French claim victory of the exact same battle,' Mr Bass adds, laughing. He turns to me and bows his head and sweeps out his arm with a theatrical flourish. 'But that was well told, Mister Martin.'

The lieutenant gazes up to the sandhill behind and gasps. I follow the direction of his stare. Standing on top of the dunes are Dilba and his friend.

'Are they alone?' the lieutenant asks.

The two Indians run down the hill, shouting. '*Raah. Raah!*'

'Have they weapons?' I ask.

I can see no spears. But do they hide some other weapon?

We rise. There is nowhere to run. I pick up the long stick used for stirring the fire, and hold it before me.

This is what it is to be a man.

A man must fight.

A man must defend, his own life and that of others.

The two Indians are nearly upon us.

Their eyes wide.

They shout and whoop.

Pelicans fly above.

Their huge wings flapping

Hawker
1822

as they land at the creek mouth. The bastard birds stir up my dogs, get them barking. The kangaroo I'm stalking thumps off as I take my shot. I curse at the pelicans. There's a holler from the native camp.

The chief and his retinue come running along the lake shore to see what I'm shooting at. I aim my fowling piece in their direction. They stop their charge, stand and stare like Bow Street Runners refusing to relinquish the chase. 'No shoot,' the old chief warned, last time he allowed his nephew to guide me on a forest trek (services purchased for a small piece of tobacco). He is not fond of rifle shooting in his dominion but will allow the odd kangaroo or bird to be taken down. The chief pretends to be in command. Most times I embrace the fiction. I've affection for the old coot. Could have shot him dead anytime, never has his guard up. But he's a man who lacks fear or malice, and that's rare enough in any place, let alone this matted rough. I lower my gun and raise my hand so the chief knows I mean no harm and soon enough he and his men leave off.

Around the edge of the lake, which spreads like a watery blue moon before it narrows to the sea, campfires are being lit, radiant markers to the thick forest. A weepy magic stirs this place at dusk. Clouds hang low, their double in water that birds glide over, as if traversing mountains deep. Everywhere, the chatter of native families and the howl of wild dogs. Nearby, a group of women are wading in the shallows, fishing. I try to pick her out. My one. A woman wades out to her waist. Is it *her*?

Before me, a pelican drifts. I could shoot it, use it to bargain. Get *her* to see my worth. I take aim but hear horses galloping, up near the cornfield. Must be the overseer, Vince Byrne, and his pack of two merry men. I yell for Lambskin. Cannot hear his axe. No telling if he's in earshot. There's two of us lifers here to tend Captain Brooks's thirteen-hundred acres, two in desperate need of freedom (or at the very least a ticket-of-leave), but only one can be relied on. Lambskin is ruining my chances of leaving this place.

'Lambskin!' I holler.

Vince Byrne won't like it if I'm not up at the field protecting Captain Brooks's corn from cockatoos or native thieves. He won't like it one bit. As overseer he is rigorous. But if he hasn't packed the grog this trip I'll be slowing down my labour till it comes.

I hike away from Mullet Creek, through the trees and up the rise to the big old fig. Stash my firearm in its hidey-hole, continue on through the forest and come in through the back of the cornfield. I see three horses cantering towards the hut. As I expected, the Byrne brothers – Vince on the stallion, his younger brother, Jed, on the brown mare – and the new man, Sam Poole (a pathetic pocket-picker when he went down), riding last.

The corn cracks as I stride the field but underfoot the soil is still damp from rain that came when needed.

'You're late,' I call, when I'm near the boundary.

'A day or two,' Vince says.

He caresses the neck of his horse.

'Trouble?' I ask.

'Always trouble.' Vince smiles.

Keeping a secret from me gives him pleasure. Irks me but I must play the fool. It's Vince I need to befriend if I'm to leave this hell and work the Appin farm. He's the man who will petition Captain Brooks. Brooks may own this land he calls Exmouth, but it's the eldest Byrne who decides its future.

The three dismount. Vince, weather-toughened and alert; Jed, as fair as his brother is dark, with shirtsleeves long enough to shield the sun; and Sam Poole, bent like an old man and still hollowed out from his sea voyage. Poole stares about him like a startled animal, while Vince and Jed make to hitch their horses to the front of the hut.

'Not there,' I say and point to the side where I've set the new rail.

There's no malice in my voice but Vince marks me all the same, turns to Poole.

'Hear that, Mr Poole? Appears that Mr Hawker don't appreciate walking out of his castle each morning and stepping in horse shit.'

'Does he not?' says Poole, joining the lark.

'Evidently, in Mother England you have horses so clean they don't defecate. That true?' Vince asks.

'In Mother England,' Poole says, poker-faced, 'our horses don't defecate and what is more, they is so intelligent they can talk. Back home a man can have a regular conversation with a horse.'

'Just as I thought,' Vince says. 'Too much inbreeding. Barking mad, the lot of yer.'

The Byrne brothers enjoy the jest but I'm not partial to being put in the same camp as the red-faced Poole. My dogs bark and run at the horses. I quiet them with a word. Rough mutts but they do what I say. Jed Byrne sets free the yapping pup tied to his saddle and it stirs mine up again.

'There is a trick to training a mutt,' I say to Vince. 'You need to think like the pack. Show them you are the one to watch.'

The pup keeps yapping like a whiny brat.

'Shut that mutt up,' Vince calls to his brother.

Jed turns, moony-eyed, offended. The pup is a sore point between them. I can use that.

Darkness settles on the forest that runs alongside the field. Cornhusks quiver in the cooling breeze. In this place the heat of the day runs into a noisy night full of jumping beasts with luminous eyes. Here, the night does not entomb the earth, instead it breathes alive ghostly shadows, as if the buried are rising up.

Poole's gelding bucks and pulls away from the rail. The man has no gift for working horses. He curses and gives it a whack.

'Hey!' Jed up and leaves the pup, takes hold of the gelding, settles it down with whispers and pats.

Poole stands back, unashamed. 'Jed, the horseman,' he says.

'A trusting touch,' I say, but that is not what I think.

When the Byrne brothers first brought Lambskin and me down to set up camp at Exmouth, an even wilder place then without pen or post, Jed spent his time in the forest collecting plants. When we went hunting Jed refused to fire his weapon. Against orders Vince trusted me with his brother's rifle (Vince does not know about the fowling piece I have since gained from a cedar cutter, traded for turning a blind eye to logging the southernmost portion of Brooks's jungle) and has done every visit. There's frailty in Jed and experience has taught me that associating with the feeble-minded is a dangerous occupation. Last month a bonded man, a decrepit fool, on his way to Appin to get medical attention, disappeared. Rumour is a fellow servant followed him up the track and hacked him to death, then threw the bloodied axe in Budjong Creek. All for the sake of a few sovereigns the fool had let know were in his possession. Out here a mind like flint and a gristly intent is needed to see a man through.

'We are out of everything,' I say, turning to the elder Byrne.

'Flour?'

'Not flour.'

'Tea?'

'Not tea.'

Vince claps his forehead. 'Lord, you mean grog and here is us and we forgot the supply!'

'Ever the joker,' I say.

Vince unsaddles his horse, pleased with his larking about. Jed takes the pup to give it water so it is Poole who unpacks the grog.

He does it slow, like he has his grave in sight.

My mouth feels like dirt.

When Poole has the grog on the ground, I don't go for it. Doesn't do to show want to any man, most especially to a spineless one, for their cowardly hearts are easily swayed to betrayal. Poole carries the grog into the hut but before I can follow, Vince orders me to join him. The rising moon spreads light across the land. Vince wants to take advantage and appraise the labours done in his absence. We stride the boundary of the first field. Vince eyes the corn but he has no nose for when it's ready. Cannot even spy the difference between what I seed here and what they seed at Appin.

'This crop should be harvested by now.' Vince speaks with the flattened tone of a born-here. A tone that tells of the true meeting between English and native.

Before I answer, I want to tell Vince a thing or two. Like, I'm not a dog. Like, don't call me the way you call a dog. But that would lead to trouble. I have to force words from my mouth, but it's not the ones I want.

'This is Indian corn,' I say. 'This crop needs two more days of sun. Got to dry out from last week's squall.'

The lie is not a lie because there's truth under it. I might have harvested yesterday but for visions of my future so unsettling I stayed indoors. It will take two days of grog to get me steady again.

'And I've got Lambskin to deal with,' I add.

'I'll tell Lambskin to pull his weight,' Vince says.

'Good.'

'I'll let him know it's you he's to listen to in my absence.'

'Thank you.'

Lambskin is the malingerer, not me. Vince knows it. I know it. The only person not to know it, is Lambskin.

'There is trouble up at Appin,' Vince says. 'Natives stealing the crop. My man there, Kent, cannot contain it.'

'Cannot or will not?'

'Kent's too friendly with the natives by half. If they've no fear of retribution nothing will stay their hand. If the crop today, what tomorrow?'

At Appin they have cool breezes, good grub (a cook to go with it) and straw beds. Kent does not know how favoured he is.

'I've nothing against a shift to Appin. Kent might serve his time better here at Exmouth, where the work is clearing land.'

'Captain Brooks is set on you staying,' Vince says.

My blood heats at the swift denial. Brooks is the cocksucker forging his fortune on my labour. A crooked captain who scored land grants by soft-soaping Macquarie – that boot-licking cussed imp of a governor who would give away his blessed wife if you named a river after him. I hold back my temper. Scoring the Appin role will take some persuading and evenness is all.

'You're the man to help him see different,' I say.

Vince eyes me. 'Kent shoulders a rifle but he's frightened to pull the trigger. What about you?'

'You've seen me hunt.'

'I need a man that can hunt then forget what he's hunted,' Vince says.

53

'Look no further,' I say, but I can tell Vince is not convinced.

'There's a native buzz at Appin that needs to be quieted,' Vince says. 'You weren't even in the country last uprising. It took men from our fields. Brooks don't want that repeated. We need to stamp sparks out early.'

Vince stares across the field (that looks less than it should for our time here) and up above the trees to Mount Hat that shimmers in the starlight, appearing more liquid than matter.

'Jed, Poole and me leave tomorrow to muster at Kangaroo Ground,' Vince says.

'Why not stay a day or two?' I ask, feigning ease.

'Brooks wouldn't like us staying longer than a night.'

'I could shoot a kangaroo. We could have a decent feed.'

I know one thing about Vince Byrne. He's a man who likes to eat.

'Brooks would never hear of it from these lips,' I add.

Vince laughs and cocks his head on the side, pretends to talk to the Captain himself. 'Captain Brooks, sir! When I were down Five Islands way my horse took lame, requiring me to delay two days instead of one.'

'A kingly performance,' I say and clap my hands.

Vince says he is of a mind to stay but his conscience pricks so he has me report about the peach trees and the potato field and the pumpkins growing at the back of the hut. I'm all thirst but he keeps me yapping. My hands begin to shake. Whether disquietude at the prospect of convincing Vince to get me to

Appin, or lack of grog, I cannot tell. I push my hands into my pockets and continue my report.

As I finish, I spy Lambskin in the distance, walking out from the blackened trees, bare-chested, with a red cloth tied around his neck.

'He's like a native man,' I say to Vince.

I need Vince to know that the fieldwork here is the labour of one man, not two. Lambskin is full of ruses. Yesterday morning he complained of shocking cramp. Spent hours squatting behind the trees. Then he could not till the potato field because his left toe hurt. Described the pain as if he were a ruddy physic. Lambskin is worse than a Black. Blacks do not pretend to work.

'Lambskin is a skulker,' I say. 'Everything you see here is my doing. It is no easy feat to clear and till a field with a simpleton for your partner. There's no telling what I could do at Appin.'

Vince is silent but I spy the shift in his eyes. We walk back to the hut, do not wait for Lambskin, who trails behind like the servant he is.

The hut is one room with a fireplace, built by Lambskin and me in our first weeks here. It was our protection from all that surrounded us, not just natives, the forest too. For the forest is thick with giant trees and ferns and vines, and also with unnatural animals and birds that screech and fight all through the night. I never feared a forest before. Back home I spent my youth trapping and hunting in one. It was the streets of London that took me down, not the forest. But this forest is different. I had not reckoned on its fevered nature, all sweaty and shaking. Had not reckoned on it whispering to me of a night. Had not reckoned on the dark days it gives me, days when I go out with a stirring to shoot everything in sight; a stirring stilled only by grog. This forest grows a part of me I never knew.

Hardly knew.

Except that one time in London.

There was that.

There are other spooks about this place I had not reckoned on: Lambskin's delirium that sends him bounding through the forest like a wild goat; birds that fly down and stare with so forceful a gaze that I feel a stranger on this earth; my yearning for the smooth run of English voices that let you know the path being taken ahead of taking it.

Poole has boiled pork to go with the grog. The man can cook. Two steadiers and the hut takes on a new shine. After we eat, I spread skins in front of the hearth and we lie listening to the spit and hiss of burning wood.

Vince tells tales of his time tracking bushrangers in the Hawkesbury.

Rain taps on the roof like it's asking permission to come in.

Lambskin rasps and we laugh. There is something in companionship. I look to Lambskin who plays the joker. He's a different kind of man now, softened by grog. I regret my turning

Vince against him. I hear my father's voice storytelling – *There's land enough for every kind of tree, even the scrawny ones.*

Jed sings the ballad of a lass who longs for the sea.

'He has our ma's voice,' Vince says softly. 'Our ma who was once an actress, yes she was, on the London stage and all.'

They make much of their elder half-brother who accompanied the adventurous Flinders on his explorations, back in the days when no one ventured far beyond Port Jackson. After his return to London, this brother pined for Sydney Cove, and so brought his ma, uncle and sister back to settle here. This half-brother's ma had two dead husbands (or so Vince claims) and soon married Thomas Byrne. Vince and Jed were born in a house with seven rooms and two parlours. They bear their father's name although he died when they were young.

I find no envy in what I hear. Listening is sweet. Night, with the fire, with grog; this land is not a gaol then.

Through the window I spy the stars, bright against the dark sky. Beneath their twinkling my hut does seem like the grandest palace. Tonight I will slumber as a king.

If I get to Appin, get my freedom, maybe I'll not return to England. I could score a land grant, work the soil myself, and wed a lass who longs for the sea. But I must first persuade Vince Byrne. If I can prove hardness, the rest will play itself out.

My turn to yarn and I tell my friends of the Surrey estate where I grew up, of my botanist brother, and of my time in London working at the paper press. I do not tell about when all went bad.

The cockatoos jolt me from slumber. I push myself up and hurry outside. Picking up the flag I have left by the door, I run with it through the cornfield to scare the birds. None can settle and I keep at it until the pests take flight. When I'm sure they are gone I return to the hut and stoke the fire. Snores and rasps but no one wakes. Weighed down by last night's liquor, perhaps. The effects never last as long with me as with others. When the fire is crackling I pick up Jed's gun and step from the smoky hut into the light.

A raven struts the patch of grass near the stringybark. A python twines the trunk, slithering to where the birds like to rest. Wagtails dive at the python, make a racket to scare it away. I yawn and stretch, call my dogs, and take off through the grey trees, gun cold in my hand.

The forest is alive with insect hum. My mutts sniff around. They know how to hunt. When I spy movement to one side, I twist to face it and the dogs bark, but I quickly lower my gun.

A bush quivers. I watch and wait. Feel like I have air under my feet.

Could it be *her*?

A brush turkey shoots out from beneath the silvery leaves. No one there.

I used to see her some mornings, fossicking about. But not since the day the deal with the chief's nephew went sour. Corn for women – that was our trade. A full peck was handed over. Lambskin had his woman picked, I had mine, but when we went to the native camp to collect what was rightfully ours, the men stood and raised their spears. They were no more than a few yards from us. I've seen natives kill kangaroos from a longer distance and I did not have my fowling piece then.

'We had a deal!' Lambskin shouted.

'Women stay here,' the chief's nephew announced.

He knew our ways by then, our vulnerabilities. The chief, who had a better sense of justice than his nephew, was elsewhere and would not return for some time.

'They never intended to complete the trade,' Lambskin whispered, disappointed.

My eyes were still on the spears pointing right at us.

'Why did you give them the corn?' I said. 'You should have waited till we had the women.'

Lambskin groaned. He ached for a woman but had done the deal the wrong way about.

The women were in canoes on the lake, watching us men on shore. I saw my one laugh. Had she never intended to come? Her wild sister laughed the loudest.

The men took another step forward, brandishing their spears.

'I want her,' I said firmly and pointed to the farthest canoe where she sat, her curly hair glistening in the morning light.

'No!' yelled the chief's nephew.

The native men ran at us and we had no choice but to back away.

We left the camp, empty-handed. Since then relations with the natives have been strained and we do not let them near our place. From now on they will *not* be getting our corn, not even one husk. I will get a full crop in, Vince Byrne will convince Captain Brooks of my worth, and I will leave for Appin.

I do not shoot a kangaroo, my steps are too heavy, but I down two pheasants. The heads for soup, bodies for stew. The meat is sweeter than kangaroo. On the stroll back to the hut, with the dogs running alongside, I feel myself swell.

'They're called lyrebirds,' Jed says when I toss the birds on the table.

'He's into birds,' Vince says. 'Has a book on them. Traded a live bird for a book, can you believe it?'

'Did not know you could read,' I say to Jed, who sits smirking, thinking he is better because he was born here, because he can roam where he likes, trade what he wants.

'Jed doesn't read,' Vince says. 'He looks at the pictures. He's real good at looking at pictures.'

On another day it would irk, Vince speaking for his brother, but Vince makes it right.

'Good catch,' he says to me. 'Hawker, the hunter.'

'Hawker the hunter,' I say and go for the grog.

Vince and I stroll to Mullet Creek to wash and get water. We put our buckets aside while we bathe. After, we run to dry off, all the way to where the creek joins the lake. The lake, by my reckoning, is twelve miles east to west, and sixteen, north to south. Shallow it is, but keen loggers can load their wares here if they have the right vessel. Pelicans and ducks abound but we have our dinner.

'Flinders called this lake a lagoon,' Vince says.

'The natives call it *Jubborsay*.'

'Look there!' Vince points.

I turn and see porpoises swimming.

'The flood tide brings them in,' I say.

The sight of their play lifts our mood.

'There are surprises in this place and much delight,' Vince says.

'Only it comes at a high price,' I say.

Vince turns to me and laughs, then again gazes at the porpoises.

'Maybe it does,' he says easily.

When we return to the hut, water buckets full, Lambskin and Poole have started on the grog again.

'No, no, no! I came on the *Prince Regent*.' Poole puts his mouth around the word like it's a ship that carries royalty.

'Thatswhattasaid!' Lambskin is still sauced from last night. '*Princeregent*.'

'Lambskin came on the *Larkins*,' I tell Poole.

'Fuckingbastardofacaptain.' Lambskin makes his mouth finish each word but the words still don't separate. The effort exhausts him and he slumps.

'Fucking bastard of a sea,' I say. 'If man was meant to be on the sea he would have flippers or fins. Legs is what we have got and they're for walking on land.'

'Give over,' says Jed.

Normally the boy will not open his mouth but he's had as much grog as Lambskin.

'Man should not be moving about as much as he is,' I say, lightly.

'We can swim, you saying we shouldn't swim?' Jed asks.

His dog is yapping again.

'Shut that mutt up,' Vince says.

'Swimming in a river, walking on land, that is natural,' I say. 'Rivers are connected to land but the sea is different. The sea is unknowable.'

Jed scowls. 'If we all thought that way there'd be no ships,' he says.

'He's a dreamer,' Vince says.

Vince is shrewd so I don't get why he treats his brother like a goddamn deity. 'Got nothing against dreams,' I say. 'Dreams are poetry. It's nightmares that bother me.'

Jed, feigning boredom, picks up his pup and cradles it. Jed is the one to watch. He is the one that could poison my name to Vince. Poison my move to Appin.

'Tell you something,' I say to Vince, 'with all your brother's animal loving, I would not take too kindly to being in one of his dreams.'

Jed is petting his pup but when he hears what I say he

makes a lunge towards me. The dog spills from his arms, squealing. Jed is all shove. I push him back and we start to wrestle. Jed is stronger than I had given him credit for and the grog has fuelled a fiery spirit. I keep my eyes on his, to unsettle his nerve. We hold each other in a rough embrace, the dog yapping at our feet. We trip over it, onto the table, and fall apart. I quickly rise and go in with a blow to Jed's jaw. Jed rolls off the table and lands on the floor but bounces up without a bruise. Vince, Poole and Lambskin are cheering. Jed comes careering for me with his shoulders bent and with such force that he lifts me from the ground and pushes me into the wall. My left hand slaps against the timber and I hear the crack of bones. Yelling abuse, I boot Jed in the stomach, push him back onto the ground and come for him with pace. I slam my foot into his face but he grabs my leg and rolls me to the ground. My left hand hits the floor and I cry out in pain. I kick Jed in the leg, then twist onto my knees, go in and strike, my right hand fisted. Blood spurts from Jed's nose onto me. Vince wades in, laughing, and pulls us apart. He pushes his brother back to the stool.

'Look after your mutt,' he says, because Jed's dog is whining like a woman taken fright.

My hand is busted up and I am in agony but don't show it.

Vince turns and grips my shoulder.

Have I ruined Appin?

Vince's eyes are shining. He's a man who likes the sight of blood.

'Next fight I'm in, I want you with me,' Vince says. He turns to Lambskin. 'Pour Hawker a drink!'

And there it is, hanging in the air like a forming thought, my place at Appin.

Two days drinking with Vince and my head is sore but I want to hunt. Vince and Lambskin come along. Jed stays to play with his yapping pup, aggrieved that Vince and I are carousing like brothers. Poole stays with him. He is so boat-fresh he cannot walk in the forest without haunting himself.

Vince hands me Jed's gun, as though he is a lord granting me a privilege. Superior attitude can wound. Take away a poor man's belief in his own potency and there are consequences. But I say nothing. Nurse my left hand that I have bound tightly.

Lambskin carries his precious stone axe, thieved from the camp closest to us. There is good coin to be made in the sale of native weaponry and before I go to Appin I will be making trades with that purpose in mind. The natives have the life. Eat and be merry. The camp has thirteen women for seven men.

'A waste of honey pot,' Lambskin says.

'I would not go it,' Vince says, as we hike through the forest.

He has his honey pot on demand and three brats to prove it so why would he bother?

I signal Lambskin to keep his mouth shut as he begins to relate past trades. We need to keep our dealings with the natives quiet. How many times do I have to tell him that?

When we were building the hut it was the chief's nephew who showed us the paths through the forest to the cedar trees. He taught us how to strip the bark of the *Couramyn* to make a fishing line, showed us what berries not to eat. Once, when our traps had caught nothing, the nephew gave us kangaroo tail. He thought he could take corn in return, said tobacco was not enough.

'That corn does not belong to me,' I explained.

The nephew went away and the chief, with complete understanding of men's desires, sent *her* back.

'Our berry grow there,' she said, pointing to the cornfield.

'Not any more,' I said, but gave over five husks.

She was as naked as the new morning but walked with the grace of someone high up. There was a tiny bump on her shoulder, mottled in colour, as though she had been recently bruised.

'Always ask and I will give you one or two corn,' I said.

That is how the trade of corn began.

But my sights were set differently then. That view has gone. It's Appin I'm aiming for now.

We walk through the trees. Captain Brooks's land is bound by Brooks's Creek to the south, Mullet Creek to the north. East his land edges the lake. The man has such good access to creek water that the farm he plans will no doubt prosper. Tomorrow I must harvest. No more days wasted. On Vince Byrne's return from Kangaroo Ground I will get him to secure a cart to transport the corn to Appin. I will slaughter a pig and barrel it, to sweeten the deal with Brooks.

We trek on through the trees, guns in hand, but sight neither kangaroo nor opossum. As we pass the giant fig where I've stashed my fowling piece, I avert my eyes. We stop when we come to the Mullet Creek bend I favour most. Green moss runs over the roots of trees, like the trailing tresses of majesty. Light sprinkles down and the water sparkles. The place has the appearance of a peaceful idyll.

'Gods of the forest,' I say.

Vince squats, cups clear water into his mouth. 'This is the place to be,' he agrees.

Lambskin runs along the bank, spotting fish. I find some wood and whittle it into a spear, like the natives. All is harder with my sore hand but I don't complain. I undress and wade into the water, waiting in stillness for my prey. Only bird chatter and the faint whirl of insects. Across from me, on the far bank, are two long rock ledges. One is the shape of a giant fish. As if once upon a time giant fish swam this creek and here lie the remains. Trailing the spear behind me, I float over to the ledge. It is the perfect place for fish to settle under. Striped fish swarm out when I stir the water up. I spy a flathead and spear it.

Lambskin builds a fire and we throw the fish on whole. I wash my muddied feet in a spring that trickles across the soft grass, and we sit down to eat. Natives appear at the top of the creek bend. Some splash in the water but they keep their distance. One young boy swims closer. He waves at us from the middle of the creek. He swims towards us, pretending to look for fish. When he is less than three feet from the bank he waves again, but when I rise he swims away.

I throw the remains of our meal in the creek, splash my arms and face, then fall back on the grass and look up at the sky through the branches of the tree.

'This is the life,' I say.

'This is the life,' Vince says, like it is me who is in charge.

Vince lies next to me. Lambskin follows suit. The three of us yawn like old men in need of napping. It's as if the forest has put a spell on us. Now our hunger is abated, hunting is forgot. Dreaming is yearned for. Soon I feel the soft hand of sleep.

It's night when we wake. The air is a wet cloth and the owls are spooking. We trek back along the creek and come out at the lake. Fires from the native camps flame all around the lake edge. Voices rise and fall, as if in anticipation of some night event.

Vince takes hold of my arm. 'What there!'

Along the shore, shapes emerge from the darkness.

'What ho!' calls Lambskin.

We raise our guns.

Then I hear the voices. 'Only women,' I say.

We lower our guns and the women pass by. They don't look at us. We are of no consequence to them. Their naked bodies shine in the moonlight. There are nine women in all and three children. I spy her, walking in the middle of the group, protected by the other women. She looks up at me as she passes, only her face is in shadow and I cannot make out her expression.

Vince and Lambskin traipse off along the path, back towards our hut.

I linger. Watching.

The women laugh.

Were I to hurry, I might catch them up. Perhaps say a word to her alone.

The women are disappearing into the forest. And then they are gone. Lost in the dark trees. An owl

Lola
1900

calling, *boo-book, boo-book*. Mary, Abe and me walk the dirt track through the forest we've yet to clear. In the starlit far, at the path end, is the long paddock. Cows huddle at the gate, dark shapes in blue light. The only sounds are our footsteps, the breeze through the tops of the trees, and small animals foraging. Before we begin the morning milking, when everything is caught between day and night, is the time I like best; even now, when it is June and cold, and we must wear coats and hats.

We come to where the trees grow tall and straight. Rope vines hang down and loop ferns that grow beneath. Mist bleeds from the trees and circles us like we are magic. A bird sings one low note and stops, spooked. Abe points to a stand of bangalay and we halt before it. From the gloom between the trunks comes a scratching sound. Could be a lyrebird but no lyrebird is visible.

'It's them,' Abe says.

'Oh lord,' Mary whispers.

Chill on my neck and a prickling all over. We open our mouths and there drifts the morning mist. Oh my! This has happened before but always it surprises.

We hold hands, each of us trembling.

Once we heard laughing voices; another time it felt like we were floating.

We wait, but soon the scratching sound gets softer, and then is gone. Our breath is no longer brumous.

'They keep coming,' I say. 'But why?'

'Want something maybe,' Abe says.

'They never harm us,' Mary says.

We stand there shivering and wondering.

'We've got milking to do,' I say, but do not move.

I am the eldest and prone to giving directions, having got into the habit from when I were young. This after we three suffered the loss of a parent, not once but twice, and before we lived with Aunty. It's Mary that leaves first. She lets go my hand. Walks on ahead, straight-backed with a slight sway, like a princess going to get her crown and not a farmer about to herd her cows.

Bud comes running along the track. He got held up at the house sniffing out a mouse, now he bounds by Abe and me and then Mary. He slips under the paddock gate, scoots around the back of the cows, and barks at their heels. It's still dark and the cows become one shadow as they stamp their hooves and bawl. The ground smells of piss and dung. Roosters crow, and kookaburras call and where it were quiet it is now noisy as hell.

I hurry to catch my sister up, half-sister if truth be known, just as Abe is my half-brother, but there is no half to how we are with each other. Mary untwists the wire that ties the gate to the post. We pull the gate open and the cows amble through, their bodies heaving. Our herd is twenty-one strong this year. All are the red Illawarra Shorthorn Mary's Otto wanted. Otto died a year ago but Mary and me have stuck to the plan made when we three first came down here from the mountain. Build up the herd from one breed.

'Get along there!' I call, hitting the rump of Bess who likes to take it slow.

'Get along there!' Mary calls.

The cow named Trigger runs off the path into the forest. Abe bolts after her. Abe is wiry and stooped but with a fierceness that is bright and wise, not sour. Like an old man and a fit young one put together. He's too tall for his age, which is why he stoops. He eats for two but the fat falls from him. I watch Abe pat the runaway cow back to the mob. He pats that cow like you would a kid. We look after our cows. Plenty about here thought Mary and me wouldn't manage without a man. After Otto died, and with Mary a widow, 'the plenty' told us to move back to the mountain. We didn't listen. Soon after, Aunty sent our brother Abe to live with us.

'Abe needs a man's job on a proper farm,' she said to Mary and me. 'I'm all right on my own.'

We disagreed but Aunty didn't listen.

'Remember it were me that taught you two girls how to shoot and ride,' she said. 'Just because I'm old, don't mean I'm unable.'

Aunty is tougher than most, and has a tongue that will lash when needed if ever she is slighted. The thoughts of 'the plenty' never bothered her. Aunty's friends are the creeks and forest and all who reside in them. And when we walk this way of a morning, through the darkest part of the track, it's clear to me 'the plenty' don't matter. For then our world seems nothing more than a painting and behind it lies another place; a between place, where our breath turns to mist and where the invisible make themselves felt in our very being.

'Get along there!' I call.

'Get along there!' calls Mary.

'Whoah up!' yells Abe.

We three are sat on stools in the milking shed, each in our stall squeezing cow teats and going at a good lick. The milking shed is open at either end, and also along one side, where the stalls are. Opposite the stalls, against the shed wall, are the hay bales and milk cans. The cows wait in the top yard, move through to be milked, then get liberated into the holding pen near the cottage. I pull on Trigger's teats and milk tinkles on the side of the bucket. Trigger shifts her feet and munches hay. I listen for how fast Mary and Abe are milking. We're having a race and the first to get their full bucket to the milk can and slap on the lid, wins. Last week I milked nine cows to Abe's seven, three days in a row. Abe were off his game. Sullen. Not telling Mary nor me what were going on. After milking he'd disappear for hours on end even though there were chores to be done. According to Aunty, boys at fifteen are like that. Have things rattling around in their still-growing body that don't get sorted in their head.

'Manhood is a tough road,' Aunty said when I told her my complaints. 'Getting there needs careful handling.'

'What about womanhood?' I said. 'That be a tougher road.'

I were thinking of my baby lost as she came from my womb. Born without a cry. That were a sin. Not her sin. One of God against me. My baby got tangled up with all that tied her to me and, at the moment she took her first breath, she were strangled. I were a tree torn out by the roots. Surely that be a tough road to womanhood. (And I'm not even speaking of how she came to conception because that were evil.)

Aunty jabbed the fire as I listed the woes of womanhood but didn't change her position one bit. 'Give Abe his breathing time,' she said. 'He's had too much loss for a boy.'

Abe and me finish milking our cows at the same time. I snatch up the milk bucket and beat him to the can, get my milk poured in first and the lid back on. So far, Abe and me have won two rounds each, Mary none. But Mary is the tortoise and we two the hares, in personality and in action, and it's often her that wins the match.

I pat Trigger out to the holding pen. Sunlight spreading on the low paddock. The middle paddock, still in shadow. Our black cat runs atop the middle paddock fence, crows swooping her. I hear the Farrell boys from across the field. All five of them are in their yard, cursing at cows. They're all lively customers – there's Niall, the eldest, he has the loudest voice; then Connor, second born and the one I like best because he will at least look at me when he talks; Padraig, never without a sarcastic comment; and the twins, Seamus and Donal, who in summer are partial to racing naked from the creek to their barn door. The Farrells are a robust family but they've got a lot of anger in them. Not only their cursing. Whenever I ride by their place there is always yelling and knuckle fighting. And they shoot off their guns at the sight of a snake. They are five boys and they are all scared of snakes.

I turn back to the milking shed that smells of hay and dung and milky dirt. Bess is already in my stall, chomping on hay from the feed box. She brings herself in there every day. No problem. She don't like to be first of the mob and she don't like to be last, she sticks to the middle somewhere. I figure she has worked out that the hay on top of the feed box is wet with dew or rain, and she likes her hay dry. If she goes first she gets wet hay, and if she goes last she gets the scraggly bits, so with the middle bit being best, she places herself in the middle.

I wouldn't put it beyond Bess to work that out. She's a clever cow. Some people think cows are dumb animals but those people don't know cows. Cows got more sense than they get credit for. And they got integrity. They work together. They know things turn out best that way.

I'm halfway through milking Bess when young Jewell comes running into our shed. She stops near me, holding her side because of the stitch, and breathing noisy and fast, as if she has run all the way from her home, which is three creeks west. She has her drawing sack in her hand.

'What's the hurry? We're not even through milking yet,' I say.

'I hate the old man is what's the hurry,' she says.

Jewell lets out a sound, somewhere between a hiss and a howl. I've never heard the like.

'I want to squash his face against the wall,' she says.

'Your old man is bigger than you so that won't happen,' Mary says, matter-of-factly.

'He's a fat old toad sat on the side of a dirty lagoon!' Jewell squeals.

Her eyes water up and I know something is truly wrong because Jewell don't cry. Not usually. We have that in common. I get up from Bess and lead Jewell over to sit on a hay bale. Abe comes too and we both coo at Jewell like we do at baby ducklings. Mary gets a cup from the shelf and scoops some milk from the bucket. She brings it to Jewell.

'What happened?' I ask.

'He says I can't come here no more and churn butter with you,' Jewell says, drinking down the milk.

'How are you to get your butter then?' I ask.

'I'm to go to Duncan's dairy and help there.'

'They don't need help at Duncan's,' Mary says.

'He has spoken to Mrs Duncan and she said if I want to I can come.' Jewell spits her words out.

'He don't want you walking as far as here, is that the reason?' I ask.

'That's not it,' Jewell says, sulkily.

Abe sits beside her. 'What then?'

'You will hate hearing it,' she says.

'Let us be the judge of that,' I say.

'He says it was all right to come here when I was twelve, and when Otto was here to keep things in line, but now I'm fourteen I can't work with no ignorant bastard girl like you, Lola, and with no half-castes like Mary and Abe.'

Where did all this come from?' I ask.

'His toad brain is where it come from,' Jewell says.

My hands are shaking. I press them into my hips to hold them steady.

Someone else might cover such evil words but not Jewell. She's a truth-teller.

There is a silence in the milking shed, even from the cows, who look back at us.

I've not heard this kind of filth talk since school days on the mountain where every day was a battle.

'Your da has got a fever of the brain,' I say to Jewell and go back to milking.

Abe and Mary do the same. I pull on Bess's teats too hard and she kicks back with her front leg. I have to pat her belly and settle her down.

'Lola, I told him he is the ignorant one – not you. You is good with your butter making, and you and Mary is both very intelligent with the cows.'

'I'm intelligent with the cows,' Abe calls out from his stall.

'Yes you are, but Lola and Mary is older and know more,' Jewell says. 'I did admit you being a bastard, Lola, but I said you was a nice one.' Jewell turns to Mary. 'I told him you and Abe ain't even half-castes, Mary, told him you is quadroon. He said back to me it makes no difference you both being quadroon because your skin tricks people into thinking you is both exotic and not two dirty blackfellas, and he said it don't matter if you, Lola, is a nice bastard, because your blood is bastard-tainted and your mother was a dirty white whore.'

'What's got on his goat and turned him mean?' I ask, pretending it don't matter to me what her da said.

'That's not even the end of it,' Jewell says. 'He announces that I got to be with people who will educate me to be more ladylike. He says no other women, and certainly no ladies, would shoot guns. I told him that ain't true, Mrs Farrell has a rifle to shoot snakes, and Mrs Duncan and her daughter Nelly do the same.'

'I don't know what world your da is living in, but it's not the same one as me,' I say.

'I know it. Anyway, I told him, I don't want to be no lady. Why should I be, when there are no ladies about Five Islands. And he said, there are ladies in Sydney. And I said, we don't live in Sydney. And he said, maybe I'll take you there. And I said, I won't go. If I go there I'll get the plague or the clap. He gave me a right old slap then and said my mouth is filthy. But Lola, the plague is in Sydney. The *Mercury* tells us that. When I say something that makes sense he always slaps me because he has no original thought in his fat old toad head.'

'Something must have set him off,' Mary says. 'What do you think it were?'

Jewell looks to where the milked cows are jostling in the holding yard. Small birds ride atop the cows, picking insects from their coats. The morning sun is bright on the yard, shadows gone.

'Jewell,' I say. 'Mary asked you a question.'

I sit back on the stool and try to catch Jewell's eye. Her jaw is set tight. She has a lot of fight in her for a fourteen year old. All us motherless children grow up that way.

'He was in a right rage because he saw me laughing,' she says.

'So he's against laughter now?' I ask.

'He's against anything I do. Lola, can I live with you and Mary and Abe? Please please please say yes. Don't make me go back to him.'

'He'd only come fetch you,' I say. 'He's your da and has final say.'

'He's a da don't deserve a daughter,' Jewell says.

'I agree with that,' I say. 'But we get no choice about our family.'

I try to get a rhythm going with my milking but Dan Dempster's words hurt worse than a slap.

Jewell gets out her drawing book, pencils and knife.

'Don't draw me,' Abe says. 'You know I don't like it.'

'That ain't true,' Jewell says, teasing him.

She sharpens her pencil with the knife and begins to draw.

'Don't draw me like I am,' Mary says. 'Make me look better.'

'I have to draw you like you is,' Jewell says. 'Mr Winter is my drawing teacher, remember. I got to draw the truth.'

Bartholomew Winter teaches at the school. He's won prizes at Kiama for his realistic portraits, most especially of farm workers. Jewell finished at school last year, but on account of her talent, Bartholomew Winter still gives her lessons at no charge.

'If you're going to draw realistic, I'm turning my back,' says Mary. 'I seen how Bartholomew Winter draws dairy maids. Prizes or no prizes, he always makes them look dirty.'

She lifts up her milking stool and sets it on an angle with her back to Jewell.

'I ain't going to make you look dirty,' Jewell says.

'I'm taking no chances,' Mary says.

I pull too hard on Bess's teats and she stamps her leg.

'Sorry Bess,' I whisper. 'Blame Dan Dempster.'

When we are through with milking, Jewell and me set to work in the dairy. It's built of stringybark, felled and planed in those first weeks after we took over the farm lease. Shelves line the walls and on them are dishes of milk that have soured overnight. We take down the dishes and ladle the risen cream into the churner. Jewell starts off cranking. She has got stronger from making butter and she's not frightened of work. That's another way she's like me. I pour the leftover milk into a bucket and scrub the empty dishes. We made our setting dishes from kerosene tins, cut in two, but Mary and me soaked and scoured those dishes for days before we let milk sit in them. We have always kept our dairy clean, you could lick the floor it is that clean. But somehow Dan Dempster's words make me feel like it is dirty. After I have dried the dishes, I wash down the shelves and rub them until they shine, then sluice the floor.

Jewell stops cranking. I help her pour the buttermilk into a bucket. We tip spring water into the barrel and it's my turn to crank. Jewell, sweating now, pulls off her woolly top. She has a brooch with a blue-winged bird at its centre, pinned to her shirt.

'I've not seen that before,' I say.

'It was my ma's,' Jewell says. 'Da keeps it in his top drawer. I stole it, Lola. Stole it from him.'

'Is that what he got angry about?'

'No, he don't know I stole it yet. When he finds out, my life won't be worth living.'

'Why did you take it then?'

'He can't keep her from me,' she says, but there is more plead than anger in her voice.

'No one can keep your ma from you,' I say to Jewell, 'unless she or God wishes it.'

My own ma wished it. She left me on my da's doorstep when I were born and then scarpered, never to be heard from again. My da took me on, bless him bless him. He married soon after so I would be cared for. He married for love but it were a union frowned upon by his family because his new wife's ma were Aboriginal, and even though her father were Scots like my da's family, and a cedar cutter who had done well for himself, it didn't count for naught. My da's parents vowed to never see him again if he went through with his marriage. When he did they kept their vow. They died before I ever saw their faces. All I know of them is that they were religious.

My da were a free-thinking man. He took me and my second ma away from the mountain to live on the coast, and he went to work in the Bulli mine. My second ma loved me as her own and I loved her back and we were a contented family. Mary were born and then Abe, but my second ma died at his birth and nothing were the same after that.

Jewell and me tip out the buttermilk and pour in more spring water. Jewell takes the crank again. I pick up the milk cloths and bucket and walk across the yard and down to the creek. Abe is shovelling out the milking shed but when he spies me, he drops his spade and catches me up.

'Did you know Jewell's da whips her?' Abe whispers.

'Dempster whips Jewell?'

'She bad mouths her da but she won't talk about that.'

'How come you know then?' I ask, as I squat to draw water.

'She showed me. There are scars all across her back.'

'Lots of das whip their daughters, don't they?' I say, and begin to rinse the milk cloths in the bucket.

'Did our da?' Abe asks.

'Maybe he would've once me and Mary had grown.'

We lost our da in a mine accident. This were two years after we lost our ma.

'He wouldn't have whipped us ever,' Abe says, stubbornly.

'No,' I say. 'Probably not. He were a good da, the best.'

When my teacher told me Da were dead I didn't cry but I stopped talking. We went to live with Aunty then, up on Mount Kembla. I didn't talk for a whole year. Aunty were really my second ma's aunty, so Mary and Abe's great-aunt, which meant she weren't a young woman when she took us on. But she never complained and treated us all, me included, like we were her own.

'We got to find a way to help Jewell,' Abe says.

'I know it,' I say.

I hang the milk cloths on the line. Mary crosses the yard from the fowl house and sets the empty scraps bucket on the ground with a thump. I know what she's thinking without her telling me.

'Dan Dempster is a bitter old sod,' I say. 'Don't worry it.'

'What if everyone thinks like him?' Mary plonks herself down on the steps of the washhouse.

After Da's funeral, when we were leaving Bulli to go live with Aunty, everyone from the school came to wave us goodbye. Not only our friends but parents and teachers too. Everyone helped everyone in that place. On the first day at the mountain school we found out life would be different. One boy called me a dirty little bastard. I punched him in the nose and broke it. I were small for my age, and I weren't speaking, but I sure had a temper. At the mountain school it were me took on the battles for our family, but Mary were the most wounded. She's always been more sensitive and kids pick that up. When Mary came home from school one day, her thin arms bruised, Aunty sat us down and told us we'd have to look out for each other.

'What happens in the playground, happens outside it too,' she said.

From that day on she began to teach us how to shoot and ride and trap. That way, she said, if anything ever happened to her, we'd be able to at least eat and protect each other.

Nothing happened to her but Mary and me did learn some hard lessons about life outside the playground. Now it seems like there will be more to come.

I sit beside my sister. There's a quiet between us. Dan Dempster's slurs have seeped inside our bones, making them feel brittle and weak.

'We don't got to care what Dan Dempster says,' I say.

'No, we don't,' Mary agrees. 'But why does he have to say it? Say it, like we are something to be trodden on. What makes him so high and mighty? He can't even spell, gets Jewell to write his letters.'

'Like Jewell says, he is an old toad. And old toads are bitter.'

Tommy Lin and me load our milk cans onto the cart, lifting together and settling them in place. Tommy's cart has tall steel sides and a canvas cover. The wheels are wooden, two big, two small, and need a good strong pull from three horses to roll along the road. Tommy carts the milk cans to the creamery twice a day and returns with the skimmed milk that we feed our pigs. Last week, no matter it were pouring down three days straight, he got my milk to the creamery. The third rainy day, when he came to pick up our cans, he were covered in mud. Tommy's uncle owns a dairy at Dapto, but his uncle's seven sons are there to help and Tommy's cart business is his way of adding to the family coffers.

I fetch a bucket of water for Tommy to give the horses. Then I scoop out two cups of milk from our home can, one for Tommy and one for me. We stand in the yard to drink.

'Dark Dragon Ridge,' he says, pointing to the escarpment.

I look up at the rock face. The clouds above, smoky; the forest-green is like a long shadowy tail.

'Firebreathing, is that it, Tommy?'

Tommy Lin gets a stick and squats to draw the name in the dirt. His long black plait falls down the back of his calico shirt.

烏龍岡

I squat down to look at the symbols.

'Dark Dragon Ridge,' he says. 'Name for town too.'

'Why not call Wollongong, Wollongong?' I ask.

Tommy Lin looks to the ground where he has written Dark Dragon Ridge. 'This one better,' he says.

'Thanks for getting me through that wet weather last week,' I say to Tommy as we stand.

'Always for Lola,' he says.

Tommy has never missed a day and is reliable, but the Farrells say he is not the kind of reliable they like, so have stopped using his cart, and have collected together with some neighbours to buy their own. Tommy has never said a word of complaint, about them or anyone else. He is different, I agree with the Farrells on that score, but not on *how* he is different.

Tommy bows and hands me his cup, and I bow in return.

'Lola McBride,' he says.

'Tommy Lin,' I say.

This is how we say goodbye to each other every day, something taught to me by Tommy. Respectful is Tommy. That's how he is different. Tommy climbs up into the front of the milk cart, adjusts his braces, and jigs the reins. The horses take off and the cart rolls away, trampling over the words Tommy has drawn in the dirt. As the cart rumbles through the gateway there is a gust of wind and brown leaves rain down on the road.

I haul our can of home milk across to the kitchen. Our farmhouse is two small buildings and a washhouse. The washhouse, store and kitchen were all built facing the creek. Alongside the kitchen is the vegetable garden and orchard which has apple, pear, quince, plum, lemon and orange trees. Set back from the kitchen is the cottage. It has two small bedrooms and a sitting room with a fireplace. One bedroom were meant for Otto and Mary, the other for me and my baby. Now Mary and I share a bed, and Abe has a room to himself. We eat at the table set on the kitchen verandah or, if it is cold, in front of the fire. Mrs Farrell next door got herself ruffled once when she saw me lay the table in the open air.

'Don't you have a dining room?' she asked.

When I told her no she sighed like it were another trouble to consider.

I place the milk can in the cool corner. Mary slides dough onto the hot hearth and covers it with coals.

'I'll take Jewell back to Dempster, have a word,' I say.

Mary stares at me. When I told her about Jewell being whipped, she got teary, but now her face opens up and she begins to laugh. 'Only if I ride with you,' she says. 'Need someone to keep things calm.'

'You worried about Dempster losing his temper or me?' I ask.

'Both,' Mary says. 'Only Dempster is bigger than you.'

'I've got my rifle,' I joke. 'If he steps out of line, I'll shoot the old bastard.'

'That's if he don't shoot you first.'

Jewell and me carry buckets of skimmed milk, bran, middlings and maize out to the pig pen. We've got two troughs. In the big trough we mix everything together. The smaller trough is for our newly weaned piglets, and in that one we mix in all but the maize. The boar and sow come running when they first hear us stirring. It takes longer for the piglets to catch on that it's feeding time, but soon they too come squealing out from their shelter. They try to get at the big trough but it's too high for them. Only when I bang a bucket on the side of the smaller trough do they come in that direction.

Jewell elbows me.

I turn and see Connor Farrell striding across the low paddock.

'Here he comes, the man himself,' Jewell says. 'You know why he comes here so often don't you?'

'To get information on our herd.'

'He's after you, Lola McBride.'

'Not interested.'

'Plenty say you *are* interested.'

'Don't listen to the plenty, how many times I told you that?'

'Look at how he struts,' she says. 'He's a horny goat.'

Connor is tall and thick-bodied like his elder brother Niall, but they are chalk and cheese in temperament. Niall explodes. Connor is like an arrow narrowed for its target. The younger brothers are all followers. It's the elder two who lead the way. Both Niall and Connor are in the rifle shooting club. Niall wins the round most weeks but it's Connor who is the best hunter. No women are allowed in their poxy club otherwise I could show them up at rifle practice any day of the week. Mary and me might not have the flash, we might not spin and twirl our rifles like they is batons, but we have the aim.

I turn away from Connor and tip the last of the sour milk mix into the little trough.

'He flirts with you. I've seen him,' Jewell teases.

'He can flirt all he likes but it won't do no good, and if you hear anyone say anything different about it, instead of gossiping with them, you tell them that from me!'

Jewell goes quiet. I spoke too harshly but I don't mend it.

Connor reaches the fence that separates the low paddock from the yard, he puts his hand on the top rail and hurdles over.

Jewell repins her brooch, which has become loose. She picks up her buckets and as she leaves she says, 'Connor Farrell, you is a show pony!'

Connor looks at her sore, which would only please Jewell all the more. He comes up to the sty and leans on the rail.

'How many milk cans this week?' he asks.

See, I want to say to Jewell, whenever Connor comes over it's straight into farm talk. That's not flirting talk. And I saw something flicker in his eyes when he looked at Jewell. He were hurt by her teasing.

'This week we're getting five of those ten-gallon cans each day,' I say. 'I'm sending most of it to the creamery except for what I keep back for ourselves.'

'Ours give us fourteen cans each day.'

'Fourteen from your fifty cows and five from our twenty-one, not much difference is there? Looks like the Illawarra stock are holding their own.'

'Da says we need a district herd book.'

'What for?'

'It's how you can buy and sell, prove lineage and whatnot,' Connor says.

'He going to get one up and running?'

'You know Da, maybe he will and maybe he won't.'

The piglets are squealing again. The sow has come to the small trough and is edging them out of their feed. I give her a tap on the nose with the bucket.

'Maybe you should do the herd book,' I say. 'You're the one that's talking to all us farmers, finding out what we're producing.'

'Maybe I will,' Connor says.

We watch the pigs.

'There's that eisteddfod coming up next week,' Connor says. 'At the town hall.'

'So I've heard.'

'It interest you?'

'It interests me.' I give Connor a sideways glance. Is he asking me to step out with him or making small talk? Thing is, I don't like not being sure of what's going on. 'Only my week is full enough without going to eisteddfods,' I say. 'We got to make a start on felling the forest beyond our long paddock.

Not to mention digging over this low paddock here and then the middle paddock. Two of our cows have sore udders and they take twice as long to milk. And we need to go to Aunty's place Saturday to chop wood for her.'

Connor's expression don't change.

'Think about it,' he says. 'We could go together. Maybe even take young Jewell along. She needs some culture got into her.'

Connor says goodbye. He climbs over the fence this time, don't leap it, and strides back across the paddock leaving me no wiser to his real intentions.

One true and good thing about Mary's Otto were his clear intentions to her right from the word go. They met when he were hired to build a cottage down the road from Aunty's place. The first day he walked past our gate and saw Mary in the yard, he came right up to her. In a thick Russian accent, and in front of us all, he said, 'Marry me?' It set Mary laughing and Mary laughing set him laughing.

'If say no I chop off head from grief,' Otto said.

Mary told him to chop off his head because she had no intention of ever getting married.

He kept asking and Mary kept saying he were a man who didn't keep his word, because his head were still on top of his neck. They fooled about like that for weeks. When he were done with building the cottage he began stopping by Aunty's house, doing jobs for her. She fed him in exchange. By talking and eating at Aunty's table we all got to know him. Otto were a big man. He took up space. That first year, he already had grey hair and he were not yet thirty. He liked to talk about the world and we would sit at Aunty's table, all five of us, and philosophise about the past and the future. We gave him a run for his money, that's for sure, especially Aunty. He had a temper of sorts, but mostly at things; not people, not animals. The saw that wouldn't cut right, or the axe that were blunt. He and Mary's courtship is the only one I've witnessed close up. Otto's heart were open, there for all to see. There were never any doubt.

Connor has a different way. He is polite enough yet in all this time he has been stopping by, I haven't ever been able to find his heart. Maybe it is wrapped deep in some hurt he can't show. Given his brothers and the way they like to scoff, he probably has good reason for that.

We saddle the horses and mount up. Jewell rides with me on Ghost, Mary on Night. Otto spotted both our horses running wild in the Snowy Mountains. He had taken a fencing job up that way. This were the winter before we took on the farm lease. Otto and Mary were not yet married. Otto spent three days tracking both horses. Once he'd caught them, it were another two weeks before he could get either bridled. They were lavish gifts for Mary and me, and we both appreciated the trouble he went to, as our old horse, Chestnut, had just died.

When I first saw Ghost, I thought she looked too tame to be wild. She stood quietly in the round yard, while Night ran amok. But trying to mount Ghost for the first time were a different matter. She's grey more than white, and sixteen hands high. Big for me. It were six months before she let me ride her, but we've made our way with each other now.

We gallop onto the road. Our dairy farm skirts the edge of the Five Island Estate that were once one large farm before it were thirty-eight small ones. North is the lagoon and south is the lake. Third Creek runs along our western boundary. We don't fence the creek and our cows go there to drink when they are in the long paddock. That creek dried out last year but the rains three weeks back have got the water flowing again. The creek separates our land from Duncan's dairy and the woodland below. Hooka Creek is beyond the far boundary of Duncan's property, Budjong runs through it. Mullet Creek follows after Hooka and after Hooka and before Mullet is where Dempster's farm is.

Jewell sings on the ride to her place. Drifty bits of sound, sweet as honey yet sad too, but when we canter into Dempster's yard and halt next to the farmhouse, she stops and hangs her head.

Dempster's place is full of straight lines. Behind the farmhouse are the sheds, and behind the sheds are his five long paddocks. He runs cattle and keeps fowls. Told me once he hates dairy cows, can't bear the sight of udders heavy with milk. Most of his land is cleared. On the far side of the paddocks runs the last line of trees. Up from that is old forest that is not Dempster's land.

I see Dempster loping across the paddock, axe in hand. He's a big man, gruff more than rough. I figure if I tackle it right, I can change his mind on Jewell helping us in the dairy. We dismount, leave Ghost and Night to graze and go to meet him by the shed. Jewell tails Mary and me like a newborn calf. Dempster stops a few feet in front of us, a firm grip on his axe.

'Jewell told us you don't want her to make butter with us no more,' I say.

'That's right,' Dempster says.

'You know we make the best butter in the district.'

'We don't need to eat the best.' Dempster's face is dull and firm, like an old bull ready to charge but in no hurry.

'But Jewell's been coming to us for two years now. She's like our own sister,' I say.

'Tell that to your brother,' Dempster says, quietly.

'Abe is like her brother too,' I add.

Dempster puts the axe head on the ground and leans on the handle. 'Not from what I've seen,' he says.

I turn back to Jewell, still hiding behind me. She is flushed. My look is like a question. She shakes her head as though she has no answer.

'What have you seen?' Mary asks Dempster.

'The two of them, down at the creek, fishing.'

It's news to Mary and me, those two going fishing, but I don't let Dempster know that.

'No law against fishing,' I say.

'It was more than fishing they were doing,' Dempster says.

'What more?' Mary asks.

'You tell your brother to keep his hands to himself and enough said.'

'Are you sure you saw right?' I say to Dempster. 'Because that don't sound like our brother.'

'They was touching,' Dempster says.

'What kind of touching?' Mary asks.

Jewell lets out a howl then. 'I was catching a fish and Abe was helping me bring it in, that kind of touching!'

Her scream quiets all the farm animals. Dempster glares at her. I worry about what Abe told me – what if Jewell gets a whipping after we go?

'Mr Dempster, our dairy is the cleanest on the estate—'

'She's of a certain age,' Dempster says, cutting me off.

I try again. 'If Jewell can keep making butter with us I'll make sure her and Abe don't behave improperly.'

Dempster breaks into a laugh and that surprises me.

When he recovers, he says, 'You two girls and your brother got your ways, but your ways can't be our ways. You can't help it, I know you can't help it. But I'm a father looking to keep my daughter safe.'

He says it reasonable, he says it with no bad words, but it's almost worse than if he had used them.

'What *ways* you talking about, Mr Dempster?' Mary asks.

Dempster shakes his head. 'I'm sorry, Mary, isn't anything to be done about bad blood.'

'Bad blood?' I say.

'That's right,' he says.

'What about bad behaviour, how do you rate that?' I ask him.

'Bad behaviour comes from bad blood,' he says.

I shouldn't let Jewell's secret out without asking her first, but Dempster has got me riled. 'Don't you think whipping a daughter so that you scar her back is bad behaviour?'

Jewell's eyes widen with surprise. She stares off into the distance.

'I don't give Jewell whippings, she gives those to herself,' Dempster says.

I laugh at that. 'No girl whips herself,' I say.

'Those that are aiming to drive out sinful thoughts do,' Dempster says. 'You may not know much about that.'

Dempster picks his axe up, walks over to Jewell and takes her hand. She don't resist but she gives me a look and it is like she is saying, *Please don't leave me here*. Did she lie or not? Does he whip her or not?

'She's a young girl, Mr Dempster,' Mary says. 'Don't forget that.'

'She's growing up and trying to find her way in the world. That's not easy without a mother,' I say.

Dempster grimaces when he hears the word mother. 'You tell your brother he ain't to come on this property again,' he says. 'Never. You girls, you're not to come here either.'

Did I hear right? We've never been banned from someone's property before.

Mary and me are stillness itself.

I am not looking at Dempster's axe but I know it's there. Something about the way he is gripping that axe, makes it seem as if he might use it if we don't leave his property now. Something about the way he is glaring at us is worrying, never mind how calm his words are said.

A whipbird calls.

'Well then,' I say, and Mary and me turn away from Jewell, go over to our horses and mount up. We nudge the horses forward and gallop out from that yard and away from that man and from Jewell.

Abe, Mary and me stand on the track, cows swarming around us.

'How come you never told us about fishing with Jewell?' I ask.

Abe is riled at Dempster banning us from his place, but I want to know why he has been lying to us.

'Do I need to report to you on everything I do?' he asks.

'It's not something you need hide,' I say.

'You seen how Dempster reacted,' Abe says, 'More like we didn't hide it well enough.'

He walks off down the track, towards the milking shed.

'Move along there!' he calls to the cows.

'They were only fishing,' Mary says. 'Don't keep at him.'

'You know I don't like secrets,' I say.

'We all got secrets,' Mary murmurs. 'You know that better than most.'

She's talking about the father of my child, whose name I have never uttered, although no one suspects the reason why.

Mary walks off along the track. I stand there for some time, staring at the muddy ground, and then I follow her.

When milking is over, I go to the kitchen to get our dinner. Mary weeds the garden and Abe herds the cows back to the long paddock. It's dark when I come out onto the verandah. I set a candle on the table and call them both. I've got potatoes and pumpkin cooked and they are good to eat hot with butter. Mary is already washing up at the side of the cottage. I call and call for Abe. Bud comes running into the yard, barking, but no Abe.

'He's gone again,' Mary says, with a sigh.

She wipes her face with a towel and goes into the kitchen.

Abe has not been right since we told him about Dempster. Didn't speak all through milking. He often goes walking at night, but this time I'm worried.

I stand on the steps and stare up at the stars that go on forever. No clouds. The moon still low. An owl hoots. Catbirds screech in the forest trees. Cockatoos flap their way towards the escarpment. Dark Dragon Ridge, Tommy Lin called it. In the starlight I see the dragon shape. The name Wollongong, I've heard it said, means hard ground near the water, or five clouds, or the sound of the sea. One group names the town for the land that is strong and solid behind it, the other names it for the water that lies before it or above it. As if one looks at how boundaries are marked, and the other at how they might merge.

Mary comes out from the kitchen with two plates of potatoes and pumpkin. We don't sit at the set table and choose instead the verandah steps. A possum scampers along the roof of the milking shed.

'Abe will be back soon,' Mary says.

In the night I wake, hear a shuffling in the next room. Abe is pulling off his boots. Good, he is home. As I drift back to sleep I hear Abe sigh.

Next morning, milking takes longer than usual because two more of our cows have sore udders and I want to try the new treatment Mr Farrell suggested. I need Abe and Mary to hold each cow while I rub on a special ointment made up from berries, eucalypt leaves and milk. Mr Farrell experiments with all kinds of unctions and some of them do work.

Wednesdays, I always check my traps straight after milking. Abe usually comes with me, but today he won't and is antsy for me to get going, says he will do all the chores on his own. No mention from either of us of last night and his vanishing trick. I keep quiet for my own reasons. Abe told me about the whippings and he meant it to be private, but I went and blurted it out to Dempster when I knew I shouldn't. It were probably that as much as anything that got us banned from his property. Whatever way I look at it, it were me that made the situation worse.

I saddle up Ghost and lead her out to the yard. Mary is raking out the milking shed. Abe is carrying the feed buckets to the fowl house. High up, there's an eagle hovering, looking for prey.

'Watch out that eagle don't get our chickens,' I call to Abe.

We have an old broom that we keep at the fowl house and when we see eagles hovering we wave it in the air and yell until they leave.

I mount Ghost and ride out along the dirt road, splash across Third Creek, then Budjong, gallop on the track below Duncan's dairy, and then over the Hooka Creek bridge. I slow Ghost down near Mullet Creek and we veer off into the forest, picking our way through the thick undergrowth. I duck branches. Some are moss green and frogs sit atop them. Small birds dart and chirp and cheep. The tree trunks are tall, like ship masts trapped in a storm of vines, the canopy their sail. We pass the narrow gully where dead cabbage trees – yellowed as old parchment – make a mat across it. I run my hand along Ghost's neck, keep murmuring to her, the way she likes. Ghost is more at home in wide-open spaces. She's always wary in the forest. It has too many noises and things she can't see.

I pull up a few yards short from the first snare, slide from the saddle. Everywhere light peeks through trees, making shiny spots on the ground. I take my rifle and loop my pack over my shoulder and walk to the snare. Damp leaves underfoot, moist soil, rot and mould. When I get close, I see the branches that I had set around the snare have been trampled. I put my rifle on the ground and kneel to reset the branches. I push them deep into the earth, so the only way for a rabbit to run is into the wire loop. Water oozes up from the soil. A black spider runs over my hand. I fix the snare, measuring three fingers from the ground. I take an apple from my pack, cut a quarter, and leave it on the grass beyond the snare to tempt a rabbit. The rest of the apple I put back in my pack. A black cloud settles above the trees and the forest goes dark. A deep quiet. I sit back and wipe my hands on my skirt. I hear a scream but can't tell where it is coming from. Were it human or catbird?

I take hold of my rifle, scramble up and listen.

Insects humming.

Is there something else? Someone else?

I strain to hear.

There. Someone running through the bush?

I wait.

Nothing.

The cloud above passes over and the forest comes alive again.

I am spooking myself.

I move on through the forest. I check the two traps set at the edge of a nearby clearing. Both are empty. There is sunshine on the water when I get to Mullet Creek. The air is warm and green leaves float down from the trees. I spy a rabbit in the trap closest to the bank. Grey and white, lying dead on the grasses, its body still warm. Only just snagged. It has its foot caught in the wire too, which must have been a feat. Fighting to escape maybe. I loosen the noose, and string the rabbit to a branch. The snares are meant to catch the animal, not kill it. I usually do that myself, because that way I do it cleanly. When Abe is with me we work together, one killing and stringing the animal up, the other resetting the snare. I am proficient but Abe is inventive. It were his idea to construct branch paths to guide unsuspecting rabbits into our traps. Something he'd learnt from the old swagman who camped by our creek last winter.

The final two traps are both untouched so I decide to hunt. I load my rifle and again hear a cry. I look along the banks. Did it come from around the bend? I stop and listen again. Nothing. Maybe just possums fighting.

I walk along the creek banks, keeping a watch out for rabbits. Milky water bubbles past. There's near two hundred men camping half a mile up in the bush, all employed at the smelting works. Most are down from Sydney and not used to bush life. They wash in the creek, stirring up the water in all the best fishing spots.

Up ahead is the smooth rock ledge shaped like a fish and beyond it the cabbage tree trunk that straddles the width of the creek. Someone placed it there to be a bridge some time back. There's another rock ledge beyond the trunk, that is uneven and full of holes. I could easily jump from the smooth rock ledge to the trunk, run along it over the creek and leap to the other bank. The property on that side were named Exmouth, once owned by Captain Brooks. He is long dead and most of the estate is taken over by the smelting works but the land down this way is too marshy for buildings. Tall trees grow on the creek banks, but walk in a short way and there are dead trees rising up out of ponds, with vines, tough like rope, curling through their branches. It's a dark watery place in there, and the insect hum sets me on edge. But the animals are less cautious, and there are patches of grass that are lush and green. It can be an easy place to hunt for rabbits. I've only been there once because when I told Aunty about it she warned me to stay away. Her mother's sister, she said, suffered a calamity in that place. She refused to say what, only that it weren't a place I should visit.

There's a whistling in my ear, unnerving. I turn quickly, my rifle raised.

'Oh you!' I say, seeing Connor.

'You going to shoot me?' he asks.

He has four rabbits bound together.

'You snuck up on me!'

Connor's face is blotchy and red. If he weren't smiling I'd have thought he'd been crying.

'You done good,' I say.

'One is Niall's,' he says. 'There's two hunters further up. The youngest of them nearly shot Niall in the foot. Niall gave them a mouthful. No joy that way. You'd do better back at the creek mouth.'

'Who is it hunting?' I ask.

'Loafers from the smelting works.'

'I met one of them two weeks back,' I say. 'He'd pitched his tent near the creek away from the others. He seemed a shifty character.'

'I don't know about shifty, but those smelter workers are all bad shots,' says Connor.

We walk back along the bank and come to where the creek empties into the wide lake. The clouds hang long and low over the water. Two wallabies drink by the creek edge but they hear us coming and are gone before we can raise our rifles. We take cover behind a coachwood tree. It's a hundred feet high and has a smooth grey trunk with branches overhanging the creek.

I look to Connor but his face is turned away.

'Something happen, Connor?' I ask gently.

He is breathing in and out like it hurts.

'Nah,' he says.

Then he looks at me.

'Niall,' he says, as if that explains it.

Niall is a nasty piece of work. I'd take Connor over Niall any day. I decide to tell Connor that I will go with him to the eisteddfod. And maybe we should take Jewell with us, and maybe Abe and Mary as well.

I spot two rabbits in the clearing ahead. Pressing my rifle into my shoulder, I take aim, and pull the trigger. I hit one rabbit, the other scarpers.

'Don't pay any attention to Niall,' I say.

I stride into the clearing, pick the dead rabbit up and string it together with the one from earlier. When I turn back, Connor is staring at the water.

'I've got to get home, Lola,' he says. 'Da wants us fencing this morning.'

He strides off quickly and is gone before I have time to tell him I've changed my mind about the eisteddfod.

I trek back through the forest to Ghost and strap the rabbits to the saddle. I mount and we pick our way out between the trees to the track. I gallop home but when I ride in through the gate the place looks deserted. In the barn I dismount and unsaddle Ghost. Night is in her stall, standing with her back to me, like she always does when I go out with Ghost and she is left behind. I brush Ghost down, lead her to her stall and give both horses some feed. I go into Night's stall and give her a brush, just so she feels included.

'We're taking you out tomorrow,' I tell her.

I pick up the rabbits and walk from the barn to the yard. Abe is nowhere to be seen, nor Bud. I can't hear the sound of an axe at work either. I walk around to the southern side of the barn, where the laying hatches are. The feed buckets for the fowls are sitting outside the fence. The fowls have not been fed. I can hear the pigs making a racket in their yard.

'Abe!' I call.

He don't appear. I hang the rabbits on a hook near the kitchen. Where's Mary? My chest goes tight. I run across the yard to the orchard. I see Mary pruning trees and feel relief. Since I heard that cry in the forest I've been on edge. It were probably catbirds. Or maybe it were Niall yelling at those hunters. Strange I didn't hear the shot that nearly got him in the foot.

There's a pile of branches at Mary's feet. She glances up as I reach her, wipes the sweat from her brow.

'You seen Abe?' I ask.

'No.'

'He's vanished again,' I say. 'And he hasn't done his chores.'

'What's up with him?' Mary asks.

'We've got to do something about it this time. He has to pull his weight.'

I grumble my way back through the orchard and across the yard. I unhook the rabbits and go into the kitchen, slap them onto the table. I fetch a cup, dip it into the can of fresh milk and drink until my thirst is gone. I take the first rabbit, turn it belly up, and picking up my knife, cut along the full length of its body.

A shadow crosses the threshold. I look up.

'Mr Dempster?'

Dempster's shirt is all mud and bark.

'Where's Jewell?' he asks, his voice low and grating.

'Not here,' I say.

'When I left for the field this morning, she was in the house,' he says. 'Jewell!' Dempster calls out like I might be hiding Jewell in the kitchen, although it is one room and there is nowhere to hide. He walks away, and when I reach the kitchen door and look to see where he has gone, he has crossed the path and is running up the steps of our cottage.

'Mr Dempster,' I call. 'Jewell is not here.'

'Jewell, Jewell!' he shouts.

I follow him across to the cottage and stand inside, watching him. Who does Dan Dempster think he is? Dempster pays me no attention. He even looks under the beds. When he is confident Jewell is not hiding in either of the bedrooms, nor behind a sitting room chair, he pushes past me, strides across the verandah, down the steps, and around to the milking sheds and dairy. He also searches the barn and fowl house. I don't go after him. I wait in the yard, so enraged I feel my whole body flush.

Mary comes up from the orchard. Dempster returns from the fowl house and stops in the middle of the yard. Mary, arms crossed, gives Dempster her glare. She's slow to anger is Mary, but once she gets there she is ferocious and does not forgive easily.

'Do you know where my daughter is?' Dempster asks Mary.

'No.'

'You swear?'

Mary gives him a sour look.

'You do anything to Jewell?' I ask. 'You do anything to make her want to run off?'

Dempster's grey eyes rest on mine, steady and cold. His skin looks jaundiced, like some babies I've seen. I remember what Connor told me, how his ma once found Dempster on the track out back of Duncan's dairy. It were early morning and Mrs Farrell were going to help Mrs Duncan with her daughter's birthing of her first born. Dempster were shirtless and calling out for his wife. Mrs Farrell didn't know if he'd been drinking or were sleepwalking.

'She could be over at her friend Lucy Needleham's,' I say, although I know she had a falling out with Lucy some months back.

'Have you seen this?' Dempster asks.

He pulls a necklace from his pocket and holds it out to me. It's a pretty necklace, made of white stones and string.

'No,' I say.

He swings it through the air. 'Jewell told me last night that your brother gave it to her.'

I catch Mary's eye. Another thing Abe hasn't told us.

Dempster pushes the necklace back into his pocket.

'If I find out that boy has been with my daughter this morning,' Dempster says, 'I'll come back here and kill him.'

Mary and me sit on the grass near the creek and wait for Abe.

'We didn't even ban Dempster from our property,' I say. 'We should have done that at least.'

'Never mind Dempster, we got to find out what Abe and Jewell have been up to,' Mary says. 'He shouldn't be courting her in secret, and not without her da's permission. That ain't right.'

'And not without telling us,' I say.

I see Abe walking down the track from the long paddock. His head is sunk low and his feet kick at the dirt.

'Here he comes,' I say to Mary.

We stand and wait.

Abe crosses the yard and stops outside the kitchen. Only then does he see us.

'Where have you been?' Mary calls as we go over to him.

'Walking.'

'With Jewell?' I ask.

'No,' he says.

We stand in the brisk winter air, sun slanting though the tree leaves.

'I'll do my chores now,' Abe says. He offers no apology and turns to go.

'Dempster has been here,' I say.

'What did he want?' Abe asks.

'He showed us the necklace you gave Jewell,' Mary says.

Abe's eyes widen with surprise. He stares out across to the low paddock.

'So I made Jewell a necklace, nothing wrong with that,' Abe says. 'You know she likes pretty things.'

'Dempster thinks you know where Jewell is,' Mary says.

'Isn't she at home?' Abe asks.

'She's missing,' I say.

Abe screws up his face, like he is trying to work out a puzzle.

'Is something happening between you two?' I ask.

Abe don't answer directly, he is a master at misdirection.

'You saw how upset she were yesterday. I promised I'd meet her today,' Abe says. 'I went to where we were supposed to meet. I called and called but she never answered. I thought she must have gone home.'

'That don't answer my question,' I say.

'I were trying to look after her, same as you,' Abe says, hotly.

'Stop it, both of you,' Mary says. 'It ain't like Jewell to go off without telling us. Something is up.'

We gallop along the shore by the lake. Abe and Mary on Night, Ghost and me, trailing behind. Jewell's been missing three days now. Everyone has been asking, did she run away or is she hurt? All the neighbours have been out searching, but Dempster made it known he don't want us part of it. He's telling everyone that Abe has done something to Jewell. Constable Black were called down but he told Dempster he can't start an investigation until he knows there's been a crime. The constable stopped by the farm and asked us all to tell what we knew. We did that and he left without giving away what his own thoughts were. Against Dempster's wishes we have been out looking for Jewell, but only at night so as not to cause more trouble. We have our own suspicion about what might have happened. Maybe Dempster whipped Jewell after Mary and I left on Tuesday, and she ran off into the bush, then fell and injured herself. If that happened she could be lying in a gully somewhere, calling out and no one hearing.

The sun sets as we turn off from the lake and ride on through the forest, up past Duncan's dairy and behind Dempster's farm. Abe says Jewell sometimes comes to this part of the forest when she wants to hide from her da. The early moon is brighter than a lamp. We halt the horses, dismount and walk through the trees, calling for Jewell, stopping to listen for a reply. Hear only night birds. A bandicoot scurries in dead leaves. Possums eye us from the trees. We creep forward to the ridge of the hill, peer through tall sedges, down over Dempster's paddocks to the farm buildings and house. Don't see no light on. Not anywhere.

We turn away and keep on walking through the forest, calling, calling, but no Jewell.

'Maybe she did catch a train out of here,' Mary says, when we stop for a rest. 'I've heard her talk of a cousin that lives in Sydney.'

'She won't have gone without telling me,' Abe says, dark eyes glinting.

He walks off through the trees, calling her name. Mary and me watch him go.

'I got this ache in my stomach,' Mary says.

'I don't know where else to look,' I say.

A catbird squeals, the sound just like a cat in a fight.

'Where are you, Jewell?' I whisper.

The next day after milking, we three ride to Aunty's place, like we do most Saturdays, but all of us are sick at heart. The storms that came in May beat potholes into the dirt road. There's a southwesterly and it's blowing cokework smoke across the plain and the stink nettles my nose.

When we were kids Aunty would bring us down from the mountain to the beach. There'd be shade all the way and chattering birds. We'd hear the sea from four miles west. On hot days we'd sit on the wet sand and let the waves rush around us. It were one jetty at Port Kembla back then, not two. Nowadays men ride coal trolleys down the mountain and scoot across the flat land like there's no tomorrow. Sometimes those men have to sit on the jetty for hours, not able to unload their coal because the ships taking it away are still hanging out at sea waiting for the wind to quiet. So the hurry is for nothing. The cokeworks are on the hill at the back of the southernmost jetty. Every day workers shovel coke into sixty-two ovens that burn through the night. On still days I hear the machines hiss and clatter, above the cows and roosters, pigs and dogs, and the slow clunk of axes.

We ride around the bend in Five Islands Road and there before us is Mount Kembla. Hat Hill it were once called. Up near the top, shrouded in mist, is Aunty's land, left to her by her da. Further along, with escarpment running between, is Mount Keira.

I press my thighs into Ghost, tip forward and begin to gallop towards Aunty's.

Abe clutches onto Mary as she pushes Night to race along beside me.

We're hot and sweaty by the time we ride into Aunty's yard. The house is in a forest clearing. There's a giant fig tree growing to one side. It has enormous roots that twist above ground and its branches spread out so far that beneath them an entire village could picnic. Five people, arms held out and standing finger-tip to finger-tip around the trunk, cannot meet to form a circle. That were something we tried one time when Otto first courted Mary.

We dismount, leave the horses to graze, and go to the kitchen, calling, 'Aunty! Aunty!' She's not about and the fire is burning low. We ladle out water from the bucket set on the table and quench our thirst. Aunty's da built the house with four rooms and a fireplace. I check that Aunty is not in any of the other rooms.

'The place is empty,' I say, coming back into the kitchen.

Abe goes out to the woodpile, takes up the axe and starts to split wood. He has not talked since last night. Mary and me take the path that leads to the caves where Aunty stores her jams and other preserves. She's not there either, so we walk down through the forest to the creek and find her sitting on a rock, dangling a line. There's a baby eel squirming in the bucket set down by her side. She has her skirts tucked up and her legs bare, and I see one is bruised.

'What happened?' I ask.

'Huh?' Aunty mutters.

'Your leg is all bruised,' I say.

'Is it?' she says, looking down at her shins.

I can't tell if she is lying or if she truly didn't know she had bruised it.

'You should live with us now, Aunty,' I say.

'How bad is your eyesight?' Mary asks.

'Nothing wrong with my eyesight,' Aunty says, reeling in an eel that is four times the size of the one she's already caught.

In the kitchen Aunty cooks while we tell her everything about Jewell. She slips the eel from the pan onto plates then dishes out the mashed potatoes. We eat but Aunty only picks at her food.

She stares at Abe like she's expecting him to say something. Finally, she pushes her plate away from her. Abe shifts about in his seat, stands and walks to the fire, then he comes back and sits down.

'I can always tell when you have a secret,' Aunty says to him.

He sighs and rubs his hands through his hair. 'Jewell and me were going to run away together,' he says. 'Go to Melbourne and get jobs in a factory and as soon as we could, get married.'

I can't believe what I've heard. 'Leave the farm?' I say.

'How come you didn't tell us this before?' Mary says.

'Jewell made me swear not to,' Abe says. 'And I've been thinking, any day now she will turn up and when she does, if I've told our secret, she will give me an ear bashing.'

Abe kicks at the chair leg with his foot. Aunty collects up the dishes.

'Were you going to tell us before you left?' I ask, unable to stop glaring at my brother.

'Jewell said it would be better for you and Mary if I didn't. She said her da would be over to see you first thing, and if you didn't know where we were, then neither of you would have to lie.'

'It don't sound like a very sensible plan to me,' Mary says. 'You don't know nothing about factory work.'

'Jewell were desperate. I had no choice.'

Aunty is washing the dishes. She nods her head as though this all makes sense, which it don't.

'Now Dempster thinks you done something to Jewell,' Mary says. 'Aunty, Dempster is telling that to everyone he can.'

'There'll be trouble, Abe, if you don't find Jewell,' Aunty says slowly.

'If Jewell could, she'd let me know where she is,' Abe says. 'It's Dempster that has done something to her, it can only be him.'

'Done what?' Mary asks.

'The worst.' Abe stands and paces about the kitchen.

He looks like he might explode.

'But Dempster were angry when he came looking for Jewell at our place,' I say. 'He didn't know where she were. He weren't pretending.'

'How can you be sure?' Abe asks.

'He might be a hard man but he is her father,' Mary says, poking at the fire.

'He has a temper,' Abe says. 'And a temper gets you into trouble.'

'But everyone has looked everywhere for her,' I say.

'A person don't just disappear,' Mary says.

'Mrs Farrell told me yesterday it were Jewell's own fault, she's always been too lippy,' I say.

'Own fault,' Abe says. 'Own fault to have her father murder her?'

'Mrs Farrell is certain she's run off,' I say.

Aunty puts down the dishcloth and turns to face us.

'There's this man I know. Toorung is his name. He can track her down. Once, years ago now, a boy got lost in the forest back behind Dapto. It were the middle of summer and hot as hell but Toorung found that boy.' Aunty goes into her bedroom and comes back with her coat. 'We got to get onto this now,' she says. 'If it rains, it will be too late.'

I help Aunty up on Ghost. We make good time, riding back down the mountain. We take the road to Illawarra Lake. Aunty taps my stomach. She points to a small track that leads to the bay and we turn onto it. Trees and thick bush on either side. About a mile along, the track twists around a gigantic tree and we come to the shore. The blue lake beyond is a big belly shuddering. Clouds are shivering ghosts on its surface. An old man and two boys are in the shallows heaving in nets. They have their pants rolled up. The boys are reed thin and bare-chested, the old man wears a shirt and vest. His grey hair is tied up in a knot. The two boys help pull the nets but the old man takes all the weight. He is strong.

'Is that old man Toorung?' I ask.

'Yes,' Aunty says.

On the sand behind, there are barrels lined up. Two kids, a boy and a girl, are running in circles around the barrels, dragging sticks behind them. Three brown dogs trail after the kids, yapping at the sticks, like the sticks are alive. There's a fire in front of a gunyah and an old woman sitting by it, a possum skin coat wrapped around her.

'That's Yardah, Toorung's wife,' Aunty says.

A timber house is set back in the trees behind the gunyah. The door is open and a woman steps through. She is older than me but not much older.

'That's their daughter, Moomung,' Aunty says. 'The kids, the older boys and the two young ones, belong to Moomung.'

Moomung stops to look at us and then goes over to her ma.

Toorung sees us now but he keeps pulling at the net.

'What do you want to do, Aunty?'

'Wait,' she says.

Toorung finishes hauling in the net. The older boys begin sorting the fish into the barrels. Toorung washes his hands in the lake and walks over. He don't smile but his face isn't mean. His vest and shirt hang open and I can see long thin scars on his chest and arms. He starts to talk in his language, which sounds familiar though I don't know a word. What gets me though is Aunty, because she speaks back to him using some of that language and snatches of English.

We sit around the campfire. The dogs have settled, two with their heads between their paws, the third rolling on its back waiting to be tickled. Yardah boils water and makes billy tea. Beneath her possum skin is a long black skirt and a white shirt, but her feet are bare. The older boys go to wash the cups. They come back and squat by the fire, line the cups up on the dirt. The two little kids grip their sticks with one hand and hang onto Moomung with the other. The older boys want to look at our rifles. Mary and me show them how to load and unload. Abe goes down to the shore, and watches the other fisher-families out on the lake work their nets. A northwesterly ripples across the water where pelicans float. The sun peeks through the clouds but the warmth is like a worn blanket.

We hear the sound of horses. I turn and see two men riding down the track. Dempster and Mr Farrell. They canter right up to the campsite and halt.

Toorung stands. Abe comes up from the shore. Yardah turns away from the men, as if disinterested, but Moomung pulls her youngest boy and girl into her lap. The campfire crackles. Seabirds on the sand begin to squawk.

The men dismount.

'Have you found Jewell?' I say.

'We found this,' Dempster says, holding out the blue brooch Jewell had showed me.

'Jewell were wearing that the other day, Mr Dempster,' I say. 'She told me she took it from your top drawer.'

'Never mind that she took it, it's where it was found,' Dempster says.

'Where?' Mary asks.

'In your milking shed,' Dempster says.

'It must have fallen off her shirt,' I say.

'What were you doing in our milking shed?' Mary asks. 'No one said you could go on our property.'

'Dan asked me to go with him to talk to you,' Mr Farrell says. 'And when you weren't there we had a look around for

Jewell, just to set Dan at ease. She could have been hiding in your barn without you knowing. Niall and Connor were with us. Connor didn't think you'd mind.'

'You know more than you are letting on, boy,' Dempster says to Abe.

'I know you're a liar,' Abe says.

Before anyone can do anything about it, Dempster steps forward and punches Abe in the stomach. Abe folds over, coughing.

'Dan!' Mr Farrell yells. 'Talk to the boy first!'

Dempster goes for Abe again, hits him on the mouth, then the cheek. Abe falls backwards onto the ground, his cheek and lip cut. Blood runs down one side of his face.

Mary screams.

'Stop!' I yell.

Mary and me run to help Abe up, but he stands, pushes us away and takes a swing at Dempster. Hits him on the jaw. Dempster's head jolts backwards. Dempster is strong and solid but Abe matches him in height and has a wily fierceness. Abe goes to punch again, but Dempster sidesteps and grabs Abe in a headlock.

'He's going to kill him,' I yell, remembering Dempster's earlier threat.

I pull on Dempster's arm while Mary hammers his back with her fists. Dempster tries to shake me off but I cling on. I can see Abe's face going red. With his free hand Dempster grabs me by the throat and tips my head back. His grip is so firm that I can barely breathe.

Above us, a white-bellied eagle hovers, looking for prey. I try to pull Dempster's hand away from my neck. I see the eagle dive to the

Bel
1998

reeds in the lake and get something in its mouth, and and and when it flies back in the air, I can see a fish dangling from its beak. I'm not in front of our house, but in front of Uncle Ray and Maxine's house. Uncle Ray is not my real uncle, he's my neighbour, but everyone in our street calls him uncle, even old people. Uncle Ray said it was okay for me to watch for dragonflies out the front of his house. One dragonfly hovers in the air like an insect helicopter. It buzzes across to the water. Behind me, I can hear Maxine shouting at Jason, 'What's going on with you?' Jason is in trouble again. He's only five and he's always pinching Maxine's mascara. He has really really long lashes and when he puts mascara on they get twice as long. Maxine can't understand why he keeps putting it on. I told her because it looks good and she told me to butt out of family arguments.

Then she said, 'Bel, haven't you got a home to go to?'

Then Uncle Ray said, 'Bel, how about you go and watch dragonflies.'

There, another dragonfly in front of me. Two now. Stick bodies, shiny blue. Glow wings that flicker in sunlight. I sneak through the grass, pulling myself along first with one elbow, then the other, like a soldier in a war film. The dragonflies don't notice because they're too busy buzzing each other because because they're mating! And, and, what happens is the tips of their abdomens touch to form an upside-down heart. It's like a wonder of nature or something.

I've seen thirteen or six or more upside-down hearts since the holidays began but most of them were after New Year's Day. It's definitely a sign. Jonathan doesn't believe in signs because he says, *Bel, a sign from whom?* Good question, Dad, how am I to know? I'm only ten. Aiko believes in signs. I do too but not because I take after her. Because there are things in the world we don't know about. Not even experts know.

Once, aeons and aeons ago, dragonflies were as big as people. Bigger. Now, they could be like the size of a hand. The dragonflies whoosh in front of me. That's a sign maybe because it's now I see the two new boys. They're rafting out from Mullet Creek. They don't row like people row in a rowboat but kneel on the raft like the painted boatmen that hang on the walls of the Berkeley Chinese. Berk-e-ley with an e. Between them is a wolf. Looks like a wolf. A white wolf.

The two boys row to the bit of water in front of me. Their raft is made from old planks of wood. On each corner and in the middle are big drums like drums from the petrol station the ones that are down the back of the garage where the mechanics sit and waste time. The two boys stare at me and so does the wolf. The older boy has eyelids that hang over his eyes like a lizard. His little brother is a puppy dog. Could be if he wasn't a human. He mustn't swim yet because he's wearing floaties. The wolf is huge and has his mouth open and is panting.

The older boy calls out, 'Need anything rafted?'

I stare back at him like I'm a mad person and make my eyes roll about. He could think I'm a ghost. If I were a ghost I might be able to walk on water.

'Need anything rafted?' Now it's the younger boy that calls out, like an echo.

They must think I'm deaf. I know they're the boys my parents talked about last night because they have funny accents. Because they've been living in England since they were like babies. Jonathan said they came back to Australia via India. According to him 'via' means road in Latin language but in English language it means travelling through one place when you're on the way to another. So like 'via' used to mean something solid we walk on and now it means pathway, only not not not a solid one.

Aiko says Jonathan is someone who knows too much and that can get on people's nerves so it might be better if I try to take after her not him because otherwise I could bore the pants off people.

'Want to *ride* on our raft?' the younger boy calls.

It's as if he knows I'm going to say yes before I say it because he makes a space for me.

Aiko told me they live in the bargain swish house at the end of our street. That house had been up for sale for a year then what happened was the price dropped dramatically because no one wanted it because it was overpriced because the people that lived there Lisa and Robert spent too much money on the renovations and thought they would make a million dollars but the the the markets were down so they didn't make much money at all. I would quite like to live in the bargain swish house because it's all white inside like a temple and has a big deck out onto the lake with a Buddha on the deck.

'Their father needed some luck,' Aiko said.

She was talking about the two boys not Lisa and Robert.

'How come he needs some luck?' I asked.

'Oh,' my mum said, 'we all need luck.'

She said it like a shrug, like, *Oh I'm just saying for saying's sake*, but she gave Jonathan one of her 'looks' so I knew there was a secret.

Whenever I know there's a secret I want to find it out. I can't help it. Aiko says I'm a nosy parker and I *am* a nosy parker because it's good to know things. I've learnt a lot by eavesdropping. That's how I found out about Lisa and Robert breaking up. This was after Lisa told Robert he was punching above his weight. I love secrets but I can't keep them. Aiko says I have to practise keeping secrets if I want people to confide in me and if I want to grow up mature. Like I didn't keep the secret that Aiko's winter boots were four or maybe six hundred dollars when she told Jonathan they were two hundred on sale.

According to Jonathan, Aiko is a cliché woman because she lies about how much her shopping costs. When I grow up I'm not going to be a cliché woman. My teacher, Miss Schubert, says I'm linguistically dexterous and have an overextended imagination so sometimes I don't listen to what she says or make up my own version of it like a novelist but if I *did* listen then I'd learn to write stories for money maybe. (She says *maybe* in a deep voice.) Miss Schubert says making up stories is the best thing I do and I think she is right because I can't do lots of other things, like I can't drive or sing in tune or tell the time properly because I can't really do numbers very well. I'm not stupid, it's the way I am.

The thing is, if you want to keep a secret, don't tell me, because somehow that secret will come out. Like the time Jonathan and I spent the afternoon watching *Chinatown,* which is a thriller and I'm not meant to watch thrillers, and then watching *Casablanca,* so two olde worlde films in a row both starting with the letter C and this when Jonathan was meant to be writing his PhD but he couldn't be buggered because words were doing his head in. And when Aiko came home and asked me what I'd been doing the first thing I said was watching *Chinatown* and *Casablanca.*

'Come on!' The younger boy pats the space next to him.

The wolf barks.

'Okay,' I say.

I roll up my jeans to wade out but then I remember the black sludge. I tell the two boys about it. Step on the black sludge and I could get cancer or die some other way. They use their oars to pole closer. The raft goes one way then the other before it comes my way. I lean out and drop my hands on the wooden planks so my body is like a bridge across water, like the Sydney Harbour Bridge, or a replica of it, but the wolf jumps up, and the raft tips from side to side and rolls away and my body stretches out.

'Isha, careful!' the younger boy screams.

'Hang on!' the one called Isha yells.

I look down and see the black sludge. Some neighbours call the lake a cesspit. But that isn't right because the water is really clear, like Gladwrap almost. MP, my old person neighbour, says it shouldn't even be called a lake, because once upon a time it was called a lagoon and that's a better name for it. The deepest bit of the lake is three and a half metres but in front of our house it never gets above a metre. MP knows history and history is specific facts about olden days only, according to Uncle Ray, MP doesn't know as many specific facts as she thinks she does. Uncle Ray says the lake was once full of fish and it was a refrigerator for everyone who camped on the banks in the olden Aborigine days before refrigerators. Aiko says, *Good news is our house sits between Uncle Ray's and MP's, otherwise it would be World War Three every day.* Along our street it goes the bargain swish house, then Betty the Greek, then the Zoia family with the one-legged cat, the Skarschewskis, Mr and Mrs Lin, the Wilsons, MP, us, Uncle Ray and Maxine, Lenny-the-biker, the Haddads (Nada and Sara live there but they're not allowed to play with me because Mrs Haddad says they are too young) and last, the two Angelas with the red car.

The older boy rams his oar into the lakebed and pushes the raft forward so it slams into the bank. I fall onto the raft and the two boys stare at me as though I'm an alien dropped down from the sky.

'You're a girl,' the older one says.

'So?' I say, sitting up.

'You look like a boy,' he says, and laughs like it's funny.

'You look like a girl.'

We squint at each other and I take three deep breaths, because that is what Aiko told me to do when I get cross.

'It's because your hair is so short,' the older boy says. 'It's like a soldier's hair.'

'My dad cut it,' I say.

'This is Zeus,' the younger boy says, patting the wolf.

I look into Zeus's wolf eyes. Not scary eyes, not friendly either. His front legs could crush me but his shaggy white fur is soft so I pat his paw and he nuzzles his nose into my neck. Which just goes to prove the old saying never judge a book by its cover.

'I'm Isha,' the older boy says, 'and this is Tarak.'

'Do you want to go scare the horse girls?' Tarak asks. 'They bring their horses down to our spot at the creek. We don't like it because it's where we put our raft, so when they come there next, we're going to run out of the bushes and go *raaah*.'

Tarak uses his hands to scratch at the air and *raaahs* like a lion.

I screw up my nose. 'That will only scare them if they're like six months old.'

'I know,' he says, 'but then we'll get Zeus to attack them.'

Zeus flops down and puts his head between his paws. I pat him again.

'He's ninety per cent wolf,' Isha says.

'What's the other per cent?' I ask.

Isha shrugs.

'Pussy cat?' I say and laugh.

Tarak laughs too but Isha lifts up his chin which I can tell is code for *I-am-not-amused*. People have codes which I'm currently fascinated to study because if I'm going to be a novelist then I need to unravel people codes. Or, I could be a marine biologist because I'm also fascinated by the virus called viral haemorrhagic septicaemia virus that attacks fish in the Baltic Sea so they die in droves and no one knows where it comes from or why the fish get it but whole populations die and then they drift, dead in the water. Only if I'm going to be a marine biologist I might have to go all the way to the Baltic Sea, or to Queensland to study dead coral reefs, and I might miss my parents.

'Do you want to scare the horse girls or not?' Isha asks like it's a challenge and I can never say no to a challenge because unfortunately or fortunately I have a competitive nature. So I agree to go and forget that I made a promise to Jonathan and Aiko to stay within cooee of our backyard.

I've never been on a raft before. No one that lives by the lake actually goes on the lake except for Lenny-the-biker who has a bathroom that is all black tiles and gold taps. His whole house was built from drug money but no one says that out loud in case Lenny's gang torches their house. Lenny says that if I drink the lake water I'll grow six fingers and if I swim in it my skin will go red, just as if I'd been burned. He thinks I'm a dumb kid who will believe anything he says but I'm not that kind of dumb kid.

I let my legs dangle over the edge of the raft to test whether they'll go red but they only get goosebumps from the cold water.

'I'm seven going on eight,' Tarak says, 'and in England I saw a hedgehog.'

He tells me all the things he and Isha have done without my asking. Like how they've been on a plane that flew over the Indian and Atlantic oceans and how on the plane they had small cans of coke half the size of the ones in the shop. Like how they've ridden elephants, which is like riding a really fat fat huge horse, and how they've fed squirrels from their hands.

I tell them all about dragonflies, like how they can flap their wings thirty times a minute and fly up and down and backwards and probably sideways as well and like how in Germany they used to get called *wasserhexe* which means water witch or *teufelsnadele* which means devil's needle.

Isha says he's never seen a dragonfly fly sideways and anyway he and Tarak have decided to be explorers when they get older and will probably go to Germany.

If I'm a novelist not a marine biologist I'm still not going to be a girl girl and have a wedding because I don't want to look like a cake and because because I want to live on my own and make up my own rules.

Tarak says they only have one rule in their house which is completely unbelievable as we have about a thousand. The one rule is no one is allowed to say no. If they get told to go to bed they can just answer with a question. One of Isha's questions might be, *Can I have one more hour before I go to bed?*

If I said that to Aiko she'd say no, but their dad is not allowed to say no so what happens is he has to say something like, *You can have one more minute.*

It must be strange in their house, question after question and no answers. It would probably get extremely complicated.

Isha says it makes them negotiate and his dad is a big negotiator.

I ask if their mum is allowed to say no and Isha shrugs as if he doesn't know the answer to that question and Tarak says, she doesn't count because she's dead.

I look at Tarak's eyes because that's a good way to guess about a human being's interior emotions. If someone's eyes go up they're thinking something serious, if they go down and to the side they're lying. I learnt that from a TV program. Lying is different to storytelling which is like a lie only a lie everyone knows is meant to be a lie. Tarak's eyes are in the middle, not up or down. I don't remember what the program said about eyes that are in the middle. Isha's eyes are squinty and up.

'Mum's ashes are on Dad's bedside table.' Tarak stops rowing. 'In a thing like a jar but not a jar.'

I glance at Isha but he turns away and pulls his oar through the water and we row in a circle.

'We're going to find a tree in the forest up on the mountain, near where Dad took Mum on their first date, which wasn't like a real date but was a big long walk, and when we find the tree we'll just sprinkle her around it,' Tarak says.

He makes a sprinkling motion with his hand as though practising for the event and smiles at me.

I wouldn't be smiling if Aiko died. I wouldn't be smiling if Jonathan died. I'd rather they went into a cocoon and became butterflies if that were possible which it probably isn't but who knows, strange things can happen in the world of science.

'Once upon a time human beings died from having a cold or the flu and now you don't,' I say to Isha and Tarak.

Isha tells me his dad is a doctor and in history in England human beings didn't know that germs made you get a cold or the flu and when doctors first started to deliver babies all the babies died and the doctors said it was because the women were immoral but later they, the doctors that is, discovered it was because they, the doctors, didn't wash their hands.

Tarak says their dad washes his hands all the time.

When we get to the bit of the creek where Isha and Tarak usually leave their raft we jump onto a rock ledge. It's shaped like a fish. Isha says it might have been carved by Aborigines or might be an accident of the weather. We walk along to the grassy bit and check the ground for footprints. The horse girls haven't showed yet. We can tell because when we look at the ground there is no fresh horse poo, only some wombat poo on a rock. The wombat poo is a cube and a cube is extremely hard to poo. We get back on the raft and row downstream to the reeds because the reeds are the best place for us to ambush the horse girls from.

I see two more dragonflies mating, which makes fourteen or ten this week. Dragonflies live in their nymph state underneath the water. When the time comes for them to transform to a grown-up dragonfly they climb up a reed or across rocks, moult one last time, which is like taking all their clothes off, begin to ~~breath in oxygen~~ ~~breathe~~ breathe and when their wings have dried, fly. I read that in *Fascinating Science* but I want to see it in real life. If I do then something magic could happen although I don't know what. Like I could change into a different person who could fly or a person who has blonde hair instead of black. Because once upon a time according to *Fascinating Science* human beings were underwater sea creatures and the journey to walking on two legs or even having two legs was aeons and aeons of time so it's not like impossible that one day we might fly.

Isha and Tarak help me search the reeds for nymphs. There's a loud buzzing by my ear. Isha grins so I see the gap between

129

his side teeth. He rolls up his sleeve and shows me the black watch strapped above his elbow. It looks like a good watch. I don't tell them about my numbers problem because I usually don't tell anyone. Everyone in my class knows but they are the only ones. Isha switches off the watch alarm.

'It was Mum's,' Tarak says. 'From when she was skindiving but she gave that up when I got pneumonia because Dad said she was too busy with her hobbies to be a proper mum and she said she wasn't.'

The watch alarm is their reminder to go home for lunch. Their dad makes them peanut butter sandwiches every day as he hasn't got a doctor's job yet but when their aunt comes over they have dhal and rice. My favourite Indian food is poppadoms. My second favourite is butter chicken.

Isha and Tarak raft me back to my place and I say yes to going with them again to scare the horse girls and rafting around the lake to look for treasure. I wave goodbye and see Nada and Sara from down the road walking along the shore with their mother. I run up and say hello and ask Mrs Haddad if Nada and Sara can have a ride on the raft tomorrow but Mrs Haddad says no. Nada is six and old enough but Sara is only four. Nada holds onto her mother's hand and smiles but Sara hides behind Mrs Haddad's dress and peeks her head out only once. I race inside leaving wet footprints on the floor so I don't start off well telling Aiko about my new friends Isha and Tarak because she is just home from her summer tutoring job at the university and not in the mood for doing housework.

'Did you know about this?' Aiko asks Jonathan in her cross voice because he is meant to be in charge of me when she goes to work only he doesn't have as many rules as she does and that gets on her goat.

'Didn't you say a few adventures would be good for her?'

Ha! Jonathan is like Isha, answering a question with a question. I can't believe I haven't ever noticed before. Now I am going to notice it all the time.

'Besides, Bel can swim,' he says.

'You said this year I could be more mature,' I say to Aiko.

'Rafting with two violent boys is not in my definition of maturity,' Aiko says.

I wish, I wish I hadn't told her about our plans to attack the horse girls.

'What is in your definition?' I ask.

'No smart talk, okay?' she says.

Aiko is quite serious for a mum. What happens next is I ask if we can negotiate and Aiko goes, *I said I said,* but then she can't speak, and she throws the Chux at the sink, and Jonathan says, *Let's all cool down,* and Aiko says, *As parents we should be on the same team,* and Jonathan says, *We are on the same team,* and Aiko says, *No we are not, Jonathan,* and Jonathan says, *We should talk about it calmly,* and he makes us all sit down on the sofa. He says the question on the table, not the coffee table, but the metaphorical table, is – *Can Bel go rafting with Isha and Tarak?*

I tell them how no one is allowed to say no in Isha and Tarak's house and explain how the rule works.

'Dumb rule,' Aiko says.

'It has some merit,' Jonathan says.

'See! Not. On. Same. Team,' Aiko says.

Jonathan sometimes uses words like merit, which are not old words but more formal than if he just said, *It's a good idea.*

'I need to be able to rely on you,' Aiko says to Jonathan and her eyebrows come together like two swords, *swish swish.*

'Dad is unreliable,' I say and laugh, because Jonathan's PhD is on people *in* stories who *tell* stories you don't believe so they can't be relied on so they are unreliable. So what what what happens when you read one of those unreliable storytelling people is you make up your *own* story alongside *their* story and get two for the price of one.

Jonathan laughs when I say he is unreliable but not Aiko. They keep talking and talking in their serious voices. Jonathan finally gets Aiko to agree to a trial period of me rafting with Tarak and Isha by saying he'll personally get us kids to comply with a rafting agreement, which is a contract.

When Jonathan speaks his voice is deep but not deep in a bad way, deep in a good way like when you're in a cave and you go deeper and deeper and everything around you is solid. Aiko's voice is around me too but then inside me also but Jonathan's voice is over and around and stays outside. He doesn't look happy when I say that but then he tells me he isn't not happy just thinking thinking because the human species knows words because of what is around a word, like not other words around the word, but the mood or something. Like *spook* has a mood and *jolly* has a different mood and so so so even if you're an alien down from Mars and only speak Martian you can maybe hear moods and get the meaning that way.

Jonathan and I go to the lake to meet Isha and Tarak. Our raft agreement is a lot of nots. Not knots but nots although Jonathan says knots could be a good metaphor for our raft agreement.

These are the nots we agree to: a) not to raft further than four metres from the shoreline (four metres is like four of Isha and four is one more than the three of us); b) not to get into strange boats; c) not to talk to strangers. We also agree to some yes things like: a) yes, we will check in with Jonathan regularly; b) yes, we will tell Jonathan exactly where we've been and exactly what we've done.

Every day, for the first week of January, Tarak, Isha and Zeus pick me up in the mornings and off we go. Sometimes we pretend to be explorers or stranded sailors or aliens or people from the future or pirates. Zeus has roles too, as a packhorse, a wild animal and a flying wolf. The flying wolf is his least favourite role as that is when all three of us climb on his back and pretend to fly. We like best to row along the foreshore, pull our raft up on land and hunt for treasure. By the end of that first week we have a huge stash: shells; animal bones; bird feathers, one white one from a white-bellied sea eagle; two street signs that someone has pulled from the signpost and thrown away; an old bike handlebar; an old tobacco tin; a brooch with a blue bird in the middle of it; and a tee shirt with Never Buy Retail printed on the front. We store our treasures in a tree hideaway that is just spiky trees growing close together around a rock, and is down a dirt path back in from the creek.

On Saturday, we crawl out of our hideaway and run along the path to the creek and there are the horse girls, five of them, walking their horses down to the water's edge.

Isha counts one, two, three and it's war.

We run towards them, half-lion, half-zombie. '*Raaah! Raaah!*'

The horses neigh and rear up like in cowboy movies.

The girls scream.

The bossiest girl shouts, 'Don't be juveniles.'

Isha gives Zeus the '*Attack!*' command.

Zeus flops down panting.

Even when we all yell, 'Go wolf, go!' Zeus won't budge.

The bossiest girl points at us. 'Grow up.'

It's an impasse, which means it's a deadlock, which means no one won the war. We take off on our raft and Tarak waves goodbye to the girls like they might have thought it was fun too, which they didn't. We know because all of them give us the finger.

We row to Swamp Park. Swamp Park isn't an official park. It's floodland that can't be built on because it floods. There's a stream that comes off from Mullet Creek and loops through the park but it's not very deep and we can just jump stones to cross it. There are groves, which is trees growing together but leaving a space in the middle that is all dark and gloomy, and the groves have the biggest spider webs I've ever seen. Some groves have smelly ponds in them and fat frogs croaking and swarming mosquitoes. All the pathways are covered with leaves and pine needles and beer bottles and paper rubbish. Away from the main path is a patch of dead spindly trees that look like burnt people with their arms out. We name it Burnt Tree Patch. Greeny twisted vines and smelly lantana loop through the branches and it could be like loops of beads on a burnt skeleton or something. Off the path and through Burnt Tree Patch, where the land goes up to a big bump, is the fig tree. It's a great tree because the roots are above ground. They look like elephant hide. Actually, it looks like lots of different trees plaited together but it's not, it's one tree. And when you sit underneath, it's like being in a huge huge tent that has all the flaps open. The branches twist all different ways and it's a really good tree for climbing. There's a big hole in the trunk that you can sit in, or hide stuff in, or you could live in it.

Isha and me and Tarak spit in our hands and squash our palms against each other and swear to do everything together no matter what. It's a really really good thing to do because I haven't really ever had best friends that I spit on my hands and make a pact with. Isha and I climb up to the third branch of the fig and wait for Tarak, who only makes it to the first branch because he looks down which is what you don't do.

'I can't climb up,' Tarak shouts.

We call down to him, 'Stop acting like a six year old.'

Tarak cries and cries because he is nearly eight so he hates being called a six year old but we only call him that to encourage him. We have to abandon the climb because someone might hear Tarak screaming and that could bring big problems because we haven't yet told Jonathan about our trips to Swamp Park. We haven't lied, we just haven't said, which is what some lawyers do, so it's legal. Why we don't tell is because Jonathan and Aiko would probably worry I'd fall into a swamp pond, especially Aiko because she's a worrywart. Swamp Park is like a secret and it's the first time I've been able to keep a secret.

We abandon our climb and go home and it's Monday before we can raft again. By then Isha has come up with the idea of a rope harness to help with Tarak's climbing terror and we raft to Swamp Park to make a second climb attempt. According to Isha you have to say attempt if you haven't climbed something yet.

After we've hauled the raft onto shore we trek along the path and through Burnt Tree Patch. Zeus is in the lead, followed by Isha, then Tarak, then me. Isha has the climbing rope looped over his shoulder which he says is what a mountain climber would do. When we come to the fig tree we stop, still as stone statues, because there on the ground, lying between the tree roots, is a girl. Her body is twisted, her legs scissored, one arm flung above her head, the other curled beneath her.

'She's dead,' Tarak whispers.

We creep closer to look at the dead girl. She has jeans on and a midriff tee shirt that's all faded and red but not tie-dye. There's a bird tattooed onto the outside of her ankle and three silver rings pierce her belly button. I see her stomach move.

'She's not dead,' I say, 'she's sleeping.'

We watch her but she doesn't wake up, not even when I fake cough. I see a wheelie suitcase shoved into the big hole in the tree trunk. It has yellow stitching on the handle and two zipper pockets at the front. We pull it out. It's heavy, heavy. Zeus sniffs at it.

'What if there's a dead body inside?' Isha whispers.

Isha is obsessed with dead things. All morning he has been trying to terrify Tarak and me with mutilated body stories.

'There won't be a dead body in there,' I whisper back.

'If there is, we don't mess up the crime scene,' Isha says.

Isha is the only one of us three allowed to stay up and watch crime movies so he thinks he is an expert on crime scenes.

We study the suitcase. Isha kneels to unzip it.

Tarak makes a scream face but doesn't scream.

'Tarak, it won't have a body in it,' I whisper. 'A body wouldn't fit in there.'

'Cut up it could,' Isha says.

We talk in hush hush voices so we don't wake up the sleeping girl.

'Don't open it,' I say.

'Bel, stop being a girl girl,' Isha says.

'I'm not being a girl girl.'

'You're acting like one,' Isha says.

'You're acting like one,' I say.

'Why does Zeus keep sniffing at it, if there's not a body in it?' Tarak asks.

Isha wants to open the suitcase but we all have to agree on account of our spit. The thing is I'm not a girl girl as in a frightened one so I have to agree to open the suitcase to prove it, only Tarak doesn't want to.

I squeeze his hand and say, 'Tarak, if there is a body in it, or even just body bits, like a finger, or a leg, we'll go back and tell Jonathan.'

'Okay,' Tarak says. 'Open.'

Isha counts one, two, three, then slowly unzips the bag and lifts the lid, but all we see is a roll of canvas and some clothes. Isha lifts the canvas from the bag and spreads it on the ground. Out roll lots of other canvases, all with paintings on them.

'It's like Aboriginal art,' I say.

'Is it?' Isha asks.

Zeus pads off. All his sniffing was for nothing.

We squat by the case and inspect what else is inside – a skimpy top, a bag of makeup, and a jumper. Underneath the jumper, there is a heavy thing, wrapped in a pillow case. Isha opens the pillowcase and pulls the heavy thing out.

'Wow,' he whispers.

'Wow and double wow,' I say.

It's a big big stone, twice as big as Jonathan's fist. It has a wooden stick that bends around it and is tied with twisty rope.

'What is it?' Tarak whispers.

'It's a stone thing,' I say.

'Yeah,' says Isha.

'Like an old ancient stone thing from a museum,' I say.

'Yeah, like a stone axe,' says Isha.

'It's not sharp enough,' says Tarak.

'But it's hard,' says Isha.

Zeus pads over to the sleeping girl and barks.

The girl moves her legs and moans.

Isha quickly puts the axe back in the pillow case and shoves it in the suitcase, under the jumper.

Zeus barks again.

The girl snaps open her eyes, like in the movies.

She sits up, a scared look on her face. It's like we spook each other. She screams and we scream and Zeus barks.

Tarak runs over and pulls Zeus away from the girl.

She looks over at her suitcase and at the rolled out canvases and jumbled belongings, even more jumbled after our fossicking.

'Hey, that's *my* stuff,' she says.

There is a big long silence.

Silences can be very uncomfortable, depending.

This one is uncomfortable.

The girl has a bruise on her cheek. It's a purple-blue lump and split in two by a line of dried blood.

'We thought there was a dead body inside,' Isha says.

The girl looks at him and her eyes roll like she doesn't believe him.

'Cut up, a body could fit in there,' he says.

Tarak and I nod our heads in agreement.

That makes her laugh. She has a really loud laugh. She twists around and crawls over to the bag and begins to roll up the canvases and put them back in the suitcase.

'Are they your paintings?' Isha asks.

'Good question,' the girl says.

The girl tells us her name is Kristie and her boyfriend's name is Ned and last night Ned had his boring friend over, called The Creep, not his real name but Kristie's name for him, and Kristie decided she was going to break up with Ned, because he is too old for her, but when she got out onto the street she had nowhere to go so she came to Swamp Park because it was a warm night and because this is where she comes a lot because no one comes here much.

'This is my secret place,' she says.

'It's our secret place too,' Tarak says.

Tarak sits down cross-legged beside Kristie.

'My dog's name is Zeus,' he says.

Kristie zips up her suitcase then leans across and pats Zeus.

'My other dog in England was called Tingle and I loved that dog,' Tarak says. 'I want to call Zeus, Tingle, but my dad says Zeus is already his name and he most probably doesn't want it changed.'

'Zeus is a good name,' Kristie says.

Isha and I squat down next to her. Although her clothes are smeared with dirt, she smells like rain.

'Zeus is a god,' Kristie says, running her hands through Zeus's fur.

'A dog,' Tarak says, correcting her.

Kristie laughs. 'Your dog has been named after a god, follow me? Hey, how long you guys been here?'

'Not long,' Isha says.

'Oh boy, I've got a whopping hangover,' Kristie says, yawning. 'I'm starving. Anyone got anything to eat?'

'I have, I have,' Tarak cries out.

He slides his backpack to the ground, unzips the front pocket and pulls out a pear. It's a bit squashed but he gives it to Kristie and she eats it quickly. She licks the juice from her fingers like it's the best pear she's ever tasted.

'How did you get that big cut on your cheek?' Isha asks.

'Is it cut?' She presses the inside of her wrist against the cut. 'It got scratched by one of those branches,' she says, and points to a small tree.

'Do you want a ride on our raft?' Tarak asks.

Kristie tosses away the pear core and pushes herself up from the ground really fast, like she is a runner in a race.

'I'd love a ride on your raft,' she says, and shoves her suitcase back into the hole in the tree trunk.

Kristie doesn't feel like a stranger, like one we should worry about. She is far too nice and friendly. Strangers can be friendly but not the way Kristie is friendly. Also, she is not too old, like she's older than us but not as old as someone older.

'Let's row to the middle of the lake,' she says, as we climb onto the raft and push away from the shore.

We have our rafting agreement with Jonathan, but going to the middle of the lake with Kristie is something not in the agreement, so it's like a special case. We row out and pass Hooka Island and then Gooseberry Island, and Kristie tells us they are nature reserves for birds and plants. We all do bird calls to see if the birds will come and land on our raft but they don't. Kristie points to the spot on land where her great-grandmother had a dairy.

'My grandmother says she was one scary lady,' Kristie says. 'Could shoot a gun and ride a horse and all that. Her first husband died and she ran the dairy with her brother and half-sister. But then she met my great-grandfather and he was like the son of this fierce Aboriginal warrior and they had a pile of kids together and one was my grandmother. The dairy was right there, see, where that factory roof is with the red stripe.'

We all look at the factory roof.

It seems small, like it's not a factory roof at all, but a roof on a toy factory.

Everything is different away from the foreshore. The bays shrink and loop alongside each other. And the trees are smaller. Only Mount Kembla and Mount Keira grow bigger, because now I can see the shape of them.

We stop rowing and let the raft drift. Kristie lies back and points at the sky.

'There's a seahorse,' she says.

We scramble to lie down next to her, four bodies spread-eagled, Zeus at our heads.

'There's a cow,' Isha says.

I see the fat bubble cloud he means.

Tarak points upwards. 'Two cows.'

'What about you?' Kristie asks, putting her hand on top of mine and linking our fingers together. 'What do you see?'

I am all hot in my chest because because because the thing is I haven't spoken since we found Kristie. I don't know why. Sometimes I get so I can't even say one word, even though mostly I can talk and talk. I point to a cloud near the horizon that has two large flaps and a long white tail trailing off into the sky.

'A stingray,' Kristie says.

Kristie has a really gravelly voice. Way too gravelly for someone as skinny as she is.

'Stare at the sky long enough,' she says, 'and you see all kinds of things you didn't see before.'

Kristie has a very pretty face, even though she has a bruise. She has this really dark spot near her lips and her lips are like really red and her eyes are like really brown.

We lie on the raft and watch clouds until Isha's watch alarm buzzes. It's time to go home. Ever since Jonathan found out that Tarak and Isha's dad was looking for a job he's been the one making us lunch. Kristie leans up on her elbows and inspects Isha's watch.

'My mum's,' he says.

'She died,' Tarak says.

Kristie sits up properly, looks to Tarak then Isha, waiting for them to say more.

'Killed herself,' Isha says.

His eyes are in the middle, not slanting down, so he's not lying.

A breeze makes tiny ripples all around the raft.

'Isha found her,' Tarak says.

'Man, that's bad, hey,' Kristie says.

She takes Isha's hands and puts them between her own but he won't look at her.

'She just got sad,' Tarak says.

'Yeah, right, thing is, some mums do get sad,' Kristie says.

She makes it sound like any mum can get sad and die. I put my arms around my knees and and and rock back and forth.

I wonder what it's like to have a mum that has killed herself.

'So hey, what does your dad say about all this?' Kristie asks Isha.

'Not much,' Isha says. 'But he left his girlfriend in England and we came back to Australia.'

'Ah,' says Kristie. 'See, right there, that says it all, doesn't it? You get what I mean?'

Isha and Tarak both nod.

I don't get what she means but I don't say that.

'Your dad's got a girlfriend, your mum's not happy. Why would she be? But shit happens between parents. Let me tell you. My parents got divorced when I was your age. Same thing. Only it was my mum left my dad. You can't take sides with your parents.'

The water laps at the edge of the raft.

'What's the best thing you did with your mum?' Kristie asks.

Isha's eyes flick sideways to Tarak. 'Run,' he says. 'We used to go running every day.'

'She was a fitness freak,' Tarak says.

'We'd run around Hyde Park,' Isha says. 'If we did the run with her then we'd get ice-cream. Dad said it was bribery but she said it was pay-off.'

'There you go – run. Or maybe eat loads of ice-cream.' Kristie lies back and puts her arms behind her head like a pillow. 'She'll be out there watching you, so make sure you do those things she loved doing with you.'

Isha looks at his watch and gasps. Too much time has passed since his alarm went off. It was only yesterday that Jonathan said we were the best, most reliable adventurers he had ever known. But now now now we are really late for lunch.

Kristie says we can just row fast all the way back and maybe not be too late, so that's what we do. First we drop Kristie at Swamp Park.

'Back to my tree,' she says, and jumps from the raft onto the shore.

'Are you going to stay here all day?' I call, as we push away from the bank.

'Maybe all night too,' she shouts.

Tarak promises he'll bring her half of his sandwich. She waves to us until we raft around the point.

When we get back to my house, Isha and Tarak's dad is sitting at the kitchen bench talking to Jonathan and the good thing is we don't get into trouble for being late.

'Ganesh, meet Bel,' Jonathan says, introducing me.

Ganesh leans down to shake my hand. He smells like Dettol. 'So this is the young lady I've been hearing so much about.'

Ganesh's lips are really pink. He has hair that sticks out all over the place, like he's just been electrified. Or like he is a wild man. But everything else about him is neat. Like he has a neat suit on and a neat white shirt and a neatly tied tie and his shoes are shiny and clean and neat. It's like his wild self has been squashed into neat packaging. Aiko says if I want I can pick up on people's personalities by looking at the way they dress but I'm not sure I can pick up on Ganesh's personality.

'I'm sorry but I have to drag the boys away for the afternoon,' Ganesh says to me. 'Their aunt has unexpectedly arrived for a visit.'

Isha and Tarak groan and I know why because now we won't be able to go back and see Kristie, but we don't say that.

'Your aunt is waiting for you,' Ganesh says in a voice like buttery milk.

Jonathan and I go with them to the gate and watch them walk down the street.

Jonathan sways back and forth with his hands folded in front of him, which is what he does when he's having a think.

'They're good boys,' he says.

He puts his hands on the back of my head and steers me inside like a cow.

By sunset clouds cover the sky. I can't see the star Venus like I sometimes can. The sun disappears and it's pitch black outside so no good for playing. I sit at the kitchen counter with Aiko and Jonathan, eating dinner – Pad Thai which is Jonathan's *pièce de résistance*. There's a lightbulb dangling above the counter and it makes a circle of light around us like in a spooky movie. Aiko teases Jonathan about his hair that he has in a topknot. She says it makes him look like a samurai. Aiko and Jonathan are already in night-time tracky dacks and tee shirts and I'm already in my PJs and the television isn't on yet so if I block out Uncle Ray and Maxine's dog barking from next door, it could just be us in the world. If my parents were gone, dead maybe, it would be like all the sound gone from the world.

'Bel?' Aiko says.

'Cold,' I say, so she doesn't know why I'm shaking.

We sit on the sofa and turn on the TV. I curl close to Aiko. She gives my shoulder a squeeze and pulls the rug around us.

'What will happen when you die?' I ask.

She wants to know where that question came from.

'My mouth,' I say.

'When I die,' she says, 'and that won't be for many moons yet, I'll be put in the earth and there I'll decompose. Worms will eat me and I'll eventually become part of the soil.'

When I ask how many moons before that happens, she doesn't answer, she just says, 'No one is going to die, okay?'

I go to sleep sitting next to her on the sofa which I like to do sometimes and later Jonathan carries me to bed and kisses me on my forehead and says, 'Sweet dreams, sweetheart.'

When Isha, me and Tarak land at Swamp Park the next day it's so dark it's almost like night. Above, there are swirls of blue-black clouds. Isha and I pull the raft onto the sand and lay the oars on top. We are all wanting to see Kristie, because she is she is she is this interesting person to us. We tramp along the path and through Dead Tree Patch.

The dark clouds part and the sun comes out and the day is full of shiny things.

Spider webs shine, like shiny necklaces.

Leaves shine a shiny green.

The wild grasses have drops of dew on them that catch the light.

But when we come to our fig tree Kristie is not there, nor is her suitcase.

At the base of the tree we inspect the damp leaves that are faded like her tee shirt. Zeus sniffs around trying to find her scent.

'She said she might sleep over,' I say.

'She probably went home to her boyfriend,' Isha says.

But we don't know where her home is.

In case Isha is wrong, because he admits he can be sometimes, we search the park for Kristie. We go into groves and stand listening to the slow plop of water. Zeus noses his way into thick bushes. He finds dirt paths we've never even explored yet. We run along the banks of the stream all the way to Mullet Creek and back again, but no Kristie.

We spend the rest of the morning looping ropes across the branches of the fig. We have to raft home for lunch but after eating Jonathan's cheese sandwiches like Speedy Gonzales – a cartoon mouse character who spoke with a Mexican accent saying *Arriba! Arriba!* which is Spanish for Go on! Go on! and who was in fact a Mexican mouse on TV when Jonathan was a kid like I am a kid – we're off again.

The sun is nearly to the escarpment, like floating above it, when we finally have the ropes set and climb the fig tree, right up to the second-to-highest branch. Standing on the branch, I can see over the dead trees, over the red and green roofs of the houses, over the tin roofs of the factories, even the one with the red stripe that was where Kristie's great-grandmother had her dairy farm, and through the Port Kembla smoke stacks, to the sea all grey and scowling.

I twist to look behind me. The escarpment cuddles all the houses and looks like a giant woman lying on her side. Like the roofs and roads and electricity wires are the swirly part of her dress, and the mountains are her curvy bits. And down from her body trickles Dapto Creek, that snakes around and becomes Mullet Creek, that twists here and there then pours into the lake where all the water swirls around like in a big shiny tub before it tips into a little stream that rushes out to the sea.

Every day for the rest of the week we row to Swamp Park and every day we climb our tree and every day I stare out at the lake. Jonathan says it's good to do things every day and that is what the long holidays are for, to get bored, so that when something comes along that is an anomaly, which is something that is out of the ordinary and not like anything else, then we, meaning we humans, appreciate it.

Kristie is an anomaly maybe, although I don't tell that to Isha and Tarak because it's a big word and before the holidays started Miss Schubert said it was my extensive vocabulary that made Julie Flint want to stick pins in me. Miss Schubert told me to keep using big words but I didn't know they were big or so big or I didn't think about them being big or not big but now I do think about it so maybe I won't use big words any more.

Every day I search for dragonfly nymphs, because because maybe something special will happen with Kristie if I am the one to witness a dragonfly's first breath.

But I don't see one.

Sometimes a stranger comes into your life and then they are gone and you miss them.

On Saturday of the second week of January, we row to Swamp Park but it's too hot among the dead trees so we go back out on the water. We row around to the next bay where there are tumbledown houses that could be great film sets for sci-fi movies. One has green palms and old rusted car parts, this other one is like a jungle, and has old tyres and and and giant plants that could eat us maybe. In the last garden – the one full of weeds – we see her. Kristie. She has her hair piled on top of her head like a crown and is lounging on a rug. A man is lying with his head on her lap. We wave and pull our raft up onto the bank and run across the grass.

'Greetings, friends,' Kristie says.

Zeus plonks himself down and rests his head between his paws, staring at the man.

'This is Ned,' Kristie says. 'Ned this is Bel, Isha, Tarak and Zeus.'

Ned opens one eye and looks at Zeus, and then at me and Isha and Tarak. 'Hey,' he says, and then closes his eye.

'He's really tired,' Kristie says. 'We've yanked out our kitchen, see there.' Kristie waves behind her to a pile of green cupboard doors tossed on top of a mountain of bricks. 'Knocked down a couple of walls. Now we're both done in.' The bangles on her arms tinkle like a musical instrument. Kristie smiles at us, then stares for ages at a piece of loose thread on her jeans.

We stand there and watch her but it's like she forgets we are there.

'Want to raft?' Tarak finally asks.

'Not today, angel,' she says.

'Oh,' says Tarak, in his disappointed voice.

Another long silence.

Isha and I look at each other. What is going on?

Tarak says, 'You sure?'

'The raft might make me dizzy.' Kristie laughs even though nothing funny has been said. 'Hey, how about I make my intrepid explorers a lemon drink?'

Kristie doesn't wait for an answer but lifts Ned's head from her lap and places it on the rug like it's a precious object. She pushes herself up from the ground, takes hold of Tarak's hand and leads him inside. Isha and I follow.

'Kristie is acting like the druggie girl that visits Lenny-the-biker,' I say to Isha.

'She's not on drugs,' he says. 'Look at her eyes, her pupils haven't shrunk to pins. That's how you tell.'

'She's acting weird.'

'You'd act weird too if you'd just pulled out a kitchen,' Isha says.

All that is left of the kitchen is bits of pipe and wire, a tap and a sink, and some rubble from the knocked-down walls. Incense is burning that smells like BO. There's a fridge and table in the hallway. Kristie fills the water jug from the tap and then squeezes lemons into it. She uses her hands to squeeze, not a plastic squeezer like Aiko. She adds six heaped spoons of sugar, and then stirs really fast, and then pours the lemon drink into glasses that have striped patterns on them. We take our drinks into the lounge room. We have to push through a plastic shower curtain to get there. There's no furniture yet because Kristie and Ned are still renovating but there are paintings stacked against every wall. Long strips of shiny material hang from the curtain rail in front of the window and the breeze makes the material swirl around me when I stand near it.

Tarak tells Kristie about the waterslides that Ganesh has refused to take him to because the cost is exorbitant.

'Everyone thinks it comes down to money,' Kristie says to Tarak. 'But money is just a way to get from A to B. Promise me you won't grow up obsessed with money.'

'I promise,' says Tarak.

'You don't get obsessed with it, but you have to deal with it.'

'How come you have so many paintings?' Isha asks.

'Because we sell them,' Kristie says.

'How do you sell them?' Isha rolls open a canvas that is just red and black lines.

'We go to a house up in Sydney and a rich lady there invites all her friends and they buy them. I am like the token Aborigine,' Kristie says. 'Only most of them think I'm not dark enough. I have to tell them my father is like royal blood, which he is, because back in the day his grandfather's grandfather was a king for the whitefellas.'

'What's a token Aborigine?' Isha asks.

'So we get all these paintings from Central Australia but these rich whitefellas want a real-life Aborigine there to authenticate them. So I get paid to say, *Oh yeah, this is a painting about the rainbow serpent* or whatever and I tell them the story and I show them a picture of Aunty or Uncle holding up the painting. And I say, *See, here is Aunty who painted this.* So I'm

153

like token. I stand in for whoever painted the painting. And these rich whitefellas don't care that it's like a different country that my people come from. Most times they go, *Oh Kristie, what an amazing story*, and then they buy the painting and then Ned makes money and then I get paid. It's a bit of smoke and mirrors, but it's for a good cause, hey, because it sells the paintings, right? Because the paintings are the real deal. Like we're not faking that bit.'

Kristie's bangles keep tinkling because she uses her hands to talk. When she holds her hands up her sleeves fall back and I see bruises on her arms.

Kristie turns to Tarak. 'Ned hasn't actually paid me yet, and believe me his bill is clocking up, but when I *do* get paid I'll take you all to the waterslides.'

We finish our drinks and go back out to the garden. Ned is awake and sitting on the back verandah steps. He looks quite friendly when he is awake. He has a lot of scars on his hands and when I say they look interesting he shows me the scars on his chest. He got them fighting in the jungle. It wasn't a war, he was just doing some defensive work, but then he got a bad back. How he got to be an art dealer is, he met a bloke who knew a bloke.

'Ned can spin a yarn,' Kristie says to us. 'So don't ask him to prove anything.'

Ned takes out his rolly packet and begins to roll some tobacco. When you roll your own it is called a rolly, not a cigarette. Ned says Zeus is quite well trained for a wolf-breed.

'Wolves don't know how to lie. Not like us apes,' he says.

'Apes!' Tarak laughs.

'Yes, apes, the lot of us,' Ned says. 'Cunning apes. It's being able to lie and plot that got us ahead of other animals. You want to know why we lie so well?'

'Ned,' Kristie warns. 'They're kids.'

Ned laughs and lights his rolly. 'Never too young to learn how the real world works. First reason we got ahead is sex. We apes *love* sex.'

Tarak laughs, but he laughs too much so I know he's embarrassed.

'But your leader wolf, see, he only has sex once a year,' Ned says. 'The rest of the pack don't have it at all, and they don't miss it.'

Isha listens to every word that Ned says.

'We apes are sex addicts,' Ned says. 'And guess what other kind of addict we are?'

Isha puts his hand up like he is in school. 'Drug addict?'

'Nup,' says Ned.

'Sleep addict,' Tarak guesses.

'We're war addicts,' Ned says. 'We love to fight.'

Ned talks to us about fighting and war strategies and we stand there listening to him because he is he is he is this really interesting person and he talks about things other people don't talk about. He says a lot of Aboriginal painting is about the war that was here in Australia in the early days, only no one in government calls it war.

'But we had massacres in this country,' Ned says, 'and where there's a massacre, there's a war.'

Later, when we raft home, we decide to keep both Ned and Kristie our secret, because it's good to have secrets.

Now I have two secrets. Swamp Park is one, Ned and Kristie is two.

For the last weeks of the school holidays we swim and scoot about on our raft and play in Swamp Park, or go to Ned and Kristie's place. Ned has muscles as big as a muscle man but when he puts on his suit he can look suave which is what he has to look like to sell paintings. Sometimes we help Ned and Kristie do renovation jobs. Like we help Ned paint the kitchen. And we help Kristie scrape paint and plaster from the bricks that are piled out the back. Once the bricks are all clean, Ned will make a paved area. Most days when we finish helping them do work, Ned makes us pancakes and Kristie makes us cups of sweet tea. Ned is an extremely good pancake cook. He's good at other things too. One time I tell Ned about dragonflies and he draws me a beautiful dragonfly that could be like a painting in an art gallery but he says it's for me to keep. I take it home and put it at the back of my wardrobe. But every now and then I take it out to look at it.

On the last Thursday of the holidays we arrive at Ned's and Kristie's place just as Kristie is locking the back door.

She has her big black sunglasses on and a roll of canvases under her arm. She's smoking a rolly.

'I've got to go up the street,' she says.

Kristie looks funny, her lips look bigger or something.

'How come you've got paintings with you?' I ask.

'These aren't paintings,' she says.

'I can see the striped bits,' I say.

'Listen, you didn't see me carrying these canvases, did you?' She says it as though she is mad with us.

We stare at her.

'Tell me you didn't see these canvases.'

'But we did see them,' I say.

She takes a puff on her rolly and blows smoke into the air.

'I know you did, Bel, but I want you to imagine I'm Ned, and you're telling him you didn't see them.'

'We didn't see any canvases,' Isha says.

'No, tell me so I believe it,' Kristie says.

Isha puts on an innocent expression.

'We didn't—'

'No, try again, I still don't believe you. And look me right in the eye. Tell it to me straight. Say, *I've never seen Kristie with a canvas. No, she didn't have a canvas.*'

Isha has another go.

'Good, I believed that!' Kristie says.

She makes Tarak and me do it too. It takes Tarak five goes and he has it, but for me, even after six goes I still don't get it right.

'Okay Bel,' Kristie says. 'In your mind, imagine me with a canvas, and then rub the canvas out with an imaginary rubber.'

I do what she says.

'Now imagine I'm Ned. And I say to you, *Did you see Kristie with a canvas?*'

'No, Ned. I didn't see Kristie with a canvas,' I say.

'Good. That time I believed you,' Kristie says. 'Best lie is the lie that doesn't get found out. And if Ned ever asks you a question and I cough like this,' and Kristie does a little cough, 'that means, leave the talking to me.'

She runs down the steps, flicks her rolly onto the ground, and stamps it out with her boot.

'Go home now,' she says, and walks around to the front of the house.

The next Saturday, after we've been at Ned and Kristie's playing frisbee with Zeus, we sit on the verandah steps. Ned is smoking and the rest of us are eating ice-cream. Kristie has her dark sunglasses on which she wears a lot because she likes them.

'Where do you kids live?' Ned asks.

'Over on Wyndarra Way,' Kristie says, and then she coughs.

'Koonawarra?' Ned asks, looking at me.

'Yeah,' Kristie says, before I have time to answer.

'Right,' Ned says. 'Posh street, that one.'

He looks out at the lake and continues to smoke.

Isha and Tarak start trying to mimic the whipbirds calling, where the male whipbird whistles its long high whistle with a crack, and the female overlaps and finishes with *choo choo*, so so so it's like one call almost. Isha is really good at whistling but Tarak can't get his lips right.

When it's time to go home, Kristie walks us down to the raft. 'Okay, you kids all live on Wyndarra Way, that is your story and you never change it.'

'Why?' asks Isha.

'Never tell Ned where you live, okay?'

'But why?' Isha asks again.

'Some people you can love, but never trust. Ned is one of those people.'

'Ned wouldn't do anything bad to us,' I say.

'Just listen to what I say, Bel.'

'She'll listen,' says Isha, even though I didn't even ask him to open his big mouth and speak for me.

February comes and Tarak, Isha and me have to go back to school. We can only visit Ned and Kristie on weekends. The weather is mercurial, which means it's like the old god from Roman times called Mercury who was really fast going here and there on messages and that's like the weather changing fast from sunny to stormy. When I walk to school it's hot like a furnace but at recess the clouds go dark and squash into bunches, and raindrops the size of grapes plop on my head and Miss Schubert is like, *Go inside, go inside, Bel, and don't you try and get wet again.* When there is thunder I stand at the windows and wait for the quick sharp cracks of lightning that x-ray the clouds and sometimes Miss Schubert stands there too. One time she tells me not to worry about what Julie Flint and the others call me.

'You play the long game, Bel,' she says. 'Do you know what I mean?'

'Yes, Miss Schubert.'

'Your time will come,' she says. 'Get it?'

'Yes,' I say.

'Good girl.'

'I'll see a nymph turn into a dragonfly,' I say.

'Sorry?'

'That's what you mean, right?'

Miss Schubert stares at me. 'Are you saying that as a metaphor?'

'It could be a metaphor,' I say. 'Or it could be something that happens.'

'Yes,' she says, and gives my shoulder a squeeze.

March comes, puff, then it's gone. April too. Kristie and Ned go to the desert to buy more paintings. Then May, June and July. But but but in all that time I don't see any nymphs become dragonflies. Jonathan says I'll just have to be patient because spring is a better time to see them maybe. School is just boring days to get through until the weekend. Every Saturday and Sunday I meet Isha and Tarak and we go rowing on the lake, or we go to Swamp Park and climb the fig, or we visit Ned and Kristie who are now our best best secret friends.

One Saturday, when we are at Ned and Kristie's, Ned and me are making pancakes. I'm stirring up the cream with sugar to put on top after the pancakes are cooked. Ned is at the stove, pouring the pancake mix into a frying pan. Kristie, Isha, and Tarak are outside, scraping paint off the last of the bricks. The patio is the only part of the renovation left to do.

'Hey,' Ned says, 'I drove along Wyndarra Way the other day, and I was thinking, now which house does Bel live in?'

I feel all my insides go cold. Kristie is not here and I don't know what to do. I don't say anything and there is this really long pause. I keep stirring the cream.

'Which one is it?' he asks.

I still don't say anything.

'Is it the two-storey white one?'

'No.'

'Is it the blue weatherboard one with the big verandah?' Ned asks.

'Ned, are you going to paint the outside of this house?'

'I might. What colour would you suggest?'

'I think blue would be good.'

'Really? Blue.'

'Yes.'

'Like your house.'

'Yes.'

'Funny thing is though, I didn't see a blue weatherboard house in Wyndarra Way. No, that was in another street.'

I keep my head down. I'm trying to think fast because the best lie is the one that doesn't get found out.

'Ned, I'll take you to my house one day.'

'I'd like that. So what colour is it?'

'You know how I'm not good with numbers,' I say.

'Yep.'

'I'm not so good with colour either.'

I think he believes me because there is a long silence but not an uncomfortable one.

I put my finger into the cream and taste it. 'I think it's sweet enough now,' I say.

'You know Kristie is a little bit nuts, don't you, Bel?' Ned says.

I stare at him.

'I virtually took her in off the streets. Gave her a place to live. I'm teaching her the art business.'

He turns a pancake over in the frying pan, then looks at me.

'But she tells a lot of lies,' he says.

'Yeah,' I say, before I even know I've said it.

'But you tell the truth, don't you?' he says.

'Yeah.'

Ned tips the pancake onto a plate and pours some more mixture into the frying pan.

'I'm missing a few paintings. You ever seen Kristie hide anything?' he asks.

I shake my head.

'Because those paintings belong to me, not Kristie. I'm giving her free accommodation, free food. I take her on free holidays, buy her Armani sunglasses for fuck's sake. You know Armani, Italian. I buy her clothes, her makeup. And all she has to do for all the free stuff is come with me to an art party now and then. Tell some of those rainbow serpent stories she loves so much. That's it. Good deal, don't you think?'

'Yeah,' I say, because it does sound like a good deal.

'But Kristie has had a rough time. She mixed with the wrong sort when she was not much older than you. Now, she doesn't trust people. But that's no excuse for lying.'

I start to stir the cream in the bowl again, even though I'm sure it is ready.

'But Ned, we apes all lie, don't we?' I say.

'Here's the thing, when I was telling you that, it was explaining general patterns of behaviour. But there's a code among friends, stronger than that, and it's about loyalty. It's about *not* lying. Sticking up for each other. You get that, don't you?'

'Like when you spit on your hands and have a pact?'

'Exactly like that. So you'd tell me if you'd ever seen Kristie hiding a canvas somewhere?'

Ned turns to me again. I force myself to look him in the eyes, the way Kristie showed me. I picture her with a canvas and then rub the canvas out with an imaginary rubber.

'I don't think I saw her with a canvas,' I say.

'You sure about that?' Ned asks. 'Because I know you're not a liar. You're like a wolf. You don't know how to lie.'

'I'm pretty sure I didn't see her with one.'

'You know I'd never tell her you told. You know that don't you? The good and true thing about best friends is, they never reveal confidences. So this would be between you and me.'

'Our secret,' I say.

'Yes.'

'Maybe I saw her with one once,' I say.

'That's what I thought,' he says. 'Only once?'

'Only once.'

'You're sure only once?'

'Maybe it was two canvases only once.'

'That makes sense. Because there is more than one missing. I think there are a few, quite expensive canvases actually, missing. And you know if I don't find them it means the artists won't get paid.'

Right then, Kristie, Isha and Tarak come running up the stairs and into the kitchen. I look at Kristie immediately because I know I've done exactly what she didn't want me to do. I think Ned will get mad at her, yell at her maybe, but he doesn't do that at all.

'Here they are,' Ned says, and he lays the plates on the table and starts to serve the pancakes and he winks at me and smiles.

When it's time to leave both Kristie and Ned walk us to the raft. Ned's never really had a good look at our raft, but now he does. He says Isha and Tarak did a really good job of making it.

They wave to us as we row away. I look up to the escarpment and watch the sun disappear. The green-leaved trees darken so they look like make-believe trees that someone has put in front of a silvery curtain. The kookaburras start laughing.

The next day, we row to Swamp Park and find Kristie waiting for us at the fig tree. She tells us she has Ned's ute parked on the street at the back of the park.

'I want you to come with me,' she says. 'But we have to hurry.'

'Where are we going?' I ask.

'Somewhere secret.'

She has her dark glasses on again. She doesn't wait for us to say yes, she just starts walking. We follow her along the path, through the trees, to the road.

'How come you're limping?' I ask her.

'Fucking boots are too tight,' she calls over her shoulder.

When we get to the road we all pile into Ned's ute. It's a four-wheel drive and has front and back seats and really good air-conditioning for when he goes to the desert to get paintings. We have to put a towel on the back seat for Zeus to sit on because Ned's ute is exceptionally clean because Ned is an exceptionally clean person. Kristie says he even cleans under the bed, which most people hardly ever do, and the weird thing is to look at him you wouldn't know how clean he is.

'He's a paradox,' she says.

'What's a paradox?' I ask.

'Like when someone is a nice person and also a shitty person,' she says, and she stares at me in the rear-vision mirror for a long time and I wonder if she means I'm a nice person and a shitty person, because maybe Ned told her I said something about the canvases. And then I remember how Ned said he wouldn't tell, because we are best friends, so anything I told him would be our secret. I believe him so I decide not to worry.

We drive along the highway and go up the winding mountain road and Kristie parks at the top of a fire trail. She takes a red bag from the back of the ute. It has a water bottle in it, and a plastic bag, a torch and the pillowcase with the old stone axe.

'What's the axe for?' I ask.

'We're going to hide it,' Kristie says.

We walk really fast along the track to be healthy, and also because Kristie needs to get the ute back before Ned knows she has taken it. Ned's doing a marathon run with his one friend, The Creep, who Kristie never wants us to meet, because he is not the kind of man children should get to know, like he is a bad man. As we pass by a big old tree I see an echidna. When I go near the echidna, it tucks its body in under its spiky coat so it is like a spiky bush.

'That's its protection mechanism,' Kristie says.

It's only me that stops to look at the echidna, so I have to run to catch the others up. We turn off the fire trail and walk along a path and come to this open area where there is a ruin of a house, and this gigantic massive fig tree. It's like our one at Swamp Park, only much much much bigger and even more knotted.

'This is the great-great-great-great-great-grandmother of all trees,' Kristie says.

The roots of the tree go all the way across to the edge of the cleared bit of land. I look up to the sky but can't see the top of the tree.

Tarak shouts and runs around the fig tree.

'Sssh, Tarak,' Kristie says. 'This is the Hill of Peace.'

Tarak laughs. 'Not the Hill of Peace any more.'

But Kristie makes him be quiet.

All that is left of the house is some wooden posts, one wall, a stone fireplace and some steps. Kristie stands on the steps and stares the same way Jonathan sometimes does when he is in his office trying to remember a word, and it's like the word is hiding in the air somewhere, and if he stares long enough he might see it.

'The old cedar house was still here when I was a kid,' Kristie says.

'What happened to it?' Isha asks, going to stand in the stone fireplace that is as tall as he is.

'Weather,' says Kristie. 'My mum used to sit on this step for hours while we played.'

'Why is it called the Hill of Peace?' Isha asks.

Kristie shrugs. 'It's peaceful.'

She jumps down from the step.

'We haven't got time today to stick around,' she says. 'Come on, let's hurry. I'll bring you back another day.'

We hike up through the trees to the rocky part of the escarpment. There's a big rock, taller than two men standing on top of each other. Kristie slips behind it.

'Spooky spooky,' she says.

We follow her and we are in a rocky corridor. We walk along and see caves. Three of them. I run ahead of Kristie and go into the first cave. It's cold and dark. Isha and Tarak race towards the back of the cave. Soon, we can't see each other's faces and have to feel our way along the rock. Tarak pikes out first, then Isha.

'I'm the bravest,' I say, when I come back to the light.

Kristie is bent down in front of the second cave. She is wrapping the stone axe in the plastic bag. Inside the bag is an envelope that has *Mum* written on it. Once the axe is tightly wrapped, Kristie flicks on the torch and walks to the back of the cave and puts the package on a narrow shelf that has bits of broken glass on it.

We come back outside the caves and Kristie says we'll go into the third cave next time we come. We walk back down to the skeleton house without speaking.

'How come you put the axe in the cave?' I ask, when Kristie stops at the clearing.

She has got something in her eye that she just needs to get out.

'It's my running away insurance,' she says.

'Running away from what?' I ask.

Kristie puts her glasses back on and turns to us and says really fast, 'Listen, if anything happens to me, you three know where that axe is, right?'

'What could happen to you?' I ask.

'Nothing probably, but if it does, just in case, I want you to do something.'

I get scared then because what does she mean.

'What do you want us to do?' Isha asks.

'I want you to tell my mother about the axe,' Kristie says. 'No one else but my mother.' She takes a bit of folded paper out of her jeans pocket and gives it to Isha. 'That's her phone number. Don't lose it.'

Isha holds the piece of paper like it's a precious jewel.

'Why don't you give the axe to her now?' I ask.

'For a start, we're not talking to each other. But also, that axe is valuable, and I might need to sell it.'

'Is it your axe or Ned's?' I ask.

'It was my uncle's,' Kristie says. 'I could sell that axe and go anywhere I wanted in the world. I could even afford to take you guys with me.'

'Would you take Ned?' I ask.

'Not if I was running away from him.'

Maybe Kristie and Ned had a fight about the canvases. I wish now I hadn't told Ned about them. 'Are you leaving Ned?'

'I don't know yet. It's complicated.'

'Why is it complicated?' I ask.

'I can't really go into it.'

'Why?' I ask.

'Why, why, you ask a lot of questions,' Kristie says, and she lights up a rolly.

'Yeah,' I say.

'I don't know, Bel. Some things are hard to talk about. Maybe you could write about that when you grow up. How there's a lot of shit in the world that we don't ever talk about. We just pretend it isn't happening.'

Maybe Ned did tell her what I said about the canvases. Kristie told me not to trust him. That is why we had to keep where we lived a secret.

'Like what isn't happening?' I ask.

'Enough,' says Kristie. She puffs on her rolly.

'I can't write about something if I don't even know what it is.'

'I thought you were going to write novels,' she says.

'I am.'

'Then make shit up,' she says.

'What if you don't like what I make up?'

'Do you have to question everything?' she asks.

'No more questions,' Isha snaps at me.

Kristie gives him a *thank-you* look and that makes me mad.

'Maybe if you didn't lie to Ned, you wouldn't have to leave him,' I say.

Kristie gives me a *where-did-that-come-from?* look.

'For fuck's sake, Bel, you don't know what you're talking about, so keep your mouth shut for once in your life.' Kristie drops her rolly on the ground and stomps it out.

I don't say anything.

Isha makes sideways eyes at me.

Kristie stares at the sky for a long time. We all stand there, hardly moving at all.

'Human beings are fucking dumb animals that think they're smart,' Kristie says. 'They're so fucking dumb they don't even realise how fucking dumb they are.'

'Yeah,' says Isha.

I kick at stones on the ground.

Tarak says, 'Fuck, fuck, fuck,' very softly under his breath, and that makes Kristie laugh.

She looks at me again. I push the stones into a pile with the tip of my shoe.

'Bel, you have to learn when to ask questions and when not to ask,' Kristie says. 'It's like you've got no social radar or maybe too much social radar, and it can be funny but it can also be fucking annoying.'

Tarak opens his mouth wide and then shuts it.

No one moves.

A hare runs across the clearing.

'Sorry, Bel,' Kristie says. 'But I'm having a bad day.'

I stop moving and stay really still. But I keep staring at my feet because I don't want to look anyone in the face, which is like a coward's way out of things or what an echidna does.

'So, I've let you know about my other secret spot and it can be your other secret spot too,' Kristie says, in a pretend happy voice.

I still don't look at her.

'Can we bring our dad here?' Tarak asks.

'It wouldn't be a secret then, would it?' Kristie says.

'No,' Tarak says.

'This place is not for dads, or for anyone else,' she says. 'This is just for you three, a place to come when you need to feel safe. It's a forgotten-about place and we leave it that way.'

Kristie hurries off along the path. We follow behind her, like we're on a safari, or like we're soldiers in a war zone, only we don't have guns, or like we're prisoners or slaves who don't have chains.

I don't ask any more questions.

The wind through the grass is making a sound like the *shush shush* of the sea.

When we get to the car Kristie stops by the door and says to me, 'Friends again?'

I nod my head but don't smile.

She takes off her glasses and I see her eye is swollen and bruised black. She lifts up her shirt and I see big bruises across her stomach.

I start to cry because now she looks like one of those battered women on the television news. Isha and Tarak just stare.

Tarak tries to touch one of the bruises. 'That's really big,' he says.

'This is why I might run away one day,' Kristie says to me. 'You made me show you this, Bel. I didn't want to show you. Ned did this to me, right? This is why you can't trust him.'

I can't work out how she got so bruised from Ned.

'Is it from sex?' I ask.

'No Bel, not from sex. From being punched. You get that? From getting hit.'

'I get it,' I say, but I can't stop crying.

We all stand by the ute not looking at each other.

'Hey, listen, Ned is not all bad,' Kristie says after a long silence. 'I wouldn't be with him if he was all bad. He loses it, but he's usually sorry after. And mostly, I know how to get out of his way before it happens, so don't worry about me. But you've got to listen to me when I say there are things we can't tell him. You know I trust you, Bel.'

'Yes,' I say.

'And you too, Isha and Tarak. You all know how to keep a secret, right?'

'Right,' says Isha.

'Never tell Ned about this place,' says Kristie. 'Deal?'

'Deal,' says Tarak.

'One day I might go away and he might come looking for information on me. Ned stores information, and one day when you least expect it, something you've told him will come back to haunt you. That's why you have to stick to your story about living on Wyndarra Way. I don't want him pestering you or your parents. Got it?'

'Got it,' I say.

But I find it hard to look at Kristie, because what if she got hit because of the canvases that I told Ned about? It's good she

173

doesn't know it was me that told him, because she trusts me, but it's also bad, because she shouldn't trust me.

Kristie gives me a kiss on my forehead, and I put my arms around her waist. I only hold on gently, because of her bruises. I hear hear

Nada
2033 & 2717

hear birds.

Hello Nada. Come in. Sit. You said you liked birds in our last session so I found this audiomem of ext—

Is it a whipbird?

Yes, excellent. You are making excellent cognitive progress.

I am Nada.

Yes. You are Nada. Very good. Your memory *is* stabilising.

I think so, yes.

Nada, I want to publicly membank what we say to each other today for our Storyland Project.

Ah.

If you don't wish to be publicly membanked you have that right. If you choose not to participate your treatment here will not be affected. Nada, may I membank?

Nada nods her head.

Nada, I can't go ahead until you *say* yes. You must verbally agree. This is a contract.

Yes.

Thank you. I'm membanking now. Do you remember the countdown?

Ten. Nine. Eight.

And if you want to stop at any time raise your right hand. Can you raise your right hand?

Nada raises her right hand.

Very good. Are you ready to go back to where you left off during our last session?

Left off? But I don't, no, I don't remember where I left—

No need to panic. You'll remember when I count you down. Hypnosis is one of the methods we use to manage the telling of difficult stories.

Difficult?

I will be here with you, prompting, clarifying. That is what I do.

Oh.

This is your personal membank. It's what is past, not you breathing now, so no need to feel fearful. We do not need to fear the past, only understand it.

I'm not frightened but you're making me feel like I should be.

Look, there. What do you see before you on the vismem?

Is it a tree? Oh, oh, yes, our ... our fig. I told you about our fig tree.

Yes, *Ficus obliqua* or small-leaved fig, I found the exact tree in our archive. I want you to look at it then shut your eyes and I'll count you down.

Yes.

Good. Ten. Nine. Eight. You're going back to that time, the time when you remember the tree. It stood very near your home. Seven. Six. Five. You're going back to that time and place. Relax and let your mind sink into that time and place. Four. Three. Two. You're nearly there. One. You are there. What do you hear?

A beating sound.

What do you do?

I switch on my torch.

What do you see?

The dripping dark around us, like the forest has slipped into the house. I shine the light on the window. A moth – pattering, pattering – against the glass. I watch its shivery dance. Then *thump*. A flash of claws. An owl snatches the moth. Grey feathers in the torchlight. Then *whoosh*. Gone. I hear myself breathing, reach out and put my hand on Ben's hip. His skin is hot. I can feel his hipbone. He's lost too much weight.

Silence.

Ben. Lost weight.

It worries me. As soon as it's light, I dress and go to the kitchen. I cram water, food bars and my inhaler into a small backpack. Esther walks in, sleepy. She stands on the other side of the breakfast counter.

Esther?

My niece was staying with us when Frank hit. After, there was no way to get her home. I stare at her for too long, thinking about how to get her back to my sister safely. My sister will be panicking.

'Have I grown horns?' Esther asks.

'Ben is worse today,' I say. 'I have to get him some Marsoral. I'm hiking to the medical centre. I can find out about food drops while I'm there.'

I zip up my backpack. Begin to rub on repellent.

'I'm coming with you,' Esther says.

'You'll slow me down.'

'What if I can ring Mum from the medical centre?' she says. 'What if they're evacuating from there?'

Evacuating?

Most people had already been evacuated. When the first cyclone warnings came Ben and I drove down the mountain to the lookout. We got out of the car and stood staring across rooftops to the ocean. Waves were running along roads and crashing through houses like they were cardboard cut-outs. Electricity poles were the new driftwood. And the sea kept coming. But our house is on high ground. We thought we'd be safe. After all, this was not the first cyclone we'd been through. We did the usual stock-up of food, boarded up the windows in the house and sheds, took the blades out of the ceiling fans. We stored away all the outdoor furniture, the potted plants, the wheelie bins – anything that might blow away in the big winds.

Only we underestimated Frank. Everyone underestimated Frank.

At first there were howling winds – a constant whooshing, then a clashing and clanging as the winds knocked bits of tin from the roof. The power went out. We heard a loud crack and then a thump as a tree crashed down. Then a second tree fell. Neither hit the house. We were bunkered down in the TV room in the basement. Every now and then we'd run up the stairs to check the house for damage. There were leaks and we found buckets and bowls to put under them. One small window in the bathroom, one that we hadn't boarded up, shattered. I taped plastic over it. Everything seemed to be holding well. We had torches and food and alcohol down in the TV room. We played board games. The rain, when it came, was like stones pelting the house. Horrible. We tried not to think about it. And then, something strange, a piercing scream. Not human. It was as if the earth itself was in horrendous pain. I've never heard anything like it – on and on this scream went and it hurt our ears. Everything began trembling, just this violent trembling. Followed by a rumbling and banging that went on and on for hours. So loud. Like standing next to a fast-moving freight train. It was like a hellish nightmare only it wasn't a nightmare it was real. There was nothing we could do. We were at the mercy of nature and nature was in a rage. Esther, Ben and I sat close together. We'd never experienced a cyclone like it. We held onto each other because we thought it was the end, the absolute end. At one point we even said our goodbyes, hugged and cried. It felt like we sat there for hours but who knows how long it really was.

And then, all of a sudden, stillness.

The commotion had stopped.

We looked at each other.

Was it over?

We couldn't believe it.

Everything was so quiet.

We crept out from the TV room, uncertain still, and slowly climbed the stairs. We opened the door from the basement into the kitchen not sure of what we'd find. All there. Our house still standing. I thought, Oh, maybe everything will be okay. But as soon as we went outside – it was like a giant had crossed the land and stepped on everything in sight. We walked down the road to check on the Castelli family. Most neighbours had evacuated but the Castellis stayed. They had the same cyclone plan as us – stock up, bunker down, wait it out. Their place was like a smashed-up toy house, just bits of roof sticking up through the rubble. We searched through the wreckage, calling their names, over and over. Couldn't find their bodies.

Everywhere we looked – roads torn up, lumps of bitumen and concrete strewn in the paddocks. Branches and tree trunks where roads used to be. Houses, cars, powerlines, all smashed. Shocking. Only four houses on our side of the mountain survived: Steve and Gina's – their farm is two properties down from us; Tom and Bill's – their place is about a kilometre to the south; the Canberra couple's weekender – next door to Tom and Bill's; and our place. Everything else destroyed. Gone. No way to drive up or down the mountain. No phone, no mobile, no internet. No idea of what was happening elsewhere. For all we knew, we could be the only people on the planet.

Those seven of us who had survived got together. We were all in a daze. Steve and Gina got us going. Nothing to do but start the clean-up, they said.

It kept raining, the rivers were flooding – the entire village down in the valley was under water. Unbelievable. It was all so disturbing. I had seen this kind of destruction on TV: seen footage of cyclones ravaging towns further north, or in other countries. I should have known it would happen here one day, but somehow I didn't. Three days into the clean-up two rescue workers arrived in a helicopter to check the damage. They reported horrific sea surges. Said it was chaotic but everyone was doing their best. Warned us about the MARS virus. They explained about the emergency clinic, how it had been set up in the school on the other side of the mountain. They told us we'd need the vaccine, Marsoral. Said they'd return with an oral dose for us all, as well as emergency food supplies, enough to keep us going until order was restored.

Often, in the days after, we'd see rescue helicopters in the sky, but none landed.

Soon, we said to each other, soon they will land here. There must be more needy areas. And none of us had MARS. How could we have it, we'd only seen the rescue workers.

And then one day, there were no more helicopters. We kept looking to the sky. Nothing. No one came. It felt like we'd been abandoned. And then, Gina got sick. We didn't think it was MARS. Not at first. Five days later she was dead. Steve was just about to hike to the medical centre. It happened so quickly.

Nada taps the side of the chair using her right hand. Her left arm hangs by her side.

You are in the kitchen. Esther wants to come with you to the medical centre.

Esther says, 'I want to talk to Mum, at least that.'

'Okay,' I say. 'Wear your walking boots and take my rain jacket. And cover yourself with repellent.'

I trudge down to Steve's before we set off. I want to ask him to check in on Ben while I'm gone. Since Gina died Steve hasn't been doing so good. He blames himself. And with the continuing clean-up there's been no time to grieve. I take a shortcut through the paddocks. The land is still strewn with dead cows, tree trunks, torn branches, rubbish, bricks, bits of tin. There's a terrible stench of death. I pass behind what used to be the Castellis' shed. Jack Castelli's red ute is now a crumpled chip packet.

The surprise of the destruction keeps coming back to me. How one night we camped in our basement while our house shook and the world was rearranged.

Steve's home is tucked into the escarpment. I tramp down the dirt driveway, stop at the back door and call out. No answer.

I look to the side of the house, to Gina's grave, there under the surviving coachwood, a chiselled rock her gravestone. I don't go over. Can't go over. Instead, I head for the shed. Steve's fortress. When I walk in he's leaning on a bench, his back to me, hunched over, like there's a great weight on top of his shoulders, pushing him down.

'I'm hiking to the medical centre,' I say.

Steve doesn't look up but his body goes rigid.

'It's Ben. He's had a fever for two days. No idea if it's MARS. But he's lost quite a bit of weight and I don't want to risk it.'

Gina's symptoms had been flu-like. She'd complained of aching bones, had a fever and a dry cough. 'Can you check on him at midday? Don't go in. Just call through the door, make sure he's okay?'

Steve doesn't respond. He's tough but everyone has a breaking point. I go and stand next to him. He's so still he could be petrified. Rosellas land in the doorway, begin picking through the new shoots of grass.

'You've lost the closest person to you,' I say.

Steve rolls a stone about with the tip of his boot. Won't look at me.

Before he bought the property he was in the army. High up. Publicity for him everywhere; the army's first Koori commander. Awarded. Esteemed. But then he'd had enough of fighting other people's wars. That's the story he told me. He and Gina bought their property and settled on the mountain. They were trying for kids.

'Not shooting the right bullets,' Steve once said.

His own family visited all the time. Kids, uncles, aunties.

'Kooris always feed each other,' Gina once said, 'just like Italians'.

Silence.

You are in the shed with Steve. He won't look at you.

Steve takes hold of a screwdriver and squats by the door. In the dirt he draws a map of the best route to take over the ridge.

'I'll check on Ben,' he says.

Nada sits forward. Short breaths.

Where are you now, Nada?

I'm hiking away from my house. Esther is with me. I need Marsoral for Ben. I need some contact with the authorities. This chaos has gone on for too long. I stop on the path and look back. Our home is long and low, with a verandah running all the way around it. A massive fig tree guards the house, its branches spread over the roof, its roots running across the ground. The greened escarpment curves behind, a protective arm around them both. The locals call our place Hill of Peace. It's always been a retreat for people. Esther was on holiday here, sent by my sister to have a break from troublesome friends, and then – catastrophe. So much destruction and yet our home, our tree, are both still standing. Was it luck or—?

Or?

Once, one of the lower branches of the fig had to be cut off because it was bearing down on the roof. We hired an arboriculturist. According to him the tree was a thousand years old. A thousand years old! That's a long time. Perhaps – perhaps this place has always been safe.

We walk along the muddy path and climb over the fallen eucalypt that blocks the driveway. Wet bark against my skin. A gossamer rainfall, no mist. As we pass through the gateway and start down the ravaged road, the *drip drip* of a dull green world. I look up. A washing machine is wedged between the branches of a tall red gum. A bra and a purple dress hang on the lower branches, as if someone has casually thrown them over to dry. Esther is slightly ahead of me. Her red backpack is strapped to her body like safety equipment, her orange hat a beacon.

The road, what is left of it, winds down the mountain, past the track that leads to the coal mine. Ben took on shift work there as night-time security when we built our house. Just to get some extra cash in. There's nothing left of the mine now. As we round a corner I look down the valley to where the village used to be. It's now a lake surrounded by torn-up trees. Bits of roof float on water, rafts for the seabirds that flock in daily. All that is visible of the church is a steeple. It looks like a buoy. Across from the steeple, where once there was a park, there's now an island. On it, skinny black and white cows huddle around a lone cabbage tree palm. Ben is building a raft to save them but that project is on hold until he is well again.

We cut down through the forest. There are three bridges crossing the stretch of river that runs along this side of the mountain, but did those bridges survive Frank? The river has swollen to ten times its normal size and the water level doesn't look like it's dropping. Impossible for us to swim across. The water is flowing too fast. So at least one of those bridges needs to be up.

Wet leaves, a slippery crust on the ground. We skid on stones. Mud and more mud and a knot in my stomach.

Why a knot?

Because even if the bridges are up and even if we cross the river, we still have to hike to the top of the escarpment, trudge along the ridge for a kilometre, before taking a route down the southern side of the range to the school where the emergency medical centre has been set up. There's a lot of dense forest to get through with trees down everywhere. And what about the medical centre? The school sits on high ground. It should have been safe from sea surges and flooding but was it?

We reach the boardwalk that runs through the rainforest. The tough plastic slats are covered with debris but they too have survived Frank. What amazes is not what has gone, but what has endured. We climb across enormous fallen trees and wade through piled-up leaf matter. If we stop, even for a moment, tiny leeches attach to our bare legs. We brush them off but they curl in tighter and cling to our skin, all wet and slimy and squishy. We can hear the river but not see it. There's barely any light because the canopy above blocks everything out. It's hard to see even a smidgen of grey sky. The air is stifling. Steamy. Everything dripping and dark. The rich pungent smell of decomposition.

Finally, we stumble into the light. Before us, water gushes past, tumbling across rocks and splashing the banks, like an animal spitting and in pain. But no bridge. The force of the water has pushed our first hope downstream. I take off my backpack and stand on the rocks, water spraying my boots. Should we give up the hike now? It seems naive to think we'll be able to get across. Surely the other bridges have gone too. FUCK! The true purpose of swearing, I decide, is to help humans come to grips with things we find difficult to grasp. Things for which there is no clear word. Esther, ahead of me, has started scrambling along the banks. She turns back. Her eyes catch mine. She wills me to continue. I think of Gina. If Steve had gone to the medical centre as soon as Gina fell ill, she'd be alive. I need that Marsoral for Ben. I might need it for Esther too. Fuck, maybe we're all infected.

The bank is muddy. Marshy. Dark clouds spit rain at us. A shifty wind wheezes along, pulling at our jackets. We use our hands to steady ourselves but it's hard going with my gammy arm. Each step is a negotiation.

When I finally look up, I see that the second bridge has gone too.

It's like I'm falling.

I have no balance.

I sink down in the mud, exhausted. Esther slumps next to me. She has her determined face on. I need a moment to compose myself so I look away. On the opposite bank, I eye three enormous rocks. These are no ordinary rocks, they are massive, their shapes worn smooth by erosion. After I've been staring at them for some time I realise I've seen these rocks before. I sketched them once, when I went hiking with Ben and we stopped for a break. Only they're in the wrong place now. They belong to a rock formation that once sat further up river. There used to be a sign in front stating that the rocks were two hundred million years old. Something that old, we think of as permanent, as never changing. This river too has changed. When I was young people called it a creek. The high rainfall these last years meant it grew in size and was renamed a river.

Esther shakes my arm. She wants to keep going, she wants to see if the third bridge, the swing bridge, is still up. We slip-slide along but halt at a strangler fig, rest on the narrow tree roots watching rain fall on flowing water. The forest canopy protects us from getting wet. The tree beneath the strangler has long ago disappeared. Now thick vine is tousled through sinewy fern-covered branches. The ferns look like jade bracelets. Insects buzz. Everything rattles. The forest is alive, as if dancing in the aftermath of catastrophe.

I take deep breaths using my inhaler. Esther sips water, but she keeps her eyes on me. She doesn't want to rest for long.

'Okay, okay, let's go,' I say.

We set off hiking again. The banks are rocky now. I can't get a good grip and keep slipping. Esther is so lightweight she streaks ahead. And then, ha, she turns to me, grinning. Such a big cheeky grin.

Up ahead I see the swing bridge.

Originally it sat high above the river.

Now water rushes just beneath it.

But it's up. It's up!

We hurry on. Esther stands on the first plank and waits for me. It's only when I reach her that I think about the journey home.

If we cross the bridge it's possible that on our return it won't be here.

FUCK!

But if Ben has the virus and I don't go?

FUCK!

The weather is holding. There are clouds but it doesn't look like rain. If we hike fast we should make it back by late afternoon. I can't risk *not* going.

I grip the thick metal rails and stagger across. Wind gusts down the gully. The bridge swings from side to side. The water rushing beneath sounds like stampeding cattle. I reach the opposite bank and jump onto the boardwalk. Esther is behind me. This side of the river the boardwalk is badly damaged. We tread along it carefully, then step off into the forest to begin our hike up the escarpment.

The ground is boggy and steep. We sink on all-fours and wriggle beneath vines that knit the trees together. Mosquitoes land on bare skin but we have our repellent on and they soon fly away. I feel something crawling on my leg and stop to flick it off. An enormous fat leech. There are leeches everywhere – on the ground, on the vine leaves. Nothing to do but grit our teeth and crawl on.

When we are two-thirds of the way up we hit a mud track. It leads south. We follow it along, below the line of the ridge.

Dark clouds gather above us. Raindrops plop onto the ground and splatter, like small water bombs. We hike up a narrow path to the top of the escarpment. Trudge through a thicket of trees to the heath. A sharp wind slaps my face.

'You okay?' I ask Esther.

She runs ahead of me – smiling. She's thinking only of the chance to talk to her mother.

We walk along by the old trees that line the edge of the ridge. Stop to catch our breath at the tourist lookout that hangs over the valley below.

I'm not prepared for what I see.

Can't speak from shock.

To the east, Port Kembla – that in my childhood had been a place of fire-blowing smokestacks – Port Kembla is gone and between where it once was and where I now stand there is only water.

Water, water, everywhere.

A few tiny islands – islands that were once hilltops – are all that remains of the land. It's like Esther and I are also on an island.

Could this have happened? Could the sea surges the relief worker told us about have covered so much land that we are now cut off from the rest of the country?

Or, has there been some bigger event further away that has caused the seas to rise?

The idea chills me.

Below us, where once there were housing estates, there is now a swirling mass of murky water.

The naked body of a boy, bloated, blackened, floats into view.

I take Esther by the hand and we continue hiking. This is a new world we're living in. We haven't had time to adjust.

Silence.

Nada raises her right hand.

Dr Koskinen counts her up.

One. Two. Three. You are coming up. Four. Five. Six. You are rising to consciousness. Seven. Eight. Nine. You are nearly with me. Ten. You are with me.

Nada opens her eyes and stares at the tree vismem.

This must be difficult for you.

I am Nada.

Yes.

But here, what is here?

Remember. You are a patient here. Taking part in our Storyland Project.

Before the project? I have no—

This is a slow process, Nada. We have to take things step by step.

We're indoors? All the time we're indoors?

It's a good place to be. The air quality on this ship is the best there is.

We're on a ship?

It is a shock for you to be here with us. We rescued you.

There are so many doctors, all asking questions. Why does everyone sound funny?

Funny?

All the doctors have old men's voices, even you and the other women.

This is a delicate time of adjustment. It is my job to steer you through this process.

Everything feels strange. I've asked to be taken off my meds but the nurse says it's too early.

You must give your mind time to reacquaint itself with the world.

Have I been in a coma?

Did they tell you a coma? Like a coma, yes.

I want to ask you something?

Go ahead.

Do you know if Ben, Esther, Steve ... is it possible they survived?

It is still possible, yes.

I can't remember what happened.

This is what you are doing now. Remembering.

Does my home still exist?

That is a difficult question to answer.

Difficult?

We can talk more at the end of our session.

I'd prefer to know *now*.

Access to the area beyond Border 29 is restricted.

Why restricted?

Nada, it *is* best if we talk at the end of our session.

I'd like to know now. Why restricted?

You said you trusted me?

Yes.

Then we can talk more when we have finished our session.

Silence.

Nada? Will you continue?

Silence.

Nada, if you will continue then I need you to say yes.

Yes.

Thank you. I will take you back into your personal membank now. Are you comfortable?

Do you need me to say yes? Yes, yes, I am comfortable.

Good. Thank you. Ten. Nine. Eight. You are returning to the mountain. Seven. Six. Five. Returning to the escarpment. Four. Three. Two. Nearly there. One. You are there. On the ridge. Esther is with you. She has her orange, no, her red backpack on. And her orange hat.

We're hiking south along the track. The heath turns to forest again.

Nada slaps her right hand over her ear.

Hunches over.

What is it?

Birds chirping. Wrens. But so many. The noise is—

You are safe. It is a memory.

Nada sits up.

You are safe, Nada.

The first day after Frank hit there were no birds. It was eerie. Just the sound of wind and water. Like the earth was having a breech birth. Then the birds started returning. Each day more and more flew in. Now, there are too many birds. On the heath especially, there is this shrill chattering. We run to get away from the noise, but when we pass several low bushes, laden with wrens, we frighten them. They fly up and we have to sprint through their fluttering bodies. We keep running and leave the birds behind. The forest becomes dense, dark. Trees so tall I can't see the tops. There are fewer birds but the air is stifling. We can barely see the path. I use the compass to guide us. We keep hiking. It's midday when we stumble out from the trees and find ourselves above the school where the emergency centre is set up. Only there's been a massive landslide and the once-grassy hill behind the gym – where kids used to build stick huts – is a heaped up mess of soil, tree trunks and branches, all crammed onto the back of the besser brick building.

But relief, I feel such relief because I can see people, hundreds of people crowded onto the small patch of land that fronts the gym.

Describe exactly what you see.

There are two long schoolroom buildings plus the gym, built around a central quadrangle, with an oval on the eastern side. In one of the schoolrooms, all the windows are shattered and most of the roof is missing, but the walls are intact. The other buildings are undamaged. Beyond the school, the land falls away. For as far as I can see there is only water and debris. Yet, I can't shake this feeling of joy at the sight of other people.

People cooking over fires.

Erecting tents.

Washing clothes.

Doing ordinary things.

And children, running between the tents as if on a camping holiday.

Some adults, some children, wear medical masks, or have cloth wrapped around their mouths, but many don't.

The oval is bare except for way over on the far corner where there is an army helicopter. Armed soldiers stand guard. Esther grabs my arm, her eyes fixed on the helicopter.

'But it's not flying,' I say.

To the west I see men, women, and children, all with bags over their shoulders, or rucksacks on their backs, trudging along the edge of the water. It's the easiest way to leave. The escarpment is steep on this side of the mountain and the mess from the landslides must be keeping people from reaching the top ridge and hiking along it as we have just done.

Can you get to the medical centre?

We have to take our time slip-sliding our way down, but yes, we can get there. The land beneath our feet feels aerated, like it might cave in at any moment. We drop to our knees to crawl through branches stuck in the soil and finally reach the gym roof. Using a drainpipe, we climb down to a narrow alley at the side of the building. As we stroll into the quadrangle we pass a queue of people snaking out from the front entrance of the gym. We're covered in mud by now but everyone here is dirty. Those standing in the queue look thin, weary.

Two elderly women, scarves around their mouths, are slumped on the ground, resting against one another, back to back.

No one pays them any attention.

People eye us warily as we walk by.

If a moment earlier I felt joy, now I'm cautious.

It doesn't feel safe down here. We halt at the doorway to the gym and look in.

What do you see?

Two basketball courts, stadium seats at either end. To our left, the queue we've just passed by splits into smaller queues that lead to individual desks. Maybe twenty desks. There are two soldiers behind each desk. One, writing information down, the other, doling out food supplies. Behind the desks, supplies are stacked on the stadium seats – sacks of something, must be rice, and also boxes, probably of tinned food. Soldiers with semiautomatic rifles guard the supplies. I think about joining the food queue but it looks like a slow process. The Marsoral is more important. I need to get it back to Ben. And the possibility of the river rising is on my mind. We've enough stocks for two more weeks, three if we are prudent. I can hike back here next week. Several people standing in the queue start to mutter but it's only when an elderly man speaks to me that I realise the problem.

'You can't push in,' the man says. 'Back of the queue. That's where you go.'

'I don't want food,' I say.

The man stares at me. He has a large scab on his forehead that he scratches at.

'I've enough,' I explain.

The man puts a finger to his lips. 'Don't say that out loud,' he whispers. 'Where have you come from?'

'Across the river,' I say.

He points to the food supplies. 'That only arrived yesterday and there's been trouble ever since.'

In the middle of the gym is another desk. Above it hangs a sign: Evacuations. Most in the queue are elderly.

To our right, in front of the stadium seats down that end of the gym, medics sit at tables. Each table has an esky beside it. In the far corner there's an enormous cool-room. I can hear a generator humming. Armed soldiers, each with their own guard dog, stand behind the medics. Before the medics – rows of chairs filled with sick people. Some hunched over, covering their mouths with cloth and coughing. One man is whimpering, the sound like a dog in pain. A soldier, holding a rifle he looks ready to shoot, patrols in front of the chairs, directing people to specific medics. Each time someone leaves the first row to go to a medic, someone from the row behind moves up to the front.

A female soldier marches over to us. Her dog patters along beside her. She's about thirty. Neat hair, cut short. Her khaki uniform is crumpled and stained. She has dark circles beneath her eyes.

'Sharp left for food distribution, centre desk for evacuations, right for medical.' Her voice is formal but friendly enough. 'Don't push in. I'll evict anyone disruptive.'

'Are you evacuating from here?' I ask.

'On foot only. Run out of fuel for now. If you need airlift you can put your name on the waiting list.'

'Where are you evacuating to?'

'Canberra,' she says, but there's a slight hesitation in her voice.

'Can I call my mother from here?' Esther asks.

'Communication is still down,' the soldier says.

Esther looks like she might cry. 'When will it be up?' she asks.

But the soldier is already walking away. 'Your guess is as good as mine,' she calls over her shoulder.

We sit at the back of the medical area. Esther's lips are pressed tightly together.

'You'll get home eventually,' I say.

'When?'

'We have to give the government time to get things running again. Could be a month.'

I think it will take longer – three months maybe – but I want to comfort Esther.

It's sticky in the gym. Efficient-looking people walk about with insect repellent, spraying mosquitoes. Others, with buckets of soapy water and wet rags, wipe down chairs and desks. They work quickly and without looking up. The smell of disinfectant is strong. A man and a woman, both unusually tall, walk into the gym. They both have shaved heads. The man has a thick neck and a face like a bulldog. The woman is all sharp angles but muscular. They wear jeans and tee shirts. Both have a piece of red cloth tied around their right arm. I have no idea what it might signify. They look fit and healthy, and I only realise now that this is how Esther and I must look too. Whereas most people here are malnourished.

Silence.

You are in the gym. You are waiting to see a medic.

Esther and I have reached the front row. A group of boys and girls saunter into the gym. I turn to watch them. They're young; only twelve or thirteen years old. They each have a piece of red cloth tied around their right arm. The teenagers walk close together, each carrying a coat or jacket or what looks like an instrument case of some sort. Perhaps they're going to put on a concert? The kids form a tight circle in the centre of the gym – like singers, huddling to get their note. The people in the food queue watch them closely. Everyone else looks away. I'm about to look away too when I see one boy turn out from the huddle. He is tall and bony, like a wading bird. He has round eyes that seem too large for his head, and orange hair. He's a strange-looking kid. There's a fragility about him that is both beguiling and frightening. I see him yank a rifle out from beneath his coat and aim it at those in the food queue. Quickly, the others in the huddle all drop their coats or jackets or open their instrument cases to reveal their weapons too. In seconds there are about twenty semiautomatic rifles aimed around the room.

There's a collective inhale, like a single breath from a giant animal.

The bony orange-haired boy has his finger near the trigger of his rifle. He stares at the people in the food queue.

The only sound in the gym is people breathing.

The boy closes his eyes, squeezes the trigger.

The bullets sound like rain on a corrugated iron roof. A man at the front of the food queue steps forward, thrusts out his hand as if he intends to halt the bullets midair but the bullets shoot through him and he shudders to the ground.

Stillness.

Breathing.

Someone screams.

Rat-a-tat-tat!

The other teenagers start shooting.

Rat-a-tat-tat!

The soldiers guarding the food supplies fire back.

Rat-a-tat-tat!

The noise – deafening.

Four boys from the huddle drop to the ground, one after the other, their thin bodies pumped with bullets.

Screaming. Scrambling.

Nearby, a thick-necked soldier slumps against an esky, a bullet through the side of his head.

I grab Esther's hand, pull her to a desk, kick it over so we can crouch behind. At my feet, the female soldier we spoke to earlier, dead. Blood trickles along her neck, slips down and pools on the cement. Next to her, a blood-splattered medic moans. He's been shot in the chest. I reach out, catch hold of his leg, drag him to cover. Eyes wide, he stares at me, then, in an instant, his eyes go flat and he is dead.

Frail-bodied teenagers, toting guns, stream into the gym, shooting randomly. They run towards the food stores. It's food they want. The soldiers guarding the food shoot the teenagers. Bodies fall.

Tables clatter to the ground as people take cover.

More teenagers come running into the gym chanting, 'Shoot! Shoot! Shoot!'

Anyone moving is a target.

Rat-a-tat-tat!

Esther and I press our bodies flat to the ground. The tall man and woman from earlier are now standing off to my right, calling instructions to a pimple-faced boy wielding a gun.

'Shoot, shoot,' the boy shouts in response, as if he has no other words, and he starts to shoot.

I look for another doorway out of the gym but there is none. Two kids are guarding the front entrance. They face away from us, but block our exit. Both have semiautomatic rifles that look as big as they are.

The elderly man with the scab, who whispered advice when I first came into the gym, is crouching opposite the kids, his back to the wall.

His eyes lock on mine – bewildered eyes, and mouth slightly open, as if taking a last gasp of breath.

A piercing scream.

Rat-a-tat-tat!

I smell shit.

I'm distracted by two women who were in the queue. They're hiding behind a desk. A kid with a gun is walking towards them, so they stand and run. Their ragged dresses balloon out. Shots hit their backs. Their bodies shudder before they fall, arms flapping, like hens trying to fly.

I pull Esther closer to me. She tucks her head into my arm, not wanting to look. Her warm breath on my skin. I spy a medical esky tipped on its side. The word Marsoral, printed on the lid. I reach over, unlatch the top, pull out the seven packets of Marsoral that are inside and shove them into my backpack.

A man hiding behind a nearby table sees me take them. He glares. I want to take Marsoral back for everyone: Ben, Steve, also Tom and Bill, and one each for Esther and me. But I'd like two for Ben. The man is still staring. There are other eskies, further away. I gesture that way but he shakes his head.

'Get your own,' I call.

He shakes his head again. He has a nasty look in his eye. I take out one pack of Marsoral and roll it across to him. He grabs it with a snarl but that's all I'm giving up.

The elderly man I spotted before now slides up the wall. He makes a sign to two old men crouching near him. They slide up too. The kids guarding the door are turned away from them. The elderly man points to the doorway. The three men sneak along towards it, but the kids guarding the doorway turn and see them.

Rat-a-tat-tat! Rat-a-tat-tat!

The old men stumble backwards, one on top of the other. Blood squirts out from their bodies and splashes onto the cement.

The two kids begin to holler, as though horrified at what they've done.

They sprint towards the food piles.

'Follow me,' I hiss to Esther.

We crawl to the entrance and scramble outside. In the centre of the quadrangle there are tottering children. Teenagers, all with bits of red cloth tied on their arms, circle them. They have rifles aimed either at the children or at parents who stand at the edge of the quadrangle. The parents are screaming; the children, crying. The gun-toting teenagers are jittery. Another bald-headed adult stands with the teenagers. Red cloth tied on his arm, two long scars across his forehead.

'Hold fire,' he yells at his crew. 'Let these people get their kids and then we'll go into the gym.'

The teenagers lower their rifles and the mothers and fathers run into the centre of the quadrangle and grab their children.

One man, running back, a child held close to his chest, trips and falls onto one of the armed teenagers.

The teenager only stumbles, but his mate nearby turns and shoots the man. The man falls, the child with him, and the child is pinned beneath his body.

The other teenagers start shooting.

Bodies fall on the concrete.

People flee. A young boy rescues the dead man's child.

One brave woman, perhaps to divert attention from the rescue, begins to shout abuse at a big-boned boy who is holding a rifle.

The boy points his rifle at the woman.

'Leave the quadrangle!' he calls to her.

The woman keeps walking forward, finger jabbing in disgust.

The scar-faced adult shouts at the woman. 'Shut it, you mad cow, and leave.'

But the woman keeps shouting abuse.

A man, tattoos over his face and body, holding two young girls behind him, stands near one of the schoolhouses. 'Kristie, get out of there,' he shouts.

The woman called Kristie turns to him. 'Are the kids safe?'

'Yes. Come back now,' the man calls.

The woman begins to walk back.

One of the young girls slips around the man and cries out, 'Kristie.'

The man grabs the girl by the arm, drags her behind him. Kristie turns back to the boy. He has his rifle aimed at the tattooed man now.

She shouts at the boy, 'Put that rifle down.'

The boy points the rifle at her.

She shouts again.

The boy shoots her.

Kristie staggers back and falls.

Soldiers, who have sprinted the distance across the oval from the helicopter, now run onto the quadrangle. They shoot the boy down.

One yells to the scar-faced adult. 'Ed, don't be a fool. Stop this now!'

The man called Ed hesitates. The gun-wielding teenagers turn to him. He has his arm raised, ready to give a signal to shoot the soldiers.

The tattooed man and the two girls run to Kristie.

'Go,' I whisper to Esther.

We sprint along the front of the gym and turn into the lane that runs down the side of the building.

I smell shit again and see a dead man propped up against the wall. We climb over him and keep going.

Esther scrambles up the side of the gym, clinging to the drainpipe, and reaches the roof. I follow but it's hard going with my bung arm. Esther has to climb back down to help me. At the top we crawl to a pile of branches and lie hidden, breathing heavily. I take out my inhaler and use it, then pull back leaves and branches to check out the quadrangle.

The soldiers shoot down the scar-faced man. He falls in the middle of the quadrangle, blood seeping from beneath his body, making a liquid map around his torso. Nearby, some of the teenagers lie dead. Others have thrown their rifles down and hold their arms up in the air. The two young girls kneel beside the woman called Kristie, crying. The tattooed man takes off his shirt and presses it to the woman's shoulder. Then he and the children help the woman up and the four hurry away from the quadrangle. A family pressed against the side wall of the schoolhouse, arms splayed like bats, turn and run.

Beyond the quadrangle, everywhere, bodies lie in the dirt.

A fine rain starts to fall.

The bony orange-haired boy runs out of the gym. The tall man and woman follow, their shaved heads glistening with sweat. Teenagers carrying boxes of tinned food and rice sacks trail behind them.

West, along a track that skirts the water's edge, men, women and children are fleeing.

'Come on, let's go,' I say to Esther.

We crawl through the branches and up the hill. I look back. See fleeing people scrambling behind us. But the land isn't stable. Small rocks fall on them. The climbers slide. Branches and dirt tumble after them.

The land feels as if it is shifting beneath our feet.

We start to climb down to help two kids and an old man who are stuck and are not sure whether to continue. We call out to them. A thundering sound from deep in the earth. *Boom.* The land starts breaking up. The man and the kids slip back down.

The thunderous sound again. *Boom.* We scramble up and are nearly at the top when I hear an almighty crack.

We continue upwards, dodging falling branches and rocks.

A crashing! A thumping!

We finally reach the ridge top.

Dirt sprays up and a thick haze envelops us.

When it clears we see there is now a sheer drop from the ridge. No way to climb up or down. The roof of the gym is covered in rubble so it looks like a pyramid. A mountain of dirt blocks the entrance. The people inside – entombed.

The dead bodies in the quadrangle are covered with a fine layer of dust. The whole place looks like some ancient ruin.

I don't cry or shout. Esther points to a place behind the school, to the southwest, where a hundred or more teenagers huddle around a boat that has been pulled from the water. The bald-headed man and woman are now hauling rifles from the boat and dealing them out. In the middle of the huddle several other adults – each with a shaved head – are issuing instructions.

All this seems unfathomable. This is not our life. Not our country.

This kind of thing happens in other places, in less civilised places, but not here.

And yet, it *is* happening here.

Esther's eyes glaze over, like she's focusing on an inner world, not this outer one. 'Come,' I say, and gently take her arm.

We half-run, half-walk along the top of the ridge and take the track into the forest. Rain falls. I pull Esther into the trees, so we run alongside the track, rather than on it. We stop, now and then, to check the way ahead, to listen. In the middle of the forest it is dead quiet. Only the flat pat-pat of our boots on wet leaves.

It is late afternoon when we sprint from the forest across the heath. Everywhere the *prip prip* of wrens. It's a frightening sound when there are so many. We don't stop running until we reach the path that we took on the way up.

We slump behind a rock to rest.

I slip my backpack from my shoulders and place it between my legs.

I see that I've left the flap open.

I try not to panic.

The water bottle is gone.

My inhaler too.

My hands rest on the Marsoral.

I know I have to stay calm. Stay alert.

Esther stares at me.

'The Marsoral is there,' I say, and do up the flap. 'I don't need my inhaler now. I want it but I don't need it.'

Esther takes out her water bottle, gives it to me. I drink, then hand it back to her. Her eyes lock on mine.

'We'll be okay,' I say.

Never before have I felt more determined.

Never before have I felt less sure about what lies ahead.

The day darkens. Mist drips across the ridge.

I stand, hoist my backpack onto my shoulders, and am ready to hike when – just in time – I see three figures emerge from the bush half a kilometre below and start up the path to the ridge. They have rifles slung over their shoulders. They wear jeans and tee shirts. Their attention is on the ground, pointing out marks to each other. I realise, with a jolt, that they're following the tracks we made earlier.

I drop down, put my hands to my lips to warn Esther. We crawl further around the rock and lie flat, waiting until they pass by.

'No, it was Mess Brother wrote that song.' It's a female voice. High-pitched.

'How'd it start then?' This is a boy, definitely.

'Turn a sally on the dead. Turn a belly on the fed.' The girl again.

'Hey, the tracks turn here.' A new voice. Deeper than the other two. Male. Older.

'We're onto them,' the girls says.

'Are these the two that did it though?' the boy asks.

I press my stomach into the wet earth. Did what? I think.

'This is them,' the girl says. 'When we sight them, give me first shot.'

Thump, pat-pat, thump. Three bodies flash by.

We keep still. They're hunting two people who have done something to them. They think those two people are us.

The trackers stop running.

I strain to hear what they're saying. Can't catch it. Have they seen our footprints coming back? I could stand and tell them we're not who they're looking for. Unless we are. No. I mustn't trust anyone or anything.

I ease myself up, peer over the top of the rock.

Two of the trackers are staring at the ground but the third, a heavy-set boy, is lifting his backpack off his shoulders. He rummages inside it; tins of food fall from the bag. He pulls out a bottle of whisky, takes a swig, then picks the tins up, shoves them in his pack.

Every muscle in my body goes rigid. They've been looting! Where have they been? Are these three connected to the bald-headed rebels back at the school? I can't see red cloth tied to their arms. Are they a different gang again? There are too many questions and no easy answers.

I think of Ben, ill in bed. I hope to God that Steve is with him. Near him.

The boy hoists his pack onto his back, follows the others who have already sprinted across the heath and are running into the forest. They haven't spotted our return tracks.

Not yet.

When they have disappeared between the trees, I take Esther by the hand and lead her further north before we descend into the forest.

I hear water. A waterfall?

There wasn't one here before. I'm overawed by the power of water. Its ability to change all that we are.

We trek down, pushing away bushes. I try not to think about the swing bridge. Whether it is still up. I try not to think about sea surges and flooding. We crawl through vines, sinking into thick black mud. Bugs squirm through our hair. We'll hit the path if we keep in this direction but it's hard going. I can hear the river galloping along, thrashing and thumping as it hits the banks. The *bizz bizz* of hundreds of mosquitoes. We slap them away.

I need my inhaler now.

My left arm aches. The memory of a pain from long ago. Metal hitting me, hot rubber, the stink of bitumen. I'm a child again, lying on a road. The car that hit me, driving away, the flash of the bumper bar in the sun.

I'm dizzy by the time we reach the path.

My chest hurts.

It's only been drizzle on the way back but has the river risen?

Has the bridge washed away?

Adrenalin floods through me. Regret too, for starting out on this journey, for leaving Ben. But what choice did I have? And we have the Marsoral. Adrenalin pushes me on, short breaths. I limp along the path in the dimming light, my arm aching like it never has before. Esther runs behind me, clinging onto my tee shirt, her fist bumping into the small of my back, her face streaked with mud. Rain spits through breaks in the rainforest canopy. The light is almost gone.

Finally, we come to the river. Water is splashing onto the planks of the swing bridge.

'It's there,' Esther whispers.

The first she's spoken since after the landslide.

We grip onto each other and run to the bridge. Clinging to the metal sides we hurry across. The escarpment melts into the night as we reach the opposite bank. Gusts scoop up leaves, and then drop them.

I take the small torch from the bottom of my pack and check the strength of the brackets that clamp the bridge cables to the rock ledge.

The brackets are strong and fixed tight.

The rock ledge is thick, wedged into the hill.

On the way over, I'd wanted the bridge to stay in place. Now we're safely back, I want it gone.

I want us cut off from those bald-headed rebels, those teenagers with guns, those looters.

Silence. Nada taps the side of her chair with her right hand.

You are at the bridge. You are nearly home.

It's pitch black as we make our way up the hill to the house. Inside, all is quiet.

I'm gasping.

I stumble down the hall and Esther holds the torch while I scramble to get a spare inhaler from the medicine cupboard.

I suck on it.

Breathe, breathe.

Esther goes ahead, to the bedroom.

I follow.

She opens the door.

A dark shape on the bed.

Esther flashes the torch.

Ben on the bed. I see the rise and fall of his chest.

Relief.

He's alive.

'Ben?' Esther says.

Ben opens his eyes. There is something hollowed out about his expression but he smiles. 'You're back,' he murmurs.

'Yes,' I say, as I come through the door.

'What is it?' he asks.

I slump down beside him.

Esther fetches a Marsoral dose from my backpack, unscrews the lid and gives it to Ben.

He drinks.

As I start to speak Esther retreats to the doorway. Stands there, listening, while I tell Ben about the medical centre, what we found there, the desperate hungry people, the sick people, the stores of food, the rebels with bald heads and red cloth tied to their arms, the teenagers with guns, the landslide, the looters.

'We're not safe here,' Esther says, when I've finished recounting.

Ben turns to her. 'The house is hidden from the road,' he says.

It's true. Our home is still camouflaged from the old road, but if someone came to it from the rainforest, they'd spot it easily.

'What if someone comes from the swing bridge?' I say. 'Looters with guns?'

'Not everyone is a looter, surely,' he says.

'People are going crazy out there,' I say.

Esther agrees.

It might seem impossible but *all of this* seems impossible. Ben hasn't witnessed the madness. Esther and I have.

'We could set up camp in the caves,' Ben suggests.

It's a good idea. The caves are well hidden.

Caves?

We used to camp in them when we first bought the property, before we built the house.

'I think we should move up there now,' I say.

'Tonight?' Ben asks.

'Ben, we do have to go now,' Esther says.

She tells him again about the orange-haired boy, and the shootings, about the birds, about the man and kids who slid away from us, about the changed world.

It's Esther who convinces Ben we need to go immediately.

'Okay,' he says, finally.

Esther and I take a Marsoral dose each. We store the remaining three doses in an esky. No ice, but we can store the esky at the back of the caves where it is cool and give the doses to Steve, Tom and Bill tomorrow. I ask Esther to pack some food boxes.

'Things we can eat without cooking,' I say. 'Or warm up on the camp stove.'

Ben, feeble, gets dressed, and we go into the storeroom where we keep the camping gear. We are dragging out the swags when he faints. I sit him up, get some water.

'I need air,' he says.

I help him out to the bench beneath the big old fig tree. Every summer we set up a table beneath the tree to eat our meals, shaded by its long gnarled branches and thick leaves. On family days, nieces and nephews always race each other to climb to the top, screaming down at the adults, *look at me, look at me*. That life seems far away now.

'Stay put,' I say, as Ben sits. 'I'll come get you when we're ready.'

I take the torch and hurry away from the house and down the track and across the paddocks to Steve's place. I want to tell Steve what has happened. Get him to come to the caves with us. I feel safer in the cover of night but also, I want everything done in a hurry. The shock of what happened at the medical centre won't leave me. But I need to push past it. I shine the torchlight on Steve's dirt driveway, jumping the potholes as I run to the house. I race up the steps to the verandah and call from the back door.

'Steve!'

No answer. The door is unlatched. I go in and walk through the kitchen to the hallway. My boots *clunk clunk* on bare floorboards. I call out, again and again, flashing the torch into empty rooms. I retreat to the back door.

Where could he be?

Ben said Steve didn't come by. That has me worried. Steve always keeps his word. Sure, he could be out shooting rabbits – since the cyclone he has started hunting again – but this morning he looked like a man with a death wish.

He keeps his rifle in the shed. I need to check if it's still there.

I run down the verandah steps and along the path. Inside the shed it smells of machinery oil and wet hay. I shine my torch across to the workshop end. Steve put everything back in its place after Gina died, as if somehow restoring order to the shed might bring her back. His old tin cans are lined up on the first bench. Above, hammers, wrenches, chisels, hooked onto the corrugated iron wall. I flash across to the second bench. A saw sits on top. The third bench has drills laid out. But on the shelf above, I see Steve's rifle. Good. He can't have used it on himself.

I stand still, staring at the rifle. This is the moment I realise that I need to be armed.

You didn't think this before?

No. I've never even held a gun. But this day has changed everything. Still, I don't immediately pick it up. I hesitate.

Why hesitate?

Ben and I have never liked the idea of storing a gun in our home. Not even for shooting rabbits.

I step towards it, grasp the cold metal, lift it down from the shelf. I don't know where Steve is, but I need his rifle.

Steve usually keeps the ammunition in the cabinet below the bench. I yank open drawer after drawer but see only nails, nuts and bolts. Fuck, where is the ammunition? I shine my torch up the walls and see boxes of bullets stashed on a high shelf. I stand on the stepladder to reach them. Clasp the boxes firmly. I'll have to keep coming back, checking for Steve's return, get him to come to the caves. And I'll need to go across to warn Tom and Bill about all that has happened, get them to come over to us too. But first, I have to get Esther and Ben settled.

As I tramp up the road my torch dims. Back at home I take spare batteries from the boot room cupboard and pile pillows, blankets, swags and camping equipment by the door. I take the medicine pouch from the hallway cupboard and go to the kitchen, the rifle still slung over my shoulder. Two food boxes sit on the counter, already packed. Esther is pulling tins from a cupboard and stacking them into a third box. She spots the rifle, stops packing. Her eyes on mine.

'Can you use it?' she asks.

'I'll work out how,' I say.

I turn off our generator then help Esther carry the food boxes to the back door. Ben hobbles into the boot room, my torch the only light.

He stares at the rifle.

'We need to be prepared,' I say.

He can't stop staring.

'It will only be for self-defence,' I add.

But something in me sinks.

Esther fetches the wheelbarrow from the shed. Into it we load one of the food boxes, the water container, our backpacks and some pillows and blankets.

'I'll come back for the rest,' I say.

Ben takes the torch. He is weak, shivering. Each step, unsteady.

Slowly we make our way past the big old fig tree, and along a track that leads through the bush up to the caves. Esther pushes the wheelbarrow.

Ben stops at the base of the escarpment, switches off the torch.

We listen.

Boo-book, boo-book. Boo-book, boo-book.

The calls are everywhere.

Hundreds of owls, their eyes glinting in the dark.

He switches the torch back on. We continue weaving through the trees until we come to a large rock. Behind it is a narrow corridor that leads to three caves.

Describe the caves.

Each cave goes deep into the escarpment. The first two are wide, like big rooms. The third is narrow and cold. All of them are dry and dark. You have to enter the corridor from the northern side. To the south, there's a small entrance, large enough to crawl through. Entry from above is impossible because it's sheer rock right to the top of the escarpment.

As soon as we have set our things down in the middle cave Ben starts to retch. He limps out to a bush. I follow him but he waves me away.

I return to the cave and lay out a blanket and pillow but the earth here is cold, too cold for an ill person. I dare not light a fire. I'll need to get our swag before Ben can lie down.

Esther is setting up the camp stove in the first cave. Ben is still retching when I go by.

I continue on down to the house but stop when I spy a fox on the back verandah. The fox stops still.

Neither of us moves.

Owls call *boo-book, boo-book*.

The fox creeps backwards, until it has disappeared out of the light and around the side of the house.

We must all be foxes now.

I continue on down. I rope one of the swags to my shoulder, pick up some towels and a bucket. Ben is sitting at the entrance when I return, his head in his hands. I put the bucket and a towel on the ground next to him, and then continue on along the rocky corridor, and set up his swag in the middle cave. I return to the entrance and sit beside him. The torch throws light on the wet green leaves scattered around. I take out my inhaler and suck on it.

'We're safe here,' I say, although I don't yet believe it.

'We've always felt at peace in this place,' Ben says.

'Don't worry. This will be sorted. Someone will come to help. We just have to be careful for the next few weeks.'

I help him to the swag. He closes his eyes and I sit, watch him fall asleep. It's strange to see him so frail. He's always had a furious energy. Illness has altered him. When I look up, Esther is at the cave entrance.

'I'm going to see if Steve's back,' I say. 'Then I'll hike to Tom and Bill's to warn them.'

I have a practice with how I can shoot the rifle. I'll need to press the butt against my stomach. Esther helps me. We work out a system and I sling it over my shoulder.

'If you hear anyone, stay quiet, don't try to warn me,' I say to Esther. 'When I return I'll flash my torch so you know it's me.'

'Don't go,' Esther says.

'We need to be prepared. We need to report to the others. And I'd feel safer if they were with us.'

I stumble through the dark to Steve's house. He's still not there.

There's no wind and the world is a dark void.

The sound of water is everywhere; the land is a body, shot full of holes.

I hike on to Tom and Bill's. Their brick house, and the concrete and steel house behind, the Canberra couple's weekender, are built into the escarpment. I bang on Tom and Bill's back door. No answer. I turn the handle. The door is unlocked.

I step inside and call out.

My voice echoes along the hallway.

I walk into their designer kitchen. The place hasn't been trashed but when I check their pantry, it's empty, except for three tins of pineapple.

Maybe they've left, hiking their way out?

But why not tell us?

Maybe an evacuation helicopter has come in my absence?

Maybe from the west?

That thought disturbs me. It's possible that Tom, Bill and Steve have all been evacuated. They'd definitely tell us if it was an evacuation. But what if they weren't given an option? What if the helicopter landed and the rescue guy said, now or never?

The idea that Ben, Esther and I are isolated terrifies me. To keep my nerve I focus on practical things. What have Tom and Bill left behind that might be useful?

I stash the tins of pineapple and some vitamin pills in a bag. I trudge up to the Canberra couple's house. I've never met them and they weren't here for Frank. I decide to see if any of their shutters are open. If this chaos lasts longer than three weeks, it might be worth taking their food stores and replacing them later. There's a broken shutter on their bathroom window. I smash the glass with a rock, lift open the window and climb in. In the bathroom cupboard I find a packet of antibiotics and some aspirin. I shove them in my pocket. On the shelf in the dining room I see a bottle of vodka. I take it and then check in the kitchen. A good stock of tinned food, pasta and rice. Big tins of cooking oil. Three packets of firestarters. Plenty that is useful. I make a mental note of it all. Decide to come and collect the stores sooner rather than later.

And then I realise what I'm doing. I've broken into my neighbour's house and I'm planning to loot all their food supplies. How quickly things change.

And yet, it feels justified.

I don't know what might be going on elsewhere in the country.

The government must be in control, somewhere.

What happened at the medical centre was madness.

Surely the army will send back-up. Surely they'll get to us eventually. But it may be a long wait until order is restored.

I stand in the Canberra couple's kitchen and think about the amount of water I've seen.

Do the rebels know something I don't?

What if we *are* cut off from the mainland?

Another thought takes hold of me.

What if there is no mainland?

Could that even be possible?

Is that why so many birds are flocking here?

When I was a child it used to be floods and bushfires. That was the nature of the country I lived in. But the cyclones mostly hit the more tropical north. By the time I was thirty, cyclones were hitting further south. They were always fierce. Temperatures rose, there were horrific droughts. The dryness had been predicted but when it arrived, it was still devastating. We thought there was a new pattern, but then the weather changed again. It rained a lot more along the coast. Rained for days on end. When there was no rain, it was hot. Plants grew like crazy. When a bushfire started, it was always bigger and more destructive than ever before. Large swathes of land, burning. It was as if the land, the sea, the sky were all living beings rising up in revolt.

I tape bin liners over the bathroom window and hike back to the caves. All night I move supplies from our house, up to the third cave. Food, matches, fuel, batteries, mobiles. No signal on our mobiles but we'll need them when the networks get back up. I make Esther stay with Ben, although I warn her not to get too close. I don't want her to take any unneccessary risks. Twice more I go down to Steve's place. He's not there. At dawn I dig up some bushes and Esther and I use them to cover both entrances to the caves. The result is good. No one will know we are here.

Esther says she wants to sleep near Ben and me.

'We don't know for sure if he has the virus,' I say. 'We should take every precaution.'

'But we've all taken Marsoral,' she says.

'The closer you are the more risk.'

'You're taking that risk.'

'That's different.'

'I can't sleep on my own,' she says. 'Not now.'

There's a look in her eye that tells me she's right. We need to stay close. We both set up our swags next to Ben.

I have a fitful sleep. When I wake, I rise and stand behind the branches we've used to disguise the cave entrance, listening for voices.

Nothing.

Only birds.

I crawl through the branches. Dull light. A black-cloud sky. I walk down to the house and over to the fig tree. I rest my head on the trunk.

'Have you ever seen this before?' I ask the tree.

When I was young I used to imagine that the trees in my garden came alive at night and talked. I'd make up all kinds of conversations for them. Because maybe we have always misunderstood the deep intelligence of trees.

I stand there, wondering and listening to the muffled sounds of the leaves, until it begins drizzling. Only then do I return to the caves, settle back in my swag and fall asleep.

Do you wake from this state?

Do I wake?

Yes.

Yes, I wake.

Nada raises her right hand.

One. Two. Three. You are slowly rising. Four. Five. Six. You are coming to consciousness. Seven. Eight. Nine. You are nearly with me. Ten. You are here, you are safe.

Who are you?

I am Dr Koskinen.

There are things you're not telling me?

You are progressing so well.

I'm remembering. You said I'm remembering. But why can't I remember?

All your cognitive functions have slowed. But they are adjusting.

Adjusting?

Nada stares at the tree vismem.

Nada?

What happened to the fig tree?

The fig tree?

Yes, our tree.

There are very few trees now.

Very few?

It is an extremely hot land out there. Nada, you have been doing so well. The research we are doing together is important.

I'd like to go outside please.

We must finish our session.

Am I a prisoner here?

You are a patient.

I want to leave!

If you finish the session, then I will answer your questions.

You will explain where I am?

Yes.

You promise.

I promise. Now, I will take you back down to your personal membank. Ten. Nine. Eight. You're sinking back down. Seven. Six. Five. Returning to the caves. Four. Three. Two. Nearly there. One. You are there. What do you see?

The rough brown rock walls of the cave.

What do you hear?

I hear Ben breathing beside me. I roll towards him. He can hardly raise his head.

'I'm okay,' he whispers.

Esther is heating soup on the camp stove.

I get dressed. We drink the warm soup and then I hoist the rifle over my shoulder and hike down the road to Steve's, alert the whole way for any human sound.

Only the drip drip of water on green leaves.

No Steve.

I spend the rest of the afternoon moving more stores from our place up to the caves. Extra blankets, extra towels, pots, cups, plates, cutlery, anything I can think of that might be useful. If looters come we could lose it all. I want to get as much as possible into our hideaway. I find a book: *Working Notes for the Future,* written by Bella Brent. She was my neighbour when I was a child. I can't believe I've never read it. My mother sent it to me some years back. I don't think I was even interested. I take it with me now. Other things, like photos, jewellery, spare clothes, laptops, I put in the wine cellar. I lock the trap door, throw a mat over it and nail the mat down.

The light is fading. Grey and listless. Night is nearly here.

Kookaburras start calling.

The noise is deafening.

There are too many birds.

I walk out to the fig tree and stand beneath it, looking up at the leaves. I've never climbed the tree before, now I do. I grip onto the tough bark and swing my legs over the thick branches. One after the other. As I near the top, the leaves thin. I can see the sky and down the mountain, to the dull water.

Not a single person in sight.

Only a liquid world.

A spark of light to the south.

I look to the sky. See a parting in the clouds. The first star of the night, Venus, shines through.

It's months since I've seen a star.

I sit on the branch and take in the glimmering light.

This is how it is now but not how it will always be. I say this to myself over and over. I need to remember that there have been catastrophes before and there will be catastrophes again. We only need to make it through a few more weeks.

I climb down and hike back to the caves. At the entrance sits a black crow. It struts away as I get nearer.

I go into the caves. Esther and Ben are there, they smile as I sit down. I don't even doubt that what we are doing is sane. The caves are our secret. Our safe place.

Esther has warmed up stock and rice. Ben is hungry, a good sign. We drink the warmed chewy brew, share some ginger biscuits. Then Ben eats a whole tin of sweet pineapple. Ben and Esther lie down to sleep. I stand near the cave entrance and stare up at the dark sky.

My star is gone.

I cry when I hear the owls calling.

The next morning everywhere is a grey mist. I can only see for three metres in front. I slip the rifle over my shoulder and hike down to Steve's to gather up any spare diesel he might have. Later, we can use it for our generator.

When I stroll into the shed Steve is there. Arms on the workbench, head down, as though he hasn't moved since the last time we spoke.

'You're here.'

He looks up as I go to hug him. The intensity of his gaze stops me in my tracks.

'I thought you'd gone,' I say.

He turns to the wall. The muscles in his neck, rippling.

'I took your rifle. If that's what you've been looking for. I'm sorry, but I took it.'

I place the rifle on the bench.

Slashes of morning light.

Dust drifting, looks like ash.

'I checked on Ben,' he says. 'Sleeping like a baby.

'Where have you been?'

'I went walking. West. Not sure where I was going. I came to a cliff. Water everywhere below. I knew then why I had come that way.'

Steve shakes his head, blows air through his teeth.

'I sat there on the edge of the cliff deciding whether to jump,' he says.

'Steve.'

'I waited for a sign. I could see way out to where the grey sea met the grey sky. A white-bellied eagle came flying in from the south. When I was young my very old Aunty told me that the white-bellied eagle knew about the meeting of water and land. She said, you must *learn* from them boy. I never understood what she meant but she said it with such gravity.' He turns to me, his eyes on mine. 'I haven't seen an eagle since the cyclone. When I saw this bird come flying in, I realised I still hadn't learnt the lesson she'd wanted me to learn. I needed to come back, if only to do that.'

'I'm glad.' I tell him what happened over at the medical centre, and what we've been doing since. 'That kind of violence shouldn't happen here.'

'It can happen anywhere,' Steve says. 'Hunger changes everyone and everything. I learnt that lesson in the army.'

We stand there in silence.

'I want to bring down the swing bridge,' I say. 'Will you help?'

Steve walks to the door, stares out across the ruined paddocks to the edge of the rainforest. 'Has Ben still got that oxy torch?' he asks.

'Yes.'

'We'll sever the hooks that hold the bridge cables,' he says. 'Then our only threat will come from those using a plane or a boat.'

I like that he says *our* threat. He'll stay. He'll help.

'Tom and Bill?' I ask. 'Have you seen them?'

'It's not like them to leave without telling us,' he says. 'I'm worried.'

I think of the looters I saw. Did they clean out Tom and Bill's cupboards? Did they do something to Tom and Bill? Did they send them running for their lives? That would mean the looters have been over to this side of the mountain. What route could they have taken?

If this is a new world we are living in, I have to function in a new way.

I help Steve gather together tools. He picks up a bag of fertiliser.

'What do you need that for?'

'It's potassium nitrate,' he says. 'Useful for fertiliser but also for smoke bombs.'

We hike up to the caves. When we get there, Ben is sitting up. He says he feels better. Esther is arranging the cave stores into neat piles.

'Look what we've found.' Esther shows us a stone with bits of twine wrapped around it and a wooden handle.

'It's a stone axe,' Steve says.

'Where did it come from?' I ask.

'Ben found it at the back of the cave,' Esther says.

'It's very old,' Steve says, taking hold of it.

He puts it on the ground between us.

We sit and talk. We decide to plan for a long stay in the caves. We agree that tomorrow, first light, we'll sever the bridge cables. Steve gives us tasks. He sends Ben and Esther to fetch the oxyacetylene cylinder from our shed and bring it back to the caves. Steve points to the bag of fertiliser.

'We're going to mix that in a pot with sugar and baking soda,' he says.

'Okay,' I say.

'Do you have any hair dye?'

'Henna?' I say.

'That'll do it,' he says.

'And toilet rolls?'

'I have a stash of toilet paper, so yeah, toilet rolls.'

'Good.'

'This is for the smoke bombs?' I ask.

'This is for the smoke bombs,' he says.

'Did you learn how to make them in the army?'

'No, I learnt at school. When I was about fourteen. We used to imagine a world just like this.'

Steve picks up the bag of fertiliser and we walk down to the house and into the kitchen. I crank up the generator and fetch the sugar and baking powder from the cupboard. Steve pours some fertiliser into a saucepan of water and heats it up. Then he adds some sugar. I fetch the henna bag from the bathroom cupboard. When I get back the mixture is turning into a yellowy paste. Steve pours in some baking powder and I rip open the henna bag and add that too.

I collect two jumbo packs of toilet rolls from the storeroom and take them back to the kitchen, where I push out the small inner cardboard rolls and line them up on the counter. Steve cuts cardboard bases from one of the boxes in the pantry and uses gaffer tape to stick them onto the rolls. We push paste into each roll. Then we collect up all the pens in the house and bring them to the kitchen. Esther and Ben join us and we stand at the counter pressing a pen into each roll. We set the rolls on a tray and wait for them to harden. Steve hikes back to his place for some fuses and I turn off the generator. When he returns we remove the pens and secure the fuses into the rolls using cotton wool. We wrap each roll with gaffer tape and cover the smoke bombs in plastic and place them in a box.

It's dark by the time we finish.

We carry the smoke bombs up to the caves. I heat up some canned soup. We don't have a fire, but eat around the camp stove.

Steve suggests we take turns at keeping a lookout.

'We can't take any risks,' he says.

The owls spook us with their calls.

Steve picks up the stone axe and puts it in his belt. He takes hold of the rifle.

'I'll take first watch,' he says.

Ben, Esther and I lie down to sleep. I'm exhausted and my sleep is so deep it is morning before I wake. Ben and Esther have slept through too. Steve has been up all night.

'Why didn't you wake us?' I ask.

'I was okay,' he says.

We pack the smoke bombs into our backpacks. Steve gives us all a box of matches to put in our pockets. We load the oxyacetylene cylinder in the wheelbarrow and take turns to push it. We trek down along the road and into the forest. When there are too many fallen trees on the track for the wheelbarrow to be of use, Ben and Steve carry the cylinder between them. We walk on through the forest to the river and scramble along the banks to the bridge. When we get there, Ben turns on the torch and begins to sever the cables. Esther and I set the smoke bombs on the edge of a rock, and stand behind it, ready to light them if needed. Steve stands as our lookout, rifle ready.

When the first cable snaps it makes a loud noise. It's a relief but also gut-wrenching. When the bridge is gone it will cut us off from those bald-headed rebels and their gun-toting teenagers, but it will also cut us off from people who might not mean us harm.

There are eight cables. Each time one is severed the swing bridge dips a little lower and the water rushing beneath splashes up onto it.

When there are only three cables to go I spot the orange-haired boy coming out from the forest. He sees us and stops, his rifle pointed in our direction. For a moment we stare at one another. Then, the two tall leaders with shaved heads appear from the bushes. More kids with semiautomatics follow. With them, the looters that had passed Esther and me on our trek back from the medical centre. The orange-haired boy runs to the edge of the swing bridge but sees it is not safe to cross. He stops and shoots. *Rat-a-tat-tat*. Steve, Esther and I drop behind the rock but Ben keeps on working the oxy torch.

Steve puts his rifle down and lights the fuses of two smoke bombs. He picks them up, runs to the edge of the bridge and throws the bombs across the water.

The bombs explode and dark red smoke fills the air.

Esther and I light two more smoke bombs.

'You keep lighting, we'll throw,' I say to Esther.

I run to the river edge and throw. Steve comes after me with another. The area on the other side of the river is now a swirling red haze.

The shooting stops.

Ben severs the next cable. The swing bridge drops further down and dangles in the water, leaving only the top edge of the walking platform and the wire rail that runs from one side of the river to the other. Two more cables to go.

The smoke is thick, but through it comes the boy. He has his gun slung over his shoulder and is edging along.

'Go back,' Steve yells.

Ben severs another cable. The bridge drops away. The boy is left hanging onto the hand railing. He keeps making his way across, hand-over-hand.

'We'll kill him,' Esther calls to Ben.

Ben looks up. 'Get that kid back!' he shouts.

'We're cutting the cable now,' Steve yells at the boy. 'Go back.'

The boy pays no attention.

Steve throws another two smoke bombs.

'Go back,' Esther yells to the boy.

'What should I do?' Ben shouts.

Through the smoke, moving quickly hand-over-hand like a swinging monkey, comes the tall man with the shaved head. He advances forcefully, as if he has been swinging on steel cables all his life.

'Sever that cable,' Steve yells.

I pick up the rifle and aim it at the man.

'Nada?' Ben calls to me.

'Ben, you have to sever the cable,' I call.

Ben looks down at the torch and then back to the man who is now getting closer to the boy.

Steve strides over and takes the rifle from me. 'Ben,' Steve yells. 'Do it.'

I run over to Ben.

'The river is running too fast,' Ben says. 'They'll die.'

'They want to kill us,' I say.

From the other side of the river, shots are fired through the smoke. No one is hit.

Steve fires back.

'Cut the fucking cable!' Steve yells.

Ben sets the torch going again. He cuts the cable and it snaps. The boy and the man fall through red smoke into the water. We hear a splash and they disappear. A few moments later their heads bob up downstream, but they are taken under the water again by the powerful current. They don't surface. Screaming comes from the other bank. We throw another five smoke bombs to keep the cover thick, then pack the remainders away and retreat into the forest, taking the oxy torch with us.

We stop and wait for the smoke to clear. When it does, there is no one on the other side.

'Gone,' I say.

'For now,' Steve says.

We hike back to the caves. No one speaks.

Esther heats up some soup and pours it into cups.

We sip at it.

'We had to do it,' Steve finally says.

'Did we?' Ben asks.

'They're murderers,' I say to Ben. 'Esther and I saw them in action, you didn't.'

'They were shooting at us,' Steve says. 'They made a clear statement and we responded to that statement.'

'I wish we didn't have to do it, but we did,' Esther says.

'If they can swim they might be fine,' I add.

'We all need to rest,' Steve says. 'There could be more trouble tomorrow. Maybe they'll leave us alone now, maybe not.'

I go to the cave entrance to take the first watch. I peer through the branches, listen to the owls.

A heavy blanket has been thrown over the world. It's as if there are no other universes, not even a sun or a moon, only this earth.

Down through the trees I see the roof of our home. But what makes a home? Not wood, not bricks; safety, surely. The year that has just passed, all the news reports, protests, referendums, were about national security, or about individual safety, but as if the threat was elsewhere. Yet the biggest danger came from our home itself, only we didn't know what our home was. We thought it was bricks and mortar, but a home is more than that, it is land and sea and sky.

Ben comes up behind me, wraps us in a doona. We stand together looking out into the darkness. I turn into him, press my hand to his heart and feel it pulsing.

'All our family, our friends, will we ever see them again?'

'Yes.'

'Will we ever meet strangers again and not be wary of them?'

'Yes.'

'You believe that? Really?' I ask.

'I want to believe it,' he says, and kisses me.

'I'm frightened I won't ever be able to tell anyone about today,' I whisper. 'And I don't know if I'm frightened because I'm ashamed of what we did, or if I'm frightened because I might not live to tell the tale.'

'We will live,' Ben says.

'But from now on everything is different,' I say.

'Yes,' he says.

The owls have stopped hooting.

A quietness settles on the earth.

We sit and pull the doona around us. Ben falls asleep. And then I fall asleep too.

Do you remember waking?

I don't – I can't remember.

Nada raises her right hand.

Ten. Nine. Eight. Seven. Six. Five. You are coming back to consciousness. Four. Three. Two. One.

Nada opens her eyes.

She stares at the tree vismem.

You did very well, Nada.

Tell me the truth. Is there any chance of finding Ben? Of finding Esther or Steve?

We will keep looking.

I can't remember what happened next. They were not at the caves, is that what you are telling me? I can't remember how we got separated. But you said everything is hot. Hot? Was there a bomb?

Nada, we've been very careful these last few days not to say anything that may disturb you. I can now deliver some information. It will shock you. Are you ready for what I have to say?

How can I be ready? But please, speak.

The narrative you've been telling today, occurred to you a long time ago. The world was different then. Your mind, your brain, was rescued.

Rescued?

Your DNA and brain data, along with compressed memory function, was stored. You are now in your second life. We have given you a new body. This information will take some time for you to comprehend.

Silence.

This must be difficult to understand.

Silence.

Nada?

I died? You're saying I died!

You've been through your first passing, yes.

This is not my body?

It is your body now. The medication is helping you understand that.

Was that my – did I just remember my last—

There may be more memories to come.

Where is Ben? Where is—

Ben, Esther, Steve, their data has not been identified as yet. Why and how your data was stored was not recorded. All transcripts and research materials connected to the data from that period, from this particular zone, have been lost. Giving you this second life is possible through new technologies that were only dreamt of in your time.

What happened to my home? What happened to the Hill of Peace?

We don't know what happened. You lived in a period of great upheaval. No one lives permanently beyond Border 29 any longer.

Can I go to my home?

The air quality there is rated high risk. No one can step outside without protective clothing and oxygen tanks. Even then it is not advised.

Silence.

I'm sorry to be the one to give you this news.

This is not real. It doesn't feel real.

Our concept of what is real is always adjusting. We are focused on making this planet a better place to live. We want to be in control of our future.

You can't control the weather.

Much has changed since your time.

Has it?

There is so much for you to discover. We are building a story library. You are what we call a living book and an important part of the Storyworld Project. You will become famous.

Silence.

You must be exhausted. Why don't you go to your berth now and rest? We can talk more tomorrow.

There. I feel it again. Wind.

It will all turn off automatically when we leave.

And listen, I can hear the

Bel
1998

whipbirds. It's hard to see whipbirds because because they aren't too big, so they can hide really well, and they like to stay hidden. They have a little black crest on top of their head, that's how I know one when I see it. I can't see *these* whipbirds though.

The clouds race above like in fast motion. They get darker and darker so I know it's going to rain soon. Aiko calls me inside for dinner. We sit at the table but the rain pelts down so loud it drowns our talking. I can't even hear the *clink clink* of cutlery. I run to the window, squash my nose against the glass and look into the dark. Hail smashes on the ground nearby. I switch on the outside light. The whole yard is covered with white ice. Then, all the lights flicker off and so does the clock on the microwave and all we hear is *bang, bang, bang* on the roof, which is how noisy the hail is.

Jonathan lights match after match to help Aiko find the candles and his eyes flash in the match flare. The hail stops but then it rains again so we finish our dinner with candles on the table, miming to each other because of the noisy rain. When I climb into bed it doesn't feel like a bed because it's shuddering because the whole house is shuddering from the rain. I go to sleep and have a dream that I'm spinning in a wave and wake with the wind hissing like a cat, lifting up bits of tin roof and smashing it down so it hurts my ears. I pull the covers tight around me but when I've had enough I run into Aiko and Jonathan's room and crawl between them, their bodies like a cave. Aiko pulls a pillow over my ear and I lie facing her and she says breathe breathe and I'm really glad that she is here and I hug her and only then can I fall asleep.

The next morning the storm is over. The quiet is unbelievable. I run onto the deck. Outside is a mess. Half a tree trunk is lying in the middle of the garden, the rest of the tree is gone. Sheets of crumpled tin from the roof of our neighbour's shed are are are jammed into the back fence. All of Aiko's saplings for the landcare group have tipped over and there is mud all along our driveway. The lake is bubbling with foamy waves and the sky is white-grey.

We put on our gumboots and Jonathan leads the way to the front of the house. It goes Jonathan, Aiko, then me. On the street, there are branches everywhere. Water gushes in the gutters like a river. Insects swarm above the still pools on the road. Uncle Ray comes out from next door and stands beside me. He puts his hand on my head, like he is stopping me from flying off.

'Who has been stirring up trouble?' he asks.

I think he is talking about me, but when I look up, he is looking at the mountains, like the mountains are naughty kids.

'Where's Maxine?' I ask.

'She's still hiding under the bed.' He laughs and I think he is joking but I'm not too sure.

'Is Jason coming over today?'

'Not today.'

'He hasn't been over for ages.'

'We have to wait for the mascara wars to be over.'

'What if they are never over?' I ask.

'Oh Bel, please, give me hope for the future.'

We're repotting the plants. Isha and Tarak pour the soil into the pots then Aiko and I place in the saplings and pat them down. *Pat, pat, pat.* Zeus is down the end of the garden. Every now and then he barks at a bird flying over the lake. Big fat blowflies buzz between the boards on the deck, like they're drunk. Next week we'll take the plants to the top of Dapto Creek, up on the mountain, and dig them into the banks. Everything the landcare group planted there last month got destroyed in the storm so we have to plant all over again. Aiko says we have to plant more trees in the world otherwise we are all going to hell in a billycart, which means we are going really fast riding down a hill towards our doom.

The day is steamy. Jonathan sits on the back doorstep, the weekend paper before him like a map. He reads out newspaper headings that sound like movie blockbusters.

'The Gingerbread Boys. Four Days in March. Great Celebrations. Here's an interesting one,' he says, 'Mystery Skeleton.'

Aiko pulls a face. 'Sounds gruesome.'

Jonathan says, 'No, it's an ancient skeleton. Found over at Sandon Point, after the storm.'

'That's not far away,' says Isha.

'An archaeological dig has been set up to gauge the age,' says Jonathan. 'And guess what?'

'What?' I say.

'Our neighbour is the Koori consultant.'

'Uncle Ray?' Aiko says.

'Yep,' Jonathan says.

'Can we go see the the the archaeological dig?' I ask.

Isha and Tarak chorus after me, 'Can we, can we?'

'It'll be roped off from the public,' Jonathan says.

But we go *can we can we* and Aiko finally says yes, as soon as we've finished repotting the plants.

At the beach where the archaeological dig is, the cars on the esplanade are bumper-to-bumper. We park seven or ten streets back. Isha, me and Tarak run ahead. Aiko and Jonathan follow with Zeus on a leash. At the shore the waves are so big they look like collapsing mountains and when the water crashes onto the sand it splashes up into frothy bubbles.

Everything is wild.

There's a huge tent covering the actual dig and it *is* roped off. Protesters are standing by the roped off bit, staring at the tent, and surfers with real surfboards are standing there too. The protesters hold like like cardboard signs. One sign says, *This is a sacred site*. Another one says, *Don't desecrate our sacred sites*. There's two, maybe six policemen lined up near them. A boy is sitting on the sandhill playing clapping sticks. He's wearing pink jeans with lace on the side. There's a news crew filming him. One woman is holding a microphone. She's talking to the camera and walking along in front of the surfies who are making peace signs with their fingers. Two fingers held up in a V means peace.

Isha pushes through the protesters to the rope. Me and Tarak follow. We see Uncle Ray step out of the tent. Uncle

Ray doesn't hear us when we shout at him, maybe because the sea is noisy or maybe because he is calling to an old man who is standing by the water's edge looking at the horizon. The old man is small but you can tell he is old because he has grey hair. He looks like a tough old hawk. He has a cool leather jacket on, like Lenny-the-biker's jacket. There's an Aboriginal flag on the back, in the spot where Lenny's has a skull.

Uncle Ray calls out to the old man again but a whooshing wind blows sand up and over the beach, like in a sandstorm. Everyone covers their faces with their hands or with a jumper or something. The sand settles but the old man keeps his arm raised like he is waving goodbye to a friend. Slowly slowly he turns away from the sea and walks to the tent. I've never seen anyone walk so slow.

When he is near to Uncle Ray he moves his hands through the air in front of him, quick, like a secret signal. I see Uncle Ray nod his head, and then Uncle Ray's hand moves, but only like a flick up, and then they both go inside the tent.

'See,' Jonathan says, when he and Aiko and Zeus have jostled through the crowd. 'I was right. You can't see a thing.'

But I have seen something. I've seen Uncle Ray and the old man speak without using their voices, like how deaf people speak. It's a secret language but it's in front of everyone.

Isha, me and Tarak sit on the front fence waiting for Uncle Ray to come home from the dig. After forever and forever, we see his ute turn into the street. He pulls up in front of his house. We run to him.

'Hey Uncle Ray,' I call, as he steps from the car.

Isha hops from one foot to the other. 'Is it a man or a woman?'

Uncle Ray jingles his keys. 'What?' he asks.

'The skeleton,' Isha says.

'Ah. *Kuradji*,' Uncle Ray says.

'What's that?' we chorus.

'A clever man,' Uncle Ray says.

Isha stops hopping.

Kuradji Kuradji it has a good sound to it.

I ask Uncle Ray how he knows the skeleton is clever, like like like is there a brain still inside.

Uncle Ray keeps jingling his keys.

'Because of what's buried with him,' Uncle Ray says. 'But some of his things, I reckon, are missing.'

'What things?' I ask.

'Some weapons.'

'Like an axe?' I ask.

Uncle Ray looks at me. 'What makes you say that?' he asks.

'We looked it up,' Isha says, and kicks me in the shins.

'Ow!' I say.

'What's going on?' Uncle Ray asks.

'Nothing,' I say.

I'm bursting to tell him about Kristie's axe that we hid in the caves but I know that I can't. Sometimes it's really

really hard to keep secrets. But what if the axe belongs to the *Kuradji*?

'Who was that old man you were with at the tent?' I ask.

'Which old man?' he asks.

'The one with the leather coat like Lenny's,' I say.

'That's Tom. He knows a lot about sacred sites. He's an important man because he can tell us what things really mean. Only not everyone is willing to listen.'

'Why not?' I ask.

We stand in front of Uncle Ray, looking up at him. He is quite tall.

'There's a company that wants to build a beachside estate,' he says. 'Right at the spot where they found the *Kuradji*. This company could lose a lot of money if they stop to listen to what old Tom has to say.'

'Who will they listen to?' Isha asks.

'I wish I knew the answer to that,' Uncle Rays says.

Tarak puts up his hand, like in school. 'How old is the *Kuradji*?'

Uncle Ray taps his fingers on Tarak's cheek like it's a drum.

'Old,' Uncle Ray says.

'Older than MP?' Tarak asks.

The sides of Uncle Ray's mouth almost go into a smile but don't. Our neighbour MP is the oldest person in the street, eighty-seven or two hundred next September, but she still gardens every day and writes her book. We call her MP because she was once a minister in parliament.

'Oh, maybe a little bit older than MP,' Uncle Ray says. 'Could be five thousand years old, maybe more.'

'That's old,' I say.

'But Bel,' Uncle Ray says, 'remember how you told me that dragonflies are three million years old.'

'Yeah,' I say.

'And remember too, this land here, this land you're standing on, how ancient it is. Compared to this land, five thousand years is like a baby.'

'It's hard to see time,' I say.

'Look at the clock,' Isha says.

'Old time, I mean.'

'See that lake there,' Uncle Ray says, looking along the side of his house to the water. 'That was here before any of us, and the creek that runs down from the mountain into the lake, that was here too, and the mountain, and the trees, and the birds. We're part of their story, not the other way around.'

'Like they were here first,' I say.

'You got it, like they were here first,' Uncle Ray says. 'But it's our job to look after all this land around here. If we don't, bad things can happen.'

I wonder what bad things might happen, but before I can ask, Maxine comes to the front door of her house and calls out to Uncle Ray, telling him to get inside and eat his bloody dinner that she spent all bloody afternoon cooking while he was gallivanting around pretending to be a warrior hero.

The next day Isha, me, Tarak and Zeus go out on the raft, searching for bones that might have washed up in the storm. Isha says that a *Kuradji* can find a murderer. How he would do it is he would talk to the dead spirit on the way to being buried, or he would look around the body of the dead person and see things about the murderer. Then he would eat stones and he could kill the murderer just by thinking strong thoughts. We don't find any bones or dead people so we raft out to the middle of the lake and lie back on the wooden slats, with Zeus as our pillow. We let the raft drift and stare up at the clouds like we did the first day we met Kristie.

'Do clouds get old?' I ask.

'Clouds are just water,' Isha says.

'But does water get old?'

Tarak says, 'Water gets old and you know it's old when it stinks.'

'That's like an answer by a nine year old,' I say to Tarak.

He looks pleased.

We row to Swamp Park and tramp to our tree listing all the old things we know – old buildings, old cars, old people, old pets, old roads, old gutters, old lamps, old beds, old tins, old milk cartons, old floors, old trees, old bits of dirt. Every now and then Zeus barks as if he understands what we're saying. The ropes we've strung around the trunk of our fig have browned with the weather. Zeus sits down between the big old roots, and we climb the tree, making monkey sounds. We perch on the high branches.

Old kettles, old cups, old shoes, old paper, old songs.

'I'm never getting old,' Isha says, when we've finally run out of ideas.

'You will one day,' Tarak says, and rests his head on the branch like it's a pillow, his arms and legs clinging around it like a baby koala.

I do the same as Tarak and watch two king parrots waddle towards me. One is female. I know because because the feathers on her head are not orange but green and cropped close, like freshly mowed lawn. She stops in front of me and lets her head fall on the side, as if trying to work out what I am.

'Everyone gets old,' I say.

The parrot whistles.

Isha stares off across the lake. 'Not everyone,' he says.

He is probably thinking of his mum.

I don't know what to say.

On Sunday we row to Ned and Kristie's. Kristie is standing outside, on the lawn. She runs down to us as we pull up on shore.

'Stay on the raft,' she says. 'Ned's going apeshit.'

We can hear Ned shouting. Zeus starts to bark.

'What happened?' I ask.

'He heard about that skeleton they found over at Sandon Point. He wants to get that axe dated.'

'But it's up at at at the caves,' I say.

'Yeah, Bel, but we're not going to tell Ned that. It's our secret, right?'

'Right,' I say.

'Ages before we took the axe up to the caves, Ned hid it from me,' Kristie says. 'He doesn't know I found it and took it away. He thinks The Creep stole it. He's in there giving The Creep the third degree.'

Kristie jumps onto the raft with us. Zeus licks her face.

'Come on, let's go to the park with the kiosk and get hot chips and ice-cream.'

Kristie is in a really good mood. We row over to the kiosk and Kristie buys us hot chips. We feed the leftovers to the pelicans. Then she buys us ice-creams, even one for Zeus. Kristie tells us she's thinking of going back to school.

'Ned doesn't approve. He's probably worried I'll meet someone my own age.'

'School is overrated,' I say.

'I thought that once too,' Kristie says. 'But I've got plans now. One day I might get a job as one of those art curators.'

We row back along the shore and Kristie tells us about this woman she met who is an art curator in the state gallery. She met her at the last art party Ned had. This woman said Kristie would make a good art curator because she already knows a lot about Aboriginal art. She told Kristie to go to university and study art history and other things about curating an art exhibition. Ned told Kristie she won't be able to go back to school because she's too dumb, but Kristie thinks she will be able to go back because she was always okay with her school work, she just didn't like the school she went to.

When we get to the house we can't hear any shouting but Kristie still won't let us get off the raft.

'You kids go home,' she says, as she pats Zeus goodbye. 'The Creep might still be inside. I don't want you involved with the likes of him.'

We row along the shore. When we get near my home, I see Jonathan and Aiko waiting down by the water.

'You're late,' Aiko says, as we pull the raft up on the grass.

'This is the third time this week,' Jonathan says.

They're not mad, but they don't smile either. Aiko tells Isha and Tarak to come inside. She says she has some sad news. She makes all three of us sit down on the sofa.

'Nada was in an accident this afternoon,' Aiko says. 'She and Sara were playing chasey in the front garden. Nada ran onto the road, straight in front of a car. Sara saw it happen. Lenny-the-biker saw it too.'

'The driver didn't stop,' Jonathan says. 'But Lenny got the numberplate.'

'Lenny called the ambulance,' Aiko says. 'Everyone in the street came out to try and help.'

Aiko can't speak for a while. She doesn't cry but she gets up and goes into the kitchen. She brings us back a cup of chocolate milk each. Jonathan stares at the floor.

'We're very worried about Nada,' he says.

We ask Jonathan about the accident and he tells us that Lenny-the-biker was crying. Aiko picks up the phone and dials a number. I hear her talking to Ganesh, asking him to come to our house after he has finished his shift at the hospital.

'They were late home again,' Aiko tells Ganesh, as soon as he arrives.

And then she explains about Nada.

'There are consequences if you don't stick to the agreement,' Ganesh says to Isha and Tarak. 'And the road is no place for games.'

'But we don't play on the road,' Isha complains.

'Is Nada going to die?' I ask Aiko.

'No,' she says.

We three kids sit on the carpet in the lounge room and play cards. Aiko, Jonathan and Ganesh talk in the kitchen, using quiet voices. They open a bottle of wine. Later, they order pizza and we all eat it, sitting around the kitchen counter.

'No rafting for a few days,' Ganesh says to Tarak and Isha when we have finished dinner.

'Why?' Isha asks.

'Aiko thinks we are giving you kids too much freedom,' Ganesh says. 'So Jonathan and I have agreed with her that you should do no rafting until the weekend. That gives us time to discuss it more.'

Isha gives me a cross look but I just shrug.

After they leave, I go to my room, lie down on my bed and put my pillow over my head.

The next day, when I get home from school, Aiko is on the pavement with Nada's mum, and both of them are crying.

'Is is is Nada dead?' I ask.

'No,' Aiko says. 'She only has an arm injury.'

Nada's mum says, 'It's a blessing from God.'

We're not allowed to go rafting until the next weekend. On Saturday morning Aiko comes down to the lake as we are heading off for the day.

'You need to come home for lunch on time or rafting is over,' Aiko says to us. 'Okay?'

'Okay,' we chorus.

Zeus barks as if he understands too.

'I mean it, over forever,' Aiko says. 'Isha, I will see to it with your father, so no mucking around. Okay?'

'Okay,' Isha says.

We go to Swamp Park and play at our tree, seeing who can climb to the top the fastest. Isha times us, using the timer on his mum's watch.

'Your mum can be scary,' Isha says, when we have got tired of climbing and are all lying spread-eagled on the ground, staring up at the sky through the tree branches.

'Yeah,' I say.

'Lots of people are scary,' Tarak says.

'I wonder what happened to The Creep,' I say.

'Let's go find out,' Isha says.

'We can't ask Ned,' I say, sitting up.

'Kristie will tell us,' Isha says.

'Maybe Ned will make us pancakes,' Tarak adds.

The thought of pancakes makes us jump up and run really fast down to the shore. We push the raft into the water and climb on. Isha and I take up the oars and start to row towards Ned and Kristie's. Tarak sits with his arm around Zeus. Gusts blow green leaves onto the lake. The clouds are dark and clump together. The air smells of peppermint.

When we get to Ned and Kristie's, we pull the raft on land and tie it up. We decide to race each other across the lawn to the top verandah step. Zeus bounds ahead, but stops at the bottom of the steps and waits for us, panting. Isha is the first to the top. He wins.

We stand on the verandah and all catch our breath.

The back door is open.

We hear shouting.

It's Ned and Kristie.

They're not in the new kitchen but somewhere down the dark end of the house. The new kitchen has a new table in it with ten seats which is strange, strange, because Ned and Kristie don't have any friends except for us, and except for The Creep. We sneak through the lounge room into the hallway. Zeus pads behind us. We walk past the first bedroom. Empty. No shouting now, but someone muttering. From outside the second bedroom I spy some of Kristie's clothes on a chair. On the bed is a suitcase. We tiptoe closer and peek in. We see Ned and Kristie over by the window.

'Where the fuck is it?' Ned says to Kristie.

He has hold of her wrist and is twisting it. Kristie looks hot and flustered. She doesn't answer Ned.

'Tell me,' Ned says.

'I don't fucking know,' Kristie says.

She tries to shove Ned away with her arm, but he's too strong for her.

'I know you've got it,' he says.

He puts his arm across Kristie's chest and pushes her back so she is pinned to the wall.

'What would I want with a stupid axe?' Kristie says. 'I want cash thank you very much. You don't fucking pay me.'

I hold on to Isha. We don't go into the room but we don't go away either.

Ned leans on Kristie, squashing her. Her face is squeezed up tight. He shakes her wrist. He's really hurting her.

'You lying bitch. You know it's worth a fortune.' Ned's voice is low. 'Tell me where it is.'

'Me, liar? You said you'd pay me. Lie! You said you'd pay the artists. Lie! Fuck Ned, if I'm a liar, what are you?'

Ned punches Kristie in the face. Her head thumps against the wall and her lip bleeds.

'Stop!' Isha shouts.

Tarak and I scream. Zeus barks.

We run into the middle of the room.

Ned keeps hold of Kristie but he turns to us. 'Fuck off, you kids.'

The veins in Ned's neck are pulsing. He's gone red all over his body.

'Let her go,' I shout.

Zeus is standing by me, low growling. He's not sure if it's a game.

Kristie pushes Ned back from her. She gets her hand free but Ned grabs it again and slams it against the wall.

'Ned!' she cries.

'Stop hurting her,' Isha shouts.

Isha runs over and tries to pull Ned away from Kristie. I want to run too but my feet won't move. It's like I'm frozen to the spot.

'Ned! Ned!' I shout.

Ned puts his hands around Kristie's neck.

Tarak screams again and starts crying.

Kristie's face is going redder and redder.

'Stop!' Isha and I yell.

I run to Ned's side and push at his stomach. Isha is on the other side, pushing too. Ned presses his arm against Kristie's neck and kicks at me with his leg.

'Fuck off, Bel,' he yells.

'Don't hurt her,' I cry.

Kristie is choking. She splutters. Saliva and blood are dripping down her chin.

Isha is grunting. He shoves his shoulder into Ned's side. I do the same. Ned lets go of Kristie's neck but keeps her pinned to the wall with his shoulder, one hand on her mouth. With his free hand he grabs my arm. His hand is big and his fingers press into my arm so it hurts. He yanks me around to where he can see me.

'Bel, tell me where the axe is,' Ned says.

I try to wriggle away but he is holding me tight.

'You're hurting me,' I yell.

'Kristie told you the axe is her uncle's, didn't she?' Ned says. 'It's not her uncle's.'

I'm not going to believe Ned. Ned knows how to lie.

'It is her uncle's,' I say.

'Her uncle should have it back then, shouldn't he?' Ned asks.

'He's dead.'

'Shut up, Bel,' Isha cries.

'So you know where it is?' Ned asks.

Ned squeezes my arm so it burns.

'Ow!' I cry.

'Do you know where it is?' Ned yells.

'No,' I say.

'Kristie stole that axe,' Ned says. 'She lied about her uncle. She took it from an artist in Central Australia.'

'She did not,' Isha says.

Ned is shaking me and shaking me. 'Tell me the fuck where it is, Bel, or I'll smack your face in.'

What did Kristie tell me to say? I can hear her gasping. Making sounds like she can't breathe. I have to say something to stop Ned hurting Kristie. There is too much noise in the room. I can't think. Zeus is snarling. Tarak is crying. Isha is grunting. Kristie shrieks. Ned is squashing her mouth. What did Kristie tell me to say to Ned? I try to think, but I can't remember.

'I mean it, Bel, I'll whack you so hard you won't know what hit you,' Ned yells.

Then I remember.

'Kristie never had a canvas,' I scream. 'I've never seen her with a canvas!'

Ned bangs my body against the wall, *owwwww*. Everything hurts.

Kristie yells, 'Stop, Ned.'

Everything happens fast, like all at once. Ned lifts me up by my arm and throws me on the bed. Kristie frees her hand and slaps Ned. He steps back from her, but thrusts his arm forward and punches her cheek. A snapping sound. Kristie falls on the floor and hits her head. I hear a *crack*. She lies there not moving. Isha screams really loud, and pushes all his weight into Ned. Ned grabs Isha's shoulder and shakes him. Zeus, snarling, lunges forward and grabs Ned's arm between his teeth and bites down. Blood squirts out. Ned howls in pain. Zeus drags Ned onto the floor. Blood splatters everywhere. Ned keeps howling.

I slide off the bed and run to Kristie. Isha is there, and together we pull Kristie up.

'We've got to go, now!' I say to Kristie.

Kristie looks at me and nods her head, but she rubs her eyes, like she's just woken up.

'Come on,' Isha says to her.

Blood is seeping from a cut near Kristie's eye.

'My suitcase,' she says.

Zeus lets go of Ned's arm and stands in front of him snarling, *grrrrrrrrr*. Ned scrambles back up against the wall. Zeus stays in front of him, *grrrrrrrrrr*. Ned kicks at Zeus and Zeus growls and bites down onto Ned's leg and starts pulling at it.

Ned screams. 'Fuck, fuck, fuck!'

I run and pick up Kristie's pile of clothes, and stuff the clothes in the suitcase. I zip the suitcase up and set it on its wheels.

Tarak is by the door, screaming and crying both at once.

I go back to Kristie. Isha and I pull her over to the door. I put the suitcase handle in Kristie's hand. 'Run, take Tarak,' I say.

Kristie takes Tarak by the hand and runs out of the bedroom, pulling the suitcase behind her.

Zeus is still biting down on Ned's leg, shaking it one way then the other. Ned is yelling. There is blood pooling on the floor. Isha runs over and grabs Zeus's collar and tries to pull him off. But Zeus won't let go of Ned's leg. I run over and both of us pull Zeus back, but Zeus doesn't budge. Zeus is a big dog.

Isha calls, 'Back, Zeus, back.'

He calls it over and over. Finally, Zeus lets go, but he stays snarling at Ned, *grrrrrrrrrrrr*.

Ned puts his arms in front of his face to protect himself.

There are bite marks on his arms and blood dripping down from the cuts, blood all over his leg, blood all over the floor.

'Fucking cunt of a dog!' Ned screams.

Isha and I turn and run.

'Come, Zeus,' Isha calls.

We run down the hall, Zeus bounding ahead of us. We race through the kitchen, out the back door, and onto the verandah. We see Kristie carrying Tarak across the lawn to the raft, dragging the suitcase behind her.

We run to the shore. I untie the raft and Isha and me push it into the water. Kristie and Tarak get on. Isha throws on the suitcase. Zeus is standing near the raft, panting.

'Raft, Zeus,' Isha shouts, and Zeus jumps onto the raft.

It rocks from side to side.

Isha and me climb on.

Kristie sits down and holds Tarak in her arms. He buries his head.

'Sssh, it's okay now,' Kristie says to Tarak.

Isha and I pick up the oars and start rowing as fast as we can, away from the shore.

We get a long way really fast before we stop rowing and look back. I see Ned limping across the lawn. He stops at the edge of the lake. He has a towel wrapped around his arm and another around his leg. He shouts something but I can't hear what he says.

'Keep going,' Isha calls to me. 'Over to Hooka.'

We row towards the island. As we pull around to the far side, we look back to Ned and Kristie's place again. Ned is gone from the shore. Only when we are out of sight completely do we stop rowing and let the raft drift.

Everything is still and grey, like on mornings after heavy rain when the birds stop singing. Kristie gets a tee shirt out of her bag and wipes her face with it. She starts to cry and then she stops.

'Are you kids okay?' she asks.

Her voice is soft, like a little kid's voice.

'We're okay,' Isha says.

'What about you?' I ask.

'Had better days,' Kristie says, and half-laughs.

'Will Ned come out on the water after us?' I ask.

'He could do,' Kristie says.

'Zeus hurt him pretty bad,' Tarak says, sniffing.

'Your head is still bleeding,' Isha says to Kristie.

'Feels like a really bad headache,' Kristie says, pressing the tee shirt against the cut to stop the blood. 'You kids did good in there.'

We don't say anything. We just stare at her.

'Hey, can you raft me over to the kiosk?' Kristie asks.

Isha looks to me and then Tarak. We're going to be late back. Rafting will be over. Aiko made that clear to us.

'Yes,' we all say.

The water is choppy. We row towards the kiosk. Kristie asks us to row as fast as we can. She's worried about Ned getting a boat and coming after us. We keep a lookout for Ned but don't see him anywhere on the lake or on the shore.

Above us, dark clouds are racing.

'What do you see in the sky?' I ask Kristie, beginning our old game.

'Rain on its way,' she says, but says it like she doesn't want to play.

'What else?'

'Change,' she says.

But then Kristie tells me she needs to be quiet for a bit.

She rummages in her suitcase and yanks out another tee shirt, and asks me to use it to clean up Zeus. I wet the tee shirt in the lake and wipe the blood from Zeus's mouth. He sits there panting. When I've finished, Kristie takes the bloodied tee shirt and throws it in the lake.

Thunder rumbles.

Rain plops down on us. Then stops.

At the park, we tie up the raft and walk to the kiosk. We are all a little bit shivery. Like after a swim or something. Our teeth are chattering.

'Do you want hot chips?' Kristie asks.

But we don't, we want ice-cream.

Kristie gives us a smile and buys us ice-creams.

'I have to make a phone call,' she says. 'Keep a watch out for Ned.'

She leaves us sitting on a bench near the pond and walks over to the phonebox by the road. She forgets to take her ice-cream with her, but Isha says we have to leave her alone while she makes her call, so Tarak has to hold the ice-cream for her. I squat next to the pond, but keep my eyes on Kristie. Isha stands looking out for Ned. Every now and then Isha runs down to the lake, to check along the shore. Kristie only makes one call. When she clicks off, she leans against the glass and doesn't turn around. She stays in the phonebox for ages. The only thing that moves is her shoulders. They heave up and down. When she comes back and sits on the bench, her eyes are red.

Tarak gives Kristie her melting ice-cream. She eats it quickly.

My head hurts when I think about what happened back at Ned and Kristie's house. It's like I get dizzy. It must be like that for the others because no one says anything. It's like we all just want it to be an ordinary day, even though we know it's not an ordinary day.

'When I was little my mum used to make her own ice-cream,' Kristie says.

'Does she still make it?' Tarak asks.

'Don't know.' Kristie munches her cone. 'Stopped going around to her place because every time I went, she would say, *Lift your game, Kristie.*'

'You can do that, can't you?' I say.

Kristie looks at me in surprise and then she belly laughs. 'I'll put that down as a future plan then, shall I?'

I nod but I'm not sure what's so funny. Jonathan is always telling me to *lift my game* and it usually means tidy my room.

'It would mean you could see your mum, wouldn't it?' I say.

Kristie nods. 'I guess so.'

The blood on her cut has dried. Her face is red and bruised. Tarak keeps hold of Kristie's leg, like she's a kite that might fly away. She gets a hair tie from her bag and puts her hair up in a ponytail.

Isha says he wants a drink and the three of them go to the kiosk again.

It's now I spy what I've been waiting for all year. A dragonfly, perched on a rock near me, trying to pull its long abdomen out from its split shell. Here it is. Just when I haven't got time to look at it properly. It takes ages for the dragonfly to get rid of its shell and a lot of effort, wriggling and squirming, but once it is done, it spreads its wings, fluttering them now and again, as they dry.

The wings are a brilliant aqua blue.

Beautiful.

I want to cry out to the others but I don't want to scare the dragonfly.

I am watching the dragonfly when they come back from the kiosk, but before I can tell them about it, Kristie says she has something to say.

'My dad's coming to pick me up,' she says. 'He's going on a road trip, over to Western Australia, and he asked me to go with him. I said yes.'

I want to tell Kristie about the the the dragonfly, but I also want to tell her I don't want her to go away.

'My dad says I've got to break the cycle of going back to Ned,' she says.

'How long will you be away?' Isha asks.

'Don't know,' Kristie says. She puts her hand to his cheek.

Not with her fingertips, like my mum does, but with the back of her hand.

'I thought Ned was going to kill you,' I say.

It's out before I know it and everything is bubbling up in me. I start to cry.

'I thought so too,' Kristie says, and now she is crying.

She puts her arms around me. Tarak is holding onto Kristie's jeans. Isha comes and stands really close to us. I see he is crying also, but quietly. Kristie takes hold of Isha's hand.

'Hey, but you guys saved me,' Kristie says, softly.

'Zeus saved you probably,' I say, and dry my tears with the end of my shirt.

'Yes,' says Kristie, and she bends to pat Zeus.

Isha is wiping his eyes too. He takes off his watch and holds it out for Kristie.

Kristie stares at it.

'I want you to have it,' Isha says.

'But it's your mother's,' Kristie says.

'Yes,' says Isha.

Kristie looks across to the lake that is all choppy waves. White foam floats into the air.

'I'm not a good person,' Kristie whispers.

'You *are* a good person,' Isha says.

'No.'

'Take it.' Isha holds it out.

Kristie shakes her head but Isha is stubborn.

'Go on, take it,' he says.

Kristie takes the watch and straps it onto her wrist. She pulls Isha to her.

'Thank you, Isha. This is a very precious gift,' she says.

Tarak has a worried expression. Kristie puts her hand onto his cheek.

I feel a pain in my chest.

Everything hurts.

A car horn beeps. Kristie looks over to the road.

'It's Dad,' she says.

We turn and watch a brown ute pull up near the bus stop. Her dad waves at her.

'Listen, don't you guys go to Koonawarra for a while. Ned will be looking for you. Steer clear of Wyndarra Way.'

'We will,' Isha says.

'Kristie,' I say, but then I don't know what to tell her.

'Hey, listen, I won't be gone for too long,' Kristie says. 'I'll get my head right, get myself back in school, and then I'll come and find you guys.'

I hug her.

'And hey, that axe, it did belong to my old uncle. My mother's uncle. I was cleaning out his place after he died and I found it. It was in a secret place. He must have hidden it there.' Kristie looks at each of us. 'No one in my family knows about it. My uncle never mentioned it to anyone. Not even to my mum. Maybe I'll tell her about it one day, maybe I won't. Maybe I'll leave it in the caves. Because probably there's a reason my old uncle never mentioned it.'

'We won't tell anyone,' I say.

'I know you won't, but I want you to know that I didn't steal it, not exactly. Probably I shouldn't have taken it from its hiding place. But that axe is from around here and whatever happens, it should stay around here.'

Kristie kisses each of us, me and Tarak on the cheek, and Isha on the lips. Then she turns and runs across the grass to the road.

She gets into the ute and hugs her dad, then he spins the car around, drives to the traffic lights, and turns onto the main road. The ute disappears into the traffic.

I sit on the rock near the dragonfly. Its wings are still held out, like it is waiting for something. I stare at it. I feel like I've got lots of heavy things on top of me. Kristie is gone and I am different. I am different but I don't know how to tell about it, and I don't know how to tell about Kristie. Too much has happened. Kristie is gone and I don't know if she will ever come back.

The dragonfly takes off and flies across the lake. An eagle with a white belly glides above it, a shadow over the

Lola
1900

water, its white head and grey claws pushed forward as it plunges towards the lake, ready to take its prey.

Dempster squeezes my neck and I cry out for help. Mary and Aunty pull on his arm. I can hear Abe spluttering. Dempster still has him in a neckhold. The dogs run around us barking. Yardah and Moomung try to hold them back. The little kids are screaming. Mr Farrell and Toorung wrestle with Dempster and finally he releases his hold on me and Abe. We fall back.

Abe stands unsteadily, gasps. Mary holds me while I recover my breath.

Dempster struggles against Mr Farrell and Toorung but keeps his eyes on Abe.

'Where is she?' Dempster yells at Abe.

'You tell me,' Abe shouts.

'My daughter!' Dempster cries out in such pain that it startles us.

'I didn't mean for this to happen,' Mr Farrell says, 'but you have got to talk to me, Abe. Tell me the truth. Do you know where Jewell is?'

'I don't know where she is.' Abe spits the words out. 'I swear.'

'And you didn't see her Wednesday morning last?' Mr Farrell asks.

'No.' Abe wipes at the blood on his cheek with his shirt.

'Not at all?'

'I told you, no.'

'That's good enough for me,' Mr Farrell says. 'Dan, you have your answer.'

Mr Farrell and Toorung step away from Dempster. The three men stand there. All are breathing heavily.

'You keep your brother out of my road,' Dempster says to me.

He strides over to his horse.

Mr Farrell says goodbye. He follows Dempster, mounts up and the two men ride off.

A mood, like a shadow on water, settles on us all.

Aunty turns to Toorung. 'We need your help to find this young girl.'

Toorung don't reply. He looks to Yardah, who is now standing silent and still.

'We help,' Yardah says.

'Where is it you went to meet Jewell?' Aunty asks Abe.

'It's like a tree cave,' he says. 'No one can see inside it. Jewell found it one time when she were out walking.'

'And you're certain she were there that morning?' Aunty asks.

'She were there but I didn't see her. She'd left me an apple to eat. I thought she had gone out to draw something and were coming back.'

'How do you know it were her that left you the apple?' I ask.

'She always did it. As a sign. It meant she were nearby.'

Toorung picks up a stone axe that is lying next to the campfire and tucks it into his belt. 'Show me,' he says.

We set off through the scrub along the track that leads to Mullet Creek, Abe in the lead. Moomung and her children stay behind to finish packing the fish in the barrels and load them on the cart when it comes. Before we reach the creek Abe pushes his way through sedge grass that grows on the side of the track, and there lies another smaller track, not visible from the larger one.

'The tree cave is at the end,' he says.

Abe starts walking but I grab his arm.

'You'd better go back to the farm now,' I say.

'No,' he says. 'I'm going with you.'

'If we run into Dempster again, there could be another fight,' I say.

'He's the one who should be looking out,' Abe says.

I turn to Aunty.

'Lola is right,' Aunty says. 'You come with me. I should put ointment on that cut on your cheek.'

'And someone needs to do the milking,' Mary says.

'I need to search for Jewell,' Abe pleads.

'Go,' Mary says.

'No!' Abe is determined.

'Hey boy,' Yardah says. 'You go *now*.' She points in the direction of the camp.

Abe stares at Yardah, but the look on her face demands he obey. He pushes past us and tramps off.

'We'll ride home on Night,' Aunty says to Mary, as she follows Abe.

Toorung and Yardah walk on but they soon stop and squat to inspect the ground.

'Look,' Toorung says.

Mary and I kneel beside them, stare at tracks in the dirt.

'That one girl,' Yardah says, pointing to some faint footprints.

We get up and follow the tracks. Yardah waves us to one side of the path. The tracks lead to a group of low trees that grow around an enormous rock. The spiky tree branches go right to the ground. This must be the tree cave Abe were talking about. Toorung pulls back the branches. Yardah steps inside and we follow.

Inside, it is magical. A soft green light shines through the leaves. There's a log for sitting on that Abe and Jewell must have dragged in.

'Stay put,' Yardah instructs us.

She walks around the tree cave, carefully looking at the ground. At the back of the cave the branches curl around crags in the rock. She finds a crevice, pokes about, and pulls out a flour bag. She brings it to us, holding it open. In it is one of Jewell's cardigans, two skirts, a shirt and some underclothes.

Mary and me turn to each other.

'She meant to come back here,' I say.

Besides clothes, the bag holds some cheese wrapped in a cloth.

Toorung sits on the log and studies the dirt. We go and sit next to him.

'That girl, in and out, a few times,' Toorung says, pointing to the entrance.

He picks up something from the dirt. Wipes it clean. A crust of bread the ants have almost eaten away.

I stare at it.

'She never ate her crust,' I say.

We leave the tree cave. Outside, cabbage tree palms grow alongside tall turpentines. Tree ferns hang down from mossy branches and ground ferns spike up between the trunks.

Yardah and Toorung stand listening. Toorung holds a finger to his lips, pushes me and Mary down behind a tree. He and Yardah crouch next to us. I close my eyes. I can hear birds and wind, frogs and humming insects. I open my eyes and stare at Yardah. She holds herself still, listening. Toorung puts his ear to the ground. I turn to Mary. She shakes her head. She can't hear anything either.

'What do you hear?' I whisper to Toorung.

'Maybe nothing,' he says. 'Come.'

He and Yardah stand and tread warily along an animal track that leads to the creek. We follow them and realise that if we hold our heads slightly back, so we catch the sun at a particular angle, we can see Jewell's footprints on the ground. Soon the track meets a wider path. Yardah points to another set of footprints.

'That girl met big fella,' Yardah says. 'Here. They stop here, them two.'

'Abe?' I ask.

'Heel gone,' Toorung says. 'See. Big man this. Not Abe.'

'Dempster is big,' I say to Mary.

We follow the two sets of footprints along the track to Mullet Creek. We come out at the smooth rock ledge shaped like a fish.

Toorung and Yardah inspect the ground. Yardah picks up some pencil shavings. 'Sat there, that girl,' she says, pointing to the edge of the rock ledge.

Toorung walks to where the cabbage tree trunk has been laid across the creek. 'Running here, that girl. See. That man, he run too.'

'Is someone chasing them?' Mary asks. 'Or is he chasing her?'

'Run up here, them two,' Toorung says, and scrambles up the bank, and around the trees and down again.

Yardah follows Toorung. She crouches near a clump of wild grasses and picks up a pencil. Yardah gives it to me.

'Could belong to Jewell,' Mary says.

'Could belong to anyone,' I say.

'Man chasing that girl, I reckon,' Yardah says.

Toorung walks back to the cabbage tree trunk, pointing out a broken branch, crushed twigs, dirt swirls on the rock.

'That one girl, she run onto log. Man pull that one girl back,' Toorung says.

Toorung steps over the trunk, onto the rocky ledge that sits alongside the smoother one, and walks to where it falls away and the ground becomes earthed bank. 'That one girl ran here,' he says.

Yardah, following behind, bends over to inspect the dirt. 'Fight, them two. Roll, them two. Both, roll and roll.'

Toorung strides to the water's edge, kneels down and tips his head on the side, peering first at the sharp corner of the rocky ledge then underneath.

'Blood. See. Hit head that girl.' He points to the rock then looks behind him on the bank. 'That man, he tried to clean up the blood that way,' he says. 'But he didn't see here. No rain. Water too low, can't get. Blood still here.'

Mary and me get down on our knees and peer under the ledge.

Dried blood is splattered everywhere.

Yardah climbs back onto the rocky ledge and squats at the edge, staring into the water.

Mary takes my hand.

'Is she in the water?' Mary asks.

'Near this place,' Yardah says. 'Somewhere here. Maybe.'

Toorung wades in. Mary unstraps her pack and rifle, drops them to the ground and follows. I do the same. We don't stop to take off our boots. It seems we might find Jewell now, but not how we wanted. I am trembling all over. The water is clear. I search the creek bed. Where is she? Where is she? We wade along. Toorung's head is above the water surface, but his arms are stretched out, feeling beneath the ledge. Slowly, we make our way downstream, back towards the cabbage tree trunk.

Bang! A zizzing past my ear. A rifle shot? Startled birds take flight. I look to the bank. Is someone shooting at the birds? A hunter or what? One of those men from the smelting works who don't know a rifle from a pistol? No one on the bank. Yardah runs from the ledge to a tree. She looks at me then points downstream, to a clump of coachwoods. Were the shot meant for us? I press in close to the rock ledge but keep my eye on the trees. *Bang!* A bullet pings off the rock right in front on me.

'Down,' Toorung says, pointing to the water.

We sink beneath the water, swim in under the ledge and back upstream, coming up where we first entered the creek. A shot comes skidding across the rock on the other side of the ledge. The shooter is guessing where we are. I can see my rifle lying on the bank. Mary's is nearby. If I worm my way along the ground, I can reach them. I look back at Mary and point to our rifles. Mary nods. Toorung sees what I am doing. He picks up some stones from the creek bed. He pitches one into the water on the far side of the smooth fish-shaped ledge to make a splash. *Bang!* Another shot fired. I wriggle up, grab our rifles and packs, and yank them down to the water's edge. I lie on my back and load up my rifle. Mary crawls up, takes hold of her rifle and loads it. I press against the ledge and eye the ferns. I pull the rifle butt into my chest, rest my cheek on the stock and take aim. I see something moving in the ferns. I don't know if I can shoot to kill – a rabbit is one thing, a human being is another. But this shooter wants us dead.

Silence. No birds tweeting now. My body rigid. Toorung has got hold of another stone and is weighing it up in his hand. He pitches the stone out along the water. It splashes on the other side of the fish-like ledge. *Bang!* The shooter is jumpy, not waiting, just reacting. I see the rifle peeking out from the ferns. I take a shot, but shake as I pull the trigger. The bullet explodes near a coachwood tree when I meant it to go above the ferns.

A loud *crack*. My arm feels like it's torn in pieces. I look down. Only a flesh wound. Blood pours from my shoulder. It throbs but then the throb goes. Toorung peels off his vest and strips off his shirt. He wraps his shirt around my shoulder to stop the bleeding. He takes the axe from his belt. Mary fires off a shot. I aim for the ferns. Take a shot. *Bang!*

A man howls.

Got him.

Yardah makes a gesture with her hand for us not to move.

We wait. There are no more shots. Quiet. Wind in the trees. Birds start to call.

What if I killed that shooter? I'm dizzy at the thought. Scared. One minute I'm thinking, *Good, I shot that bastard*, and the next minute I'm thinking, *Oh no, what if I shot that bastard?* We wait and wait. Nothing. We wait and wait. Toorung wriggles up close. He nods in the direction of the tree nearest to us. He wants to run up behind it.

I search the ferns. Nothing moving.

'I'll cover,' I say, and aim my rifle at the ferns.

Toorung hunkers down behind the rock ledge, then he takes off, running up to the tree. He hides behind the trunk, waiting. Nothing stirs. Yardah peeks out. Toorung waves her back. Mary and me push ourselves up from the ground and run over to Toorung, bending over as we do. My arm, like a dead weight. We stand with Toorung, flat against the trunk, listening, then edge around it. Toorung in front, with his axe, Mary next, rifle ready, me last. We slip out at the place where the shots came from.

Nothing there. Only fern fronds rustling in the breeze.

'Gone,' Toorung says, lowering his axe.

He goes forward and inspects the dirt, frowns.

Yardah hurries along the bank to us and she too examines the ground. She looks to Toorung.

'This one, same one,' Yardah says.

'That him,' Toorung says.

Mary is shaking.

I put my arms around her. 'He's gone,' I say. 'We'll be safe.'

'It's not that,' Mary says. 'But if he's shooting at us, something bad has definitely happened to Jewell.'

Warily, we follow the shooter's tracks, jumping at every twig snap. We come out at a clearing.

Toorung and Yardah poke around, talk to each other in their language.

'That big one, had him horse. Rode that way,' Toorung says, coming back to us but pointing to Hooka Creek.

Yardah is already walking off in that direction. 'Come,' she calls.

We follow her through the bush all the way to Hooka Creek. Toorung scrambles down the bank, wades across to the opposite side, then swims back.

'Rode along creek,' he says, pointing upstream. 'You want follow?'

'Is Jewell back there in the water?' Mary asks.

'Could be,' Yardah says, wiping Toorung's face with her skirt.

'Must be,' I say. 'Why else would we be shot at?'

'Or maybe she's not dead,' Mary says. 'Maybe he is holding her somewhere near there.'

'There were a lot of blood,' I say, carefully.

'We've got to go back,' Mary says.

'Don't we have to get Constable Black?' I ask.

'What if whoever shot at us, wants to lead us away from Jewell long enough so that he can move her away,' Mary says. 'If Jewell is there, dead or alive, we've got to find her first, don't we?'

Mary is right.

'You think the shooter were only trying to scare us?' I ask Toorung.

'Maybe,' Toorung says.

'We go back,' Yardah says.

We take the track through the forest to the creek.

We search again along the banks.

'Jewell!' Mary screams out, hoping against hope that our dear friend is alive.

We listen but only hear the birds.

At the fish ledge Toorung takes off his boots and vest and splashes into the water. Yardah walks along the edge of the rock, Mary and me following.

Toorung dives under the fish ledge, swims from one end of

the ledge to the other. Stripy gudgeon dart out from the weeds, their hiding place invaded. Toorung comes up for air.

'Not this place,' he says.

I jump from the fish ledge onto the tree trunk. Mary paddles into the water and feels around beneath the trunk. I climb over to the other side, and wade along, downstream, beyond the fish ledge, pushing back overhanging tree branches. I get on all fours in the shallows and reach in beneath the low bushes. Toorung and Mary wade over to help me and we crawl along, feeling our way. We don't find Jewell. We stumble out, dripping from head to toe, and sit on the bank next to Yardah.

'Maybe the current took her,' I say.

'But no one has found her body,' Mary says. 'There's leisure cruises on the lake every day.'

Yardah is staring downstream. She points to where the roots of a tree sit part way in the water, the rest of the trunk on land.

'There,' she says.

Mary, Toorung and me splash back in and over to the tree trunk. Toorung holds his breath and ducks his head under water. A moment later he bursts up.

'Eels,' he says.

'On, on,' Yardah calls.

She points to a bed of thick reeds.

We make our way over, through the water, and I pull apart the reeds. Further in I see some white cloth. Like a woman's blouse?

'Here's something,' I say.

We wade to where the reeds are higher than our heads, clearing away fallen branches. I pull back thick reeds, and see her. Jewell. Face down in the water. She is tied to an old rotten boat that has sunk. Tied there with some vine.

'She's been here all this time,' Mary whispers.

I peer out through the reeds to the creek bank.

Want to see if anyone is watching.

No one is there.

Toorung pulls his axe from his belt and cuts the vine. We turn Jewell over.

Here she is. Our Jewell. Bloated. All white and blue and purple. Her clothes are torn and there's a gash across her forehead.

Jewell, sweet Jewell.

I run back to the camp. Moomung, the kids and dogs are further down along the shore. Too far away to see me. I mount up on Ghost, ride up the track and take the road to Duncan's dairy. I spy Tommy Lin in his cart, coming from the other direction.

'Jewell's dead,' I say, as he pulls up alongside me.

Tommy Lin stares like he don't believe what I've said. I don't believe it myself.

'Someone murdered her,' I say.

Ghost turns in a circle as she settles herself.

Murdered. It's not an easy word. Tommy Lin shakes his head. I tell him about the shooter and about finding Jewell's body in the creek.

'No good world,' Tommy Lin says.

I pat Ghost's neck, as she can't seem to settle. I can't speak. There is nothing to say.

'She young,' Tommy Lin says. 'Too young.'

Magpies choralling.

Wind shaking the trees, like a baby's rattle.

'Can you help us take Jewell's body to her da?' I ask.

'Dempster not like.'

'He's got no choice,' I say.

Tommy Lin agrees to take his cart to the Mullet Creek mouth. I ride on to Duncan's dairy. Mrs Duncan is in the yard when I canter in. I dismount and go to her. She holds her hand to her heart while I tell her what's happened. Mr Duncan and his daughter, Nellie, come running from the dairy. I sit on the bench by the back door while Mrs Duncan repeats all I've said.

'Nellie, you ride into Wollongong and get Constable Black,' Mr Duncan says. He picks up the rifle leaning on the wall near the door. 'Take this because who knows where that lunatic has ridden to. I'll go with Lola.'

'Come in Lola, I'll bandage your arm first,' Mrs Duncan says to me.

'It'll hold until we get Jewell,' I say. 'Someone needs to tell Dempster about his daughter and it can't be me.'

'I'll tell Dan Dempster,' Mrs Duncan says.

Getting Jewell to the cart is a miserable task. Tommy Lin, Mr Duncan, Toorung and Mary stumble along the banks with her stinking body. Yardah and me walk behind. As we are putting Jewell into the cart, the leisure boat sails past. Some passengers wave. They can't see what we're loading. Mary climbs into the back of the cart with Jewell. Toorung and Yardah sit next to her. Mr Duncan hauls himself up next to Tommy Lin.

'Whoah up!' Tommy jigs the reins and the horses take off along the track. I follow behind on Ghost.

We stop at the camp. Toorung tells Moomung to take the kids to Mickey Johnson's place, at the point. He wants them to go now, no delays. 'Bad man near here, got rifle,' he says.

The older boys try to see inside the cart but Toorung clips them behind the ears.

'Off, off,' he says. 'Go with Moomung.'

The boys pick up some buckets. Their mother is already walking along the shore, the two little ones running ahead. The older boys hurry after them.

Mrs Duncan is standing at Dempster's front gate when we arrive. She comes to the back of the cart and holds her hand on her heart for some time, just staring at Jewell. Finally, she says, 'I'll get Dan.' Then she adds, 'After he's seen Jewell, we'll take her back to my place so I can ready her body for mourning. Dan's kitchen is filthy and I'll not be preparing a body for the afterlife in a place like that.'

Mrs Duncan goes inside the house to get Dan Dempster. Soon after, he comes out and walks down to the gate, looking stiff and shaky, Mrs Duncan following behind. Dempster does not look at any of us, but stares straight ahead, until he reaches the back of the cart. He howls when he sees Jewell and bends over her body, weeping. If I thought him a harsh father, I know now that he loved her as well. It could not have been him that did this to Jewell, although I check his boots all the same. There is no chunk missing from the heel, and when I look to the dirt, his footprints are not like the others we saw. Well, a man can have two pairs of boots, but I don't believe this man could murder his daughter.

Mary is sitting by Jewell but Dempster keeps his eyes averted. When Mary expresses her sorrow he cuts her off curtly, saying only, 'Do not speak.'

He takes a handkerchief from his pocket, wipes his face, and walks away from the cart.

'Come by mine in an hour, Dan,' Mrs Duncan says, going with him to the front gate. 'I'll have the body ready for viewing then and we'll call in some of the neighbours.'

Dan Dempster nods his head gravely and walks inside. No one could begrudge him his pain, for Jewell is a sad loss to this world.

Before we depart the wind blows up fierce. Strips of bark fly through the air. Black clouds gather above us. A deep rumbling from the sky.

'The storm will wash away the killer's tracks,' I call to Toorung.

Toorung tips his head out of the cart and looks to the sky. 'That big fella storm not stop here,' he says.

Tommy Lin jigs the reins and the cart rolls on towards Duncan's dairy. I nudge Ghost forward and follow.

At the dairy we carry Jewell into the washhouse. Mrs Duncan covers her with a sheet. Tommy Lin has to go to his uncle's farm to help with the afternoon milking. He says he will come back after. Mr Duncan leads the rest of us into the kitchen as we will need to stay and give our depositions to Constable Black. We warm ourselves by the fire. Toorung, Mary and me dry our wet clothes. Yardah rests in a chair. Mrs Duncan stitches up my arm and Mr Duncan serves out bowls of stew. He eats quickly then leaves to herd in the cows. The Duncans are very late with the milking and the cows are bawling. Nellie arrives with Constable Black, and after scoffing down some stew, she goes to help her da. Mrs Duncan takes Constable Black to the washhouse so he can view Jewell's body. She'll prepare the body for mourning after he has seen it. When she returns she collects up her cloths and ointments. Mary and me ask to help wash the body.

'Dempster said he don't want either one of you touching her. So I need to respect his wishes,' she says. 'But I'll call you to come see her when I'm done. You'll have time to say your goodbyes.'

'You two can shoot,' Toorung says to Mary and me when Mrs Duncan has gone. 'That fella found his possum legs after.'

'But who were it?' Mary asks.

'Had him farm boots,' Toorung says.

'A farmer then?' Mary asks.

'Maybe,' I say, 'but it could be someone like Bartholomew Winter. He's not a farmer but he wears farm boots.'

'Has he a rifle?' Mary asks.

I feel my heart quickening. 'He's in the shooting club.'

'Whoever that man, he know that water,' Yardah says.

'That one been swimming in creek many time,' Toorung says. 'Got to be one of them men from around here.'

Constable Black returns and warms his hands by the fire. He has a long scar that runs from his forehead, down the right side of his face to his neck. It makes him seem like someone to fear, yet there's a stillness about him that is calming. Mary and me have the shivers. We can't get warm. Yardah stirs the coals with a poker to liven up the flame, while we tell Constable Black all that has happened. He nods but don't say much. Holds his cards close to his chest. I show him the pencil we found. He examines it and puts it in his pocket.

'I need to see where you found the body,' Constable Black says, turning to Toorung.

'I can show,' Toorung says. 'Rain coming. Now go.'

Constable Black asks us to stay by the fire until he returns. He will take our depositions then.

The two men leave.

Yardah falls asleep, sitting up, her legs stretched out on a cushion. Mary lies down across two chairs and puts her head on my lap, like she used to do when we were kids.

We stare at the flames.

'I don't like to think of Jewell gone,' I say.

Her going leaves a great emptiness that chills me. It's like when I am standing alone in the long paddock in winter and a cold wind is blowing fierce.

After an hour, Mrs Duncan calls Mary and me to come view the body.

'Take your time,' she says. 'I don't think Dan will let you back for the mourning. He didn't speak kindly of either of you, and I won't repeat what he said about young Abe.'

Mrs Duncan hurries over to the milking shed. Mary and me walk to the washhouse. Two chickens scratch the ground near the doorway. I shoo them away.

Jewell is inside, on the table, her body glistening in the afternoon light. Her skin is puffed up but clean. Her hair is washed. Mrs Duncan has made an effort to find our Jewell again. We stand close to the table. Neither Mary nor me tremble or cry but our bodies are slumped with sadness. I can't bear to see all the life gone out of Jewell, yet somehow her sweetness is still there.

What is a life if it must come to this?

I wave away the flies and the mosquitoes that want to feed on Jewell still. We all prey on each other, is that it? Is that what God planned?

'Goodbye dear friend,' I whisper. 'No one is meant to leave their life this way.'

'It's a wrong that needs to be righted,' Mary says softly to Jewell. 'I promise we'll right it for you.'

We cover Jewell with the sheet, but stand there listening to the insect hum. My first ma ran away and my second ma died. Then my da died, whose love were strong. My baby that were dear to me, she died too, and Mary's Otto, who we all loved, and now Jewell. The world is a lonely place.

We hear Constable Black and Toorung return but we stay with Jewell, quietly standing by her side, until the light starts to fade. Only then do we come out of the washhouse. Mary goes back to the kitchen. Constable Black is sitting on the bench under the tree, smoking his pipe and watching two scaly shrikes in the grass. I go and sit next to him.

The wind is coming in waves, low down, beneath the tree tops. Tunnels of leaves twist up from the ground and fall again.

The earth is a body breathing.

I glance up at the sky. Toorung were right. The storm passed over us and is breaking out at sea. Out there, thunder is rumbling and lightning is splintering the clouds.

'I don't understand evil,' I say.

'Evil is evil,' Constable Black says, puffing smoke into the air. 'Evil is a mystery.'

'Evil is a horror, I'll grant you that, but I don't see it being a mystery. Tell me what you mean?'

'When I go riding of a night, like I sometimes do, Ghost will pull up all on her own, in the middle of the track. Just stop. She's behaving like there is something evil before her, when all I see is the dark road ahead. I know she's hearing things, seeing things, things I can't hear or see.'

I turn to Constable Black and watch him draw back on his pipe as he considers what I have said.

'Her hearing is better is all. Her night vision may be better too,' he says. 'She is most likely concentrating hard on what is coming along the path.'

'There are, what shall I call it, aspects, there are aspects of this world that we don't know about because we see in a particular way.'

I want to make a serious point but Constable Black laughs.

'We don't know about but the horse does know about?' he asks.

'Yes,' I say, looking ahead and trying not to be offended.

'Because of the way the horse sees?'

'Yes.'

'Are you talking about ghosts?'

'A sensing of a world that is different to our sensing,' I say.

Constable Black turns to me now, his face suddenly animated.

'So would you go to Madame Vichy's séance?' he asks.

'Madame Vichy is a sham.'

'You had me worried,' Constable Black says. 'So you believe in science?'

'Science is how we've improved our butter. But there are things science don't know,' I say.

'But will know.'

'No, Constable Black.'

'Call me Joe.'

'Some things are unknowable, Joe. Like evil.'

'Things can be forgotten, I'll give you that,' Joe Black says. 'They once had great waterways in Rome. Systems for getting water to houses where there was no well. No river nearby. Aqueducts they were called. But the knowledge of how to build them got lost.'

'Aqueducts? I've not heard of them.'

The two shrikes have been darting back and forth across the grass but now, suddenly, they fly away.

'A civilisation is built too,' Joe Black says. 'We build it. We make our minds up to right and wrong. Good and evil. Evil is not a thing that exists before we decide. But once we decide, once we have named it, it is there.'

'Good and evil exist before we decide on names,' I say.

'But naming is powerful,' Joe Black insists.

'Evil don't come from being powerful, it comes from being weak,' I say.

I am not one to give up on my own ideas easily. I got well used to arguing when Otto were courting Mary.

'Weakness yes, evil does come from weakness, but from someone weak who wants to feel *power* in their own hands,' Joe Black says.

'But why do they need to feel that?' I say. 'That's the mystery I'm talking about.'

Suddenly, I want to tell Joe Black the secret I have held inside me for three years. Tell him about the many fathers of my child. Tell him my shame. Tell him how these men grabbed me as I walked home one night after finishing work at the hotel where I'd been employed as a cook's assistant. Oh, I knew them all, I had been at school with some of them, but I didn't know their evil, not until that night.

'I think you're making too much of mystery,' Joe Black says. 'There's good fruit and bad fruit. People are like fruit. Sometimes they go rotten, sometimes they are born rotten. It just is. There's no mystery about it. The cause can be not good soil, or it can be weather, it was too hot or too cold say, and this delicate thing, this fruit, had a time when it tasted good but then it went bad. The way I see it, there's been a lot of bad weather lately and the fruit is not tasting good.'

Black and purple clouds drift across the sky. The yellowed moon is rising. Joe Black takes depositions from Mary and me in the Duncans' kitchen and we sign them. He says a court won't take any notice of what Toorung or Yardah might have to say, but he listens to what they tell him. After, Toorung and Yardah leave to walk home. Joe Black says he will go to their camp tomorrow, in the morning. They have agreed to help him trace the shooter's tracks up Hooka Creek and see where he might have come out of the water. Dempster has not arrived, so Mrs Duncan shuts up the washhouse, says she'll go over to his place and see if he is all right. We give her our thanks. As we mount our horses, Tommy Lin comes rolling through the gate at speed. He pulls his cart up alongside us.

'Trouble at farm,' he says to me.

'What kind of trouble?' Joe Black asks.

'I meet Mr Farrell on road. Mr Farrell say Dempster went around and around. Tell everyone they got to help him get justice for daughter. Now they all go to Lola and Mary's farm.'

Tommy Lin lifts up his shirt. He has a pistol stuck through his belt.

'Never shot gun,' Tommy Lin says. 'Had gun since cousin got held up in shop. Remember?'

'Don't shoot it now,' I say.

'Might need,' Tommy Lin says. 'Saw Niall Farrell walking across paddock to farm. He had rifle.'

Joe Black loads his rifle. Mary and I do the same.

'I don't want you shooting those,' Joe Black says.

'We been shot at already today,' I say. 'We got to defend ourselves.'

'Have them, but don't shoot unless I say. Agreed?' Joe Black says to me and Mary.

'Agreed,' we say.

Mrs Duncan calls out to her husband to get his rifle and then climbs up into the cart next to Tommy. Mr Duncan comes running, rifle in hand, and hauls himself up next to her. Nellie comes running behind him, but he tells her to stay put. 'I'm too scared to stay put,' Nellie says.

'Lock yourself in the storeroom,' Mr Duncan says. 'Don't move until you hear my voice.'

We kick into our horses and gallop out through the gate and along the road, Tommy Lin's cart rattling behind us. A possum scrambles up a darkened tree. Kangaroos thump through the shadowy bush. A wombat, its squat tub body brown like a rock, waddles off the road.

We make good time and soon we see our farm up ahead, lit up as if for a gathering. I look to the paddocks and see neighbours trailing across, lamps or firesticks guiding their way.

'There's a mob there already!' I call back to Tommy.

We gallop through the gates. I see a circle of men and women forming in front of the kitchen. The flames of their firesticks are bright orange. Grey smoke drifts into the night sky. As we ride closer I see that some carry lengths of wood, some rifles, one an axe. Bartholomew Winter is on the verandah, holding Aunty. He has one hand clapped over her mouth. I can hear Bud barking from behind the kitchen door.

The mob turns to us, as we ride up. Ghost snorts and flicks her ears back. There's a howling from inside the circle. *Thwack! Thwack!* I can't see what is happening. Do they have Abe? I search for faces I know, spot Mrs Farrell and Niall and Padraig, and the two youngest Farrells, Seamus and Donal. There are people from the estate I recognise but also people I don't know.

Joe Black, rifle in hand, nudges his horse forward and the circle opens up. *Thwack! Thwack!* I see Dempster whacking Abe on his leg with a length of wood. Abe cries out in pain, limps, holds his leg.

Mary and I yell, 'Stop!'

Dempster wallops Abe on the back. He falls to the ground. Joe Black shoots his rifle into the air. *Bang!* The horses rear up and neigh. I aim my rifle at Dempster while Joe Black reloads.

Niall Farrell steps into the centre of the circle, yells at Joe Black, 'This is a father's revenge.'

'He's got the wrong man,' I scream at Niall.

There's blood running down Abe's face. He sinks into the dirt.

Dempster goes to hit him again. I shoot just above Dempster's head. No time to wait for Joe Black's permission. Dempster turns and stares, eyes yellow in the flame light. I reload. There is so much human noise, it crashes around us.

Mary shoots her rifle into the air. *Bang!*

The horses snort and neigh.

Someone calls out from the crowd, 'There's more of us than them.'

A sharpness.

Everyone taking a breath in.

Niall and Padraig point their rifles at us.

Mary yells at them, 'Niall and Padraig Farrell, we are *neighbours*.'

Joe Black aims at Niall.

'I am ready to shoot you dead, Niall Farrell,' Joe Black says. 'You want to go to gaol. Go ahead and shoot me. This boy ain't the murderer.'

I see Mr Farrell and Connor running across the paddock. Mr Farrell yells and it breaks the spell on Demspter who has been staring at us. He swings around and hits Abe again and again with his length of wood.

Thwack! Thwack!

I shoot at the ground near Dempster. Dirt spurts up.

Dempster stops hitting. Which is lucky, because I'm ready to shoot him dead.

He stares at us again, saliva dripping down his chin. I reload.

Joe Black, holding his rifle steady, shouts to Dempster. 'Enough.'

Abe is lying on the ground, moaning, gripping his leg. Blood pooling.

'Abe needs help, he is bleeding bad,' I say to Joe Black.

'You let his Aunty go,' Joe Black calls to Bartholomew Winter. 'She needs to get this boy bandaged.'

Bartholomew Winter holds Aunty tighter, like he's going to defy Joe Black's order.

Mr Farrell and Connor climb over the fence and come up on the verandah, alongside Bartholomew Winter.

'Let her go,' says Mr Farrell.

I hold my rifle steady on Bartholomew Winter, who tries to stare me down.

There's snarling and muttering from the mob.

Bartholomew Winter pulls his hand away from Aunty's mouth, but he still don't let her go.

Aunty wails. Her cry is sharp and violent. It pierces the night. Stirs the mob.

Suddenly, Bartholomew Winter releases Aunty and stretches his arms out wide, like he is a victim.

I lower my rifle. Aunty starts down the steps, shaking her fist at the mob. She kneels beside Abe.

'You people all go home now,' Joe Black yells, keeping his rifle aimed at Niall.

The men and women don't move.

Our horses, restless and wary, pin their ears back.

Mary dismounts and walks over to Abe, glaring at the faces surrounding her. She turns to Dempster.

'Any one of these men could have murdered Jewell. It don't take long to get to Mullet Creek from any of these farms hereabouts. We found the footprints. It were a big man, bigger than Abe. If it weren't you, Mr Dempster, then who? It could have been Niall or Connor? They're both tall. How about Mr Winter? No one is a match for him in size. Or one of you others here.' Mary points to men in the crowd. 'Maybe one of you knows what happened and is not speaking up.'

'You were at the creek, Connor Farrell. You said you saw men from the smelting works hunting, it could have been one of them, couldn't it?' I ask.

'Yes,' Connor says.

'What about you, Niall, you see anyone?' I ask.

'Not there,' Niall says. 'So I couldn't say.'

'You were there!' I say, affronted. Connor told me you were hunting with him. He showed me the rabbits you caught.'

Niall looks to Connor. I can't tell what is passing between them, but something is not right.

There is a hush now.

Everyone is looking at Connor.

'Connor? You said Niall were there,' I say.

Connor's face is flushed and I remember it were like that last Wednesday.

Suddenly, it is like the smoke has thickened the air. I can't breathe so well. I keep my eyes on Connor.

'Were it *you*, Connor?' I say, quietly.

Connor stares at me. He goes to say something but no words come out.

'Speak up,' Joe Black says.

'Were it you murdered Jewell?' I ask.

Connor shifts his weight from one foot to the other, as though he don't know how to settle. The light catches his eyes. But there is nothing there, blankness. Were it him or not?

'It was not my Connor,' Mrs Farrell cries out.

'Then why can't he tell us what happened?' Mary asks.

'Connor, was it you that killed Jewell Dempster?' Joe Black asks.

'Or were it Niall?' I ask, because maybe Connor is protecting his brother.

Connor glances at Niall.

'Were it you that shot at us over at Mullet Creek?' I ask.

'Or Niall?' Mary asks.

'Were it you I shot, Connor?' I look to his chest. Both he and Niall are wearing jackets and I can't see if either is hurt.

Connor's eyes are on mine again now. Sad. Soft. Not like a murderer's eyes. He can't be the one, can he?

'Were it an accident?' I ask.

Tommy Lin runs forward from his cart and points his pistol at Connor. 'Take Connor Farrell to gaol.'

Niall turns his rifle on Tommy. 'Don't dare point a gun at my brother, Mr Yellow Swine.'

'You leave him alone, Niall,' I say, swinging my rifle in Niall's direction.

'Shoot me, shoot me,' Padraig sniggers, and raises his rifle at me.

'All of you, hold fire!' Joe Black yells, trying to calm us down.

'Someone here is a murderer,' I scream at Joe Black.

'And you are not the law!' Joe Black shouts at me. 'Rifles down, rifles down,' Joe Black orders everyone.

We don't let them drop completely, but we lower them slightly.

'Did you see Jewell on Wednesday morning, Connor?' Joe Black asks.

'No,' Connor says.

'Were you down there hunting?' Joe Black asks.

'Yes,' Connor replies.

His eyes seem to want to say more, or am I just inventing?

'Niall, were you down there hunting?' Joe Black asks.

'No,' Niall says.

'See, someone is lying!' I say.

297

'It was not one of my boys hurt young Jewell,' Mrs Farrell shouts, her big body heaving with emotion.

'Someone lying or looking guilty is not the same as someone guilty,' Joe Black says to me. 'You should be the first to know that.' He turns back to Connor and Niall. 'I'll want both you boys to go home now. I'll be over shortly to take your depositions.'

'You can't let them go home!' I say.

'My boys have nothing to hide,' Mr Farrell says.

'Then they'll do what I say,' Joe Black says. 'Now all of you, go home! There's a young girl been murdered and it's my job, and only my job, to find out who murdered her. But it's your job to mourn her. '

Grimaces. Still no movement.

Aunty stands. 'Go home,' she says. 'There's already been one murder, we don't need any more.'

There is such authority in her voice that people begin to step away.

Niall and Padraig let their guns fall to their sides. They turn and walk to the fence. Seamus and Donal follow. Donal picks up a lamp that has been left in the yard. They stand and wait for Connor. He follows, giving me a final look as he leaves, a look that is unreadable. Then all five boys climb over the fence and walk across the paddock into the darkness. Soon the lamp Donal holds becomes a bouncing glow.

'It's one thing to protect your brother,' Mr Farrell says to me sternly. 'It's another to slander our sons.'

'It was not one of mine done anything to Jewell,' Mrs Farrell says.

The Farrells leave, walking the long way home, out through the gate and along the road. Some of the neighbours walk off along the road, back to their houses. Others go to their horses and mount up. Some ride off but a few sit and wait for Dempster. Dempster stays put, like he don't know how to move.

'Dempster, you've stirred up enough trouble for a lifetime,' Joe Black says. 'Your daughter is waiting for you over at Duncan's dairy. She's waiting for you to do your mourning. You go do that now and don't do more damage to your name.'

Dempster twists around to face Abe.

'You might not like that boy,' Joe Black says. 'But he ain't your killer.'

Dempster turns to Joe Black, his lips pressed tight.

'The clues point in other directions,' Joe Black says.

Dan Dempster glares at Joe Black, then he shakes his head, walks to his horse and mounts up. He rides to those that have waited for him, and they gallop off down the track.

I dismount and run over to Abe.

'You all right there, Abe?' I say, crouching by him.

One of his eyes is swollen and won't open. He turns his head so he can see me with his good eye.

'Jewell really dead?' he murmurs.

'We found her in Mullet Creek.'

Abe moans for the loss of Jewell. Aunty checks his body for broken bones.

'Warm water,' Aunty says to Mary. 'Brandy and bandages.'
Mary rises and runs up the steps to the kitchen.

'Does this hurt?' Aunty asks, touching near Abe's stomach.
Abe rears up in pain.

'There's crimes been committed here, more than murder,' I
say to Joe Black.

'Let me handle it,' he says.

'This beating is a crime,' I say.

'I heard you the first time, Lola,' he says. 'And I know who
was here.'

'This boy needs a doctor, now,' Aunty says. 'He has bones
broken and his kidneys are damaged.'

'Can you take Abe in your cart, Tommy Lin, take him to the
hospital?' I ask.

'I can take,' Tommy Lin says.

Aunty settles Abe in the back of Tommy Lin's cart. Tommy
waits, reins in hand. I sit in the saddle and stare into the trees.
Joe Black checks the footprints in the yard. None match those
by the creek, although some are the same size.

'I'll come by tomorrow,' Joe Black says, mounting his horse.
He rides up to me.

'This will be sorted,' he says.

'I'll make sure of it,' I say.

He half grins, reaches out and touches my hand. He kicks
into his horse and rides off through the gate and along the road
to the Farrells' place.

Mary mounts Night and rides up to me. 'You think Connor did it?'

'He's not saying all he knows, that's for sure,' I say.

Perhaps it were both brothers. But how come there were only one set of tracks? Perhaps one of them did it, and the other watched, unknowingly as far as the murderer were concerned. Or perhaps that morning I met Connor, he made up a story about Niall being with him, and he alone killed Jewell.

'Bad man,' Tommy Lin says.

'But which bad man,' I say, because maybe it *were* someone else and not either of the Farrells. But why won't Connor speak?

'We're set,' Aunty calls from the back of the cart.

'We go!' Tommy Lin jigs the reins and the cart rolls on out through the gate.

In the back of the cart, I see Aunty wrap a blanket around Abe.

A mizzling rain begins to fall.

Mary turns Night in a circle. 'Nothing can be the same,' she says. 'Not after tonight.'

'No,' I say.

'But they're not going to scare us away,' Mary says to me. 'They tried to after Otto's death, and they'll try it again now, but we won't budge.'

'We won't budge,' I say.

I button up my coat, pull my hat onto my head. Mary does the same.

The rain is softening up the dirt and the tracks made by our neighbours are washing away. The forest trees that edge the gate and run down to the long paddock, shake in the swirling wind, but between the trees, it is still and dark.

Suddenly, I feel it. That chill on my neck. I look to Mary. Her eyes are already on mine.

We open our mouths and breathe out mist.

'They're here,' I whisper.

'Yes,' Mary says.

'Can you hear the sound?' I ask.

'Beneath the rain. Listen.'

I hold still, but hear nothing.

We wait.

Nothing.

Mary sighs, nudges Night forward.

'Come on,' she says. 'Tonight, we've got to look after Abe.'

She rides ahead, out along the road.

I keep staring at the dark between the trees.

I shiver, nudge Ghost forward and gallop to catch Mary up. An owl

Hawker
1822

hoots. She and the women are gone. The dark forest has taken them. I hesitated too long. Only now do

I wonder what they are up to. All the campfires are around the lake, yet the women were moving inland. Why? This place has too much mystery. I don't understand it, only how I came here. I turn and follow Vince and Lambskin. We tramp up to the hut in the watery dark as the full moon sails through ghost trees. My mood is heavy, as if I am sinking down into a pool of thick black mud.

Back at the hut we drink the last of the grog. Poole and Jed are already asleep, lying on rugs in front of the fire. Lambskin joins them. I tell Vince that come dawn I will harvest the corn. He claps me on the back. He is in good cheer. I spread out our sheepskins to one side of the hearth. Vince lies down, and is soon lulled into the land of dreams.

I can find no rest and sit in the open doorway. Watch an owl perched in the tree. Its bright eyes staring. There is no grog left to blur my vision and all I see on the road ahead is luckless. For what purpose must I work my time out in drudgery? I will be a cripple when I get my ticket of leave, never mind my freedom. There must be another way.

I am a fool. Building up hopes and visions, but of what? A warm bed and food for my belly. Even a dog gets that.

Too much has been stolen from me.

What kind of justice transports a man from his land? What kind of justice treats a man like a dog? What kind of justice treats a man worse than a dog?

Manhood suffrage is what is needed. Laws made by your own kind could be some kind of fairness. One vote one man and no buying your way to parliament. That would be the start of something. But if manhood suffrage arrives it will be after my time, not before.

Night visions stir the sleepers. I turn and gaze at their faces. The firelight makes them men I might choose to be with instead of blackguards I am bound to while I wait out my time in a prison land where the heat hurts more than English damp ever could.

It was not manhood suffrage that had me transported here. It was one spark of passion in a London lane, late one night when I should have been back to Surrey. When I had planned to be back to Surrey. One spark of anger after drinking two days straight so my wits were against me, and the spark against a man who refused to pay what he owed, owed fair and square for a business sold, from me to him. A punch at his refusal to pay, and a falling that landed wrong so his head smashed on the stone. The sentence I got was to end my life away from all human kindness.

That money I was owed was for a future with a lass who knew how to shed light on even the darkest days. The arrangement was made with her father. I was meant to return to Surrey and set up a new press close to her home. But that wife and the family I should have had is lost to me forever. The final blow came when I learnt that my brother took up where I left off. He married my sweetheart. The bitterness of that news lost me a brother too.

I get up to search for grog that might be left in the packs. Poole must have some stashed as his thirst is unquenchable. I peer into bags, rummage through the stores, but if Poole has grog hidden I cannot find it.

Back I go to the doorway, look up and see dark wings, hundreds of them, flapping in the night sky. Pelicans flying free to some unknown destination.

And here I am trapped on land.

The birds are freer than I will ever be.

The new day will bring no more than a march to nowhere.

Each day the same.

Each day my prison.

I stare at the gun, heavy in my hand, and know what I must do.

In the field, corn tips catch the light, like thousands of candles lit as if to herald my departure.

All good feeling has leaked away.

It is clear to me now that I will not see the sunrise.

One pull of the trigger and I'd be as free as the birds.

What might Appin ever offer that could compare? Nothing.

True freedom comes from death. Only death.

I should do it now.

Pull the trigger now.

I turn to the sleeping men.

They look in pain.

Miserable faces.

Why not end their misery too?

Why not do them this kindness?

It would be a mercy to us all. The kindest mercy. They would know no more fear. Their sweet departure could be my best purpose in life.

I rise and load my gun. It takes time with my banged up hand but the idea of freedom has taken hold. Every man must leave his mark and destiny has claimed this as mine. There is a shiver going through me.

They would be confused in waking after the first shot. I would have time to reload.

I set myself ready and settle the gun on my shoulder. The dogs rise from the steps outside and start barking. I turn to the doorway.

Vince wakes, rolls over.

'What is it?' he asks.

'What?' I say.

He is looking right at me. A brother better than my own by blood. I could take all his pain away now. Shoot him right through the eyes. It would be over quickly.

Then shoot Jed, then Poole.

It is our actions not our fears that make us a man. I can be a good man, a man who is a true friend, who does what no one else dares. I can free us all from the slavery of life.

'Hawker?' Vince says.

Freedom is always hard fought for.

'Hawker,' Vince shouts.

My gun is aimed at him.

The others stir from their grogged dreams.

Bats flap past the open door and wing it across the field. Dark agents of the night.

The night harbours possibilities not gleaned in the day but it also illuminates the boundaries that shape us.

I hear a call, like a bird but not a bird.

I walk to the door, keep my gun aimed at Vince. In the field, several natives are plucking corn.

Man is never free, always he is manipulated through physical coercion; if not coercion, there is hunger, brutality, or the misinformation that is distributed in pamphlets or pulpit. But now is the opportunity I have to free us from false living.

'HAWKER!' Vince shouts.

He cannot make out what is happening.

I look down. My mutts barking at my feet. I realise, as if in a dream, that they have been by me for some time.

My finger is on the trigger.

What is this wild place that fills me with terrible purpose?

It is some dark magic turning me away from my aim.

I shake my head to rid myself of cursed thoughts.

It is the *place* I must leave and those who inhabit it, those who work its dark magic. I must shoot the natives in the field and get to Appin. Leave this forest and never return.

'HAWKER!' Vince screams.

'Blacks!' I cry and swing my gun towards the open door.

The dogs run ahead as I stride from the hut.

'Go,' I shout, running down the steps.

The dogs sprint off in pursuit of their prey.

I walk across the dirt and on through the corn. It slaps my body like a tide on the turn. Leaf crunch underfoot.

Up ahead I spy wretched thieves still slashing husks.

The cheek. They think I won't shoot.

I lift the gun, wedge it into my shoulder, pull the trigger. I almost fall from the blast.

'I have one,' I shout to Vince.

But I am not sure I have.

Vince comes up behind me. 'Reload.'

I want to go on but he drags me back to the hut.

'Reload man, reload.'

Inside the hut the others are shadows shouting.

'Blacks,' I yell. 'Arm yourself.'

There is new purpose to my actions.

I kick at a chair, grab the ammunition, as if in a fever.

How many Blacks can I shoot?

I bite off the top of the cartridge and I am pouring the powder into the pan as I run back out. Jed blocks my path.

'We will tell them to leave,' Jed shouts.

Vince comes forward, he is tying a knife on the end of his gun.

'It is our weapons they will answer to,' Vince says.

He pushes Jed aside, runs across the threshold and down the steps. I follow Vince and we, two men in search of justice, stride into the field. My left hand aches and I must stop to pour the rest of the powder into the muzzle, shove in the ball and stuff down the paper. My ramrod sticks and I have to wriggle it out.

When I get it free I ram the paper, ball and powder down to the breech of the barrel, pull out the rod, and return it to its hold. I pull the lock to full cock, wedge the gun into my shoulder, and walk on. Alongside me, to the right, Lambskin holds a spear in one hand and a native axe in the other. Poole, on my left, swings a horse whip through the air. Vince, further on from Poole, has shouldered his rifle. Only Jed has stayed in the hut.

I spy a Black, moonlit and still on the edge of the field. Does he taunt me? The devil to that!

'Name, name, name,' I call.

No answer.

I aim and pull the trigger.

Vince calls, 'A hit?'

'Yes,' I say.

This time I am certain.

The Black has fallen between the cornfield and the trees. He is moaning, so not dead.

Vince runs to me. 'Are there more?'

I peer into the gloom.

Nothing moves.

'Any more?' Vince asks again.

'They have gone,' I say, fired up by my hit.

We walk to the edge of the field.

Vince runs ahead to the whimpering Black.

'Damn,' Vince shouts.

'What?' I yell.

'A woman.'

The woman screams. A warning perhaps.

I reload and fire into the trees in case any of her kind are lingering. 'Scat now or I will shoot you dead,' I shout, and stride up to Vince.

Lambskin and Poole run to us.

The woman starts to sob, the sound fills the night air.

The dogs bark at her.

Vince tells Lambskin and Poole to scout the forest boundary.

'I do *not* want a spear through my chest,' Poole says, his face packed with fear.

'If they were still here, there would be a spear in you now,' I say.

There is authority in my voice. I am the man that protects the cornfield.

Vince orders Poole and Lambskin on their way.

They slink off, searching the nearby trees. The dogs run with them. But Poole and Lambskin are quick to return.

Vince picks up the net of corn that lies alongside the woman.

'Nearly a peck,' I say. 'Would have wiped us clean.'

The woman's body is twisted, hair over her face. She is lying in the dirt. Her back arches as she tries to crawl away. She cannot go far. There is blood pooling beneath her. She must have been facing me when I shot her.

I want to know which one it is and go to turn her over.

'Do *not* touch her,' Vince says.

'What?'

'You will have to report at Appin tomorrow. To the constable.'

What is Vince doing? Making it all seem wrong.

'Brooks would not want his corn stolen,' I say.

The dogs run around the woman, barking.

She screams into the dirt.

Poole and Lambskin back away and stand at the edge of the cornfield.

'Better if you had shot a man,' Vince says, between gritted teeth.

'What difference?' I say, but do not believe it.

'There's a difference in the eyes of a magistrate,' Vince says. 'Easier to handcuff a woman. That is what the law now asks us to do with native thieves. Give them warning.'

'This is their warning,' I say.

At least Brooks will know I am a hard man. At least that. I *will* leave this place. Why not? Others have done worse than I have done here, and there has been no penalty.

Vince stares at the woman as she struggles to crawl forward, scratching at the dirt, whimpering. She makes no progress and emits one long moan, then slumps down, muttering in her language.

Vince turns to me. 'I know what to do,' he says.

He whistles to the dogs. They come to him. He gets down and rubs their necks.

'Set to it,' he says, kicking the woman's leg.

The dogs lick him, not understanding.

'What you doing?' I ask Vince.

He grins at me.

'Dogs mauled this woman,' he says.

'I shot her,' I say. 'Brooks needs to know that.'

'No. Listen to me. The dogs mauled her is what we will tell the magistrate,' Vince says.

'Tell the magistrate?'

'Leave Brooks to me,' Vince adds. 'I will get you to Appin.'

I see it now. See what Vince is doing. The fault for murder will lie with the dogs, not me. He has proved it now. He has proved he is a true friend.

'Get her, get her,' I shout to the dogs.

The dogs bark at me. Then they run around the woman, snarling and growling and pulling at her arms, so her body slides in the dirt.

'Get!' I say.

My biggest dog, the best hunter, rolls her over, snarls and rips at her stomach, tearing the flesh. The smaller dogs, drooling, bite into her thigh. She screams and gasps but has no power in her limbs to push them away. The dogs lift their blood-covered snouts and bark.

'Good dogs,' I say.

The woman turns her head to look at me.

She is muttering.

The hair falls from her face.

Only then do I see.

Her.

There, on her shoulder, the mottled bump that once so concerned me.

I squat down, feel something soft in me churn about.

Her.

I press my hand to the dirt, steady myself.

She groans and then sighs.

I see her eye flicker.

Her eye, judging.

Her eye, unforgiving.

I shake my head, clench my teeth.

There is no room for weakness in this place.

'Not guilty,' I whisper.

The dogs drag her away, but her head rolls back so she is facing me.

'We must live by the quick not by the deed,' Vince says.

'Yes,' I say.

I stand and look back to the hut. I do not want her eyes on me. It is too late now. It is done now.

But I stamp my feet because there is a lightness in my head that I must heave away. I am some other kind of man now. The man Vince Byrne needs at Appin. The man Captain Brooks needs to protect his fields from thieves.

I spy Jed in the doorway, lit up by the firelight. I raise my rifle, so the moon catches it. I want to show him that we have shot a Black. Want to show him what men do here.

Jed turns and walks inside. Perhaps searching for his pup.

'This night he is shaming me,' Vince says.

He turns and with his knife, slices his wrist. Blood slithers out, like a seeping tide.

'Hold out your arm,' he orders.

I do as he asks. He cuts my skin and presses our bloodied wrists together.

'Brother,' he says.

'Brother,' I say, and feel a rush of heat.

'We will say nothing of this deed,' he says, solemnly looking towards the woman.

'Agreed.'

I turn towards Poole and Lambskin, who are striding through the corn, making for the hut.

'What about those two?' I ask.

'They will do what I say,' Vince says. 'They dare not do otherwise if they want an easy ride. Jed too. He may be weak but he is loyal.'

I do not tell Vince what I did to Jed's pup.

It was yapping until the last bit of earth was shovelled on top.

One day I might tell Jed, tell him when he least expects it, tell him when the blow will hit hardest.

Or maybe not.

Vince never liked the pup and Jed's whinging about the loss will set him on edge. Vince will be glad of my company. It is a small plan compared to the events of this night. A silent story for this unsilent night.

Human events are like rivers, they change course depending on circumstance.

I am safe now.

Safe.

Vince will get me to the Appin farm. No matter what magistrates may say. I am the man that saved the corn. I say that to Vince.

He orders the dogs back from the woman. They come away.

I stare at her.

She lies in the dirt, the moon soft on her face.

Her red lips are parted, her eye still flickering.

She is staring at my boot.

She thought she could outfox me and that led to her downfall.

She should have known I would win out.

If she had done what I had told her, this would never have happened.

Her fault, not mine.

Hardly a breath in her now.

Not long and she will be gone.

The wind stirs the trees.

The flap of wings above, pelicans flying

Will Martin
1796

across

the sky. The Indians run along the sand and stop, several yards from us, all sun-smiles. We are as still as gravestones. Mr Bass and the lieutenant have had no time to gather a weapon. But I am ready, a burning stick in hand.

The natives keep dimpling. Is it a trick?

The Indian named Dilba steps forward. The lieutenant and I step back, but Mr Bass does not. Dilba, gabbling in his language, and jabbing a finger northwards, seizes Mr Bass's arm and pulls him along the shore.

'Ah,' Mr Bass calls back to us. 'He thinks we do not know where Port Jackson lies.'

The lieutenant said we were going north, but we went south. We cannot tell Dilba about our stratagems, yet he thinks us clodskulls.

If your enemy thinks you a clodskull, what then? Might it not make them braver? Is it not better for them to fear you?

'Thank you,' Mr Bass says to Dilba, who I remember cannot be our enemy after all, as he speaks the Port Jackson tongue like Na and like Baneelong.

The lieutenant mimes how we must first sup before we sail. Dilba and his friend watch closely, then laugh.

We are stood around the campfire.

The green sea is shiny.

The yellow sand is warming.

The scissors that Mr Bass has used to scale the fish lie on the ground, glinting.

Dilba's friend picks them up and walks away, his feet on the sand go *whoosh, whoosh* like silk on a lady's dress. The lieutenant mimes what you can do with the blades. Then, with friendly gestures, but with a nervous air, he grasps the scissors from Dilba's friend. His move is too hasty and the Indian knows it.

Dilba steps forward, his tall figure towering over the lieutenant.

For a tick-tock all is wave crash.

Eyes back and forth.

The lieutenant, laughing in pretence, takes hold of Dilba's beard.

Dilba swipes away the lieutenant's hand, darts back. Eyes toing and froing.

The burning stick is still in my hand. I wait. Are we friends or enemies? It is yet to be confirmed.

The lieutenant grabs a clump of his own hair. He snips it off and offers it to Dilba who takes it, stares like a mute. The lieutenant again reaches for Dilba's beard. Dilba, wary. The lieutenant raises the scissors and snips. He holds a clump of Dilba's beard in the air.

Tick-tock.

Dilba grins.

The lieutenant leans forward, takes another snip. Dilba's friend laughs and points. The lieutenant snips and snips until Dilba's beard is trimmed and his hair cut. The friend doubles over he is laughing so much.

The Indians laugh like us, only they laugh more. This is my discovery.

Dilba's friend wants his hair shorn now. We all come closer as the lieutenant snips. Mr Bass sings a barber's ditty, and Dilba sings it after him, in perfect English, in perfect tune. It is no mean feat. Uncle Hilton and Mama would be astonished at his skill. The Indians are our friends, it is clear.

Gulls circle above, and the fire spits. The fish is cooked. We sit and eat, pulling the flesh from the bones. We invite our friends to join us. They eat the same way we do. This is proof that they are not cannibals.

'*Bādo?*' Mr Bass asks Dilba, scooping up imaginary water.

Bādo is the word we learnt for water.

Dilba points south. 'Water,' he says, copying Mr Bass's action for scooping water.

'River?' Mr Bass asks.

'River, there,' Dilba says.

Dilba speaks only some words of English, but his accent, Mr Bass says, is splendid. Dilba raises his head the way Na does to indicate direction.

'River?' Mr Bass points south again, to confirm.

'Yes,' Dilba says. 'River, there.'

Mr Bass and the lieutenant look to each other. Maybe *this* is the river Henry Hacking has talked about? Or if not, it may be another river, not yet seen by Hacking or any other, except for Dilba and his ilk. The thrill of it. Maybe this is the river that, with waters deep, will lead us to the heart of the land. Maybe this is the river that will make rise our monument.

What strange twists of fate. We would not have come this far south if not for water spoiled by storage in a wine barica. And where I had felt bad about the troubles we have endured, now the fate of those actions may lead to a great discovery.

But this swelling does not last long, for, as Mr Bass and the lieutenant debate the river, I spy Dilba's sly look to his friend.

A look of malice?

I remember the cannibal story from Calcutta. I remember also the lieutenant's words. Do not let your enemy know your next move. Could these Indians be feigning friendship? What might be their next move? Dilba's eyes are half-open. Eyes half-open mark men that are slippery in their thoughts. Uncle Hilton told me this for he has always played Iago with a half-open eye. The lieutenant and Mr Bass, not having stage skill, see none of it.

'Mr Bass, the wind is the wrong way about for returning north,' the lieutenant says.

'It is indeed,' agrees Mr Bass, with a wink to me. 'Lieutenant Flinders, are we not in desperate need of water?'

How to tell them what I know about Dilba without giving away the game?

'Impossible to return north without water,' says the lieutenant.

'Agreed,' says Mr Bass. 'Unquestionable that it is impossible to return north without water.'

Lieutenant Flinders and Mr Bass both turn to me. 'Mister Martin?' they chorus.

They are speaking as if I am to decide. I am baffled. I nod my agreement, we need water. My throat is so dry it is hard to swallow.

'So be it,' Mr Bass says and rubs his hands above the fire.

'So be it,' Lieutenant Flinders agrees.

'We will sail to the river,' Mr Bass explains to Dilba who has not understood.

Now I spot their ruse. They are rehearsing what to say to the governor. If the governor asks, *Why did you disobey my instructions and sail further south?* Their reasons will be practised. True, we are all in desperate need of a drink. But Mr Bass and Lieutenant Flinders have a greater intention. That intention lies between words, or behind them. This river could change our destiny is what they think.

Lieutenant Flinders mimes us all getting in the boat and sailing south. Dilba claps his hands and points. He will show the way. Mr Bass and the lieutenant begin to pack our things.

I stand by the fire. If I do not move, Mr Bass will notice me. Then, I will signal by my eyes that we cannot go. But Mr Bass and the lieutenant continue packing. Reckless with ambition, they pay no heed to me or the Indians. I run to Mr Bass.

'Sir, what if the Indians mean to trick us?' I whisper.

'It was we who asked them to assist in our search for water,' Mr Bass says. 'And I lie not when I say I am blasted thirsty.'

'Must we not obey the governor's orders to the letter?' I ask.

Mr Bass gives me a sour look. 'And that was to find a river.'

'A river that joins the sea just south of Botany Bay,' I say. 'We are a long way from that mark.'

'Are you afraid?' he asks me.

'No,' I say, for I will not have him think me cowardly. But I curse the day I did not check the barica was clean. Curse the day I asked to crew *Tom Thumb*. Curse the day I left England.

As I stomp out the fire I spy Dilba watching me. His hand flicks up. A signal to his friend? I pretend not to see.

We shove off from the shallows, Mr Bass at the helm. The lieutenant and I step the mast, and we set sail. Dilba sits next to Mr Bass. Mr Bass has put on his red coat, as if to mark the importance of the occasion. Dilba's friend sits silent at the bow, as if he does not like to travel by boat. I will have to watch them both, for my elders, in their rashness, are like babes.

Out on the ocean, the water is choppy. All around us is blue sea. In the far, on the horizon where the sun rises each day, strings of clouds in neat rows, like the sheet music Uncle Hilton uses to sing. Over on shore, for a very long way, it is scrubby bush and high sand dunes. Beyond the dunes are two hills, Hat Hill, and the other, not yet named perhaps, and running between the hills and on either side of them, the green escarpment.

The wind picks up and we are sailing fast.

'To the river,' Mr Bass says.

Dilba watches him. '*Yoorongi*,' he says and points south.

'Wild duck?' Mr Bass asks.

'*Yoorongi* in water place?' the lieutenant asks.

'*Moremme*,' Dilba says.

'He says yes,' Mr Bass tells the lieutenant. 'What else?' Mr Bass asks Dilba.

A wave comes crashing over the side of *Thumb* and when I look up, wiping water from my face, Mr Bass and Dilba are laughing.

'What?' Lieutenant Flinders leans forward to hear.

'Dilba tells me that at this river there is Indian corn and potatoes,' Mr Bass says. 'But more than that, he swears there is a beautiful white woman who tends it all.'

'Ah,' the lieutenant shouts. 'Then he has known explorers before us. Or whalers.'

Dilba points to me and this makes Mr Bass laugh louder. My cheeks flush with heat. I turn away. Usually it is Moore, the ship's master, who stirs me about women. I always feign boredom. I know what goes on. It is all over the cove. If a man has stirrings, no mind the flavour, anything can be supped. White or black, woman or boy, even child, all is there and up for trade. If no coin is had, spirits will do, even flour. When Mr Bass lets me have free roam, Na and I kick around the campfires at night. We see those that go cock-a-hoop for a bit of flesh. Hoary Bogarty growls as he distributes goods from the store, but to see him with a woman by firelight and watch how he fondles her bosom is to see how he fair turns into a dribbling pup.

Mr Bass calls to the lieutenant. 'Matthew, Dilba is offering you the white woman.'

'No white woman could live so far from civilisation,' the lieutenant shouts over the splash of waves.

I look across the sea to the scrubby land. Before we left Sydney Cove two escaped convicts were reported to be living with Hawkesbury tribes. But there are farms on the Hawkesbury that the escaped men raid. This far south, there are no farms to be had. Few animals. That is why there are cannibals. To live here would be too great a risk. Even Cook did not land in this wild place.

Seawater spurts before my eyes. I lean over the gunwale and spy the sleek back of a dolphin. More romp in the water alongside, swim under the boat and to the front of *Thumb* where they rise up through the air with newborn squeaks. I eye one for his scarred back and swear he eyes me in return. The dolphins swim off in haste. I look starboard and see, in the water beyond, a feeding hubbub. Silver fish jump from the water to feed on smaller prey. Circling them, dark-finned sharks. Above, gulls swoop to pick off what they can. It is as if all creatures of the sea and air have come to join a flipping, flapping dance of death.

I grip the gunwale. This sight is a bad omen, surely.

We sail towards the beach. The escarpment runs along the land like a giant's arm, cradling trees from hilltop to shore. No river is visible beneath the canopy of green, but I spy the glint of water trickling through the sand dunes. The others see it too.

'Our river,' shouts Mr Bass. 'Soon we will be drinking fresh water.'

We strike sail and take up oars.

Splish, splash, splish, splash, to dare is to do.

'It is no more than a stream,' the lieutenant calls as we get closer, disappointment dripping from him.

'It may widen past the bend,' Mr Bass replies.

The entrance to the stream is a yeasty beast, and the wind howls like a child in tantrum. No way to enter yet Dilba, pointing and waving, his language his own, gives directions like a ship's captain. We navigate the surf as if it were a rocky path – straight towards the mouth, then one side, then the other. Soon we are through and rowing upstream against a strong tide.

Dilba and his friend jump from *Thumb* and splash through the shallows. They begin to stride the wide sandy bank beside us. They call out. I cannot catch their words.

Our boat scrapes the bed of the stream and I turn my attention to pulling. The lieutenant joins with me. From shrubs on the shore, men appear, like tricksy spirits: first one, then another and another, as if the land is coughing them up. Dilba and his friend have their backs to us. I cannot spy their countenance. The Indians from the bush stand and stare at us, then at Dilba and his friend. I count the Indians. Ten have gathered. The men have grizzled beards that go to their navel and sharp bones through their noses.

No one speaks. They have a spirit way of talking. It must be that.

All is still.

And then, when I think they must be threatening even to Dilba and his friend, the Indians begin to shout and laugh and stroll along the bank. Their dogs run to the shallows but do not bark. Are they devils in dogs' bodies?

The Indians wave and call to us, *Soga, Soga!* – but could their *friendly* be a trap?

Mr Bass says they call out *Soga* for soldier and it is because of his red waistcoat that is the same colour as a soldier's. Dilba, striding the shallow water, points to the hills. We look that way and now spy a shimmering lagoon.

'But the stream is scarce deep enough to get us there,' says the lieutenant.

'Once there, we would have to wait for the tide to get us back down,' Mr Bass says. 'We are too vulnerable,' he warns, eyeing the men on shore.

'We must dry our powder and clean the muskets or else we have no safety,' the lieutenant whispers. 'Then, if we are armed, we could walk to fresh water.'

Mr Bass studies the men on shore. 'The mood appears light. Perhaps we could risk going ashore here.'

'Or turn now, go back now,' I say.

'We need water,' the lieutenant says. 'Without it we will die.'

'They mean us harm,' I say.

'To show fear would be a mistake.' The lieutenant ships his oars. 'We have no arms in working order. If we retreat now they could easily overcome us. But their intentions may not yet be formed. If we keep them friendly, go ashore, find water, dry the powder, we will be prepared for attack on land or sea.'

Birds swoop across the stream, catch buzzing insects in their beaks.

'Are we for shore?' Mr Bass asks.

'Yes,' says the lieutenant.

Mr Bass turns to me. 'Will?'

The Indians are shouting. I go to speak but all is slow and heavy and I hear only insect hum. No, I am *not* for it. Yet Mr Bass will think me cowardly if I say so.

'Good,' Mr Bass says, as if I have answered.

He jumps from *Thumb* and, splashing through the water, begins to haul the boat to shore. The lieutenant and I clamber over the gunwale and join him. As soon as we step on land the Indians circle us. They touch our hair and finger our clothes.

'*Bādo?*' Mr Bass asks for water, his question almost a command.

I haul the barica out of the boat.

Dilba points to the lagoon, wants us to walk that way.

'No.' The lieutenant hits the gunwale. 'We stay with our boat.'

Dilba runs along the sand, pointing and jabbering, but too on the hop for me to catch even one word.

I stand away to observe the belly of water he indicates.

An old Indian grips my arm, bends it back, and pushes me into the shrubby trees. The surprise takes my voice away.

This is it, I think, I am soon to meet my end!

In his hair I see yellowed teeth. Human? Such as cannibals wear?

A few steps into the trees, I stumble. When I look up the old man is pointing to a small pond. He smiles, revealing the pink of his mouth. It is water he is showing me! He has no evil purpose. The teeth, I now see, are kangaroo teeth, like those our Port Jackson natives wear.

I kneel on the sand and put my lips to the water to test for salt. I have had worse at the Tank Stream. I drink in all I can. The water cools my face. Leaves dance in the air. The old man sits next to me, runs his hand through the sandy soil, then pats it.

'*Bamal*,' he says.

'Soil,' I say. I have played this word game before.

I fetch a rough stone and rub down the barica, sluice it with water and fill it as far as I can. The old man babbles in his own tongue. I talk to him with the Port Jackson speak I learnt from Baneelong, but he does not understand.

The old man lays a rock axe on the ground. I spy it at first with caution and then with interest, because Indian tools fetch a high price back in London. The hewn rock is many interesting colours, bluish green and brown, and the handle is made from a strong dark wood bound with twisted vine. I offer to trade my hat, but the Indian shakes his head. The more I look at the axe, the more I think how useful it would be on the journey home and how it would impress all on the *Reliance*. I offer to trade my shirt but still the Indian shakes his head. I try to impress him with our expedition.

'We are looking for a big river.' I make my arms bend, like the flow of a river. 'Swoosh, swoosh,' I say.

The old man pats the earth.

'No, no, river,' I say. 'Big enough to sail ships down.' I stand and move in the wind, like the sail of a boat. The old man laughs and shakes his head as if it is me who is the halfwit. I mime unloading a large vessel but he is no wiser to our purpose.

He refuses the deal, and I know I must give it up. As we go to leave I help him stand to show I have no bad feeling about our lack of trade and that makes him laugh even more. They can be a jolly lot, the Indian men.

When we come out of the shrubs Lieutenant Flinders and Mr Bass are in a huddle with Dilba and the other Indians. The old man lopes over to them. I follow but get seized by a branch and stop to untangle myself.

The lieutenant shouts my name. He and Mr Bass stride over to me.

Mr Bass runs his hand through my hair. 'Will, do not scare us like that again.'

The lieutenant says he is pleased to see my scrawny face.

'I was getting water,' I explain.

'Water!' they say, delighted.

Mr Bass and I hold the barica up. The lieutenant gulps water from the spout. Then Mr Bass takes his fill.

'If water has been close by all this time,' Lieutenant Flinders whispers, 'why has Dilba been luring us to the lagoon?'

'To meet a darker purpose?' Mr Bass suggests.

Now is the time to say the old man has shown me the water, but I do not because there is a hollering from the Indians. Their number has now increased to twenty, with more following. The old man points at me. My fears return. Could the old man be full of trickery?

Mr Bass drinks again. 'Good work, Will,' he murmurs.

'Stow the barica in *Thumb*,' the lieutenant says. 'We will dry the gunpowder, then depart.'

But as we walk to the boat, the Indians stop their yabbering and watch our every move.

'Reveal no haste,' the lieutenant says.

Slowly he takes hold of the powder horns. Slowly Mr Bass retrieves the muskets. Slowly I stow the barica beneath the thwart then fetch some twine as the oar needs repairing. I hear the sea roar and wish us back on the ocean. Back in the spray and the open air and not watched by these many eyes.

The lieutenant, like the fairy godmother in a pantomime, sprinkles the gunpowder on a cloth to dry in the sun and lays out the wet paper beside it. All is ease.

Mr Bass sits to clean a musket, tips it up between his knees, but at that action the Indians holler and run at him, waving spears.

I jump to and grip the oar as a weapon, but Mr Bass halts me with his eyes. Steadily, he lays his musket down on the sand. His careful action quiets the Indians. But still they hold their spears high, eyes shooting back and forth, from Mr Bass to the musket.

Mr Bass calls for the twine and oar. I take them to him. He places the oar across his knee and begins to wrap twine around the split wood. I stare at the Indians with their raised spears. Hear only my breathing. Then, birds in the shrubs, their faint twittering. Insects drone. An ant the size of a beetle crawls across my foot.

The Indians lower their weapons. One of them, no older than me as he has no beard, comes closer and sits on the sand, observing Mr Bass's task. Another sits next to the first, picks up the ball of twine and threads it out as Mr Bass twists it around the oar.

The lieutenant calls me over. 'This is the shock of the Indians,' he whispers. 'Savage one moment, child the next. Keep alert, Will, keep alert.'

But an easier mood settles upon our temporary camp.

A long-bearded man now points to Dilba's short beard. Dilba, smiling, jabbers how the lieutenant has snipped it. He speaks fast. I can pick out some words. *Yarrin*, the word for beard. *Dewarra*, the word for hair.

'*Boodyerre*,' Dilba says, miming the scissors cutting his beard.

'You have become famous, Matthew,' Mr Bass says. 'These men want their beards cut.'

The lieutenant walks to *Thumb* to collect the scissors. I find myself a sturdy stick. These Indians are warriors and I will be ready to fight if this request for beard cutting be a ruse. To dare is to do. To dare is to do. I say this over and over.

All the Indians watch the lieutenant who sets up a log

330

as his barber's chair and points to it. The old man who took me to the pond is the first to sit. The lieutenant grips the old man's beard that lies like an arrested waterfall upon his chest, and makes to snip the end of it. But the old man, surprised by the blades coming towards him, leans back and falls from the log.

The Indians holler. I raise my stick.

Dilba, knowing what scissors are, picks the old man up, jabbering to him all the while. The old man raises his eyebrows, nods and grunts, then sits again on the log. He stares straight into the eyes of the lieutenant who again takes hold of the old man's beard and now begins to cut.

The Indians murmur, watching the lieutenant's actions with surprise and laughter. Soon shouting, like a soldier's huzzah, accompanies each snip.

'Mr Hogarth would find this man a fascinating subject for his canvas,' calls the lieutenant.

'It may be beyond Hogarth,' replies Mr Bass.

'Never,' says the lieutenant.

'Oh, I know he creates portraiture true in its reveal, but to divine the Indian nature might need a different sort of man,' Mr Bass says.

The Indians clap and shout as the lieutenant snips.

'Perhaps the void between us *is* too great, even for an artist such as Hogarth,' the lieutenant calls above the noise.

The sun beats down. The sand is hot. Insects nip at my skin. Indian dogs sniff at my feet.

The first barbering is finished. The lieutenant bows like an actor on the stage. The Indians surround the old man. Some reach out to touch his shortened beard. Others laugh and jabber as if this shorn beard is some wonder of the earth.

A second Indian steps forward. The lieutenant snips a lock of this man's beard and holds it to his own beardless chin. The Indians clap and holler.

A tall man with many teeth twisted through his hair, and with muscles as tight as a barrel, reaches out and wipes some sweat from the lieutenant's forehead. The lieutenant starts back, gripping the scissors. But the Indian is still, all his attention given to his fingertips. With his left hand he reaches up to his own forehead, thickly covered in fish oil, and wipes at it, then holds his two fingers out in front of him, as if comparing.

'A fellow scientist,' Mr Bass suggests.

'Or a cook checking his ingredients,' the lieutenant jokes.

Lieutenant Flinders continues with his barbering, but the tall Indian's interest has bothered him and he calls me over.

'Will, pack that powder now. Wet or dry I think we must be satisfied and take our leave. The natives are friendly, but my suspicion is they are too friendly.'

With internal quivering such as I dare not display, I filter the gunpowder back into the horns (wet in one, dry in the other), then gather the near-dry cartridge papers, wrap them in hide, and with bravado make my way across the sand to *Thumb*. Mr Bass, understanding the lieutenant's intention, brings the muskets and mended oar. The lieutenant takes his last snip.

Then he too makes his way to our trusted vessel. The Indians, astonished at their new beards, do not notice our preparations for departure. Except for Dilba who comes running. He grips the lieutenant's arm and hauls him towards the lagoon.

'Lagoon,' Dilba says, having already learnt our word for it.

The lieutenant, spooked, shakes himself free with a growl. The savage glares and makes to again take the lieutenant's arm, but the lieutenant signals against it and steps backwards towards our boat, careful never to let his eyes leave those of his assailant.

The savage's arms begin to circle the air, like a watermill in a fierce wind.

'Why is he so violent in his request?' the lieutenant whispers when he reaches us.

'It is strange,' says Mr Bass.

'We must put the Indians off in a friendly way and make our escape without them suspecting,' the lieutenant decides.

Mr Bass calls to Dilba and gestures our friendship by palms held forth, flat and open.

'Tomorrow, we will visit the lagoon,' he promises.

Mr Bass turns away from Dilba, beckons me, and together we push *Thumb* into the water using idle chatter and false laughter to disguise our proper purpose.

Meanwhile the lieutenant, aiming to calm Dilba, points downstream to a green bank that is near the bend in the stream. He puts his folded hands to the side of his face, feigning sleep.

'We must rest. We go to that green bank there,' the lieutenant says.

This news, however, has the opposite effect to the lieutenant's intention. Dilba runs back to his fellow savages in alarm, and the men stop admiring their beards and turn to stare at us.

'Get *Thumb* into the middle of the stream,' the lieutenant calls. 'I will keep them occupied.' He walks towards the Indians with exaggerated leg movements, as though exhaustion has set in, and again he puts his hands to his cheek and repeats our need for sleep. The lieutenant has a feel for the comic and could be the best of actors if he took up the trade.

But the wily Dilba is not to be distracted. The savage shakes his head and points at our desired location in disgust. He does not want us to go there, that much is certain, but what is his objection? It is a bank like any other bank. A cacophony of shouts erupt from the natives, whose numbers continue to increase, and twenty or more of their dogs run to the shoreline.

Mr Bass and I, having waded to the place where the water is deepest, clamber on board *Thumb*.

'Matthew, come now,' Mr Bass yells.

Still carrying on with his antics the lieutenant splashes into the water and makes his way to us. I pull him on board.

'Show no fear, Will,' the lieutenant orders as we take up our oars.

With smiling faces we begin to row and are nearly away when four spear-holding Indians hasten into the water after us, wade out and jump into *Thumb*. There are seven of us bearing down on *Thumb*'s creaking timbers and, in consequence, our little boat sinks lower in the stream.

I row faster, fearing for my life, praying that Mr Bass, with his great strength, will push the natives off. But there is no escaping our terror. A howling erupts from the shore. All the savages standing there raise their spears up high and, in a single burst, hurtle into the stream, hooting as they splash their way to our boat, surrounding it. The lieutenant and I pull and pull but, still, I am surprised when *Thumb* glides along easily. How is this possible? Then I see the cause. For the natives are pushing our boat and it is their strength that is giving us pace. The Indians begin to whoop and sing, the din unnerving.

Mr Bass bursts into a sailor's shanty.

'Sing, Will,' he calls out, sternly.

Soon we are all singing and such a savage clamouring I have never heard. There is much laughter, but there is *too* much laughter. Shall we survive our ordeal and leave this place alive?

When we are near the green bank, those Indians in the boat jump into the water. One, as he departs, snatches Mr Bass's hat and, dropping it onto his own head, makes for shore.

Mr Bass, unthinking, shouts, 'My hat!'

The Indian turns and raises his spear, ready to throw. He has no bone through his nose and no teeth in his hair, but his expression is all wildness. I let the oar rest and grip the sharpened stick I have kept by my side. My old native friend, the same who revealed the pond, hollers at the wild one who, fierceness in his countenance, wades towards us. I plant my feet, ready to fight but, to my surprise, the Indian stops, takes the hat from his head, and tosses it into the boat with a laugh, as if the whole event had been nothing more than a lark. He bows to Mr Bass, a perfect copy of the theatrical flourish the lieutenant exhibited earlier.

'Shove off, Will,' the lieutenant hollers. 'Make for the ocean.'

I use my oar to push us into deeper water. We begin to row at pace towards the mouth of the stream, but the Indians, still in good spirits or pretending so, and still believing the green bank to be our destination, and now seemingly happy for that occurence, begin again to haul the boat to shore.

'Stop there!' the lieutenant yells.

'Halt. Halt!' Mr Bass joins in.

The Indians – intent on getting the boat to shore or howling so loudly that they themselves cannot hear – do not stop. Again it is my old friend who sees our red faces and, taking his hand from the gunwale, shouts an order to his fellow savages.

The Indians stop and stand like statues in the shallows. More than forty eyes staring. More than twenty muscled bodies with spears aloft. And dogs aplenty. We are but three. Sea roar and insect buzz. The boat drifts on the current.

It is the lieutenant who shakes us from our stupor. 'Pull, Will, pull!' he shouts, dipping his oar into the water.

Mr Bass takes up a musket from beneath the thwart and aims it at the Indians. A ruse, as the gun is still clogged with sand. But it does the trick as the Indians do not move. We row towards the sea. My eyes steady on the savages as they become smaller and smaller.

'That was well suffered,' Mr Bass says when we round the bend and the sight of the Indians is lost to us.

'We are not out of it yet, George,' the lieutenant replies.

'They have the numbers. They have the spears. If they wanted they could kill us all,' Mr Bass says. 'They do not and the why escapes me.'

'They have no definite plan, no strategy,' the lieutenant replies.

'What was their laughing about?' I ask Mr Bass.

'Indian mood shifts like the weather,' the lieutenant says. 'It cannot be explained.'

We ride the stream to where it meets the sea. The salt breeze slaps my face, the ocean noise, thunderous. Waves crash over us. *Whoosh* goes one wave, *whoosh* goes another.

'Blast! We cannot cross the sandbar till the tide turns,' Mr Bass shouts.

'Anchor,' orders the lieutenant.

We ship our oars and drop anchor. The water around our boat is deep enough, thanks to the current running out from the stream, but white foamy waves keep whipping us. It is fifteen yards on either side to the shore. We are safe for the time from savage attack.

The lieutenant and Mr Bass begin in haste to clean the musket barrels that are still full of sand. We will need arms if the Indians come for us again.

I pour some of the dry powder onto a scrap of paper and place a musket ball in it. I make up two cartridges this way, but there is no more dry paper. I begin to tear strips off my shirt. If we need to fire more shots we will have to use cotton to stuff the balls down the barrel.

We are all working at a feverish pace, our boat lurching as waves sluice over the gunwale. I keep a steady eye on the stream, the white sand and the scrubby trees.

No natives appear. Gulls flap on the shore. My breath slows.

Tick-tock.

I keep my eyes peeled.

Tick-tock.

We may be out of the horror yet.

Tick-tock.

But then I spy Dilba tramping around the bend, ten savages following. 'Here they come,' I shout.

The men wade across the stream from the northern bank and stand on the point to the south of us.

Dilba puts his hand to his mouth. 'Lagoon?' he calls.

'Why is he still at us?' I ask.

The lieutenant shouts, 'Yes, yes! If the wind and surf doesn't abate, then we shall go.'

'Lagoon!' shouts Dilba.

'When the sun goes down,' Mr Bass calls.

Several times the lieutenant, Mr Bass and Dilba shout in this way, like noisy magpies saying goodnight.

'*Coing burregoolah. Coing burregoolah,*' Mr Bass finally calls.

It is the Port Jackson speak for the sun setting.

'That may steal us some time,' Mr Bass says.

Why does Dilba insist we go to the lagoon? If I was to kill someone I would not flag it so.

'What is at the lagoon?' I ask Mr Bass.

'Death,' Mr Bass says to me. 'Nothing more than death.'

The lieutenant has his barrel clean and is wiping sand from the trigger. Mr Bass has freed the rod from his musket, but his trigger is still clogged with sand.

The Indians sit on the shore, staring at us. The sun drops behind the hills. The sea flickers with fading light and the clouds redden.

There is no movement from the south but, just when I again think we are safe, I see five Indians come out from the scrub to the north. They splash into the water.

'Look there,' I warn.

The men wade towards us. What to do? I still have my stick.

Mr Bass raises his musket, but it is all pretence for his trigger is still jammed.

'Round,' the lieutenant orders and pulls the lock of his musket to half cock.

I hand him a cartridge. He bites the top off the measure, salts the pan and closes it. He casts over and pours the rest of the powder down the barrel of the gun, pushes in the ball and paper.

The lieutenant's actions are fast and I know he is an excellent shot. He takes the rod, rams it down the barrel, shafts the rod and pulls the hammer back.

The Indians make good time. The seawater is soon frothing at their sides. One of them looks like Dilba's friend, but as there are five coming for us – with water splashing between them, and our boat in motion – I cannot be sure.

'Present,' shouts Mr Bass.

The lieutenant twists his body and lifts his firearm to his shoulder.

'It will fright them enough even if you miss,' Mr Bass says.

'We cannot be sure.' The lieutenant keeps his gun steady. 'Have you a second cartridge, Will?'

'Yes, sir,' I say.

'Fire,' Mr Bass hollers.

'Mr Bass, leave this to me,' the lieutenant snaps.

'They are getting closer,' I shout.

'Fire!' Mr Bass cries out.

The Indians are up to their chests in water now.

'Lieutenant!' I shout.

'A few more yards,' the lieutenant says coolly, holding his aim.

'Lieutenant Flinders, fire!' Mr Bass is screaming now.

'You would be no good in battle, George, with that temper.' The lieutenant is strangely calm.

'They are nearly upon us, sir,' I yell.

Seagulls scoot overhead, squealing. *Karr! Karr! Karr!*

'Fire!' Mr Bass cries out.

Thumb rocks in the waves.

The lieutenant steadies himself, and shoots.

Boom! Smoke drifts up from the musket. A mad hollering from the Indians. They fling their arms into the air.

The lieutenant makes to reload his musket but now his lock jams.

'They are going,' I cry out, as the Indians turn and splash towards the beach.

The lieutenant spits on his rag and cleans around the lock.

The Indians reach the shore. They do not look back at us but disappear into the scrub.

'Excellent execution, Matthew,' Mr Bass says.

The lieutenant's face is drained of colour. I grip the gunwale.

To the south of us, Dilba and the other Indians stand and begin to wail. The waves lap at their feet, but none dare enter the water. Then, one by one, they leave the beach until only Dilba is left, a lone figure, tall against the shadowy bushes. When the light is almost gone, he too turns and walks into the scrub.

'And it is done,' the lieutenant says.

'They will not return?' Mr Bass asks.

'I doubt it,' the lieutenant says.

Waves crash onto the shore. One lone gull rides the surf. The beach blackens. The lieutenant, more used to battle, lies down to sleep and is soon snoring. Mr Bass says he cannot sleep. The day has had too much charge. He and I sit in the moonlight, watch the darkened banks, and wait for the change of tide.

When the moon is part way in the sky, the water calms and the currents are for us. I wake the lieutenant. He sits up with a start, rubs his face then slaps it awake. He and I take up oars. Mr Bass stays at the helm. We pull towards the first of the small islets north of the stream.

Splish, splash, to dare is to do. *Splish, splash*, to dare is to do.

When we are near the closest islet it is clear there is no place to land. Mr Bass and I push the anchor over the side. I look to him. He is smiling, glad to be alive, but I do not feel the same gladness. Every part of me is shaken. If the Indians wanted us dead why did they not throw spears? What was up at the lagoon? Mr Bass says death. But why must we go to the lagoon for death?

I sit staring at the shore.

'Have some melon,' says Mr Bass.

But I have no stomach for it. *Splish, splash*, to dare is to do.

'We will call this islet after you, Mister Martin,' says Mr Bass.

The lieutenant agrees. 'You handled yourself well today, Will.'

I look about me. The islet is the kind that might vanish in heavy surf. *Splish, splash*. I remember the old man patting the earth. There is a question in his action. I remember Dilba's dark figure standing on the shore. I look up to the stars that shine. All about me there is a vast unknowing. Mr Bass and the lieutenant jabber on. I ache to know what might be the Indians' purpose. Would they have eaten us? I start to shake. I am not frightened now but I am in awe at the mysteries of this strange world. Sometimes being alive is too much. It is like a new rope-knot that I have never seen before and cannot untie.

I wish that I were home. At least with Mama and Uncle Hilton adventures into the wild are always fictions shaped for pleasure and death comes with fake swords.

I put my arms around my head. Mr Bass and the lieutenant continue with their discourse, but their voices are far away. Despite the cold, I fall into a deep slumber.

Monday, our fifth day. The morning is bright, and the breeze is up. According to the lieutenant, I have faced a foe and survived.

'We left them puzzling our very nature,' agrees Mr Bass.

Yesterday is like a dream. My spirit, again hungry for adventure, soars.

We step the mast and hoist sail, but the breeze soon shifts, blowing one way, then another. The sea becomes a bubbling soup, and the clouds lumpy dumplings.

We strike the sail and pull for land.

When the sun is above us, we row through a gap in a reef, enter a shielded bay and haul up on the beach. We climb out of *Thumb* like old men, our arms sore from pulling and our bodies aching from three nights sleeping on a boat. Yet the sun is warm on my skin, and there are no Indian footprints on the sand.

Carefully, I help Mr Bass undress. His shirt sticks to his body where his burnt skin has blistered. I ease him free. He runs into the sea, ducks below the waves, shoots up out of the water and bellows. The lieutenant and I look to each other and laugh. We strip off our clothes and race to join him. I dive into the cool water and swim as far as I can, then turn to float on my back.

Seabirds, flying low, pluck insects from the air. A cool breeze washes over me. Mr Bass swims out and circles me like a shark; the lieutenant paddles his way. When he reaches us, he grins as though pleased to have made it, then dunks me beneath the sea. We three wrestle in the water, like brothers. I have never known such happy abandonment. I stroke my way to shore, run out of the water and bound along the sand to dry off. Then I collect sticks, light a fire beneath a shady tree and boil a soup cake.

Mr Bass and the lieutenant stay an age in the water. Eventually they wade out. Mr Bass gently rubs his body with a cloth. The lieutenant hops in circles around the fire, his teeth chattering like a child. Mr Bass suggests I rinse the salt from the pork and add the meat to the soup.

'A neat culinary trick,' he says with relish.

Mr Bass looks forward to every meal as if it is his last. Food is pleasure. For the lieutenant food should not be savoured, for anything savoured is missed when in short supply. Instead, he suggests, food should only be thought of as necessary sustenance.

'Come, Will, we will search for fresh water,' says the lieutenant. 'What we have is good enough, but still a little briny for my liking.'

Mr Bass watches the soup while the lieutenant and I, naked as the Indians, scramble over slippery rocks. We find a place where water is trickling down from the cliff.

I tip my head back to taste it. Sweet and clear.

The lieutenant does the same. 'This will do,' he says.

He leaves me there to fill the barica. Slow drips but I am in no hurry. I spy a gecko run across a rock. A spider drops down on a fine thread of web and dangles before me. Seagulls land on the cliff above, squawking.

I stroll back to camp happy to have my feet on firm ground. My sad spirit from the night before has withered and a new one has grown in its place.

Perhaps a man must always ride the waves of turmoil before finding peace. Perhaps it has always been so.

I make bread the way our cook showed me. The lieutenant scribbles in his journal. Mr Bass fossicks in the scrub, picking up insects and inspecting plants and bones. He stores his collection in the shade.

We are a pleasant camp, and our spirits are much restored. I dish out soup and we sup.

'How would it be if all they wanted was to show us a river?' I say, thinking of our trials the day before.

I dip some bread into my soup but, before I bite into it, I spy Mr Bass and the lieutenant staring at me. They have both stopped eating. I need to explain myself.

'Because what if a larger river ran into the lagoon?' I say.

Is this such a strange thought? Surely not? Mr Bass looks to the lieutenant but the lieutenant does not take his eye from me. I am sure that fright crosses his face but then he banishes it.

'Impossible hypothesis,' the lieutenant says confidently. 'A river of any strength reveals itself at the coast.' He turns to Mr Bass. 'We must make sure the governor realises that too, else he might doubt us for further endeavours.'

The lieutenant continues eating, but I have unsettled Mr Bass, who sits staring into the fire.

Later, I walk in the scrub collecting more sticks. The wood is dry and smells of the sea. The sun sets and the dunes take on new shapes. The sand cools. Small animals rustle in the grasses. The stars come out, like lamps in a faraway town.

I make a vow, yet again, to hold my thoughts, because the lieutenant was not pleased with my river contemplations and I now feel a wedge between us where an hour earlier there had been none. I trail away, further than I mean to and, when I come back to camp, my arms full of sticks, Mr Bass and the lieutenant are at each other.

'The primitive mind,' Mr Bass says angrily, 'does not *just* belong to the primitive but to us all.'

'Yes, my point exactly! Take the French,' says the lieutenant.

'Take them where?' Mr Bass snaps.

'Take their inclination to rise against their king.'

'But we must all rise,' Mr Bass says. 'Man is like bread. To improve the quality of his mind, he *must* rise.'

I feed some sticks into the fire.

'Progress needs order and order needs hierarchy,' the lieutenant argues. 'It is the ladder of civilisation, with a top and a bottom. You cannot climb in disorder, George.'

Lieutenant Flinders lays out his thoughts, like neat piles of sand.

'If you know where you are placed, top or bottom, king or subject, you know about civilisation,' he says. 'These Indians mock us because they have no idea of our superiority. Their ignorance makes them arrogant. They have no understanding of order. The French did a great disservice to their country, trying to rid their society of the order of things. Their revolution proved they were no better than the native.'

'The French have some of the best minds in science and philosophy!' Mr Bass thumps his hand on the sand. 'They build the best ships too. Belief in equality is not only mouthed by them but felt in the heart.'

'Equality will never aid progress,' the lieutenant says. 'Such a belief dooms humanity as it seeks to elevate it. The French thirst for the destruction of order *is* primitive.'

'Such arrogance, Matthew! That same destructive force is in the English.'

'But we control it.'

'You talk of top and bottom, Matthew, as if you have no place in it. But what about the middle, you forget the middle, to which you belong.' Mr Bass is all afire now.

'What concerns me is not the middle, George, but the future. The future into which we are sailing. And how it will be for men of England.'

Mr Bass shakes his head and stares up at the sky. His hand, in a theatrical gesture, stirs the air.

'Sometimes I look at men and see the flourishing of all that is good,' he says. 'But evil exists in the civilised as well as in the savage. We English do not control it, but we do disguise it.'

Dark waves slurp at the shore. It is all very good, I think, them talking about top and bottom and middle, about good and evil, order and disorder, but think of it as water in a bucket, and what if that bucket has a hole? Then soon there would be no top, bottom and middle. No good or evil. No order or disorder. Only an empty bucket.

I am about to say this to Mr Bass when he rolls on his side and groans at his blisters. He stands quickly and walks away.

The lieutenant bends his head towards the firelight and writes in his journal.

I lie on the soft sand to sleep. The breeze tickles my cheek and despite my disturbed mind I sink into a sweet dream. I am at a theatre where Mama and Uncle Hilton are to perform. They cheer when I walk onto the stage and stoop to admire my gold buttons.

I awake to the sound of water lap. The sun is in my eye. The sand is the white-blue of early morn. In my dream there was an Indian, covered in crow feathers, sitting by me. The Indian said: *Bird from far away, fly home.*

I was so in fright of him that I did fly. But when I was in the air, wind tugging my hair, I recalled how far from home I was and began to fall. Falling woke me.

I sit up. Mr Bass is cross-legged, staring at the fire. I tell him my dream and then, remembering the talk from the night before, speak of water in a bucket. I tell him this in earnest but to my surprise he shoots dagger eyes at me.

'You know nothing, boy, do not pretend you do.'

I turn away and begin to prepare our food. Why does Mr Bass disregard me so? It is the sixth day of our sail and have I not shown great courage and faced foes never dreamt of by most men? And did I not warn him of the Indian danger? Never mind it was a warning he took no heed of. I think now that he too often dismisses advice from the less lettered. He did it with our first *Tom Thumb* and lost that vessel to fairweather friends. I have heard more wisdom in a corn jobber's speech than in some of Mr Bass's sermons. And for all their fine sailing, did not he and the lieutenant miss their mark the first day of our journey?

Mr Bass talks to the lieutenant in a sour voice. 'The soldier I attended before we embarked had been flogged for stealing peas from the store. His wounds were so deep they needed special care.'

'I am sorry to hear that,' the lieutenant says, evenly.

'That is what hunger does, Matthew,' says Mr Bass. 'It turns us all into savages. The Indian cries out in pain when he sees a flogging. He must turn away from it. But we stand and watch, unflinching. Who then is the savage and who is the civilised?'

'An interesting point, George,' the lieutenant says. 'Why not write it up in your book?'

'I just might,' snaps Mr Bass, and walks off.

I want to shout at Mr Bass. If so easily he raises up the Indians who might have killed him, why not those men who are with him day and night?

The wind blows along the beach, tumbling driftwood down to the sea. There is a silence among us three. Us three? The lieutenant's theory of top and bottom is on my mind. I am thinking, if he is right, then I am not in the middle, as he is, but on the bottom. And it is not a good place to be.

I stow our provisions into *Thumb*. Mr Bass sits far away, on a rock.

'The tide is for us, George,' the lieutenant calls.

Mr Bass does not deign to reply, but he joins us. We shove *Thumb* into the water, push across the wave break and climb in. Mr Bass and I pull out through the reef. *Swish, swash. Swish, swash.* The breeze picks up enough for us to hoist sail. It rustles and flaps and is scooped up by a wily wind.

As we sail past the point I hear birdsong but see no birds. Not even when I squint my eyes to the thickest bush. The birds here know how to find cover when they need, as if constantly wary of hunters.

Thumb skims the top of the waves.

'Look there, Barn Cove,' calls the lieutenant.

He is being his jolly self, attempting to pull Mr Bass out of his temper, which is much like pulling a dying horse out of thick mud.

'Will, you were there at its naming,' the lieutenant shouts. 'You must tell that to your family on your return.'

I look to the cove that is not really a cove. A falcon hovers above a rocky ledge. Squawking seabirds settle on the sand below. This land is a forever land. Here, the clock ticks to a different time.

Perhaps, yes perhaps there *is* something in being at its naming. Perhaps I am rising. Man must rise, was that not what Mr Bass said? And when he writes his book about the colony, as he has promised to do, my own name will be known to the world and men will marvel at our journey.

The breeze turns, whipping so strong from the north that it blows us about. To escape it, the lieutenant steers through a reef near a headland. Mr Bass and I pull towards the cliff where we will be shielded from the wind. We drop anchor and sit idle in the rocking boat, waiting for the weather to change.

'And there is no river found,' Mr Bass says, face like a basset hound.

'We may come to it yet.' The lieutenant starts to repack our stores.

He has not stopped pretending all in our little boat are merry, hopeful that by the force of his pretence we will become so, and for the first time I see some merit in his strategy. For things without resolve are best left unattended.

I think back to the lagoon. That sweep of water spied from the stream must have come from somewhere. Yet, if there was a river in that place, we will not be the ones to find it.

Is this what disturbs Mr Bass? Makes him twist and turn in anguish? Makes him huff and puff and sigh? Or is it his eyeing the vastness about us, of the sea and sky and land? Against which we, in our boat, are like a thimble in a grand house. For such an awareness is more present when sailing in *Thumb* than on the *Reliance* where each day is busy with duties.

Our boat sits low in the water. I stare at the sandy beach and the tall trees that surround it. Waves bump us about. I have voices in my head like a hundred young ones calling. What is to be discovered there on the shore? Maybe a river flows behind the trees? Maybe some other treasure is to be found?

'Mr Bass, may I swim to shore?' I resent the asking.

'What for, Will?'

'To see what is there.'

Mr Bass stares at me, but I glare back.

He will not frighten me again. I have seen more than most men twice his age.

'If you wish,' Mr Bass says eventually, closing his eyes, as if dismissing all around him.

The lieutenant smiles as though pleased with my spirit. I strip off and dive into the water, swim like a shark until I ache to breathe. Only then do I surface.

When I reach shore, I stagger out and glance back. Mr Bass and Lieutenant Flinders are dwarfed by the rocky cliff and the swirling sea.

I tramp the sandy beach. The cliffs at either end are the colour of clay. No bush grows on them yet behind me trees come all the way to the edge of the dunes. I jump over black weed that lies on the beach in thin bands, then paddle in the sea. Boulders, like the tiny islands of an archipelago, are spread through the shallows. Some covered with green slimy seaweed, others with colonies of shells – fan shells, brown and purple; cup-like shells; and small grey button shells. Seagulls rest on the boulders and survey their kingdom, or strut in the shallows, plucking tiny sea creatures from the wet sand.

There are no other footprints but mine. Only shells and driftwood.

Halfway along the beach I discover a stream whistling out from the trees. It narrows in places and can easily be jumped. I kneel to drink. The water is fresh.

If I could name it as I pleased I would name this stream for the new sister Mama wrote me about. A sister who seems more dear to me now than when I first heard the news, for I worried at who the father might be. My own father was a captain who sailed to the Americas and was never heard from again.

As I spin on the sand I name the bay for Mama, and the cliffs for Uncle Hilton. I wade along the stream that is cooler than the sea, and spy two long-bodied insects hovering. Wings gleaming. If I had wings where would I fly? I follow the insects upstream into the forest, and wade out of the water to rest beneath a giant fig tree with roots so large they curve around my back. With a shell I scratch my name into the bark, WILL MARTIN, then the date, MARCH 29, 1796. My stomach churns with all that has happened and weariness takes hold of me. I settle against the tree and doze. I dream I am running from Indians and when I turn to discover if they are upon me, I am startled to see that Mr Bass is one of them. I wake and yawn and then climb up the tree to the top branch. So many trees in one place! I spy giant fig trees that run in a pattern from the shore all the way up the mountain, their shiny leaves glinting in circles of green like women's dresses twirling on the dance floor. I think of Mama and her way of gabbling about the world. Always imagining herself into faraway places, places she had never even been. Now I have my own story to jaw, only it is not imagined.

When I return to the *Reliance* I will recount how I swam to this beach on my own and discovered a stream and was not frightened of cannibals. The lieutenant's brother, Samuel, will pretend not to listen, thinking I am beneath him, but others will slap me on the back.

To dare is to do.

I will not tell of Mr Bass's moods, of how he thinks less of me than the natives. For to do so might lower the opinion others may have of me. For, as Mr Bass has often said, *Slander sticks, no matter where it comes from.*

Ha! I feel emboldened by my thoughts.

I shift about on the high branches, and take in all that is around me, land and sea, mountain and sky, tree and bird, and find in me another stirring. One I may also never be able to tell, because there are no words fit to describe it. A quiet stirring, with its own magic, like a small candle burning on a dark night. Here I am. It may be nothing more than that but it seems, at this moment, much more.

After a time I climb down from the great tree and pat it goodbye, for it has given me solace. When I bolt into the sea, I dive beneath an enormous wave, to cheat it of its power, kick along the sandy bottom then surface to tread water. I look back at the shore. The white sand curves around the land; the dunes in the late light are dark mountains and valleys; the forest behind is thick green to the sky. This is a wild place. Too wild for civilisation. It is a place for adventure.

I will remember this place in my dreams. I will remember it in the stories I tell. For in this place I first realised that if I am to rise, it will come not only by what I tell of what I dare, but also by what I don't tell.

I kick out my legs and swim towards *Tom Thumb*.

Mr Bass hauls me into the boat, greets me like a long-lost friend, his mood much improved. The sun has fallen behind the cliffs and dark is descending.

'What did you find?' Mr Bass asks.

'A stream of fresh water,' I say, wiping my face.

Neither he nor the lieutenant question the length of time I spent on shore.

The lieutenant glances about him. 'The wind is for us,' he says. 'We must make use of it.'

Mr Bass and I get upon the oars and pull out through the gap in the reef. *Swish, swash, swish, swash.* We step the mast and haul sail.

At first the wind is strong and steady and we make good time, but soon it gusts, tipping us about. The sky is heaving with inky clouds that threaten to burst as we ride the waves.

A great clap of thunder sounds right above our heads.

Boom! Boom!

The thunder makes me jump.

Boom! Boom!

Giant spider legs of light rip through the sky. Night comes in a hurry, and the moon is hiding.

'We need shelter,' I call to Mr Bass over the drumming sea.

'Matthew,' Mr Bass bellows at the lieutenant.

The lieutenant points to a piece of land that juts out from a beach to the north. We strike sail and row in that direction and find shelter beneath a cliff. We heave the stone anchor up and toss it in the sea. The lieutenant leans over the gunwale, peers into the gloom to estimate our distance from the rocks. He can see nothing.

Lightning blazes. The lieutenant quickly surveys our position. 'We are too close to the rocks to stay long,' he shouts.

The light goes, and again we sit in the dark. Waves drum the nearby crags. *Thump, thump, thump! Thump, thump, thump!*

Which gives the greater danger – the monstrous rocks so near to us now or the ocean waves?

Another burst of lightning and the sky crackles with light. Mr Bass holds the anchor rope as if it might race away. The lieutenant at the helm, ever watchful.

Dark again. We wait. *Whoosh, whoosh,* goes the sea.

The wind shifts and smacks into our boat.

The lieutenant shouts, 'Pull now. Or we will smash upon the rocks!'

Mr Bass and I haul up the anchor – haste, haste – get on the oars – haste, haste – and row. The ocean waves it must be. *Swish, swash, swish, swash.*

Out from the cliff we boat the oars and hoist sail. Soon we are rolling on the sea. Lightning whips the sky. High above us the crest of a wave is bearing down. We sink to the dip of the wave. I spy harsh-faced crags barely more than an arm's length away; then, just as we seem sure to smash onto them, we rise up and ride to the wave top.

The boat is filling with water. I slip and scramble, fetch the bucket and begin to bail. Lightning sizzles and snaps. Again *Thumb* tips towards harsh-faced crags and again we rise up and ride the wave. I push my body into the side of the boat to steady myself and bail. All is cold and hard and urgent. Time is measured by waves and lightning.

We again fall towards the rocks.

I cry out.

But yet again, yes, yes, we rise and ride away. In a crack of light I see the lieutenant, iron-faced, as the waves, like shape-shifting ghouls, emerge from the noisy dark to chase us. It is death coming but we will not be taken without a fight.

To dare is to do. *Slap, slap and roar.* To dare is to do. *Slap, slap and roar.* Glory for us, not death.

Lightning crack!

A monstrous wave hovers above like a magnificent dark angel. This is not a battle of my daring. No, this is nature laughing at me. Ideas of manhood and mankind are nothing now. There is no leveller that can beat this. Mankind is no more than a squib that hisses and dies.

Everything hurts. My arms scream, but my legs hold on. Water crashes over me, *swoosh, swoosh.* I am thrust from one side of the boat to the other. My body whacks against the timber, against all that lies between me and the hungry sea.

Bail, bail, I must bail.

I dip my bucket in the water and bail. I spy in the distance, through the sheeting rain, the white water of a break. Could it be?

'Reef! Reef!' I shout above the wind howl.

The lieutenant and Mr Bass follow my pointing arm.

'We can make it,' I shout.

'Get ready to strike sail!' Mr Bass hollers.

The lieutenant leans back on his steering oar and *Thumb* flips into the wind. Waves smash over us. I stash the bucket and heave on the sail rope, my strength stretched like in a tug-of-war. Mr Bass and I leap up, strike sail and unstep the mast. The rain pummels us as we get on the oars. We wait for the slow between racing waves and then pull, hard and fast.

Every muscle in my body screeches in pain. We pull and pull.

Rain slaps my cheeks. Pull, pull.

My feet start to slip. Pull, pull.

My hands clench the oar. Pull, pull.

Again and again, pull, pull.

To dare is to do, to dare is to do, to dare is to ... We slip through a gap in the reef and are delivered – magnificently – into smooth water.

An immense quiet crowds in as though my ears are muffled in wool.

We keep on pulling, but the ease is so far from the force we have just been rowing against that it must be a dream. I see a sliver of flickering white. Oh my, it looks like the edge of the world. Is this, perchance, death's sweet ride?

But then the flickering white becomes a beach. I laugh inwardly at my foolish thought.

Mr Bass and I slide away the oars. Slipping on the wet wood, we muddle about in the dark, heave up the stone anchor and drop it over the side.

We stop still in the pitch black. I listen to our breathing, the sound like an untuned instrument. Oh, but I am thrilled by the sound.

The moon comes out from behind a cloud, and I spy the lieutenant. He looks like a cat that has caught a mouse. It is infectious.

We laugh, quietly, then loudly, at the surprise of being alive.

'My God, there is grace in our protection,' the lieutenant says as our laughter subsides.

'Not God, it was chance gave us safety,' says Mr Bass.

'Perhaps,' says the lieutenant.

'We had only the option to choose movement or not,' Mr Bass says, his voice joyful and sad together.

'And all the while we knew not where movement would take us,' I say.

'This time to safety,' the lieutenant whispers.

'Yes,' I agree.

The lieutenant grabs Mr Bass's hand. 'This place is providential, do you agree, George?'

'It feels that way,' Mr Bass replies.

'Providential Cove, that is what we must name it,' the lieutenant says. 'Will, do you agree?'

'That be the name,' I say, 'that most fits this place.'

I see now what it takes for me to be one of them. It is not about blood, but something wrought by a higher force. It was the dark angel who came to us. We battled her, and now, here we are, us three, alive and together, together and alive.

I bend back and watch clouds that race the sea currents below. The stars peek through, like children behind fingers. All is childish wonder. It is a night not to be forgotten. We sit there remembering the storm, remembering wave after wave, jawing as though it were a story anew. It is some time before we attempt to sleep.

'Our seventh day,' I say, as I jump into the shallows and help Mr Bass and the lieutenant haul *Thumb* onto the shore.

I stand and look about me. The rocky cliffs curve to a headland on each side of the beach and set a frame for the sea beyond. The water is magnificent, like a turquoise jewel. Behind, spiky green bushes grow in the sand and tall trees cast shadows across tidal pools. I see a stream at the back of the cove and without waiting for instruction I run up the sand hill.

The stream snakes through the dunes. There are Indian footprints leading down to the water, yet my feeling of gladness cannot be dampened. This is a cove of peace. I spy the ashes of a fire and dare myself to nudge a burnt log with my toe. Ah, it is cold. Nothing bad can happen here. There is nought to fear, not from man or beast or sky or sea.

It is late morn when we leave our peaceful cove. We push off and row, then pick up a light breeze and sail. Our spirits are high.

When I was young, my mama would tell me stories about Jamaica and Calcutta and other places that may or may not have existed. Once, I asked her, 'How do you know about such places? You, who have never been from England?'

'You have missed the point of the story,' she said. 'I have been to many faraway places, the future as well as the past.'

But here am I, and I have been to places beyond imagining.

We sail on with Point Solander in sight. Point Solander is eleven miles from Port Jackson. The cliffs turn low and sandy as we breeze into an open bay. The sun beats down upon the still water, and a tired wind pushes us along. The sky is pale blue, like faded uniforms, and on the scrubby shore the green bush is flecked with silver.

It is near noon when we see it. We are sitting in *Thumb*, coasting the northeast of the bay.

'There is our river,' the lieutenant says.

We do not whoop for joy but eye it like seasoned travellers.

'So it is,' I say.

'It was a long journey here,' adds Mr Bass.

We strike sail and row up the river. Our river. It is scrubby on either side with rock ledges that hang over the water like bushy eyebrows.

Mr Bass sighs. 'It will not do for large vessels.'

It is a river, but not one that will please our governor. Not one that will easily transport a new community to clean water and good pastureland.

'We might name the river after Hacking, who guessed it was here,' the lieutenant suggests.

This river will not make monuments of our names but, after our stormy night, each day is monument enough. We row back out to the bay and sit rocking in our boat.

'This place feels older than time,' Mr Bass says.

'Yes,' agrees the lieutenant.

'It should be our care, not so much to live a long life, but an honourable one,' says Mr Bass.

'Well said,' agrees the lieutenant.

They look to me and smile and, in their serenity, I see something of what it means to live. For in the tumble of all that is life, there are moments that lift a man into a quiet place, where the wonder is in the drawing of each breath. Our journey has been worth this discovery alone.

We row to the north side of the cove, drag *Thumb* up onto the sand. The fan leaves of the palm trees give us shade. I gather sticks from the back of the beach, flint a fire and lay out our clothes to dry. Then I stretch my arms and legs, and rub my toes in the sand.

I turn and spy two Indians standing in the trees. How long have they been watching? The two men smile. One is older than the other. No spears. Must have left them in the grasses.

Mr Bass calls out a welcome in the Port Jackson speak and slowly the Indians walk across the sand, as if we are the wild things and not they. The lieutenant, down by the water's edge, hurries up to join us. He tells the Indians we are from Sydney Cove, yet they seem not to know the name. We offer to share what food we have but, to our surprise, they wave it away.

Instead, they look us over from head to toe. The older man touches the freckles on my nose. The younger one strokes Mr Bass's waistcoat.

I sit to tend the fire but, when I stand, they are already leaving, as quietly as they arrived. I watch them go.

We push *Thumb* into the water and row to the middle of the bay to fish. I look to the hilltops, but there is no sign of the Indians. Sharks slide alongside and watch us, as if curious to take a bite. We sit with our lines. Catch nothing.

We leave off fishing and row back to shore.

Mr Bass and the lieutenant gather sticks for the fire. I rinse the salt from our piece of beef and then boil it. We eat a small supper. Later, I pull up soft grass and throw it on the ground to make our beds.

The night is all stars. I pick out *Warrewull*. I hear the bird that sings in the moonlight.

Our eighth day. Gulls wake me. *Carick, carick!* We breakfast in the morning cool then again push *Thumb* into the water – *splish, splash* – and the lieutenant and I pull around Port Hacking. Mr Bass is at the helm, his long legs stretched out before him.

We boat our oars. The lieutenant scrambles to the bow and ferrets out his compass and journal. He sketches the final part of our journey onto his map.

Mr Bass and I rummage for hooks and line so we can fish. We talk about what we will say on our return, about the currents being too strong so that we overshot our mark, about the dumping on the beach where the thin trails of smoke from the forest alerted us to danger, about the cannibals that we nearly met, and our trading with the Indians and the barbering of their beards.

'And our escape from their clutches,' the lieutenant adds.

'Was it escape?' Mr Bass asks.

'You know it was,' the lieutenant says.

They look to each other, then to me, and for a tick-tock I hold my breath.

Carick, carick! the gulls call out.

The lieutenant and Mr Bass are waiting for me to speak. And what shall I say? What will be the story of how we met this land?

Carick, carick!

From a single tree a forest can grow but only if the seeds are well spread. Yet not all stories can be told.

'We were dead men in that place,' I say.

'We were,' says Mr Bass.

'Indeed,' agrees the lieutenant.

Mr Bass claps me on the shoulder. The lieutenant takes hold of my neck and squeezes it, which is his dearest form of affection.

We three talk on about our battle with the storm.

'What a story we have to tell,' I say.

Mr Bass laughs and ruffles my hair.

'I am too old for that,' I shout, pulling away.

'Yes,' he says. 'You are too old.'

He ruffles my hair again, and we start to wrestle.

'My journal!' the lieutenant shouts, as the boat rocks.

Mr Bass pushes me, but I push back. He is stronger but I am faster. We grip arms, breathing close, poised for a fall.

'The sharks will get us,' I dare.

'You think I am frightened of sharks?' he asks.

'You tell me,' I say.

We stay, both holding tight. My heart beating fast. He pushes me as I push him. We tip together and fall into the cool water.

Down, down, down, I go, drift with the current, then swim up to the surface.

I stroke away from *Thumb*, dive under again, swimming beneath the surface back to the boat and bursting up for air at the bow. I climb in, quicker than I might normally do, for a dare is a dare but I do not want to chance sharks any more than I have to.

Mr Bass stays in the water a moment longer to prove that he can.

'Look there,' I say, pointing to a spot beyond him, where my imaginary shark is circling.

Mr Bass is in the boat in a tick-tock with me sitting on the thwart laughing.

In the early morn of our ninth day, I wake to a sky full of majestic ships. All is glory up in the clouds. It is a future portent, perhaps?

Mr Bass and the lieutenant are still sleeping. Loud snores.

I rise and walk the beach, gathering sticks, but when I have a pile I dump them on the sand and bound off along the shore, through the shallows. When my breath is short I stop to rest, then splash into the water to swim.

Soon I will be back on the *Reliance* and my time will be measured. What is unmeasured is unknown. A secret that can be discovered by no one.

I swim back to the shore and run in circles to dry off, feeling the soft sand beneath my feet.

The sun is skimming the water when I walk back to gather my pile of sticks. I return to the camp where my elders are still snoring, as if they have not a care in the world. I light a fire, setting a pot to boil, so we can feed on the last of our soup cakes. The flames dart up into the air. Mr Bass and the lieutenant finally stir, and we sup as though at a feast. Later, we pack and then heave *Thumb* into the water.

I gaze back at the wide bay as we pull out through the entrance. Will I ever see this sight again? The sail flaps in the breeze and we head for Port Jackson.

At sunset we are in Sydney Cove, clapping the shoulders of friends on board the *Reliance*. Our excitement is so great that we must report to the governor at once. We climb down to *Thumb*, pull to the dock and hurry to the governor's house.

He is in the garden listening to an owl.

'I am pleased to see you,' he says to Mr Bass and the lieutenant. Then he turns to me. 'Young Will,' he says.

He shakes my hand and his grip is firm.

'A drink is in order,' he says, but by the colour of his nose he has had several already.

The governor leads the way into the house. We all follow, but at the door Mr Bass turns to me. 'You must want to see your friends,' he says.

'No, sir,' I say.

The governor and the lieutenant are walking down the hallway.

Mr Bass goes to ruffle my hair then thinks better of it and folds his arms.

'Go. Enjoy yourself, Will. I must report our adventures but you have earned the night off.'

Mr Bass turns away, thinking he has done me a favour but it is not the favour I wished for.

I walk away from the governor's house and stride along the shore, kicking stones.

The sky is clear and the half-moon is bright. I search for Na at the campfires near the Tank Stream. Drunken wretches singing lewd songs. A man facedown in the dirt. No Na.

Na would have seen *Thumb* come in, I am sure of it.

I scout along the edge of the stream, cross it, and then go along to the hospital. Buckley, the surgeon's mate, is outside smoking a pipe. His dogs bark as I arrive. Na is not there.

'Na has your dog with him,' says Buckley.

I search down along the shore but Na and my dog, George the Fourth – that is kept at Mr Palmer's place, Palmer's gift to me – are nowhere to be seen.

I climb around the cliff to an outcrop of rocks and shrubs. Last spring Na and I came here to watch the chicks of a honeyeater. The chicks are long gone, but the nest is still here as if waiting for new occupants. I sit on a rock ledge.

If I were born into a tribe like Na, what I would have to do to be a man is have my tooth pulled. Is not my journey, in a small boat, facing wild seas and treacherous cannibals, equal to tooth pulling?

They will be toasting at the governor's. There will be a fire blazing and they will tell the story of our journey.

I lie on the rock and eye the water slapping the shore. Now I am a man, and a man is his story told. I say this out loud, but only the nightjar answers.

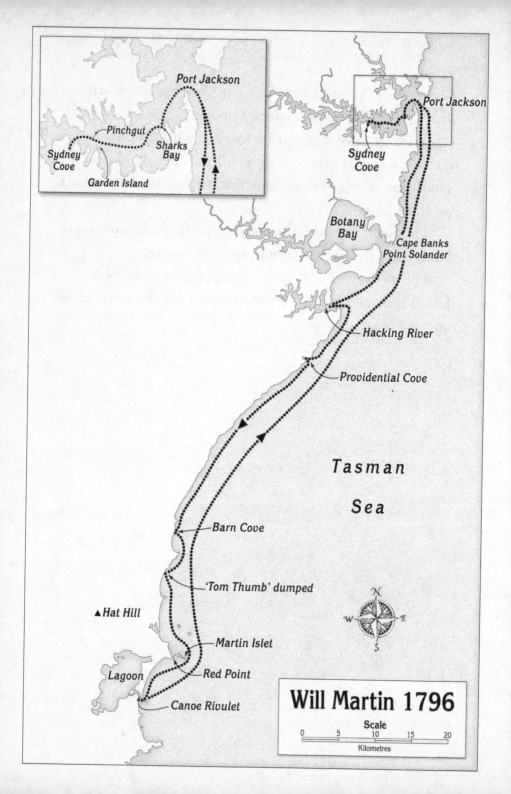

Port Jackson

Pinchgut

Sydney
Cove

Garden Island

Sharks
Bay

Port Jackson

Sydney
Cove

Botany
Bay

Cape Banks
Point Solander

Hacking River

Providential Cove

Tasman

Sea

Barn Cove

'Tom Thumb' dumped

▲ Hat Hill

Martin Islet

Lagoon

Red Point

Canoe Rivulet

N
W E
S

Will Martin 1796

Scale

| 0 | 5 | 10 | 15 | 20 |

Kilometres

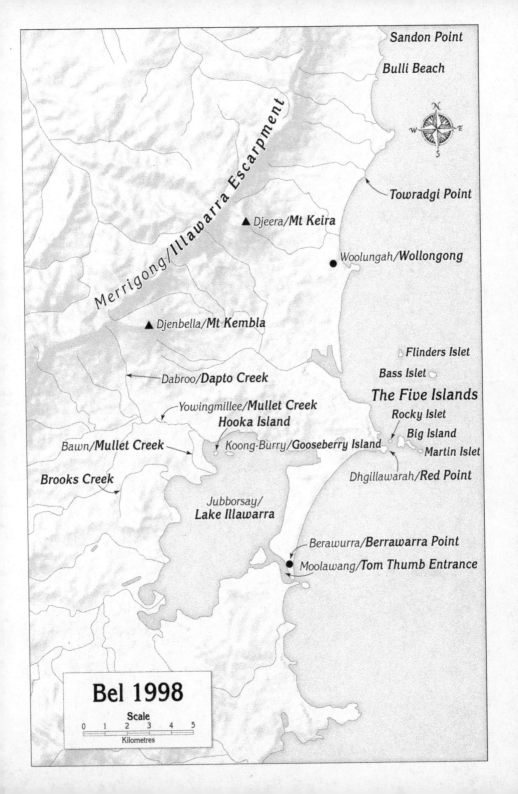

Sandon Point

Bulli Beach

Merrigong/Illawarra Escarpment

Towradgi Point

▲ Djeera/**Mt Keira**

● Woolungah/**Wollongong**

▲ Djenbella/**Mt Kembla**

↙ Flinders Islet

Bass Islet ⌐

The Five Islands

Dabroo/**Dapto Creek** ←

Yowingmillee/**Mullet Creek**
Hooka Island

Rocky Islet
Big Island
Martin Islet

Bawn/**Mullet Creek** → ↓ Koong-Burry/**Gooseberry Island**

Dhgillawarah/**Red Point**

Brooks Creek ↘

Jubborsay/
Lake Illawarra

← Berawurra/**Berrawarra Point**

● Moolawang/**Tom Thumb Entrance**

Bel 1998

Scale

0   1   2   3   4   5

Kilometres

Author's note

Storyland is a work of fiction but certain characters and situations have been inspired by documented events. I have stayed true to history and geography whenever doing so served the story, but when it did not, I have used my imagination.

I first came across William Martin when reading Miriam Estensen's *The Life of Matthew Flinders* (2003). In the late eighteenth century, it was common for boys as young as eleven to be employed on ships. Martin was thirteen when he first stepped on board the *Reliance* to become George Bass's servant and loblolly boy; he had only just turned fifteen when he took the second *Tom Thumb* journey in March 1796. (The first journey, on a different *Tom Thumb*, took place during the previous year, when Flinders, Bass and Martin sailed to Georges River.) Flinders wrote down a narrative of this second exploration trip, and his version of the tale has been recounted by others ever since. In the Flinders account, Dilba is presented as having malicious intentions towards the Europeans. This controversial point of view, persuasively put by Flinders, occurs in most of the retellings. In fact Flinders wrote two versions of the journey. Historians suggest that the longer journal version, which includes the meetings that took place at Red Point and later at Canoe Rivulet, titled *Narrative of Tom Thumb's cruize to Canoe Rivulet,* was written in the year following the exploration trip. After Flinders died, the manuscript was passed down through his family and eventually edited by Keith Bowden, and published in 1985. The second account (a remodelling of the first) appears in the introduction to *A Voyage to Terra Australis* ([1814] 1966), which Flinders wrote at the end of his career, after his return to England from his *Investigator* explorations. Flinders was, by the time he wrote the second account, a mature man, and this second version reflects his change in status from a young second lieutenant to a respected captain, explorer and navigator. The 1796 narrative in *Storyland* closely follows the first Flinders nonfiction account, but imagines it from Will Martin's perspective.

Many people have sought to pinpoint the locations where Flinders, Bass and Martin landed. For those who have an interest, see *Earliest Illawarra by its explorers and pioneers* (1966) edited by W.G. McDonald. McDonald suggests Barn Cove might be Bulli Beach, or Woonona Beach; the *Tom Thumb* dumping might have occurred south of Towradgi Point; Saddle Point is Red Point; Hat Hill is Mount Kembla; Canoe Rivulet is the entrance to Lake Illawarra; Providential Cove is Wattamolla.

In 1822, on Captain Richard Brooks's farm at Exmouth, an Aboriginal woman was shot and then mauled by dogs, after she and others had picked corn from a field. A convict, Seth Hawker, who worked for Brooks, was tried for murder and acquitted. I read about this tragic event in Michael Organ's *A Documentary History of the Illawarra and South Coast Aborigines: 1770-1850* (1990). The evidence presented in the trial transcripts is chilling. The woman who was killed was not named either at the trial or in the covering newspaper reports. The trial Judge Advocate suggested the deed had been unfortunate, but was validated by the need to protect Captain Brooks's property. Quite early on, as I was thinking about how to narrate such a disturbing tale, I had a conversation with local poet and elder, Aunty Barbara Nicholson. Among other things, we talked about stories and ownership. It was this conversation that made me realise how important it might be to portray the events from Hawker's perspective.

When researching *Storyland*, I'd often spend the mornings reading books and articles about the future of the planet, and in the afternoons, I'd visit libraries and pour through old historical records, personal accounts, letters, diaries, maps and newspaper archives. I discovered the changing use of the land around Lake Illawarra. At the time when Lola begins her narration, there were many small farms operating on what was then called the Five Islands Estate, and in the nearby Dapto area, there were at least two dairies run by Chinese immigrants. Milk, cheese and butter were an important part of the regional industry.

The railway had arrived in the last breath of the nineteenth century, and life began to alter for locals. For a heartbeat, butter from the region was exported to London, and there was talk of deepening Lake Illawarra so that it could harbour ships. This was also the period when Australian women were seeking their right to vote (gained in 1895 in South Australia and 1902 in New South Wales). Lola's narrative isn't about voting, but women were beginning to fight for their rights, and a little of that impetus finds its way into her story.

During the year that Bel recounts her tale, 1998, an ancient skeleton was found at McCauley's Beach, Sandon Point, discovered after a storm. A couple of years later an Aboriginal Tent Embassy was set up there, and there has been a long running battle since, between some of the residents and the Aboriginal Tent Embassy representatives.

Thinking about the near and far future has always interested me. Roy Stanton provides a compelling perspective in *Learning How to Die in the Anthropocene: Reflections on the End of a Civilisation* (2015). Stanton recounts how, as an American soldier serving in Iraq, he learnt (from a Samurai manual written in the eighteenth century) to meditate daily on death. Stanton suggests that in our time of climate instability such a practice might be useful for everyone. An understanding of what the future might hold for us as a species can help us plan for it, forewarned is forearmed. Yet the future, as Will Martin says, is unmade, and the potential for surprise, ever-present.

Indigenous language and historical sources

As Lieutenant Watkin Tench observed, Europeans often misunderstood the meaning of Aboriginal words. In his journal, Tench writes, 'We had lived almost three years at Port Jackson ... before we knew that the word bèeal, signified "no," and not "good," in which latter sense we had always used it without suspecting that we were wrong; and even without being corrected by those with whom we talked daily.' The Aboriginal words and their meanings used in *Storyland* are representations of what the Europeans may have understood at the time. Where there is discrepancy among historical sources for a particular language group I've chosen the word that seemed appropriate to the knowledge of the character. Resources for this novel were numerous and wide-ranging but important for language were *An Account of the English Colony in New South Wales: with remarks on the Disposition, Customs, Manners, &c. of the Native Inhabitants of that Country*, vol. 1 ([1798] 1971) by David Collins and The Notebooks of William Dawes, available at www.williamdawes.org. For knowledge specific to the Dharawal people I continually went to *A Documentary History of the Illawarra and South Coast Aborigines: 1770-1850* (1990) edited by Michael Organ; *Dharawal: The story of the Dharawal speaking people of Southern Sydney*, a collaborative work by Les Bursill, Mary Jacobs, artist Deborah Lennis, Dharawal Elder Aunty Beryl Timbery-Beller and Dharawal spokesperson Merv Ryan (2007); *Murni Dhungang Jirra: Living in the Illawarra*, compiled and written by Sue Wesson (2005). Always close at hand was the thorough and illuminating *The World of the First Australians: Aboriginal Traditional Life: Past and Present*, by Ronald and Catherine Berndt (1999).

Acknowledgements

I would like to acknowledge the *Elouera* and *Wadi Wadi* (also *Wodi Wodi*) people of *Dharawal* Country. The Aboriginal Elders of this land, past, present and future, hold the memories, the traditions, the culture and hopes of Indigenous Australia.

In getting this book to publication my heartfelt thanks go to publisher Catherine Milne for her generosity, intelligence and vigilant editorial oversight and input. Without Catherine this would be a different book, and one I'd be less happy with. Likewise, thanks to Nicola Robinson, for her detailed and comprehensive editing (and for posing great questions); to the HarperCollins team, especially Jaki Arthur, Lara Wallace, Tom Wilson and Lucy Bennett; and to Bronwyn Sweeney for proofreading. I am most grateful to my literary agent, Jo Butler, from The Cameron Creswell Agency, for her excellent advice on all things book related and for her care and thoughtfulness, and also to Sophie Hamley who first championed this novel.

Thank you to Gary Christian for reading drafts, offering suggestions, and keeping an eye on the 'bullshit factor', and to Aunty Barbara Nicholson for reading, local knowledge, and for generous advice both early on in the process and nearing completion. Many thanks also to Julianne Schultz, John Tague, Susan Hornbeck, Jerath Head, from *Griffith Review*, to Brian Johns, Jacqueline Blanchard and Cate Kennedy who selected Will Martin in 2015 for *Griffith Review: Tall Tales Short – The Novella Project III*, to CAL, and to Aviva Tuffield, who was the guest editor. A thank you must also go to Gillian Dooley, founding general editor of *Transnational Literature*, who first published the 'Will Martin' story online in 2011.

My appreciation goes to Flinders University for supporting this project, most especially to Julie Holledge, for her inspiration and wisdom and to Mary Moore and Jonathan Bollen. I also owe a debt to those Illawarra locals — Ed Dion, Jade Kennedy, Roy (Dootch) Kennedy, Nikki Harris, Beth Harris, Lotte Latukefu and Dorothy O'Keefe — who made themselves available for interviews and chats about past and current events.

Many thanks to University of Wollongong writers and researchers who read the manuscript or contributed to discussions about it: in particular Shady Cosgrove and Luke Johnson (both pitched in with terrific comments); Wenche Ommundsen and Cathy Cole (both provided concise overviews); Joshua Lobb, Jan Wright, and Sharon Athanasios. For the research and writing retreats and for ongoing discussions on all things writerly and ecological I cherish time spent with colleagues from both the Material Ecologies (MECO) research network, steered by Su Ballard, and the Centre for Cultures, Texts, and Creative Industries (CTC), directed by Sue Turnbull. I am also most grateful to the University of Wollongong for supporting ongoing research for this novel, especially the encouragement and advice provided by Sarah Miller, Amanda Lawson and Vera Mackie. Also thanks to James Phelan for discussions related to the work and for his own writings on unreliable narrators.

I am greatly indebted to the historians and researchers who have written about the Illawarra, especially Michael Organ, Carol Speechley, and Peter Charles Gibson, and the many local writers, both Indigenous and non-indigenous, who have shared their stories with the public. While writing and researching, much time was spent at the Mitchell Library, New South Wales, the State Library of New South Wales, the University of Wollongong Library, the Wollongong City Libraries, the Flinders University Library, and the State Library of South Australia. I am grateful to the many excellent librarians who work at these institutions.

Many friends kindly read drafts of the novel and gave opinions, advice and support and these include: Sue Walker, Charmaine Moldridge, Rachel Healy, Alan John, Karen Norris, David Carlin, Linda Mickleborough, Melissa Reeves, Sue Temby, Merrilyn Temby, Bea Christian, Robin Hopf, Shaar Christian, Peter Kelly, and Nelly Flannery. The writing of this book was made easier by those who offered or shared peaceful homes in meditative locations: Ruth Nicholas, David Goode, Georgie Goode, Hugo Goode; Peter Barge and Kinchem Hegedus; John and Anne McKinnon; Janne and Gerald Coughlin; Brigid Kennedy and Michael McConnell; Susie and James Fitzpatrick. Also thanks to Friederike Krishnabhakdi-Vasilakis and the South Coast Writers Centre for support, and to Jenny Kemp for her 2016 writer's workshop and Clare Grant for organizing it.

Thanks to my family but most especially my parents, Des McKinnon and Dawn McKinnon, for inspiring a love of stories and instilling an ongoing fascination with what makes people tick.

Catherine McKinnon lives in rural New South Wales with her husband, sculptor and painter Gary Christian. She grew up in South Australia, studied at Flinders University, then worked as a theatre director and playwright. In 2006 she won the *Australian Women's Weekly*/Penguin Books Award for her short story *Haley and the Sea*. Her novel, *The Nearly Happy Family*, was published by Penguin in 2008, and in 2015 she was a co-winner of the *Griffith Review: Tall Tales Short – The Novella Project III*. Her plays have been performed nationally and her short stories, reviews and articles have appeared in *Transnational Literature*, *Text Journal*, *RealTime* and *Narrative*. She teaches performance and creative writing at the University of Wollongong and is currently working on her third novel.